Valentine's Day
Seekers: Book Four

Josie Jaffrey

CONTENT WARNINGS

There is a full list of content warnings at the back of this book.

By Josie Jaffrey

The Solis Invicti Series

A Bargain in Silver
The Price of Silver
Bound in Silver
The Silver Bullet

The Sovereign Trilogy

The Gilded King
The Silver Queen
The Blood Prince

The Seekers Series

Killian's Dead (short story prequel, free to Josie's
subscribers)
May Day
Judgement Day
Winta's Day
Valentine's Day

Silverse Short Stories

Blood Brothers
Blood Work
Bad Blood
Ex Marks the Spot
Cara Mia (free to Josie's subscribers)
Bella Donna (free to Josie's subscribers)
Dead Road Rules
Ungilded
The Blue Empress
The Red Lady

Other Novels

The Wolf and the Water

Other Short Stories

Ring The Bell
Last Christmas
SnapShot
Peyton's End

For Asha

For Ashla

1

'HAPPY VALENTINE'S DAY, Valentine.'

'Yeah, sure, whatever,' I say. 'Are you coming inside, or what?'

Killian Drake, the Baron of Oxford and perennial pain in my arse, has just arrived at my shitty little bedsit – in a city I won't name for my own protection – for his monthly visit. If that makes it sound like he's about as welcome as my period, then you've got the right idea. Unfortunately, I need him. Just not in the way he wants me to.

'Miss me?' he asks as he walks into the flat.

'Nope.'

'Liar.'

'Megalomaniac.'

'Flirt.'

'In your dreams.'

I slam the door behind him, which relieves some of my frustration, but none of my irritation. The problem is, the irritant is still here, standing in front of me with a sly grin that tells me he's not buying a word I just said.

It's not that he isn't attractive. Between his effortless charm, his tailored suit and the sharp edge of danger that's always lurking just behind his eyes, he's basically a wet dream in a billionaire vampire wrapper, but the way he looks isn't what's holding me back. There are a million reasons not to let Killian Drake too close. The smug expression on his punchable face is just one of them.

He shrugs out of his expensive wool coat and slings it over the arm of the stained sofa that doubles as my bed, then hands me the duffel bag he's carrying.

'Supplies,' he says.

I unzip it and empty its contents – the cash into my satchel and the blood bottles into my fridge – then I hand back the duffel and say thank you, like the well-mannered lady I am not. This is the easy bit of our planned interaction this evening. The rest is going to be trickier.

'You still have blood left?' he says.

'I don't use much.'

He got a good look in my fridge while I was stocking it up. With the bedsit as tiny as it is, the kitchen is nothing more than a few units along the wall opposite the sofa-bed. The bathroom is a cupboard in the corner. You'd have to be really friendly with someone to be comfortable spending extended periods of time with them in a space this small, and Drake and I… we aren't all that friendly right now.

'Tell me the news from home,' I say, but he just shakes his head, as I knew he would. He thinks it's safer this way, that the less I know the better, and I couldn't disagree more.

'Shall we have a drink?' he asks, pulling a bottle of wine from a pocket of his coat.

'Can we just get this over with?'

'No preamble?' he asks. 'Straight to business?'

'What do you think this is, exactly?' I ask. 'I need you to heal me, and that involves you kissing me. That's all this is, Drake. This isn't a date.'

'And how long do you plan to keep deluding yourself

about that?'

'I'm not the one living in a state of delusion. How long is it going to take to get that through your thick skull?'

He just smiles in response, and just like that I want to punch him again.

Here's the problem: on New Year's Eve, I got into trouble and ended up stuck on a rooftop in central London with lethal, infected blood in my veins. I would have died that night if Drake hadn't healed me with a kiss, which he can only do because of his bond to me, which is a whole other can of worms that I won't go into right now. Unfortunately, it turns out that the infected blood's still inside me and, slowly but surely, it's trying to burn me up from the inside. My own supernatural self-healing abilities do nothing for it, Drake can't heal it all the way out of me, and I can't work out how to neutralise it by any other method. That means I need him to keep kissing me, just once every few weeks to keep the fire at bay, and it's giving him the wrong idea.

'You can't take back what you said,' he says.

Which is the other problem: it's possible that just before he healed me that night, I told him I loved him. Just sometimes, and just a little, but in typical Killian Drake fashion, he's let it go to his head.

'You can't hold me accountable for things I said when I was dying,' I say.

'In the circumstances, you can't expect me not to.'

'Just shut up and kiss me.'

'Gladly.'

I take pains to ensure that the kiss that follows is perfunctory at best – a peck on the lips that doesn't even leave a scent mark – but it serves its purpose. My blood is healed, the burning in my veins is cooled, and I no longer feel like my life is draining out of me with every breath.

Sweet relief.

This is the second time that Drake's healed me since that night on the rooftop, and the first was just like this: he tracked me down by following the pull of the bond, we argued, he kissed me, then he left. And it works. We don't have to make it all messy with emotions. We can carry on like this forever, and I'll never have to think about what the bond means, or how he makes me feel, or what else I did on the rooftops that night to make the healing necessary in the first place.

Job done, healing performed, temptation resisted. Now I can throw Drake out of my shitty residence and continue being on the run with minimal inconvenience to both of us.

Or so I think, until he steps back and I see his face. He's looking at me with his silver-veined eyes, and with the evidence of his feelings right there on his face it's impossible to ignore what this means to him. What *I* mean to him.

All us vampires have silver in the whites of our eyes, tracing the lines of our blood vessels; it's why we call ourselves the Silver. We hide that silver most of the time so humans won't cotton on to what we are, but Drake isn't hiding his now, and he has more than the usual amount. In his shark-black eyes, the silver extends into the iris, filtering along its spokes to circle around his pupils. It's the outward sign of his bond to me, and the reason he can find me wherever I am. It's also the reason he has the power to heal me, and the reason it matters to him so much that he does. It means that he... likes me. More than likes, really, and more than a little bit.

He looks into my eyes, then his glance flicks down to my lips, which are now stained silver from his healing mojo, and I can pinpoint the exact moment that he decides that today, a peck on the lips is not enough.

I should push him away, and he gives me the chance, but although I promised myself I wouldn't and although I know

4

I'll hate myself for this later, I don't. I can't. After six weeks on the run on my own, with nothing but two tiny teasing kisses by way of contact, I want him more than I have ever wanted anything in my entire life. I want to taste his lips. I want to smell his skin. I want to feel his flesh dimple under my fingertips as I pull him naked against my body. I want—

'Valentine,' he whispers.

When our lips meet again, his hands are at my waist, sliding up my back, pulling me against his chest in a grip I can't resist. My hands are in his hair, messing up the perfect dark waves, grabbing fistfuls of it so he can't pull away. He's not trying to, either. His mouth tastes of wine and blood and spice, then the air fills with the same scent and I know we've just fucked up. That's his scent mark swirling around us, and all over my skin, and it's not the only one. I can smell my scent on him too.

Brilliant. Just brilliant.

'Shit,' I say. 'The marks—'

He kisses me again before I can say more, not that there's any point in resisting now. The marks have been made, and there's nothing either of us can do to change that. Despite the potential consequences, I can't deny that I like the smell of him on my skin, and the knowledge that I've marked him gives me a surge of possessive arousal that's so strong it worries me. Whatever the bond suggests, he isn't mine, even if I want him to be in that moment.

I'm conflicted, is what I'm trying to say, which is the only way I can explain what happens next.

Instead of pulling away, which is still what I should do, I catch his lips with mine, fist my hands into his shirt and use that grip to slam his back into the wall, pinning him between it and my body. I think I've dented the plaster, because there's white powder in his hair when I pull back to assess my next line of attack.

I want to rip off his shirt. No, I want to rip off his trousers. No, both. All of it. However it happens, naked would be better, and quickly. I've seen Drake gloriously in the buff once before, and to say I'm keen for a repeat performance would be a criminal understatement.

'Does this mean you'll be my Valentine?' he whispers with a smirk, and suddenly I want to thump him again.

Why does he have to ruin everything?

'Do me a favour and fuck off,' I say, pushing away, but it's a little late for that.

'Because you can't resist me otherwise?'

I laugh scornfully, pretending there isn't more than a little truth to his words. It's a hollow gesture given the Drake-shaped dent in my wall.

'Anyway, I can't,' he says, dusting the plaster from his shoulders. 'I'm wearing your scent mark. If I leave now, everyone will know I've been with you, and they'll follow my scent back here. It's not safe.'

Which is, of course, the whole reason I was trying to resist him in the first place. There are a lot of powerful people out there who want me dead. I'm supposed to be keeping a low profile, which is pretty fucking difficult when I need to receive regular visits from the bloody Baron of bloody Oxford, and extra difficult if he's wandering around wearing my scent mark.

'You did this on purpose,' I say.

'You think I can resist this any more than you can?'

'Yes.'

'That wasn't on purpose, Valentine. If you want to see what it's like when I mark you on purpose, well—'

Then suddenly it's *my* back against the wall, plaster dust in my hair, and my mind is once again calculating the most efficient way to strip him before I've even begun to kiss him back. Whatever else Killian Drake might be, he is an excellent kisser. He persuades me with his lips and with his fingertips, coaxing me towards revelations that I would kill to suppress.

'Tell me you don't want this,' he whispers against my mouth. His hand is slipping under my top to stroke the bare skin at the base of my spine. 'Tell me to stop.'

I should, because every minute this continues is just delaying the twenty-four chaste hours we'll have to wait before he can leave, but his words remind me so much of the first time we kissed – in the dark, in his car, when I still thought I hated him – that I can't contain the quiet moan that escapes me.

'Tell me,' he says, and then he's kissing the edge of my jaw, down my throat, and his mouth is on my neck with his teeth gazing the spot where—

'Stop,' I say before I self-combust. 'Drake, stop.'

He stops dead, as though I've hit a button to turn him off. Then carefully, as though he's afraid he'll break me, he pulls back from me and steps away.

'Did I do something wrong?' he asks in a voice so full of pain that I want to kiss it away.

But I can't trust that desire. This is what the bond does: it pulls me towards him. Now that I'm wearing his scent mark, it'll be worse. I shouldn't have given in to the temptation to kiss him properly in the first place, because for the next twenty-four hours, all I'll want to do is kiss him again – and more – to bathe myself in the inimitable and sublime scent of Killian Drake until I forget where I end and he begins. And if he's going to spend those twenty-four hours here while he waits for my scent mark to dissipate…

Well, that's a unique kind of torture.

'This isn't what I want,' I say, kicking myself for letting it get this far. 'That wasn't supposed to happen.'

'But you enjoyed it,' he says, looking for reassurance that

I can't give him. 'It's what you wanted.'

'It's what the bond wanted,' I say. 'Not me.'

'Right,' Drake says, but there's a new sharpness in his voice. 'Blame it on the bond. Blame it on the mark. Blame it on anything that allows you to convince yourself that it has nothing to do with me at all.'

'Drake—'

'I'm not *Drake* to you, and you know it. I'm Killian.' He wraps his hand around mine as he says the name I have only ever whispered to him. 'I'm *your* Killian.'

'You're the Baron of Oxford,' I say with a laugh, trying to snap him out of this mood, because I can't let his words derail me again. 'You don't belong to anyone, least of all to me. You're the one in charge. Speaking of which, I know you're busy. You really don't need to come and find me as often as you have been. I have plenty of blood, and cash, and the burning really isn't that bad—'

'I can feel it through the bond,' he interrupts. 'I can feel when it's making you weaker.'

'*Weaker*. Not weak. It's dangerous for you to make contact more often than you have to. We can leave it four, five, maybe six weeks.'

'And leave you vulnerable?'

'You're already making me vulnerable by refusing to tell me anything about what's happening back home,' I say, frustrated.

'Let me worry about that. You can trust me to handle it. You just need to concentrate on hiding, and on keeping strong enough to fight if you have to.'

'But every time you track me down, you risk exposing my location. Isn't that worse than letting me get just a bit weaker?'

'And leaving you unable to defend yourself? No,' he says. 'And I don't think you believe that either.'

He's right to be suspicious; my problem isn't with the risk of discovery, it's with the risk that he presents to me. The more I see him, the more likely I am to give in to temptation. Again.

'The less often you visit,' I say, 'the better off I am.'

For a moment, he is speechless. Then he says, 'Is that what you really think?'

I shrug.

That's what tips him over the edge. I'm not sure why exactly. Maybe it's that he knows I'm avoiding the real issue, or that I'm being flippant about it, or maybe he's just looking for a way out of here that doesn't involve spilling whatever news he's keeping from me, but either way it's enough to cloud his expression and have him reaching for his coat.

'Fine,' he says. 'I'll go.'

'You can't go. You're still wearing my scent mark,' I argue, quite reasonably I think. 'You said it yourself: they'll use it to follow you back to me.'

'Do you really think that little of me?' he says, and he's properly pissed off now. 'Do you seriously think that I'd endanger you? Quite apart from anything else, have you forgotten that my life is tied to yours through the bond?'

'Then what are you doing?'

'There are other places I can go to wait out the scent mark. I'm not stupid, Jack.'

'So it's back to Jack, now, is it?' I say, unable to stop myself. I regret it instantly.

As if he wasn't riled up enough. But I can't take it back.

He slams the door on his way out.

I'm left standing alone in my shitty little bedsit, wreathed in the intoxicating scent of spice and copper that makes me ache, wishing things were otherwise.

But this is for the best. I've made my bed, and I have to lie in it, alone. I promised myself that I wouldn't drag him down into it with me. I seem to be doing a piss-poor job of that so far, but I resolve to do better in future. I will clean up the mess I have made, and if he's determined to keep me in the dark, then I'll do it without him.

2

I WAKE IN the middle of the night with my pulse racing and the feeling that I've forgotten something awful in the darkness of my subconscious. I realise that my throat is sore, then I remember what happened on the rooftops in my dreams, and in reality. I've been screaming in my sleep again.

Fucking night terrors.

There's a knock at the door, and I go back on high alert.

I'm not expecting visitors. I check the time on my retro radio alarm clock: past three in the morning. Not a time that anyone would knock on someone else's door, unless they had a very good reason.

I don't have a dressing gown, so I pull a jumper on over my pyjamas and walk the scant four feet to the front door to peer out of the peephole. An innocuous-looking woman is standing on the other side in her nightwear. She, I notice, is enough of a grown up to have not only a dressing gown, but matching slippers as well. She's about my age, which is to say about forty, although she's wearing every one of those years, while I'm stuck looking like I did when I turned Silver at eighteen. She smiles at the peephole and waves.

'Hi,' she says quietly through the door. 'It's Louise from next door.'

I recognise her now, vaguely. We've said hi along the length of the hall a couple of times, but she certainly doesn't know me well enough to be visiting at this hour. Still, she's harmless and I'm loaded up on blood and Drake's healing mojo, so I open the door.

'Hi,' I say. 'What's up?'

'Is everything okay?' she asks me. 'I heard screaming.'

'Oh. Shit. Sorry,' I say, rubbing the sleep from my eyes. 'Nightmares,' I explain. 'I didn't mean to disturb you.'

'No, it's fine. It's just that I heard arguing last night and I worried—' I must look horrified, because she interrupts herself to say, 'I'm sorry. I didn't mean to pry, but this place has thin walls, and I wanted to make sure you were okay.'

'No, *I'm* sorry,' I say, mortified, and worried about how much of my conversation with Drake she might have overheard. I'm racing back through our argument in my mind, trying to sift out anything incriminating. Louise is obviously very human, and it would be a whole different kind of nightmare if we'd unintentionally clued her in on the Silver with our shouting. 'I don't know if you heard what we were arguing about…' I say, fishing.

'Not the words,' she says, and I relax a little. 'Just tones, you know. And… thumping,' she adds, doing some fishing of her own.

'Not the bad kind.' I smile.

'Oh. *Oh.*'

'I'm fine, really. Thank you, though. It's really kind of you to check on me.' And brave, I think, for a human woman to investigate my screaming on her own in the middle of the night. 'And I'm sorry for disturbing you; I'll try to be quieter.'

'All right,' she says. 'I'll say goodnight then.'

'Goodnight, Louise.'

'Goodnight...'

She leaves a significant pause. I scramble to come up with something to fill it with.

'Naia,' I say.

Okay, fine, it's not exactly original, but it's nearly four in the morning. What do you want from me?

'Night then, Naia,' she says with a smile, then she turns to go back to her own bedsit. 'Nice lipstick, by the way. Different.'

My hand flies to my lips, which are still stained silver from Drake's healing. Like the scent mark, it takes a day or so to disappear. In the fog of sleep, I had entirely forgotten about it.

'Um, thanks,' I say.

She waves and carries on down the corridor. I don't close my door until I know she's safely locked up behind her own. I've just heard something outside our building, and I don't want lovely, brave Louise to get mixed up in what happens next.

3

WHEN I GET back inside the bedsit, gravel is raining gently against my second-storey window. Then pebbles. Then a stone big enough to chip the glass.

I rush to the window and throw it open.

'Mina,' I whisper. 'Mina. Is that you?'

'That depends,' a voice calls up, less softly than I'd like. 'How many clothes have you got on, and how many of them are you willing to take off?'

Prurient, unnecessarily sexual and completely unprofessional. Yup, that's Mina.

Mina Parchek is a private investigator, and she's Silver. We had a brief dalliance a couple of years ago that has, unfortunately, set the tone for the rest of our relationship. She used to work in Oxford, but after a few too many run-ins with the local authorities – by which I mean Drake and the Seekers and me – she was persuaded to take her enterprising investigative skills elsewhere. When I needed help with my current situation from someone with no respect for the law, either human or Silver, she was the first person who came to mind. She's unethical, she's aggressive and she's off-puttingly predatory, but she goes after a problem like a

Chihuahua after a Rottweiler's bone, and she gets the job done.

'I'm staying fully clothed,' I whisper back, 'and so are you.'

'Spoilsport.'

'Just get up here, will you?'

I'm expecting her to go to the front door so I can buzz her in, but instead she takes a standing leap from the pavement up to my windowsill.

'Subtle,' I say. 'You do know that I'm in hiding, right? And you nearly broke my bloody window with that last rock.'

'If you got a phone then I wouldn't have to resort to less orthodox methods of communication, so that's your own fault, really.'

'I repeat: I'm in hiding. Phones can be tracked.'

'Then I'll get you a burner,' she says, stepping down through the window and into the room. 'Well, this place is a shithole. I thought you were running on the baron's money. Can't you afford something less... condemnable?'

'It's fine. I won't be here for long. And I don't want a burner phone. They can be tracked, too.'

Mina takes a moment to have a proper look around the bedsit. I only moved in last week, and I never unpacked, which will make the fleeing-for-my-life thing easier when it's time to move on again. Not that there would be much unpacking to do: just a change of clothes and a handful of toiletries in a bag. The only traces of my presence are the small pile of belongings in the satchel on the floor and the blankets laid messily over the fold-out bed. The mattress is somehow paper thin and at the same time exceptionally lumpy. It's enough to make me miss my creaky college single.

While Mina assesses my living space, I assess her. Her

15

dark hair is styled in a slick little bob and the burgundy red of her coat sets off the gold in her olive skin. She's dressed for a night out in heels, dark trousers and a top cut so low I can practically see her stomach. Altogether, she's looking good enough to remind me why we tumbled into bed together in the first place. That's unfortunate, because I'm still more than a little frustrated from Drake's visit, and Mina's sense of smell is sharp enough to pick up on the pheromones. She can tell that she's making me thoughtful.

'I heard you scream,' she says, looking at my rumpled sheets. 'Having trouble sleeping, Jack? Need some company?'

The best policy with Mina's propositions is to ignore them, so instead of responding directly, I say, 'Tell me what you've found out.'

'Well, that explains the sexual tension,' she says, ignoring me in return as her gaze lands squarely on my silver lips. 'Looks like someone's been smooching a baron. A baron with a dangerous secret.'

'Yes, I am aware of that, Mina. Tell me something I don't know, about one of the things I'm actually paying you to investigate.'

When you hire Mina, you don't always get to control where she points her devious little mind. It only took one visit from Drake for her to piece together the truth about the bad blood, the healing mojo, and therefore the bond. She knows her Silver lore and she's good at what she does, which means she's now one of only four people in the world who know that Drake has silvered for me, the fourth being his most recent ex, Carlotta Arden. The bond is a secret that could kill him if it gets out; if someone wanted him dead, all they'd have to do is kill me, and the bond would make sure that the two of us left this earth together. Since I've been Silver for far fewer years than him, and since I already have one foot in the grave, bumping me off would not be a particular challenge. It's why Drake is so concerned for my safety: our lives are bound together now.

And I guess there's the other reason too, but I'm not thinking about that.

'Looks like you did more than smooch him, too,' Mina says, clocking the dents in the plasterboard.

'The landlord's renovating,' I lie. 'What's going on in Oxford? Have you got any news on the Invicti, or Yolande Leclercq, or Khalyed's blood?'

'No kiss and tell with the baron, then?' Mina asks. 'He's still not cluing you in?'

'He won't.'

'Tight-lipped bastard,' she says. She flops down onto the sofa-bed, then sits forward again, pulling Drake's bottle of wine out from behind one of the cushions. 'Hmm, good vintage. Maybe you're not living so badly after all. Grab us a couple of glasses.'

The best I can find in the cupboards is a pint glass and a coffee mug shaped like a frog, but we make do.

'The Invicti are hanging around the mansion most days,' Mina says, selecting the frog for herself. She fills it to the top. 'They've got the baron pinned down pretty tightly. I'm surprised he managed to slip away.'

'I'm not. He's as slippery as they come.'

'Well,' Mina snorts into her wine, 'you'd know.'

'Jesus, Mina. Can we please try to stay on track?'

'Fine,' she says, knocking back her wine like it's beer. 'Then here it is: you're not just top of the Invicti's most-wanted list at the moment, you *are* the list. If they find you, they're going to kill you on sight.'

'Fuck.'

It's not as though I expected anything different. After all, I did try to kill the Primus – the most powerful Silver in existence, and basically our king in all but name – but I was still hopeful. The last time I saw him I got the distinct impression that he has a soft spot for me, even though I was trying to stab him with a syringe full of poisoned blood at the time.

'You won't want to hear this,' Mina says, 'but your old mates from the Seekers are helping them. Naia and Cameron.'

I nod while my heart breaks. This is no surprise either, but it hurts. When the Seekers were disbanded at the beginning of the year, my old partner and bestie Cam was promptly inaugurated into the ranks of the Solis Invicti – the Primus's elite guard – and Naia wasn't far behind. They didn't have many other options, so I didn't blame them, and anyway that was before everything went to shit. They didn't know then that they were pitting themselves against me, because I hadn't told them what I was planning.

Cam knew a little. He knew that I'd been living in the house where the last in a line of exsanguinated students had been found. He'd been loyal enough to move my things out of the house before the others arrived to investigate, and he wanted to help me clear my name, so he took a blood sample from me to compare against the DNA of the dead students. Back then, before the attempt on the Primus's life, I'd thought it might actually work. But then I remembered the bottles of anonymous blood that had been given to me in that house, bottles I thought had been stolen from the college supply, and I started to wonder if I'd made some seriously flawed assumptions about their origins. Which all goes to say: it's possible that the results of that blood test might give the Invicti more reason to go after me, not less.

'What about Raul?' I ask.

Raul's an old drinking buddy who joined the Seekers shortly before the end. He was something of a protégé of mine – I know, right? Who'd trust me with a protégé? – but I somehow doubt he's Invicti material.

'He's gone back to his old life,' Mina says.

This isn't a surprise, but I'm still disappointed. I wanted him to get out from under the shadow of his past, and that isn't going to happen if he disappears back into a bottle, or a pile of his drug of choice, or both.

'And Boyd?'

'He's not with the Invicti either.'

That *is* a surprise. Boyd was once the deputy, and then acting captain, of the Seekers. If anyone's uptight enough to make it in the Silver equivalent of the military, it's Boyd.

'Then where is he?' I ask.

'Buggered if I know. Seems like he's lying low. Did you want me to find out?'

'No,' I say. 'It's not important. I was just wondering.'

Unexpectedly, I miss him. I miss them all, my old team. My old friends. Without them, all I have left is a permanently randy ex-fling and whatever the hell Drake is.

'It must be hard for you,' Mina says.

'Hmm.'

'You can talk to me about it, if you like. You don't even have to take your clothes off if you don't want to.'

'Pass. Tell me about Yolande Leclercq.'

Mina shrugs and pours herself another glass of wine.

'What's that supposed to mean?' I ask.

'It means I've got nothing on her. And believe me, I've looked. She's good at staying hidden, that one. Better than you. I don't know where she is or how she's going to come at you, but I think we can assume that you're in the shit.' Mina pulls up a photo on her phone and hands it to me. 'Solomon College quad,' she says.

'Oh shit.'

'*Oh shit* is right.'

I never would have pegged Leclercq as an artist, but there must have been some skill involved in getting her graffiti to look that angry and spiky. The paint is blood-red – actually, it probably *is* blood – and it reads *Valentine will die*. Going by the height of the windows in the quad, I'd guess the writing's about six feet tall, scrawled across the entire length of one limestone wall. It's signed *YL*, which is a stupid thing to do when you're committing an act of wanton and bloody vandalism, but she obviously cares more about getting her threat across than she does about whatever repercussions will follow from a little petty criminality.

She wants me to be scared.

Which takes us back to the rooftop, back to ancient history, and back to the things that wake me up screaming in the middle of the night.

Winta.

'Do you know how she found out?' I ask, my mouth suddenly dry.

The only people who should know what happened on that rooftop are me and Drake – and, after she somehow finagled the truth out of me in a dark moment, Mina. Leclercq shouldn't know that I... about Winta, so she shouldn't have any reason to want me dead.

And yet.

'From what I can gather,' Mina says, 'it seems like the baron is trying to swing things in your favour by pretending you were a double agent who was actually there to *foil* the plot to kill the Primus. As proof of your apparently-true allegiances, he told the Invicti what you did to your supposed co-conspirator. It must have leaked out.'

'But the Primus saw me. I mean, he was right there. Right *there*.' I gesture at a spot less than a foot away to make my point. 'He knew that I was trying to inject him with the syringe.'

'Yeah, well. I didn't say the baron's plan was working.'

'And now Leclercq knows what I did.'

'Apparently so.'

'Bloody Drake.'

'Good thing he's so fuckable, right?'

I scoff.

'Come on,' she says, pulling one knee up as she slouches back into the sofa. 'That devilish smile, those strong arms, that biteable—'

'*Mina!*'

'Fine. Forget it.'

The problem is, I don't disagree with her assessment. In fact, I had almost exactly those thoughts myself last night, and now that she's reminded me of them, Drake's mark on my skin is doing strange things to my senses and all I can think about is pulling on my coat and chasing the shadow of his scent out into the dark until I can track him down and throw him against the nearest wall and—

'You haven't touched your wine,' Mina says.

'I'm not thirsty.'

'Could have fooled me.'

'What I am thirsty for,' I say, with all the dignity I can muster, 'is a cure for the bad blood in my veins. Can you give me any news on that?'

'No good news,' she replies, filling her mug again. 'The baron was meeting with Dr Castell at Solomon College for a while, and I think they were working on something together.'

'Drake's working with Ed?' I ask, a little bubble of hope rising up in my chest.

Ed worked on the formula that created the poison in the first place. His colleague Dr Jay Khalyed infected himself with it, acting as a guinea pig for a formula that went terribly wrong. The blood I was planning to use to kill the Primus, and that ended up in my veins and Winta's, came from

21

Khalyed's body. If anyone can find a way to cure me, it's Ed.

'They were,' Mina says. 'But now Dr Castell's mostly in London with the Invicti, and they're keeping the baron busy at the mansion.'

'Can you get to Ed?'

'I don't know. I can try, but are you sure you want me to?'

She's right: I have no idea what side he's on. Chances are, it's not mine.

'No,' I say. 'No. For now, let's focus on getting another sample of Khalyed's blood, so we have something to work with. Can you do that?'

'Sure, if you give me some time to work my way into the baron's spooky basement.' She pauses to drain her mug, then gives me a curious look. 'Is it true that he used Khalyed's blood to kill a bunch of the psychopathic Silver who were boxed up down there?'

I blink. 'Where did you hear about that?'

Mina shrugs. Like I said, she's good at what she does. If you're doing something you don't want anyone to find out about, odds are Mina Parchek already has a file on it.

'Is it?' she asks again.

'Yes. So be careful.'

'And is it true that one of the rogues he killed was Elise Santiago? The one he used to go out—'

'Can we get back to business, please?'

'The two of you have a lot in common, you know,' she says.

'No. I don't.'

'Well, you both have strong personal morals but a kind of wishy-washy approach to the actual law, you both killed the women you thought were the loves of your life – with the same poisoned blood, no less – and on top of all that, you both want to rip each other's clothes off.'

'Mina—'

'I'm just not sure I see the problem here, is what I'm saying.'

'I'm not talking about this.'

I can't. I can't take myself back to that rooftop, not here and now, not by choice. I only go back in the darkness against my will.

'You've got to talk to *someone* about it, and you're clearly not talking to him.'

'I thought you were trying to get me naked?'

'Always.'

'Then this is a really weird way to go about it. I'm not talking to you about Drake.'

'But you *are* going to take your clothes off?'

'No! Jesus, Mina, please. Try to focus for just a few minutes, will you? I need you to find the doctor. Okay?'

'All right. But I'm going to need a cut of that pile of twenties the baron left on your night table.'

'Here,' I say, handing her a bundle of cash from my bag.

She licks her thumb, counts the stack, slips it into her bra, and says, 'That'll do nicely.'

'And it's not like that. Me and Drake, we're not—'

'Fucking?'

'Definitely not.' Not at the moment, anyway.

'But you want to.'

'No!'

'Tell that to the spicy little scent mark you're wearing tonight. I hope you're not planning on leaving this room for a while, because every Silver in the country knows that scent, and if you happen to meet one in the street, they'll know who you belong to right now.'

'Come on, Mina. The mark doesn't mean anything. You know we have to kiss for him to heal me.'

'Yeah, but you don't have to like it,' she says with an evil glint in her eye. 'And you do, don't you? Maybe a little too much. Maybe so much that when he leaves, you lie in bed alone, and you toss and you turn and you moan, and then maybe you kick off your trousers and—'

'Out!' I say, pointing to the door.

'Struck a nerve, have I?' she says. 'You know, Jack, I'm not afraid of Baron Drake. If you've got an itch that needs scratching, then I'm more than happy to oblige. So if you'll just step out of those pyjamas—'

'Goodbye, Mina.'

'All right,' she says, getting to her feet. 'But just so you know, I haven't forgotten how to make you scream.'

She gives me a wink that's filthy enough to make me blush, then hops back out of the window and into the night.

Maybe I could use that drink after all.

4

BEING ON THE run is both far too boring and far too exciting, all at the same time. I have to stay hidden inside most of the time, because otherwise the chances of Leclercq or the Invicti finding me are vastly increased, but I'm too anxious to read, and I can't touch the internet for the same reason I can't have a phone: too easy to track. If this was a film then I'd be busy limbering up for some final confrontation, doing press-ups and pull-ups, then I'd go undercover to find the evidence I needed to clear my name, but I've never been much for exercise, and if I'm being perfectly honest, my name deserves to stay dirty. I did what I did, but I'm not willing to do the time, so instead I waste the next couple of weeks day-drinking Massacres alone in front of the television and regretting my choices, while I wait for the door to crash open at any moment and put an end to my freedom, such as it is.

When I hear the footsteps in the corridor outside early one morning, early enough that I haven't yet dragged myself out of bed, I think this is finally it. Louise and Drake are the only other people I've ever heard walking down that corridor, so I can only assume that two sets of large, thumping footsteps are bringing bad news. It turns out I'm right about that, it's just not me they're here for.

There's a knock at a door that isn't mine, then a man's voice shouts, 'Louise Cahill?'

A pause, then a woman says: 'Mrs Cahill, it's the police. Open the door, please.' Another pause. 'Your mother's worried about you, Mrs Cahill. We just want to check that you're all right.'

Pause.

Knock knock.

'Mrs Cahill?'

Footsteps come back along the corridor, and this time the knocking is at my door.

I shouldn't answer it. I should stay exactly where I am, pretending that the flat is vacant or that I'm out or that I'm too wasted to come to the door, but the truth is that I'm curious, and a little worried. I like Louise. Ever since the night she came and checked on me – a couple of weeks ago now – we've had a quick chat whenever we've bumped into each other, and she's never been less than friendly. If something's wrong, I want to know about it, so I pull on my new dressing gown and open the door to the police officers.

There are two of them, a man and a woman. The woman has the build of a rugby player, with muscular thighs that are straining her trousers to their limit, while the man is skinny with a ratty moustache that makes him look like a sex pest. But who am I to judge? I'm standing here in my pink fluffy charity shop dressing gown with – I'm just noticing to my horror – dried blood smeared up my arm.

'Good morning,' I say, pulling down my sleeve as I blink in the sunshine. It's streaming in through the window behind them, and it's brighter than I expected it would be.

'Good afternoon,' the woman says.

'Afternoon?' I ask.

'Afternoon.'

'Huh.' That would explain the problem with the sun. Maybe it's time I knocked the day-drinking on the head. 'What's going on? I heard you next door.'

'Is this your residence?' the woman asks, then she looks down at my bloody arm. I follow her gaze and see there's red caked on the sleeve of my dressing gown too.

Perfect.

'Cut myself shaving,' I say. 'And yes, I live here.'

'Shaving your *arm*?' the man asks.

I turn to him. 'Some women are hairy. What about it?'

Great, Jack. Antagonise the fucking police when you're supposed to be flying under the radar. That'll help.

But the woman says, 'Ignore him,' and moves on, for now at least. I guess she's Good Cop. 'We're performing a welfare check on your neighbour, Louise Cahill. Do you know her at all?'

'Yeah, enough to say hello. Is something wrong?'

'Have you seen her today?' the woman asks, trying and failing to make it sound like a genuine question; we both know I've only just got out of bed. 'Or yesterday?'

'No. I haven't seen her for a few days.' Or heard her, now that I think about it, and with my supernatural senses, I should have done. 'Did something happen?'

'She missed an appointment yesterday, an appointment she would have kept. Do you happen to have a spare key to her place?'

'No,' I say. 'I've only lived here a few weeks. We don't know each other that well.'

'And your name is...?' the man says, pulling out a notebook.

'Ms Balls,' I say, giving the name on the fake I.D. Mina sorted out for me last week.

'First name?'

Christ.

I clear my throat and say, 'Ophelia.' Then I have to go and fetch said fake I.D. from my bag because neither of them believes me.

Mina thought it would be funny. I think it's worse than reckless to draw attention to yourself with a joke name when you're on the run – a sentiment that I expressed to Mina with far more four-letter words – but she just laughed and said it suited me, so here we are.

The man squints at my fake driver's licence for a moment before handing it to the woman. She does the same, then hands it back to me with a sympathetic grimace.

'What happens now?' I ask, chucking the card back into the flat behind me. 'Do you bust down the door, or whatever?'

'No,' the man says, scribbling something in his notebook before flipping it closed in a way that feels performative. Who even uses a notebook anymore? 'We go back to the station and make a report.'

I'm waiting for him to continue, but apparently that's it.

'You just walk away without even checking if she's in there?' I ask. 'What if she's dying on the floor right now?'

The woman's gaze narrows on me. 'Do you have any reason to believe that she might be?'

I think back. There's nothing, but I can't let them leave without checking on her, because I'm sure as shit going in there myself if they don't, and it feels like a bad idea to get myself mixed up in this if I don't have to.

So I lie and say, 'There was a thud.'

'A thud?' the woman asks.

'Like someone falling over. Yesterday, I think. A thud, crash, bang. She could be trapped under the furniture, or she could have had a heart attack or something. Either way, you really should check on her.'

The man looks at the woman and says, 'Is that enough?'

She walks a little way down the corridor and spends some time on her radio, then comes back to my door and says, 'Thank you for your help, Ms Balls.' It's a dismissal.

'You can't just leave,' I say.

'We won't,' she promises. 'But you should go back inside.'

So, out of character though it is, I obediently step away from the action, back into my dingy little flat, and lock the door behind me.

But I'm still a detective at heart, so I listen. I listen while the two police officers hang around in the corridor outside instead of breaking into Louise's flat, and my frustration builds with each passing minute. About half an hour later, someone from the management company comes over with a spare key, and I realise that even if they do believe my story, they think it's too late for it to be worth breaking anything to get to Louise.

The moment they get the door open, I know they're right.

Poor Louise.

The scent of rot is new enough not to have made it through the walls, but it rolls under my door like a foul tide. The humans don't notice it. They don't even realise she's dead until—

'Holy shit!' a man yells. It's not the police officer – this guy sounds younger and posher – so it must be the agent.

'Oh dear,' says the woman. 'I've got a syringe here.'

'Drugs?' says the agent. He sounds horrified. 'We don't house druggies. This isn't some low-rent establishment.'

The piss in the lift and the graffiti on the front door would tend to disagree, but it's true that my weekly rent is extortionate for what this place is, so I guess he's technically correct on that point.

'Her mother told us she was in recovery,' the woman says.

'Eight months clean,' her colleague replies, and I can hear his notebook snapping shut. 'It's always the relapse that gets them. They lose their tolerance for it, don't reduce the dose enough, and that's the end.'

'Poor woman.'

There's a moment's respectful silence, then the agent says, 'Fucking hell. Now I'm going to have to pay to get this cleaned up.'

People are in and out all that day, and the day after, clearing away what remains of my former-neighbour's life.

Her death has affected me in ways I didn't expect. I'm drinking, of course, because I always drink these days, but I think I'm hallucinating too. Late on the second day, I swear I get a waft of a scent that I recognise, something like oil and burning rubber, something that makes me feel like I should be jumping into action, but then my special blood cocktail hits and takes me away to a numb place where I can't smell much of anything anymore, let alone remember a scent.

A voice in my head says, *Maybe you should pack up and get out of here. Move on.*

It says, *Bad things come in threes. This is only number one.*

It says, *Remember the last three? One: the bungled assassination attempt. Two: the bad blood in your veins. Three: you murdered Winta.*

It says, *Maybe your drinking is becoming a problem.*

It says, *You murdered her.*

I tell it to shut up and I pour myself another.

I should feel worse than I do, and I feel guilty about that.

I feel guilty about Louise, too: that I didn't know her better, and that I didn't know anything about her struggles, but then you don't move to a place like this unless you want anonymity. She was here for the same reason I am: she was running away. And though her demons were purely psychological, while mine also take the form of supernatural revenge-seeking Silver, it's difficult to ignore the fact that I'm not exactly stable at the moment either, mentally speaking. That's pretty evident from the empty booze and blood bottles scattered around my flat, and is it even safe for me to be mixing Valentine's Massacre cocktails using my own poisoned blood? Who knows, but apparently I don't care, because that's exactly what I've been doing.

I've been trying not to think too hard about why this is. There's the nightmares, of course. And I'm bored, I guess, but that can't be the whole story. I'm scared too, but that's not quite it either. And I'm in pain, because the more time that passes between one healing and the next, the more the bad blood starts to burn me from the inside out – and I'd swear it's worse this time that it was the last – but I'm worried that's not why I'm craving Drake's kiss. The truth is that I have an addiction of my own, and it comes in a package six-feet tall with a wicked smile and shark's eyes. Given that our lives are now tied together through the bond, it's selfish as shit for me to be taking risks with my blood. I know this, but I'm still doing it, and I don't know why. Maybe I'm trying to drink us both into an early grave so I can summon him back here sooner through the bond. Maybe I just want to numb the pain and forget about the rooftop.

Either way, I can't succumb to Drake, not again. It's like the policeman said: it's the relapse that gets you.

5

EVENTUALLY, I RUN out of booze. It was bound to happen sooner or later.

I nip out to the local off-licence to grab a few more bottles of gin, but on the way back to my flat I get an itchy, tingly feeling at the back of my neck.

My footsteps have an echo. It's a soft one, but it's there. I swear someone's following me. I can't get a scent, because they're downwind from me, but I can hear a heartbeat that isn't human.

This is the point at which I should book it back to the flat, or run away entirely to a new city, or a new country even, but I'm still a little drunk, so instead I decide to turn a corner, then nip into the first alley I pass and see if I can get eyes on the person behind me. It's not the stealthiest move I've ever made. Either I don't move quickly enough to fool them, or they're tracking my scent – which, frankly, I should have thought about before attempting the manoeuvre – because they're right behind me when I turn back towards the mouth of the alley, silhouetted against the streetlights on the main road. They can see my face, but I can't see theirs.

It's at this point I realise that Massacres make for bad

planning.

'Don't take another step,' I warn the shadow. 'I've got—' I look down at the bottles in my arms and do a quick count '—five bottles of gin, and I can afford to lose at least one of them bashing your head in.'

The figure doesn't move. But then I recognise something in the height, in the shape of the shoulders, in the wave of the hair, and in the gangly Labradorishness of the limbs.

'Cam?' I whisper.

'Hello, Jack.'

He turns slightly sideways, so the light falls on his face. It really is him. He's a little more muscular, a little more chiseled around the jaw, and the Invicti have tidied up his hair, but here he is: my partner, my confidante, my best friend.

And now he's one of them.

'Look, Cam,' I say, backing away as I clutch my gin bottles to my chest, 'I know I did some bad things, and I ruined your admission ceremony to the Solis Invicti by trying to murder the Primus, but I'm still your best friend in the world, right? You don't have to do this.'

'I'm a little insulted by that.' And he doesn't look amused, either.

'You're loyal, I know,' I say, scrambling for ideas as I trip over random detritus. 'And I know being in the Invicti has always been a dream of yours, and I wouldn't want to jeopardise that, but maybe you could just... let me go?'

His face twists. The light isn't great, but I don't think he's impressed.

The alley is a dead-end and my back's against the wall. I could try to run, but I know Cam's faster than me. There's no point.

'For old times' sake?' I say, desperately.

'You think I'm here to capture you?' he asks.

'Are you... not? I thought the Invicti had orders to kill me on sight.'

'You are a complete idiot, do you know that? Firstly, give me a little credit: I know your scent like I know my own, and I could track you halfway around the world and back if I had to. If I wanted to bring you in, I would have done it back in January. Secondly, if you're wandering around in the open like this, then frankly you deserve to get caught. And thirdly, I'm your best friend in the world and you haven't seen me since New Year's. Are you going to make me beg for a hug?'

It takes a moment for all of this to filter through my addled brain.

'A hug?' I whisper.

Then I drop the bottles of gin and start crying.

Cam wraps me up in his arms and I let him. 'Oh, Jack,' he says, holding me close. 'You're a mess. Have you been drinking?'

'Yes,' I sob, 'of course I've been drinking. But that's not why I'm crying.'

'Is it because you smashed one of your many bottles of gin?'

'No,' I sniff, wiping my nose on my sleeve. 'And I'm blaming you for that.'

'At least you didn't waste it bashing my head in.' He pulls back from the hug to get a good look at me, then wipes away my tears with his thumbs. 'Who did you think I was, anyway?'

'I don't know, but I was worried you might be Yolande Leclercq.'

'Oh, yes. I saw the graffiti in the college quad.'

'And you're not even a little bit tempted to join forces with her?'

He just laughs at that and retrieves my unbroken bottles from the piles of rubbish at my feet.

'I hope you're not expecting me to share those,' I say.

'Only a little,' he replies, and the smile fades from his face. 'Look, I can't stay long.'

'Why are you here?' I ask. 'Not that it isn't amazing to see you, but if you aren't here to bring me to justice...'

'I can't just be missing you?' he says innocently, but I know it has to be more than that.

'You wouldn't risk it unless it was something important,' I say.

'All right. I'm here to warn you about—' He glances around and doesn't seem satisfied by what he sees. 'Is there somewhere we can go to talk?

'If you're sure you weren't followed.' I go up on my tiptoes so I can peek over his shoulder to scan the street behind him.

'Okay, now I'm feeling insulted again,' he says. 'I might need another hug.'

'You can have all the hugs you want once we're inside,' I say, taking his hand. 'Come on.'

It's only when I've already got Cam upstairs with the door half-open that I remember what a state my flat is in: the blood I've spilled on the floor, the empty bottles, the Drake-shaped holes in the plaster... It doesn't exactly give the impression that I'm doing well.

'Rough night?' he says, looking around at the flotsam I've left in my wake.

'Rough month,' I reply.

I pick up everything that's piled on the sofa and chuck it on the floor, making room for the two of us. Cam sits without judgement. He's seen enough of my college rooms over the past couple of decades not to expect good housekeeping from me.

'Just so we're clear,' he says, 'you don't have to worry

JOSIE JAFFREY

about me. I'm not going to tell anyone where you are. The Invicti don't know I'm here, and they never will. Actually, let's just say I was never here in the first place, and we never had the conversation we're about to have. Okay?'

'Okay, super spy.'

'Okay. Gin?' Cam offers me one of the bottles he's just dumped on the sofa.

'I think I'd better take a break until you've told me the bad news. Is it Leclercq? Has she found me?'

'You're really that worried about her?' Cam asks, surprised.

'Of course I am. She moves like a ghost. You remember what it was like that night at Crimson when the place got lit on fire – I'm pretty sure that was her doing the clandestine fire-starting. And then there was that time she blew us up.'

'And shredded your leather jacket,' Cam adds.

'Right, and I loved that jacket. My point is, she knows explosives. Also, you know, she might be nursing a misguided grudge against me.'

'Misguided?'

'A bit,' I say, then for the sake of fairness I add: 'Not entirely.'

Leclercq has every right to hate me for what I did. I can accept that – I hate myself for it too – but she doesn't know the whole truth. Leclercq doesn't know that Winta double-crossed her at the end. As far as she's concerned, Winta wasn't *my* girlfriend, who was about to screw Leclercq over and run away with me. No, she was *Leclercq's* girlfriend, and I ruined *their* happily-ever-after. In those circumstances, I can understand why she might want me dead.

'What's wrong with your skin?' Cam asks, watching me rub at the spots on my arm where it's started to burn. Thinking about all of this makes it harder to ignore the pain, and it's been four weeks since my last healing. It'll only get

36

worse from now on. 'Did you hurt yourself?'

I debate the merits of lying to him. Technically, he works for the enemy, and anything I tell him could end up being leaked back to them, but I don't think he'd do that to me. Not Cam.

'When I used the syringe of Khalyed's blood…' I say, but I'm not sure how to finish the sentence. 'You heard about that, right?'

He nods, and I'm grateful that I don't have to go into details.

'It broke in my hand,' I go on, 'and some of the blood got into me. It burns, from time to time.'

For a moment, Cam says nothing, he just stares at me, scanning my body in a panic for signs of imminent combustion. Then he says, 'Are you serious? How are you still alive?'

'I can't really go into that.' Since telling him the truth about the bond and the healing mojo could endanger Drake, it doesn't feel like it's my secret to share.

'You have to.'

'No, Cam. I don't. I don't have to do anything.'

'No, Jack, listen. It's important,' he says, leaning forward to take my hands in his. 'I came here to warn you: you're fixating on Yolande Leclercq, but the person you really need to be worried about is Adewale Ladipo.'

'Oh, trust me, I am. I'm worried about all the Invicti. Except you, of course.' Not anymore, at least.

'But Adewale isn't working with us on this.'

'Excuse me?'

'You killed his sister, Jack. He's gone off on his own with his friend Alistair Jameson. The rest of the Invicti are trying to bring you in alive, but if Adewale and Alistair find you first and you accidentally end up dead, no one's going to blame them for it. They're older than you, they're stronger than you, they've got gizmos and gadgets galore, and they've been trained by the Invicti, who – and you can trust me on this – know what they're doing when it comes to boot camp. You are in trouble. Do you hear me? *Trouble*.'

'I was already aware of that, actually.'

'But if you've got a cure for Dr Jay's blood, and by extension his serum,' he goes on, ignoring me, 'then that could be enough to buy you a way out of this.'

'What are you talking about?'

'Ed told you the story. Remember? Dr Jay bit Adewale's father and infected him with an earlier version of the serum. If you can offer Adewale whatever you're using to treat Dr Jay's poison, then maybe it'll help his father, and maybe that'll be enough to get him to call off this witch-hunt against you.'

'But Winta and Adewale's parents are dead,' I say, confused. 'Adewale told me so himself. The Invicti killed his parents because his mother tried to steal Khalyed's blood to develop a cure for his father. They're gone.'

'He told you that?'

'Yes.'

Cam shrugs. 'Then he was lying.'

'He was— Wait a minute,' I say. '*You* told me that too.'

'I don't think I did.' Cam crinkles his face into an expression of such fake puzzlement that it wouldn't fool anyone.

'You did, too!' I insist. 'When we were down in Drake's basement, just after we'd been to Khalyed's box—'

'You mean after you tricked us into going down there and showing you where he was, so you could come back later and steal his blood to kill the Primus?'

Bugger. I forgot that part.

'Never mind that,' I say.

'I do mind that,' he replies. 'I mind it a lot, and I'm not

sure Ed's ever going to forgive you for it. Dr Jay was his friend.'

'Yes, and you said Ed had been working with Winta's parents to make a cure, but they didn't manage it because the Ladipos died,' I say, talking over him. 'You *lied* to me, Cam.'

'Oh, *I* lied, did I? If we're having a competition about who's the biggest liar out of the two of us, who do you think is going to win that?'

Okay, he might have a point, there.

'Because one of us secretly got back together with her ex,' he goes on, 'then pretended she'd been kidnapped by her *other* ex, while she and the original ex plotted the downfall of Silver society as we know it, all while lying through her teeth to her best friend about it, while the other one of us told a tiny white lie to keep a friend's confidence. Which of those sounds worse to you?'

'Cam—' I say, holding my hand out to him.

'No,' he says, crossing his arms over his chest so I can't reach him. Then he sits back into the sofa and looks at the floor. 'Now you've reminded me how angry I am with you. I'm going to need a minute to calm down.'

'Okay.'

I can't say I don't deserve it, so I let him take the time he needs.

After a long silence, he says, 'You know, the results of your blood tests came back at the beginning of January.' He's still looking at the floor instead of looking at me.

'I guess they weren't good.'

'No. They weren't. You had the DNA of the last three victims in your blood.'

This isn't exactly a surprise, but I still feel like I've been punched in the chest.

I knew in my heart that it was true, but now I have proof:

Winta killed all those students in Oxford last year and drained them for her own personal blood supply. Probably Leclercq was helping her, but Winta was at least aware of what was happening. She knew where the bottles of blood in her fridge were coming from, and she still gave them to me to drink. She wanted me to be complicit in those murders, but why? As a kind of insurance? Or for some sick thrill? I'll never know now, but the possibilities turn my stomach.

'Cam,' I say, swallowing back my nausea, 'you know I wouldn't—'

'I didn't think you'd try to kill the Primus either, but – whatever Baron Drake says about it – I'm pretty sure you did. Didn't you?'

'Yes,' I admit. 'But I didn't kill those kids, and if I'd known their blood was in those bottles, I never would have drunk them.'

He stares at the floor for a few more seconds, then he folds. 'I know that. And I know you must have thought you were doing the right thing. But Jack,' he says, finally meeting my eyes, 'why didn't you tell me? You could have told me.'

'No, Cam. You were joining the Invicti. I couldn't.'

'I'm Invicti now and you don't see me turning you in, do you?'

'And if I told you I was actively planning an attack on the Primus?'

He looks alarmed. 'You're not, are you?'

'No! It was a mistake I'm not going to repeat. But if I was, you'd tell him.'

'Not necessarily.'

I give him a look. 'Cam…'

'Yes, fine,' he concedes. 'I would. But I still wish you'd told me, and maybe then I could have talked you out of it.'

'With Winta in my other ear? I don't think so. I thought I

was in love. I would have done anything for her, Cam.'

'Then why did you kill her?' he asks. 'Or was that just another lie?'

'No,' I whisper. 'It's true. I killed her.'

It's the first time I've said the words out loud, and they hit me in the chest like arrows. Just like that, I'm back on the rooftop with my first love in my arms, her face fracturing along glowing red cracks that break her open and burn her to ashes, right in front of me.

I did that. I immolated the woman I loved.

'But why?' Cam asks. 'You didn't really do it to save the Primus, did you?'

'No. Not him.'

When I don't elaborate, Cam just looks confused. 'I don't understand,' he says.

'I'm not sure I do either,' I say, but I've already said more than I should have done. 'So what's going to happen now?' I ask. 'About the students, I mean.'

'If the Seekers still existed then we'd be hunting you down and boxing you up, but they don't, so I guess it's up to the Baron of Oxford, since it happened in his city. You'll have to deal with him, but something tells me that won't be a problem. You know he's been asking the Primus to pardon you?'

'What?' This is news to me.

'The Primus seems pretty interested in you, actually. He's been asking me to tell him about you. I've not been saying anything bad, I promise.'

'Then you can't have said much. Is he angry?' I ask, wincing.

'Weirdly, no. But Drew is, and Benedict's livid.'

Oh hooray, two of my least favourite members of the Super Squad: the Secundus and the Tertius, first- and second-in-command of the Solis Invicti. I'm pretty sure that

Benedict, at the very least, would kill to see me boxed. Or vice versa.

'They didn't much like being blinded by your laser device,' Cam goes on, 'or being knocked out by whatever alcoholic cocktail you put in their drinks. They're pretending it's all about protecting the Primus, but honestly I think you just pissed them off. It's a talent of yours,' he adds, not without affection.

'It wasn't just me!' I protest. 'I hope they're looking for Leclercq as well. She's the one who blew up Solis Invicti HQ, you know, and if you could lock her away, then at least it would get her off my back.'

'Wait,' he says, his brow furrowing, 'why did Yolande Leclercq blow up our building?'

Our building. How quickly he's become one of them.

'Funny you should ask that,' I say, 'but she was actually looking for Winta's parents. Winta didn't believe they were dead – with good reason, apparently – and we were supposed to be rescuing them, but Leclercq couldn't find them.'

'*Rescuing* them? Jack, they don't need rescuing. The whole reason they're with the Invicti is that they were hiding from Winta.'

Now it's my turn to do some brow-furrowing.

'Why would they be hiding from their own daughter?' I ask. 'That doesn't make any sense.'

'Because she wanted to take her father's infected blood and turn it into a weapon, just like she ended up doing with Dr Jay's,' Cam says, as though this is the most obvious thing in the world.

By this point, I'm more than a little confused. I know Winta wasn't one hundred percent honest with me, but over the past couple of months I thought I'd managed to unravel her true motives: she told me she wanted to dismantle the elitist structure of Silver society, but all she really wanted was revenge against the Primus and liberation for her parents. Or so I thought.

'But if her parents weren't imprisoned then she wouldn't have needed the blood in the first place,' I say. 'The whole point of using it against the Primus was to get Leclercq into Solis Invicti HQ to release them.'

'They don't need or want to be released, Jack,' he insists. 'I promise you. Her mother Adinde Ladipo was my closest friend in the Seekers before you came along. I was the one who had to break the news about Winta.'

'Cam—'

'They're sad, of course, but honestly I think it was kind of a relief. They've been hiding for so long, even from the people they loved.'

'But from *their own daughter*?'

'From everyone. Adewale didn't know they were alive either, not until he joined the Invicti, and Winta wasn't who you thought she was, Jack. I know she was your sire, and I know you loved her, but... You know how sometimes we'd work cases where a scab would keep stalking humans to drink from them, over and over, however many times they were offered bottles as an alternative, or warned or punished for it?'

It was something we used to see a lot of in the Seekers. In fact, it was such a common type that we even gave them a name: Biters. And yes, it's not a particularly creative or funny name, but then we were called the Seekers, so what do you expect? Shakespeare?

Anyway, we thought Biters were crazy for taking the risks they did, because they must have known we'd catch up with them eventually. There was a horrible inevitability to the cycle. It would start with a little nip, maybe by accident, or maybe just because they were curious to see what it would be like. Then the attacks would get serious, and dangerous, and they might even start attracting human attention, which was an absolute no-no from our perspective. And then, finally, they'd get reckless and kill someone, and that was the end of their freedom. I always wished we could intervene in the cycle sooner, because we all knew where it would end up, but that's not the way the Seekers worked. We were hamstrung by the Primus's rules, which didn't give us a mandate to intervene before there was an actual risk of the Silver's revelation to humanity. If we'd been able to be more proactive, then maybe the Silver wouldn't be on the brink of that revelation, and maybe the Seekers would still exist.

'Are you seriously saying that Winta was a Biter?' I ask.

'Knowing what you do now about the deaths of all those students last year, and the ones she killed with Elise Santiago before you were even turned, are you seriously going to argue that she wasn't?'

When he puts it like that, it's hard to deny.

'Okay,' I say, 'but even if I'm willing to accept that, what has it got to do with the fiery-death blood serum?'

'Everything, Jack. It has everything to do with it. If you're a Biter who wants to keep on biting, in defiance of all the other Silver who are trying to stop you from doing it, then what do you need?'

'A weapon,' I say, as realisation dawns.

'A weapon strong enough to kill any Silver who's stupid enough to come after you, and scare the rest. Winta had been trying to get away with murder for years. When she tried to steal Dr Jay's blood two decades ago, she got caught, but then she got lucky and you set her free.'

'By accident, Cam,' I say in my defence, though we both know I would have freed her deliberately if I'd been able.

'The Invicti never stopped tracking her, though,' he says. 'I've seen their records. She left a trail of scab murders across the world, but she never stopped looking for her father, because she knew his blood was the key to making her invincible. Then she got the bright idea of breaking into the baron's basement again, using you as her key, and you know the rest.'

'But you never told me the beginning,' I say.

I'd badgered Cam for news about Winta for years after I joined the Seekers. In fact, the only reason I'd joined in the first place was to help them find the first love of my life. My reasons were different from theirs, but the mission was the same. But even back then, Cam and the others knew better than to clue me in.

'I thought I was doing the right thing by keeping this from you,' he says, 'but now I wish I had told you about it years ago, because maybe then this wouldn't have happened.'

'I wouldn't have listened,' I say. 'This isn't your fault, Cam. It's not like you didn't try to warn me. All those years you spent trying to get me to move on and keep me out of her orbit... Well, if what happened at the end of last year proves anything, it's that you were right to keep us apart.'

'You say that, Jack, but you're the one who finally stopped her. Maybe you were the only person who could.'

I don't have anything to say to that. I know Cam expects it to make me feel better, as though it wasn't all for nothing, but instead I just feel hollow.

'*Ophelia Balls?*' he says. He's been kicking through the pile of detritus on the floor as we've been talking, and he's just found my fake I.D. 'Jack. Really? You're running for your life and you're not even taking it seriously. Remind me, exactly how long is the list of people who want you dead right now?'

'One longer than I thought it was, apparently. Thanks the warning about Adewale.'

'It probably won't be enough to keep you safe, I'm afraid. The way I see it, your only option is to clear your name, or you'll be in hiding forever.'

'And how do you propose I do that?' I say, giving up and reaching for the gin. 'I tried to kill the Primus, and he knows it, so I guess I'll just have to stay hidden forever. Or maybe I'll get lucky and Khalyed's blood will kill me before Adewale and Leclercq find me.'

Cam looks alarmed. 'Wait, you mean you're still dying?'

'Maybe. I don't know. It feels like it sometimes.'

'Then why the hell are we still here?' he yells, taking away my gin and pulling me to my feet. 'You need to let me take you in. Get your jacket. We're going to see Ed. He can take a look at your blood, and if you show him what you've been taking for the burning then maybe he can combine it with his research on the serum, refine the formula and—'

'No, Cam,' I say, flopping back down onto the sofa and taking him with me. 'I'm not going anywhere, and you are *definitely* not going to say a word to Ed about any of this.'

'But—'

'Listen to me very carefully,' I say, turning him to face me. 'You're not going to tell him you saw me, you're not going to tell him I'm infected with Khalyed's blood, and you are not – I repeat, *not* – going to tell him that I have any kind of treatment for it *at all*.'

'But Kayode Ladipo—'

'Can't be helped with what I'm using.'

'He's a friend, Jack,' Cam says reprovingly.

'And I would help him if I could. I promise I would.'

'But you only have a limited supply of the stuff, is that the problem?' he says, his voice tinged with desperation as he tries to puzzle out my reticence. 'Because if you just gave a sample to Ed, then I'm sure he could make enough to—'

'No! No, Cam, he couldn't. Ugh.' I don't want to tell him the truth about the healing mojo. I'm still scared to admit it to myself, and the fact that Mina knows... It's already too much. But I can't bear the thought of him leaving here believing that I might be holding out on him about something so important, so I say, 'Remember what you said, about telling a white lie to keep a confidence to a friend?'

'Are you telling me that you're lying about this too?' He looks as though his heart is breaking.

'Only by omission,' I say quickly, 'because it's a secret that doesn't belong to me. But I'm not lying when I say that I don't have a cure, or a treatment, or anything that would counteract the effects of Khalyed's blood—'

'Then how are you—'

'—for anyone who isn't me,' I add significantly.

Here's the thing about Cam: he might look like an overgrown puppy, but he pays attention, he sucks up information like a sponge, and he's brighter than most people give him credit for. He's also been around for a long, long time, so he's soaked up even more Silver lore than Mina. He knows all the ways that the Silver can heal themselves, and each other, and he knows that the number of people I have left in my corner – and for whom I'd keep secrets even from him – is almost zero.

Almost.

His eyes go wide. He's worked it out.

'Are you telling me that Baron Drake has silv—'

'I'm not telling you anything!' I interrupt. 'Nothing at all. But I really hope you'll keep the thing I haven't told you to yourself, because if anyone who might want to usurp a certain someone finds out, then I'll have even more people trying to kill me than there are already.'

Cam leans back into the sofa and tips his head back to look at the ceiling, exhaling.

'Jack,' he says, turning in my direction. 'This is big.' His tone is soft with awe or fear, I'm not sure which.

'I don't know what you're talking about,' I say.

'Are you playing with me, or are you genuinely in denial about this? Because I know how you are with him, but this is serious. It's rare and it's precious. It's a gift.'

'And I *still* don't know what you're talking about,' I say emphatically. 'Now can we move on, please?'

'Have you talked to him about it?' Cam asks.

'I don't know what you mean.'

Since Cam confiscated my last one, I pull another bottle of gin from the pile. He swipes it, along with the rest, and puts it on the floor out of my reach.

'Jack,' he says, taking my hands in his. 'This is big.'

'I know.' I snatch my hands back and clamber over him to get to the gin. 'Why do you think I'm drinking?'

I manage to snag a bottle, but he just takes it away again.

'Because you're trying to forget about what you did,' he says. Damn him and his uncanny perspicacity. 'It's not going to work, you know. When you sober up, it will still have happened.'

'I know,' I whisper.

'But you're still here, and you'll get through it. You're strong, Jack,' he says, pulling me close. 'If you could just stop fighting against yourself, you'd be unstoppable. You know that?'

'I don't feel very strong right now.'

'Maybe not, but you will be again.'

I snuggle up next to him on the sofa, his arm around my shoulders, enveloping me in the comforting scent of Cam. It feels like the old days, when we'd stay up all night on the tiny little sofa in my tiny college rooms, eating pizza and watching terrible films. That was all only a few months ago, but it feels like a lifetime.

'I missed you,' I whisper.

He presses a kiss into the top of my head, and suddenly I can't bear the thought of him leaving.

'You have to go, don't you?' I ask.

'Yes. I shouldn't have stayed this long. And I probably won't be able to come again.' I can feel his shame, and I know his reluctance to visit has more to do with his divided loyalties than it does with his ability to slip away.

'It's okay, Cam. I don't want to drag you down with me.'

'You could always change your mind,' he says hopefully. 'If you let me bring you in—'

'I think I'd rather burn to death.'

'That's not true.' He takes me by the shoulders, suddenly serious. 'Don't say that, Jack, and don't you dare do it. It's not just your life on the line anymore. Promise me you'll let me bring you in before it gets that bad.'

'Cam...'

'Promise!' he demands.

'Fine,' I say. 'I promise.'

'Good. Call me on this number,' he says, passing me a piece of card with nothing on it but his first name and a telephone number, and on the reverse, the symbol of the Solis Invicti.

'The Invicti have *business cards*?' I say. 'How very nineties of them.'

'Just call, okay? It's a private line. No one will answer it except me.'

'But I'm guessing you won't be the only one listening.'

'Just me, though I don't expect a conspiracy theorist like you to believe that. Anyway, if you get to the point that you need to call, I think you'll be willing to take the risk.' He checks his watch. 'I'm sorry, Jack, but I really do have to go. They'll miss me.'

I pull him into my arms and hug him tight. '*I'll* miss you,' I say.

'You'll see me again soon,' he says, kissing my forehead. 'Baron Drake will work something out with the Primus, we'll deal with Adewale, we'll find Leclercq, and you can come back home.'

'I don't have a home anymore, Cam.'

'Then we'll make one for you. Don't give up,' he whispers, then he squeezes me tight one last time, says his goodbyes and leaves me alone in the dark.

Despite the clutter, the flat feels empty without Cam in it. I know that seeing him and talking to him about all of this should change the way I feel. Perhaps I should even feel a little healed. I know that I should be filled with a sense of purpose and determination, at least enough to tidy the place up and throw out the booze, but that's not how it goes. Instead, I crack a bottle of gin, and a bottle of blood, and I cut my arm until the heat bleeds out of it into my cocktail.

I tell myself I'll just drink until the burning stops, or until it gets so bad I can't drink anymore, but instead I do what I always do: I drink until there's nothing left to be drunk.

6

'CHRIST ALIVE, IT smells like something died in here,' Mina says as she lets herself in through the window.

'My neighbour,' I mumble into my blood cocktail. 'My neighbour died. A few weeks ago.'

'Oh.' She stops short with one foot still on the windowsill. 'I'm sorry. Were you close?'

'No. Not really.'

'Then what the fuck, Jack?' she asks, waving her arms at the space that used to be my flat and is now not much more than a rubbish tip.

It's been no time at all since Cam was here – a week ago, was it? – and that night with him is already starting to feel like a dream. Maybe I should have been cheered up by his visit, spurred into dynamic action, but I just miss him. I miss them all. I miss my home and my job and, god help me, I miss Drake – and not just because the burning is starting to getting really, really bad.

I miss the life I had, and the dream of the life I thought I might have had with Winta, and I miss the version of me that had never taken a life, much less the life of the woman who made me what I am. I owe Winta for everything I became, and I blame her for everything I have become. At the same time, I blame myself for being naïve enough to believe that everything she said was true, and for being stubborn enough to believe that just because she lied about one thing, everything she said must have been a lie. But most of all, I blame myself for killing her before I found out the truth. My ignorance haunts me.

Was what she said on that rooftop true? Did she really love me? And does it even matter?

I'm not sure I'll ever know.

'I was only here last month,' Mina says, oblivious to my inner torment, 'and suddenly you're buried in empty pizza boxes, blood bottles and... Was that a rat?'

'Probably. I've been calling him Eric.'

A look of horror crosses her face, quickly replaced by a look of stern resolve that is not like her at all.

'Up!' she yells, grabbing me so roughly by the arm that she makes me spill my drink all over myself.

'Hey!'

'Don't you *hey* me. Will you look at yourself? You're living in filth, moping around like a sulky teenager while I'm out there doing all the work.'

'I'm in hiding.'

'Well, you're doing such a good job that you're starting to moulder into the sofa, and mould isn't sexy, Jack. Not sexy at all.'

She crosses the room to the little kitchenette and starts rootling around in the cupboard under the sink, then throws me a roll of bin bags and pulls out a load of cleaning supplies that were there when I moved in.

'Clean,' she says. 'I'll be back in two hours, and if you and this place aren't spotless – *spotless* – then I'm walking straight back out again without telling you what I found out about Khalyed.'

'Mina—'

'Clean!'

When she returns, she comes through the door this time, and she's carrying coffee. It calls to me like a siren song. Apparently I respond better to tough love and blackmail than to Cam's softer variety of intervention, because I've showered and changed into clean clothes, the tiny flat is sparkling and the whole place reeks of bleach so strongly that it's burning my nostrils. There's even a load of laundry spinning in the rickety old machine in the bathroom. But the Massacre is still churning in my stomach and in my veins. Doing super-speed cleaning has burned through the energy in the blood from the cocktail, so I'm exhausted, but I'm still not quite sober. I feel ragged and nauseous, and on top of it all, the constant burning from the bad blood is becoming hard to ignore.

'Here,' Mina says, handing me a cup. 'Quintuple shot, and I chucked a handful of caffeine tabs in there to give it some kick.'

I down half the coffee in one go, then flop down onto the sofa and say, 'Tell me about Khalyed.'

'Did you wash this?' Mina asks, squinting suspiciously at the sofa cushions.

'All the blood was on my blankets, and I'm washing them. Now will you tell me?'

Mina sits gingerly on the edge of the sofa, grimacing at the wet stains on the armrest, and sips her own coffee.

'I did my best to scrub it out, okay?' I say. 'Now can you just tell me, please?'

'Khalyed's gone.'

'What? What do you mean, *He's gone*?'

'I mean he's gone. He is no longer there. Disappeared. Poof.'

'He can't be gone. He was locked up in a box in Drake's

basement.'

'Yeah, well,' she says, finally settling back into the sofa, 'maybe someone took him out again. After all, you got in there, didn't you? So it can't be all that hard.'

'Excuse me?' I'm a little insulted. 'It is quite hard, actually. If I hadn't had access because of my role in the Seekers, and if I hadn't charmed my way in there—'

'By banging the baron, you mean?'

'What? No!'

'And anyway,' Mina goes on, ignoring my protests, 'if it's so very hard, then how did I get someone in there to find out that Khalyed's box is empty?'

She's got me there.

'I don't know,' I say.

'And you never will. Have to protect my sources, don't I?' She taps the side of her nose like a car boot salesman hocking a box of jeans that fell off the back of a truck – wink wink, nudge nudge – and grins a self-satisfied grin. 'You can take it as gospel, though. Trust me. He's not in there.'

'Then where is he?'

'Buggered if I know.' She gets up and walks to the kitchenette to chuck her empty coffee cup in the bin, then she starts looking through the cupboards. 'Is there anything left to drink, or did you neck it all?'

'Top left,' I say. 'Emergency stash.'

She goes up on her tiptoes to reach behind the vases and eggcups, and comes up with a half-empty bottle of strawberry vodka that's so heavily sugared she struggles to unscrew the congealed cap. That doesn't stop her from taking a long drink straight from the bottle.

'Ugh.' She squints at the label. 'How old is this shit?'

'Who knows? It was here when I moved in.'

'It's revolting,' she says, but she brings the bottle back to the sofa and keeps drinking it. 'I've got some good news, though.'

'Oh?'

'I had an idea.'

'I'm listening.'

'Right, okay,' she says, gesturing excitedly with the bottle. 'You know how you were saying that the baron used Khalyed's blood to kill a bunch of the boxed Silver?'

'Actually you were saying that, but yes.'

'Right, well, I was thinking, if that was me and I was bumping off murderous Silver on the regular, I wouldn't want to keep going back to Khalyed, with his potentially deadly bite and all, and risk going up in smoke every time I needed another shot of blood. You know?'

'Okay…'

'So, if I'm the baron, what I'm thinking is, why not take a whole load of blood in one hit, then I've got a stash that I can put somewhere safe, and I only have to wrestle the fiery super-vampire once, you know?' She gestures with such expressive finality that the sticky strawberry liquor splashes all over my clean floor.

'I think you've had too much coffee,' I say. 'How many caffeine tablets did you put in yours?'

'A couple of packets, but my point stands.'

And I have to admit, it does seem like a reasonable theory. It's what I would do if I were Drake.

'So you can ask him about it the next time he comes to visit,' she says. 'Which should be soon, because you're hurting, aren't you?'

I shrug, making light of the screaming pain. 'It's been five weeks.'

'Then he's already overdue. I'm sure he'll be turning up any day now.'

'Usually, but I told him not to.' I grimace. 'I told him to leave it at least six.'

'*Six?* Are you crazy?'

'Maybe. I don't know. It seemed like a good idea at the time.'

'You're such a bloody martyr. You can't just fuck him and have fun, can you?'

'It's not that easy.'

'Yes, it is. Look: you take your clothes off, he takes his clothes off, you rub your bodies together a bit and, hey presto, everyone feels better. What's so hard about that?' She smirks. 'Except the obvious, of course.'

'Mina...'

'You're missing out, is all I'm saying. Or was it so awful the first time you banged him that you can't bear to repeat it? Is that it?'

'No!' Unfortunately, the whole Silver world knows about the one-night-stand I had with Drake last year. I made the mistake of taking a walk of shame through the centre of Oxford the next day wearing Drake's scent mark, and that was that. I will never live it down. 'I just don't want to give him the wrong idea. Speaking of which,' I say, 'I need you to look into something else for me.'

She shrugs and says, 'You're paying. Or rather, the baron is.'

'You make it sound like I'm a kept woman.'

'Well, aren't you?'

'No! I'm going to reimburse him for every penny.'

'And how are you going to do that without a job? With all those savings from your entry-grade Seekers salary? Even if you do – by some miracle – manage to get out of this mess and back into Silver society, you know no one's going to hire you after you tried to kill the Primus.'

'I'll sell the flat,' I say.

'What flat?'

'I have a flat in Oxford. My ex bought it for me.'

I've never lived there. In fact, I didn't even find out about the flat until Tabitha and I had already broken up under less-than-amicable circumstances. I don't have any intention of going back to it.

'Oh, so you're *her* kept woman?' Mina says.

She's only teasing, but I'm starting to get angry now. The pain is grating at me, and I'm so tired and drained that my nerves are fraying. In the circumstances, that last comment is enough to make me snap. I'm about to yell at Mina, but she senses the temperature in the room and jumps in before I can.

'Look, Jack,' she says. 'I don't care where the money comes from as long as I'm getting paid. Just tell me about the job.'

I take a deep breath, knowing this is a big ask, and say, 'I need to know how to break Drake's bond to me.'

'And you want to use his own money to find out?' She clicks her tongue. 'That's cold.'

'Mina! You just said—'

'Yeah, I don't care where the money comes from, but for that, I think the baron probably would. Don't you?'

'Are you going to help me or not?' I say, louder than I meant to.

'Fine,' she says, holding up her hands in surrender. 'I'll see what I can do, but I wouldn't get too excited.'

'You think it's impossible?'

'Breaking a bond? It's definitely not easy. You could always kill him, I guess,' she suggests.

'Not helpful.'

'Well, that's the only way I know.'

'There must be another. I'll do the research, I just need you to get the sources. I want everything you can find. All the books, all the papers, whatever there is. Just bring it here and I'll go through it all.'

Because, as I finally resolved during my cleaning whirlwind, it's time for me to get proactive. I'm sick of sitting around in this prison and sending Mina out to do everything for me, unable to help myself. It's so frustrating that, even if it weren't for my poisoned blood, I know my skin would still be itching. I need to start working towards a solution on my own, and if I have to do that by reading shit – far from my favourite activity – then I bloody will.

'Question,' says Mina.

'Yeah?'

'You realise that if you do succeed in this long shot of yours, and somehow you break the bond, there'll be no one around to heal you anymore. What happens then?'

'I guess I die. But what happens if I don't break the bond, and the shit in my blood kills me anyway?'

'Why would it do that?'

'It's getting worse, Mina,' I whisper, finally saying out loud the words that I've been afraid even to think up until now. 'Every time Drake heals me, the pain comes back faster. What if, one day, the healing won't be enough? What if my death – and Drake's – is inevitable, and we're just delaying it? At least if I break the bond first, Drake doesn't have to die too.'

'Shit,' she says, then she empties the bottle of rancid liquor in one big swallow. 'How bad has it got?'

'At first, I barely felt anything at all between one healing and the next, but this time it only took a couple of weeks for the tingling to start, three for the heat, four for the burning, and now, after five, I feel like there's lava building up underneath my skin, trying to burst it's way out.'

'Do you want me to call him?'

'No,' I say quickly. 'No, Mina. Do not call Drake.'

'You're clearly in pain.'

'I'll be fine. It's just a burning sensation in my veins and up my spine and under my skin, all over my body.' I rub at my arms, pushing the sleeves of my T-shirt up to my elbows. The heat's getting so strong that I feel like I should be able to see it glowing from inside my flesh, but there's just my normal arms and the pain. 'I can manage,' I say, more to myself than to Mina. 'I'll be fine. It's only a week. But what I'm saying is that I need a cure, not a stopgap solution. So just find the doctor, okay?'

'I'm looking. And in the meantime, you know you can call me, right? You have my number. If it gets really bad, find a payphone, or go to the library and email me.'

'They'll be able to track it.'

'I know, but better boxed than dead, right? If it gets bad enough that you get worried, then don't wait, Jack. Promise me you'll call.'

I'm hearing that a lot lately.

'Fine,' I say, 'but he'll be here in a week. I can wait that long.'

Turns out I'm right about that, but only just.

7

'HAPPY EASTER, VALENTINE.'

'Fuck off, Drake.'

It's been six weeks to the day, and here he is on my doorstep again, all smiles, as though we never argued at all. I'm not smiling back, though. With the pain of the bad blood twisting and burning inside me, it's all I can do not to cry.

Six weeks was too long.

I want to snatch him to me, to steal the healing kiss I need so badly, but I hold myself back. I can't let him know just how much I need him, or just how much I regret keeping him away so long.

'So you don't want the chocolate Easter egg I brought you?' he asks.

'Well if you're stooping to bribery, then you'd better come in,' I say, biting back the pain as I open the door wide.

'If I'd known all it would take was confectionery, I wouldn't have bothered with the cash and blood,' he replies, handing me the usual duffel bag as he crosses the short distance to the sofa bed. 'You're still here, then?' He looks around the room as though trying to discover what appeal it holds. He can look all day if he likes, but he won't find what he's looking for.

'For the time being.'

I empty the duffel back on the kitchenette counter – blood, cash, chocolate – and hand it back to him. My hand's shaking, and he notices.

'I need you to bring me something else next time,' I say.

There's no easy way to ask for this, and he's going to fight about it however I phrase the question, so I may as well get straight to it. Besides which, I don't have the strength for patience right now.

'What do you need?' he asks.

'Khalyed's blood.' His face clouds over, so I interrupt before he can reply. 'I'm not planning to hurt anyone. I just want to have someone look at it to see if they can help me, and I'm sure you have a supply.'

'What "someone"?' he asks, his eyes narrowing with suspicion. 'I told you, Valentine: I'm taking care of it.'

'With Ed and the Invicti?' I roll my eyes. 'Because they're going to be so concerned about curing the person who tried to kill the Primus. Oh, god, please tell me you haven't actually told them I'm infected with Khalyed's blood.'

'Of course not. You and I are the only ones who know about that.'

That's what he thinks. He doesn't know about Mina, or Cam, and the circle is getting worryingly large, now I come to think about it, particularly since those two also know about the bond.

'If Ed and the others don't know about me,' I say, 'then why do they think they're working on it?'

'You're not the only one an antidote could help,' he says, and I wonder then if he already knows about the Ladipos. He's probably known this whole time, just like the rest of them. 'Your assassination attempt stepped things up a little, and they're working hard on a cure. As soon as they have it,

I'm getting it for you, one way or another. But I'm not giving you Dr Khalyed's blood.'

'Drake—'

'No, Jack. Don't ask me again.'

I drop the subject, for now, and concentrate on stowing the blood bottles away in my fridge. By the time I'm done, Drake has moved on to other thoughts.

'There was a Silver scent outside when I arrived,' he says suspiciously. It was probably Mina's, but I've been staying inside doing research like a good little fugitive, so I can't say for sure. 'You should think about moving again.'

'There are Silver all over the country,' I reply. 'Just because there's one in the area doesn't mean they're here for me.'

'You've not had any visitors, then?' he prods.

'Why, are you jealous?'

It's the wrong thing to say. I know it the moment the words are out of my mouth. I'm supposed to be keeping things professional between us – as professional as they can be when I need his kisses to keep me alive – but yet again my mouth has got me into trouble. Drake's eyes have gone as dark as I've ever seen them, his pupils swallowing his irises whole, then he flashes his silver at me for a moment in a gesture that, for the Silver, is partly flirtatious and entirely predatory.

'Do you want me to be?' he asks, crossing the room towards me in slow, deliberate steps. The room's so small that I have to back up against the kitchen cabinets to avoid touching him. It's a visceral reminder of what happened on Drake's last visit, and I know I have to shut this down right now.

'Fuck off,' I say, putting my palm flat against his chest to push him back, but he catches me by the wrist and holds my hand to his heart.

'Not yet,' he whispers. 'I haven't done what I came here to do.'

Then he leans forward to kiss me. The second his lips touch mine and I feel the healing mojo spread through my body, tamping down the inner fire in a wash of cool relief, I jerk away. He's still holding my hand against his chest, but I'm determined. I've been psyching myself up for this day for weeks, and I'm not going to let this descend into a scent-marking orgy, not again, however much my body is thrumming with disagreement.

'It's not safe for you to wear my mark,' I say by way of explanation. I speak more softly than I want to because his hand is now locked in a death grip around my wrist and I don't want to provoke him into a fight that I'd probably lose. 'Let me go, Drake.'

He does, immediately, with a bewildered look on his face, as though he wasn't aware that he'd tightened his hold.

'Okay,' I say, walking past him to the door and pulling it open. 'Well, thanks for coming and all that. I'll let you get back to your life.'

He just stares at me for a moment.

'Thanks for the Easter egg,' I add, trying to smooth his exit.

He's confused, that much is obvious. He's looking at me as though I'm a puzzle he has to solve, and I don't like that one bit. I just want him out of here so I can get on with my work. I've been immersed in old Silver lore and bonding theories ever since Mina delivered the research stack last week, and if I can just concentrate on that then maybe I can distract myself from the smell of Drake's skin, and the irrational desire I have to press my face against his neck and sniff.

No sniffing. No marking. And definitely – *definitely* – no anything else. I have to stick to the plan.

'Don't you want to ask about the news from Oxford?' he asks, a transparent play for time.

'Would you tell me anything if I did?'

'No.'

'Well, then.' I gesture to the doorway.

'But you always ask,' he says.

'Definition of madness, Drake: doing the same thing again and again, and expecting a different result.'

'So you're not going to ask anymore? You're just going to trust me to take care of everything, the cure and the Invicti and all of that?'

'Sure, if you like.'

He gets close again, looking into my eyes as though he'll be able to read my thoughts in them.

'I don't believe you,' he says.

'That's not my problem.'

He's silent for a moment as he scans my eyes again.

'What are you doing?' he asks softly. 'Where's all this coldness coming from?'

'I'm being perfectly pleasant.'

'Yes, you are, and it's not like you at all. I don't like it.'

'Would you be happier if we were fighting?'

'Yes, actually. We're good at fighting,' he says, dropping his voice as he steps in closer, close enough that I can feel the whisper of his breath on my cheek. Then he says, 'We're good at making up too.'

'Goodbye, Drake,' I say, putting a hand on his shoulder to swivel him away from me and out of the door.

'See you in a month, then?' he asks.

'Six weeks.'

He stops and turns back to me, bracing himself in the doorway so I can't slam the door in his face, however much I might want to.

'Why are you playing this game with me, Valentine?' he

asks. 'There's no point. It's just the two of us.'

Just the two of us, from now until forever.

'I don't know what you're talking about,' I say, blinking away the echo in my head.

'I'm talking about the fact that I can feel how much Khalyed's blood is affecting you. You know I can feel it through the bond, so why are you trying to pretend that six weeks isn't too long?'

'It isn't,' I lie.

'Then you weren't biting back tears of pain when I arrived?'

'Absolutely not.'

'Liar.' He reaches out and strokes his thumb down my cheek, tracing the tracks of the tears I refused to shed. 'You can't lie to me, not about this.'

'And we can't do this,' I say, pushing his hand away, 'and you know it.'

'Why not? Why can't we?' he asks, his voice filled with frustration.

'It's too dangerous.'

'At the moment,' he says, 'while you're in hiding, but this won't last forever. I'm going to make it right, so you can come home.'

Home.

The problem is, I'm not sure where that is anymore. With the Seekers disbanded, Solomon College claimed by the Invicti, and all my traitorous friends now working for them in London, there's nothing left for me in Oxford. I've destroyed it all. I destroyed *her*.

From now until forever ~ W

He's all that's left.

'You're not just talking about the scent marks, though, are you?' Drake says, his expression darkening. 'That's not the only thing you think is dangerous about being with me.'

'No.'

'Then tell me what you really mean.'

I killed her for you.

'I'm grateful for your help,' I say. 'Thank you. But now I think you should leave, before we do something we'll both regret.'

For a moment, he looks genuinely shocked. Shocked enough to let go of his grip on the doorframe.

'Valentine—'

I take my chance and slam the door shut. He could break it open if he wanted to, but he doesn't. Instead, he says, 'I'm not waiting six weeks.' Then he stands there for a few seconds on the other side of the door, perhaps hoping I might change my mind, before giving up and walking away down the corridor, out of the building and away.

Every step hurts.

I wish I could let him hold me, but it's not right. I can't make him believe that we're in this together when I don't intend for us to continue that way.

I've already killed one ex. I can't handle repeating the experience, particularly not when it would put us both through a cycle of healing and hurting that would make death feel like a series of tiny, incremental cuts. I can't see a way to extract the poison from my veins, but maybe I can find a way to break the bond. At least then, when I meet my inevitable demise, I won't have to feel guilty about killing him too.

8

I GET THE letter out from its envelope again that night. I've read it so many times that the ink is becoming paler, as though the act of my reading it is causing the words to fade at the same rate as they're burning themselves into my brain.

I hope you don't mind that we're not going to Argentina, but you'll like Vancouver, I promise. I've got us a house on the coast, just for us this time. Just the two of us, from now until forever ~ W

It's been months, and I still don't know how I'm supposed to feel about it. She was my first love and the woman who turned me Silver, but she was also a murderer who killed at least twenty-six humans, at a modest estimate. That's all confusing enough, but it gets more complicated.

I thought she'd betrayed me for Yolande Leclercq, but in fact she'd betrayed Leclercq for me.

She told me to kill the Primus, but I failed.

She told me to kill Drake, but I wouldn't.

I killed her instead.

At the time, I believed I was doing it to escape her and everything she'd done to me: the manipulation, the pain, the abandonment. She disagreed.

It was me or him, and you made your choice.

I didn't believe her at the time, but now it feels blindingly obvious: I killed her for him.

There's a rain of gravel against the window and I shove the letter back into its envelope, stowing it away in the pocket of my leather jacket. Drake bought me that jacket, a present from a trip he made to Italy with his latest ex, Carlotta, back when they were still together. I remember when he gave it to me, the way he wrapped it around me, along with the coppery spiced scent of his skin. Those memories, and so many others, are woven into its lining. It's remarkable, the weight these simple objects carry: a piece of paper, a jacket, a betrayal, a murder, and five broken hearts.

'Sorry I'm late,' Mina says as she climbs through the window. 'I had to wait until I was sure the baron had left.'

'That was hours ago,' I say.

'He hung around outside for a bit. What did you say to him?'

'Nothing.'

'Keep it to yourself, then,' she says dismissively as she throws herself down onto the sofa. 'Did you ask him about Khalyed's blood?'

'Yes,' I say irritably. 'He wouldn't tell me anything.'

'Because you obviously gave him nothing in return. I can't help but notice there's no scent mark this time, so you obviously didn't give him any kind of proper seeing to.'

'We need to get Khalyed's blood,' I say, ignoring her. 'If we're going to make a cure, we'll need it. Can you get back into the mansion and have a look around, find where Drake is hiding it? It's got to be there somewhere. I can't imagine he'd keep it anywhere else.'

'Sure, but since you're not wearing his scent mark and I've got a free evening... How about it?' She waggles her eyebrows at me in a way I'm sure is supposed to be alluring, but looks faintly comical. It's endearing nonetheless, but I'm hardly in the mood.

'Not tonight, Mina.'

'But another night?'

I sigh. 'You're persistent, I'll give you that.'

'You have to be, in my line of work.'

The lift pings out in the corridor – it hasn't worked the whole time I've lived here, so it takes me a while to place the sound – then there's the rumble of suitcase wheels passing my door. It stops at what was once Louise's apartment. Keys jangle. The lock tumbles next door.

'New neighbour?' Mina asks.

'I guess.'

I haven't heard anyone looking around the place, so the agent must have rented it out unseen. That's unusual, but not much of a surprise – only an idiot would move into this block after they'd actually seen it.

Mina's brought a load more books and papers for me about the Silver bond, so she pulls them out and the two of us sit together on the sofa sifting through them, trying to pick out the ones that look promising. Meanwhile, outside in the corridor, footsteps go back and forth, accompanied by various rattlings and rumblings that suggest someone's moving an entire truck full of shit into the crappy bedsit next door.

'Where are they going to put it all?' Mina asks after what must be my new neighbour's tenth trip.

'The real question is, how are they going to secure it?' I say. 'This building has rubbish locks.'

It's a good thing I'm in hiding, because if I ever left the place for more than an hour at a time, I'm pretty sure I'd be cleaned out by the time I got back.

'You shouldn't keep this lot here if you can't lock it up properly,' Mina says, waving at the papers spread out across our laps, and the sofa, and the floor.

She has a point. If anyone were to break in here and find out what I'm researching, whether they're Silver or not, it could be a serious problem.

'I could get a safe,' I suggest.

'Or you could just move out of this shithole,' she counters. 'It's not like there's anything keeping you here. Speaking of which, when you do move – and frankly it's past time – I have a suggestion about where you should go.'

'Why?' I say, shoving aside the papers I've been reading so I can give her my full attention. 'Did you find something.'

'No.' She tips her head, equivocating. 'I've just got a feeling about a lead I'm tracking.'

'Where?'

'North.'

'How far north are we talking?' I ask, catching on.

'About as far north as you can get without hitting the sea.' Mina smiles, and I know exactly what she's found.

'Are you serious?' I ask, so elated that I briefly consider kissing her, but that would only encourage her.

'I'm not sure how easy it would be to hide you there, though,' she says. 'It's not a big place, and we're not in tourist season yet—'

'I can find a way to make it work. You're sure about this?'

'Not yet. But I will be soon.'

I'm about to press her for more details when the footsteps in the corridor stop outside my door. There's a knock.

I groan and get to my feet.

'Probably wants a cup of fucking sugar,' Mina says in a whisper. I'm already walking to the door when she whispers, more urgently this time, 'Jack.'

'What?'

'Your mouth?'

'Shit.' Since it's been less than twenty-four hours since

Drake did his healing mojo, my lips are still all silvery. 'I forgot.'

'For a fugitive, you're not very good at this clandestine shit, are you?' Mina sighs, then she gets up, pulls a lipstick from her pocket and says, 'Go like this,' making a face that stretches her lips.

She applies the lipstick quickly, a blood-red shade that would not have been my first choice, then steps back to assess her work.

'It looks a bit pearly,' she says, 'but it's passable.'

There's another knock at the door – apparently my new neighbour is an impatient bastard – and I go to open it.

'Hi!' says the guy waiting on the other side.

He's mid-twenties, average height, average build, average brown hair and eyes, but he's wearing the loudest multi-coloured neon T-shirt I have ever seen, paired with black jeans, but similarly blinding trainers. He gives me a little finger wave by way of greeting, and I see that all his nails are not only manicured, but also extended with acrylics and painted to match his shirt. He's wearing so much aftershave – an aggressively floral and woody scent – that I wonder if he's used it as soap.

'Um, hi?' I say.

'Hi! I'm Mikey!' he says excitedly. This is a man who clearly only comes with one setting, and it's LOUD. Since everyone who moves into this building seems to have some addiction or other, I'm guessing his is coke. Or caffeine. Or both. 'I've just moved in next door!'

'Hi, Mikey,' I say. 'I'm—'

'I'm Mina,' says Mina, joining me at the doorway. Neither her expression nor her tone is friendly. 'This is Ophelia.'

Mikey looks a little taken aback, but he recovers quickly. 'Oo!' he says. 'So you two live here together, then!'

'I'm visiting,' says Mina, openly hostile now. 'We're

busy.'

'Oh, okay! Sorry to disturb you! Nice to meet you both!' Mikey says, then he heads back along the corridor, waving all the way.

Mina slams my door and returns to the sofa.

'What was that about?' I ask her as soon as I hear Mikey close his door. 'You didn't have to be a dick about it.'

'He was too cheerful,' she says. 'I got a weird vibe from him. Didn't you?'

'Not really. Mostly I was wishing for sunglasses.'

'Peacocking,' Mina says, dismissively.

'Excuse me?'

'It's basic psychology. He dresses all bright and showy so you only look at the things he wants you to see – the things he's drawing attention to – and you ignore everything else. I don't trust people like that. It makes me suspicious.'

'Of what?'

'Of what exactly it is that they *don't* want you to see.'

'Maybe he's just a friendly guy who likes neon,' I say.

Mina snorts derisively and turns back to the stack of papers in front of her. After a quick look through the peephole to check the corridor – empty now – I join her.

We read peacefully side by side for a couple of hours in a strangely companionable silence. I'm not used to having that with Mina. Usually she's a frenetic ball of sexual tension, lobbing out innuendoes and propositions with startling regularity. In fact, I don't think I've ever spent this long in her company without her trying to get me naked, except for that brief window in our acquaintance when we were asleep together, or already naked, or both. I realise then that this is part of what makes her a great investigator: when she focuses on something, that focus is razor sharp. It's just that most of the time when she's around me, she seems to be focusing on sex. The study session is a refreshing change.

Not that we find anything. We pack it in around ten o'clock because Mina has a party to go to – I don't ask for details, but she shows me the whip she's brought with her anyway – and I walk her out as I take out the last bag of rubbish from this morning. On my way back to my door, I bump into Mikey again, taking out his own rubbish from the move.

'Sorry about Mina,' I say. 'She's not usually so prickly.'

'Don't worry!' he says, waving my concerns away. 'I totally get it! Little disappointed, got to admit, because I'd be lying if I said I hadn't hoped we might make an awesome double act the moment I heard her name – I mean, Mikey and Mina? Can you *imagine*! And that outfit of hers with the corset and the dark leather would just look incredible next to all *this* on the stage – but still, I'm not everyone's cup of tea, like they say, bit over the top sometimes, I know – and talk about *chatty*, right? – but what I'm saying is that it's totally cool! I should be the one apologising for interrupting you!' He laughs aloud for so long and with so much force that I'm left wondering, not for the first time, if he ever actually breathes.

'Well, anyway,' I say, blinking a little to clear my head, 'I'm sorry. I'll see you around.'

'Hey, I was actually going out in a bit if you wanted to tag along – awesome party in this place by the river that has this soundproofed basement with full-on DJ and lights and foam and *everything* – free booze!'

'Um, no thanks,' I say. 'I was actually heading to bed.' Not to mention that the party sounds like a nightmare, and that's even before you factor in the ominously soundproofed basement. When is that ever a good thing? 'But have a good time.'

'Thanks! I'll be as quiet as a mouse when I come back in, promise!'

JOSIE JAFFREY

'Okay. See you around, Mikey.'
'See you around, J— Ophelia!'
I try not to react.

Instead I force a smile, wave goodbye and close my door firmly behind me. Later, when Mikey leaves for the party, I'm on the other side of the wall, listening for a heartbeat that's less than human, but I can't be sure either way. Maybe he's a human with a slow pulse – not all that unusual – or maybe he's a Silver with so many stimulants in his system that they're masking the usual signs.

Maybe I'm paranoid.

After all, it was only a tiny sound, that "J". So tiny that I could have imagined it, and even if I didn't, it could mean nothing at all. Just a slip of the tongue. Nothing out of the ordinary about that. Still, it's enough to make me do as Drake suggested.

I pack my bag, ditching most of my clothes to make room for the research materials, and leave through the window that same night.

9

FINDING PLACES TO stay at short notice without a paper
trail – or, more appropriately, electronic trail – is pretty
tricky in these days of online bookings and AirBnB.
Fortunately, I can be pretty fucking tricky myself when I put
my mind to it. This part of the Scottish coast is mostly
populated by local folks, but the Easter break has brought a
bunch of visitors that wouldn't normally be in residence, so
everything online is already booked anyway. I have to
improvise.

'Glamorous,' Mina says, looking around my caravan.

Yes, a caravan. I said I was tricky, not that I was a
miracle-worker.

'Watch that bit of flooring there,' I say, just as Mina's foot
goes right through the carpet.

'*Really* glamorous,' she says.

I help her out of the hole. Her foot is soaking wet; the
caravan is sitting on the edge of a farm in the middle of a
small pond of muddy water that's collected during the recent
April showers. Or, more accurately, April torrents.

It was all right when I moved in, chucking a handful of
cash at the farmer so he wouldn't ask too many questions,

but in retrospect I understand his willingness to accept such a small amount of money for such a beautiful coastal view. The caravan can now only be accessed over a series of makeshift plank-and-breezeblock bridges, which keep falling over into the drink, and since it's currently tipping it down outside, there's a constant dripping racket as water seeps through the roof and into the twenty-or-so receptacles that are dotted around the interior to collect said water. When that noise combines with the hammering rain on the thin roof, it's a little difficult to hear myself think. Mina and I are practically shouting to hear each other, which isn't exactly clandestine.

'Couldn't you have found a nice coastal cave to hole up in for a few days?' Mina asks.

'A cave, Mina? It would be freezing.'

'I'm not sure anything could be more freezing that this tin can.'

It's true: there's not much by way of heating. But there are blankets and privacy, and the farmer lets me use his kitchen to make cups of tea, so it'll do for now.

'It's only for a couple of days,' I say.

'Yes, and I'm telling you that for a couple of days, a cave would be more comfortable.'

'Oh, shut up and have a biscuit.' I throw a packet of Hobnobs at her and curl up on the bed, wrapping the slightly mouldy duvet around myself to keep out the cold. Mina joins me tentatively, but makes sure not to touch the duvet.

'It isn't exactly a love nest, is it?' she says through a mouthful of biscuit.

'Is that why you haven't asked me to take my clothes off yet?'

'Well, I wouldn't want you to get cold. Besides,' she says, grinning wickedly, 'there are plenty of things we can do with your clothes still on.'

Ah, there's the Mina I know and tolerate.

'Anyway,' she says, ignoring my sigh, 'I was actually thinking about Baron Drake. Next time he visits, are you sure you want it to be here?'

'It doesn't matter where he visits. How many times do I have to tell you? Nothing is going on between us.'

She pops the remaining bit of biscuit into her mouth then sucks her fingers, cleaning them thoughtfully. 'Is it because he's a murderer?' she asks. 'Is that what's bothering you?'

'*I'm* a murderer,' I point out.

'Yeah, but you were in a bit of a situation at the time. His way's colder and more calculating. There's a hell of a difference between killing someone in the heat of the moment when the tension's high, and making a choice to procure a poison and then use it to execute someone.'

'Which is exactly what I was planning to do to the Primus. It would be a bit hypocritical of me to object.'

'Yes,' she insists, 'but the Primus wasn't locked up in a box at the time, was he? He wasn't drained of all his blood and left totally defenceless. Because that's what the baron did to his however-many victims, right? Then one injection in the darkness and *poof*, up in smoke. Like an angel of death, you might say.'

The thought turns my stomach, but then when I think of Winta – *poof, up in smoke* – I get a little nauseous too.

'Why are we talking about this?' I say, desperate to change the subject. 'Haven't we got better things to be doing?'

'Oh, speaking of which...' I'm expecting another proposition, but instead she says, 'I've found the doctor.'

'What? Really? Where?'

'It's close. Just like I thought.'

'Then why didn't you say?'

'I just... You're sure you want to do this?' she asks.

'We've been looking for months,' I say. 'Of course I want to do this.'

'Yes, but are you sure you're ready? I mean, we don't have to go right now. You could wait until you've settled in here,' she says, looking around at the caravan sceptically, 'or until you're better rested. I'm sure you're not sleeping well on this thing.' She prods the inch-thin mattress that forms my bed.

'Why procrastinate? In fact, why are you procrastinating?'

'Because I have a bad feeling that you're about to fuck this up.'

'Just give me the address, Mina.'

'Whatever you say.'

She shows me an address on her phone. It's less than ten miles away.

I pull on my boots before I have time to talk myself out of it. The truth is, I'm worried that Mina might be right.

10

THE NEAREST TOWN isn't so much a town as it is a slightly larger collection of buildings than you usually get in the Scottish Highlands, combined with a shop and a post office and not much else. It's also on the top of a bloody enormous hill, where the wind blows so savagely and in so many fast-changing directions that even with my supernatural strength, I'm getting buffeted about. I'm also bloody freezing.

Scotland – and I say this with the greatest respect for kilts and shortbread and haggis, and lobbing tree trunks about and pretending it's a sport – can fuck right off.

Thankfully, my target isn't far: just on the other side of this rise, stepping out of the local supermarket. I approach with caution, anticipating trouble.

'Hello, Tabby,' I say.

'Jack.' Dr Tabitha Ross glares at me over her glasses. 'I've got to say, this is a ballsy move. Even for you, hen.'

She deploys her former pet name for me with all the subtlety of a siege weapon. Needless to say, she is not pleased to see me, and who can blame her? When I found out Winta had kidnapped her, I did nothing to set her free.

JOSIE JAFFREY

Worse, I made her out to be a kidnapper herself and, to top it all, I got her boxed up in Drake's basement as punishment for a crime she didn't commit. I *did* also make sure that Winta didn't kill her, and that Drake got her out of the box again when the assassination attempt against the Primus went tits up, but I'm not expecting that to win me any points. In fact, given her antipathy towards Drake during the time that she and I were together, Tabby was probably less than thrilled to be released by him anyway.

Suffice it to say, a quick apology isn't going to cut it.

'I know I have some explaining to do,' I start, but she cuts me off before I can get going.

'I don't want to hear it,' she says, walking away.

I fall into step and try to keep pace with her, but despite Tabby's short stature, she can march faster than you'd expect. In the flow of oncoming pedestrian and animal traffic – the town is full of sheep for some reason – I'm having to dodge to stay alongside her.

'Tabs, please,' I say. 'I know that nothing I can say will ever make up for what I did to you, and if I could take it all back then I would, believe me, but I can't, so all I can say is I'm sorry. I'm so very, very sorry.'

She stops so abruptly that I'm not ready for it, and I trip over my own feet trying to stop next to her. She reaches out to steady me without thinking, then snatches her hand back as though I've burned her. With the bad blood burning in my veins, that's actually not beyond the realms of possibility, but from the look on her face I suspect she's just angry at herself for helping me.

'Thank you,' I say.

'Look here, Jack Valentine,' she says, waving a finger in my face. 'I warned you. I begged you not to go through with that asinine plan, but did you listen? No. You were so set on doing whatever that… that… *woman* told you to.'

'I know,' I say, grabbing her wagging finger and taking her hand in mine. 'I was an idiot. I'm sorry. If I had my time again, I would do things differently. It was a mistake.'

She snatches her hand away and laughs, bitterly. 'Where have I heard that before? Oh, yes, that's right. I was in a cage in your girlfriend's basement, only you weren't saying those words to me, I was saying them to you. So I'll give you the same answer you gave me: You can't kick a dog then complain when it turns around and bites you. Goodbye, Jack.'

She starts walking again and I have to run to catch up.

This is not going well. Between her and Cam, this is starting to feel like the Jack Valentine apology tour. I clearly need to take a different tack with Tabitha.

'Did you hear what happened that night?' I ask.

'I didn't need to,' she says, her gaze fixed forward. 'I can guess: your plan failed, you got caught, and given that you're here instead of locked away in a box – like I was, by the way, for *no reason at all* – I imagine you're trying to hide from the Invicti, and you want my help with that because I used to work for them, which I only stopped doing because of you, I might add. Well, hard cheese, buster. You're on your own.'

She might have done some questionable things in her time, but I'll say this for Tabitha: she's adorable when she's angry.

'I killed her, Tabby,' I say quietly, and that's what finally stops her.

'I don't believe you,' she whispers, but her eyes say otherwise. 'It's not possible.'

'With Khalyed's blood. I injected it into her heart and she burned to ash right in front of me, then blew away on the breeze.' I don't mean to, but I'm tearing up.

Tabitha presses her lips together tightly for a moment,

then she says, 'Oh, hen,' and this time the word is gentle. 'You'd better come with me.'

Tabitha's house is the exact opposite of everything I've come to expect from her. In stark contrast to her cottage in Nash Lee, this place is a grand bay-fronted Georgian country house with sash windows, wooden floors, antique furniture, and ceiling roses that anchor light fittings at least eleven feet above our heads. It's enormous.

'You really are loaded, aren't you?' I say as she ushers me into what I can only describe as a parlour.

'It's vulgar to talk about money, Jack.'

'You used to like it when I was vulgar.'

'I did,' she smiles, just a little, and just for a moment, before the sadness returns. 'But I don't think that's why you're here. Is it?'

'No. It's not.'

'Sit,' she says.

I perch in the spindly-legged chair she's directed me to and she takes the one next to it. I think they're supposed to be armchairs, but they look like a sudden wind would disintegrate them and they're stuffed with something that's poking me uncomfortably in the bum cheek. These are chairs designed for comportment, not for relaxation.

Stupid antiques.

'I know I have no right to ask this,' I say, 'but I'm in trouble, and I need your help.'

'I'm not helping you kill the Primus,' she says immediately. 'I might not agree with him on everything, but —'

'That's not what I'm asking.'

'Then what?'

'I need a cure for Khalyed's blood.'

Tabitha scrunches up her face, nudging her glasses up her

nose in a way that reminds me why I fell for her the first place.

'Why would you need a cure?' she asks. 'You know you can't bring her back.'

'Bring her…' She's talking about Winta, I realise. 'No, Tabby. Not… not her. She's gone. I'm not sure I'd want to bring her back even if I knew how.'

'Then why?' she asks, leaning forward.

The motion sends a gentle waft of her personal scent my way – nectarines and honey – and floods my brain with memories.

It's funny how it's the mundane things I've missed the most: the angle of her smile, the sound of her breathing, the way she fiddles with the collection of random objects that are holding up her hair. When I'm face to face with her like this, confronting the reality of her rather than the things I've turned her into in my memory, I have to remind myself of the reasons we broke up. She's bewitching like that; she makes it hard to remember the bad.

But this is neither the time nor the place for reminiscing about my relationship with Tabitha. It's in the past, and it's going to stay there. It *needs* to stay there. Let's face it: my life is already complicated enough.

There's a knock at the door and I lock eyes with Tabitha.

'Who did you tell?' I ask.

'No one!' she says. 'When would I have had a chance to? Who did *you* tell?'

'I'm in hiding, Tabby. I'm hardly going to announce to everyone— Oh, no, wait, there is someone. But she's actually the one who told me.'

'Jack!' comes a shout from the front of the house. 'I know you're in there. Open the bloody door. It's pissing it down out here and the rain's going to fuck up my suede boots!'

I follow Tabitha out into the entrance hall, where the

thumping against the door is getting louder by the second. If it carries on much longer, I'm worried the whole thing is going to cave in. Tabitha gets there just in time, swinging the door open to reveal a drenched Mina on her doorstep, complete with inverted umbrella and soaked hair.

'Well, that's it. I'm never going to be able to salvage them,' says Mina, then she pushes her way inside, leaving puddles in her wake. Once she's a few steps in, standing on the increasingly-muddy cream carpet, she pulls off her ruined boots and throws them unceremoniously to the floor, where they leave long scuff marks against the skirting boards.

'This is the soggiest country I've ever been to,' she says, shaking herself like a wet dog. It doesn't make her much drier, but it does cover me and Tabitha in a shower of secondhand rain.

'I don't believe we've met,' says Tabitha, her expression stony.

'Mina Parchek,' says Mina, thrusting out a hand.

Tabitha ignores it and says, 'Mina... the private investigator? The one who Jack—'

'Why are you here, Mina?' I interrupt, intuiting that a trip down memory lane isn't going to help anyone at this point.

'I don't know,' Mina says. 'Just trying to keep you honest, I guess. And chaste.'

'That's rich, coming from you.'

'Jack,' Tabitha says, taking a step back, 'whatever this is between the two of you, I don't want to be stuck in the middle of it, so if you'll excuse me—'

'Have you asked her yet?' Mina says to me, ignoring Tabitha entirely.

'Asked me what?' says Tabitha.

'I was just getting to it when you barged in and started making insinuations, as usual,' I reply, then I turn to Tabitha.

'Mina's been helping me with everything. There's nothing going on between us.'

'Yet.'

'Mina, you are not helping.'

'What? It's not like you're planning to jump into bed with her either, are you? You're too busy with the Baron of—'

'Mina! Will you please shut up?'

'She's not telling me anything I don't already know already,' Tabitha says, and I can hear the exhaustion in her voice. 'You and the baron? That's hardly news to me. But I *am* still in the dark about why you need a cure for Dr Jay's blood, so maybe you could get to the point.'

'Okay,' I say, taking a deep breath. But I don't know how to phrase it, and I hesitate. While I'm trying to find the right words, Mina gets impatient.

'The syringe broke while she was stabbing her ex,' Mina says, 'a bit of his blood got into hers. She's been healing it by—'

'A process we don't need to bother Tabby with,' I interrupt.

Mina shrugs and leans back against the corridor wall, crossing her arms over her chest in a gesture that says she's prepared to let me have the floor, for now. I can already see the water stain from her contact spreading across the wallpaper.

'The problem is,' I say, 'the treatment isn't working as well as it used to, and it's not a cure. I think I'm still dying, I'm just doing it more slowly.'

I'm sure I'm not imagining the flicker of sympathy I see in Tabitha's eyes before she locks it down. She cares, and more than she's willing to let on.

'If you told me about the treatment—' she starts saying, but I interrupt her.

'I can't do that.'

'I won't be able to tell whether or not it's working as you say it is unless I know what it is.'

'Trust me,' I say. 'It's not relevant.'

Tabitha seems sceptical at best.

'Will you at least take a blood sample from me and see what you think?' I ask.

She looks at me for a few seconds, then at Mina, and the wait for her judgement feels like an eternity.

'All right,' she says eventually. 'But only out of professional curiosity, you understand. And I'm not making any promises.'

'Thank you so—'

'Save your thanks. I don't know what's in your blood, or what you've been taking. For all I know, it might already be too late.'

'Then what are we waiting for?' Mina says cheerfully. 'Stick a needle in her already.'

Tabitha glares at Mina, then turns back to me and says, 'I'll get my kit.'

11

THE BLOOD ANALYSIS is not a quick process. Tabitha has a lab in the back garden of her Scottish home, and it's even more sophisticated than the one she had in Nash Lee, but the fancy equipment doesn't seem to be speeding things up at all. I'm not sure exactly what she's doing, but it involves putting things in machines and adding drops of things to other things and generally doing the sort of stuff you'd see in the montage of a murder investigation show. Ed would be all over it, but to me it's just a long, boring process that's delaying the answers I so desperately need.

There's one question on the table: am I going to die?

Tabitha's wearing one of those big plastic anti-contamination suits, which I take as a bad sign. With potential doom hanging over me, it's difficult to muster up any enthusiasm for the scientific method. My toe is literally tapping as I sit at one of the high stools at the end of the bench in Tabitha's lab and watch her work. I'm so impatient that I can't stop myself from asking her how long it will be, over and over again, until I feel like a child on a holiday road trip.

One small blessing is that Mina got bored waiting and

decided to ditch us hours ago. She's back off to wherever it is that she lives now – she enjoys the power imbalance in our relationship too much to give me her address – and back to work. I hope that work is tracking down Khalyed's missing body and blood, or finding a way to break the bond, but I suspect she's busy making some poor adulterer's life miserable. I'm paying her well, but not well enough that she can afford to drop all her other work.

Part of me is a little annoyed that she doesn't care enough to hang around and find out whether or not I'm going to die soon, but I can't say I'm sorry to see her leave. It's not that I don't appreciate her help, but having her here was putting Tabitha in a distinctly uncooperative mood. It seems like the only people who are willing to associate with me these days are people who've slept with me – and Cam, though I'm not sure a single visit counts – and despite the fact that my liaisons with Tabitha and Mina are both ancient history, that history makes everything a little fraught. In future, I will be trying my damnedest to keep them apart.

'Okay,' Tabitha says eventually, pulling off her helmet and suit now that my samples are safely sealed away. 'I've tested it every way I can, and your blood is… It's not good, Jack.'

'Details, please,' I say, sitting up straighter.

'I'm not sure I can give them to you,' she says. 'I mean, I can tell you what's happening, but I can't tell you why.'

'Then let's start with the what, for now.'

She comes over to sit on the stool next to me and drags her laptop over to the bench in front of us, swivelling it so I can see the screen.

'Here,' she says, pulling up a photo.

It looks like a magnified image of blood cells in black and white, until Tabitha zooms out and I see that that the photo is actually in colour, it's just that only half of the cells in the shot are red. The others are mostly a light, dusty-looking grey, but there are a good number that are pitch black and weirdly-shaped.

'These are healthy blood cells,' she says, pointing to the red ones, then she points at the black ones. 'These are the invasive serum cells from Dr Khalyed's blood. And these—' She points at the suspiciously ashy-looking cells. '—are cells that have been destroyed by contact with the blood from Dr Khalyed.'

'I don't like that ratio.'

'Which is the problem,' Tabitha agrees. 'Somehow, the cells from Dr Khalyed are either replicating in your body, or they're infecting healthy cells from the blood you drink and mutating them into cells like themselves. I suspect – but I can't be sure without further testing – that when you receive this healing treatment you're being so cagey about, it's either eliminating or repairing these damaged cells—' She points to the ashy grey ones. '—but it's doing nothing to repair or slow the replication of the infected ones.'

'That sounds bad.'

'I'm sorry, Jack, but I think you're right: it's only going to get worse. I'm not really sure how you're even still alive, because with most people the replication would be instant. At this point a single drop of your blood would be deadly to any other Silver.'

'Shit,' I say, making a mental note to be more careful with Drake next time I see him.

'I'll need to take another sample from you after your next healing treatment to be sure, but even though it's happening much more slowly for you that it would for anyone else, if we can't find a way to remove the infected blood from your body, or to kill the infected cells, then I think the cells are just going to keep multiplying until there are so many of them that you can't heal at all anymore.'

It's bad news. Terrible, really, but I'm fixating on one little word, and it gives me hope.

'We?' I say.

Tabitha looks away for a moment, fiddling with the display on her computer screen.

'You said *we*,' I prompt. 'Does that mean you're going to help?'

'Of course I'm going to help, Jack,' she says softly. 'I'm not saying all's forgiven. I'm not sure we'll ever get past what we did to each other, probably not even enough to be friends, but I'm not very well going to sit on my arse and just let you die, am I?'

I pop up off my stool and throw my arms around her neck. Maybe I've been a bit blasé about the whole imminent death thing up until now, but that was when it was only a risk, one that I was ignoring. Now, seeing the proof of my impending demise so clearly on the screen, I am overwhelmed by the strength of my desire to live.

And Tabitha's going to help me do that.

'Thank you,' I whisper, breathing every ounce of sincerity I can into the word.

'We'll get you through this, hen,' she says, squeezing me tightly for a moment before gently pushing me away. 'I was close to a cure, you know. When you and that woman had me locked up in the basement—'

'I'm sorry about—'

'I'm not fishing for apologies, Jack. But you know I'd already been working on an antidote for the serum before she snatched me, and then I spent more time working with the formula while I developed the imitation serum that she used on Matthew Felton. I know it backwards and forwards. I was very, very close. I just need to run a few more tests.'

'You're serious?'

I had no idea it would be this easy.

'Deadly,' she says. 'I managed to reverse-engineer the

serum, but there must be something about the way it interacts with Dr Khalyed's particular genetic code that makes it behave the way it does, and I haven't been able to replicate that.'

'You're going to need a sample of Khalyed's blood,' I say.

I saw the notes Tabitha was keeping while she was Winta's prisoner, so I was expecting this. It's why Mina and I have been working so hard to track down Khalyed's blood.

'Exactly,' she says. 'If you can get me that, then I think I could finally crack it.'

'Oh, I can get it,' I say, thinking about Drake's secret stash.

It has to be somewhere at the mansion. He'd want it somewhere close, within his control. And if Mina can't find Khalyed's blood in the meantime, I could trying asking Drake for it again the next time he comes to visit. Maybe he'll be more cooperative now that I have an actual solution in the works.

'Then your cure is as good as done,' says Tabitha. 'I'll probably only need a couple of days.'

I grin. 'That's the best news I've had all year.'

'I don't want you staying around here while I work on it, though, hen. It's too close, and that's not good for either of us while you're in danger. Plus,' she adds, going a bit coy, 'I think we've both moved on now, haven't we?'

'You're seeing someone?' I say, surprised that I'm feeling ambivalent about that prospect.

Tabitha and I are done – more than done – but while I want her to be happy, I still get the tiniest echo of jealousy at the idea of her being with someone else. I know it's just an emotional hangover, which is hardly unexpected given that we only broke up six months ago, but I wasn't aware that I still felt anything for her at all. It makes me wonder how I could have repressed my feelings so easily when I was under

Winta's influence. Maybe it had something to do with Winta being my sire, but the truth is that I still don't understand the control she wielded over me. I don't think I ever will.

'I'm not seeing anyone in particular,' Tabitha says evasively. 'Not enough to be talking about it to you, at least. But is there anything you want to tell me about?' she asks.

We both know what she's implying, but I'm not going to acknowledge Drake openly, not to her. Maybe in a few days, if we get a cure and I don't have to worry about killing him anymore. Maybe then, once I know he's safe and the bond is no longer a death sentence, but not before.

So I say, 'No. But you're right, it's not a good idea for me to hang around. I'll get Khalyed's blood – shouldn't take more than a day or two – and then I've got a place on the coast where I can stay for a few days, just until you're done with the cure.'

'The coast is too close,' she insists. 'I've got a place you can use.'

'The Invicti know about all your places,' I say. 'They gave me a list.'

'Well, they don't know about this one. It's there and it's empty, so use it,' she says, then she roots around in her lab coat for her keyring, takes one key off and hands it to me. 'It's secure, it's private, it's central, and it's yours for as long as you want it.'

'I'll think about it.'

She gives me the address, but I have no intention of taking her up on her offer.

When I get back to the farm, I knock at the farmhouse to see if I can use the kettle, but no one answers the door, and when I try the handle, it's locked. I go to bed without my hot tea. It's only the next day, when I can't get inside to make my morning coffee, that I begin to worry.

I tromp around the outside of the house in my wellies in the rain, wading through mud so deep that it pours over the tops of my boots and straight into my socks. I'm shouting the farmer's name and getting no response, but there's an increasingly ominous smell that I'd initially assumed was the septic tank, though now I'm not so sure.

When I look through the window at the side of the house, peering into the sitting room, there's poor old Mr Inman slumped down in his armchair with his whisky glass tipped over onto the floor, his dead eyes staring straight at me. He liked a tipple, but I already knew from his sickly frame and his rosacea that it didn't like him. It was really only a matter of time, but I'm sad nonetheless. He was a decent sort.

I clear out of the caravan and call in an anonymous tip from the phone box in the village. I can't afford to hang around for another encounter with the police. They're bound to have questions that I can't answer.

Thankfully, I have somewhere else I can go.

12

MINA WASTES DAYS trying to track down Khalyed's blood at Drake's mansion. Apparently she – or whoever is working for her – gets in there easily enough, but they search everywhere they can think to look and find nothing.

'I don't think it's there at all,' says Mina one evening as we sit out on the balcony together in the moonlight, drinking too much wine.

I've been here a couple of weeks now, and I've happily settled in to Tabitha's shiny new penthouse apartment. It's located in a central U.K. city that shall remain nameless for my own safety, but is well-served by transport links so I can scram sharpish should the need arise. It's also bloody enormous and has every modern convenience you could possibly desire, including a weird multi-room music system that I can't work out and may possibly have broken in the process of my various attempts. I'm hoping I won't have to confess that to Tabitha until after she's created a cure.

Which will, of course, be impossible if I can't get my hands on a sample of Khalyed's blood.

'Where else would he have hidden it?' I ask.

'Why are you asking me? You're the one who knows

him.' Mina smirks, so I know the joke is coming before she lets it drop. 'Inside and out.'

'Yes, har-dee-har, but I don't know anywhere else he would keep it. I've never seen him comfortable anywhere other than at the mansion. He doesn't have any other property that I know of.'

'I checked,' Mina says, draining her wineglass. 'There's nothing else registered to him or his company that isn't commercial property, and I don't think he'd hide anything there.'

'Then maybe you were wrong,' I suggest. 'Maybe he never had a secret stash of Khalyed's blood.'

'But he didn't deny it when you asked him.'

'He didn't exactly confirm it, either. Not in so many words. Maybe we jumped to conclusions.'

What a depressing thought. It seemed like a perfect solution when Khalyed went missing. Given my access to Drake, it actually felt like an easy alternative, but it's not turned out like that at all.

For a moment, we just sit and drink in silence.

'This is getting us nowhere,' I say. 'We need to look at our other options. Can we find Khalyed?'

'Yeah,' Mina says, shifting in her chair. 'I heard something unsettling about that.'

'What?'

'I heard that the Solis Invicti took him.'

I groan.

It makes sense, of course. The Invicti were all over the mansion in the days after I ran. If what Cam told me about Winta and Adewale's father was true, and if Mina was right about Ed being in London with the Invicti, then of course they would have taken Khalyed there to run their own tests and create their own cure. Mina's information isn't surprising so much as it is a confirmation of our expectations. But it's still awful fucking news.

'Maybe they'll crack it,' Mina suggests. 'Maybe they'll make a cure and then the baron can get it for you.'

'They're hardly just going to give it to him though, are they? And Tabitha's so close to a cure. They don't have her research. It could take them ages.'

Neither of us needs to mention that we don't have time to wait for the Invicti to meander towards their own cure; that's clear enough from the way I'm itching at my arms. It's not even been three weeks, and I'm already feeling the burn.

'Then you'll just have to try asking the baron again,' Mina suggests. 'We both know you can be very persuasive when you want to be.'

I ignore the insinuation and say, 'I'll try.'

But I already know he's going to refuse. He'll give me some bullshit about it not being politically expedient or whatever, and he'll insist that he has it all under control. To be fair to Drake, he doesn't know that the situation is becoming more urgent all the time, but I don't want to worry him with that until it's absolutely necessary. If I do, I'm worried he'll work out my back-up plan.

'What about the bond?' Mina says. 'Did you trouble yourself to do any reading while I've been out doing your dirty work?'

I want to snap back with a snarky comment, but I can't think of one, and anyway I do actually have some news on the question of the bond.

'I was reading this thing this afternoon,' I say eloquently.

'Thing?'

'Not a book, not one of the print outs. A manuscript? I don't know. It's a few pages of crinkly paper in a version of English so old that it took me ages to understand it, but it said something about stretching the bond until it snapped. Give me a minute to find it.'

By the time I come back outside with the papers, Mina has finished our bottle of wine and opened a second. I have no idea where she magicked it from, because I swear it wasn't there when I left, and I wasn't gone for more than a minute, tops. I finish my own drink and have her pour me another, then I show her what I've found.

'Here,' I say. 'This bit. "*Yif that the lengthe bitwene the tweye encresseth in espace and in understondynge the bondemark mot strecche and at mooste destresse breke*".'

'You what now?'

'As far as I can work out, it says something like: "If the length between the two increases in space and in understanding then the bond can stretch and eventually break".'

'Okay,' Mina says sceptically. 'But this is some medieval shit. Are you sure this word "bondemark" even means "bond"? It looks weird.'

'What else could it be?' I ask. 'All of this stuff around it is definitely about us. Look: the super-speed, the way the Silver heal, our heightened senses. In the context, this bit has to be about the bond.'

'But this is the only reference you've found?'

'I've looked through everything,' I say. In fact, I've looked through everything three times, burning through my blood supply to read at high speed. 'This is it.'

Mina squints at the paper, shaking her head.

'"If the length between the two increases in space and in understanding",' she quotes. 'So, what? You have to move to Australia and piss him off?'

'Or something similar.'

'I don't know,' she says, pouring us both another glass of wine. I'm not sure where the last ones have gone. 'It seems pretty thin to me.'

'But it's all we have.'

'Then what's the plan?'

I know what I have to do, but the thought of putting it into action makes me feel a little sick. If I keep pushing Drake away, then maybe I'll break the bond, which would be a good thing for him, but would mean no more healing for me. For that reason alone, I don't want to do it until I've given up on the cure, which I'm definitely not ready to do yet, and the best way to get the blood we need to make that cure is by bringing Drake closer.

That sounds mercenary, and I guess it is. It's not that I don't have feelings about it – just thinking about being closer to Drake is enough to make my skin tingle – it's just that I really can't think about those right now. I have to ignore the way he makes me feel and try to be practical. I might not like the idea of manipulating him into giving me Khalyed's blood, but I can't pretend it would be the first time. Also, he's a mass murderer, so perhaps morality shouldn't be my guiding star here. Really, he should be expecting this.

But we still have other options to explore.

'You keep trying to find Khalyed,' I say to Mina, sounding more decisive than I feel. 'I'll ask Drake about the blood again.'

'So you're not going to try stretching the bond until it—' She snaps her fingers.

'Not yet.'

Mina swills her wine thoughtfully around her glass before downing the lot, then she says, 'You know that if the Invicti have Khalyed, the chances of me getting in there and getting out again with the blood are close to zero, particularly since they tightened security after your little coup.'

'I know. But we don't know for sure that he's at Solis Invicti HQ. Can you find out for certain?'

Mina shrugs. 'I'll try.'

'Good.'

'There's another way, you know,' she says slyly, rolling her empty glass around in her hands. Apparently her hidden supply of wine is gone, and I'm all out. 'Your mate Cam.'

'No,' I say, swiping her glass so I can take it inside with my own. We might not be mixing our drinks with blood, so neither of us is actually drunk, but I think we've had enough chit-chat for one evening.

She follows me in from the terrace, chasing me across the open plan living room to the kitchen.

'You should think about it,' she says.

'I'm not getting him involved in this.'

'In your life and death struggle, you mean? Don't you think he'd *want* to be involved?'

I slam the glasses down on the counter next to the sink, breaking one of the stems in my hand. The glass splinters into my palm, giving me flashbacks that frankly I could do without right now. Apparently I have a habit of holding on too tight.

'I'm not bringing him into this,' I say to Mina as I run my hand under the tap. The water's red for a moment, but I've drunk enough blood today that the cut heals quickly. Not as quickly as it should, though.

'You said he gave you his number,' Mina points out. 'He's expecting you to call.'

'Only if it gets too bad, and it isn't, not yet.' I dry my hands roughly with a towel then crumple it up and throw it onto the counter. It doesn't make me feel any better. 'Maybe the healing mojo will be able to keep the fire at bay for longer than Tabby thinks. Maybe Ed and the Invicti will actually come up with a cure. Who knows? But I can't involve Cam, not until I have to. It wouldn't be fair to him, and with the Invicti baying for my blood, it wouldn't work out well for me. However close we were, he's one of them now. I'm just going to have to deal with this on my own.'

'All right,' Mina says, holding her hands up in surrender, but the tone of her voice is far from satisfied. 'Whatever you say. You're the boss. Speaking of which…'

She rubs her thumb and forefinger together.

'World's tiniest violin?' I ask facetiously.

'Money, Jack,' she says. 'Bribing people costs money, and I'm running out of it. If you want me to see if I can track Khalyed down in the Invicti building, I'm going to need more of it.'

'You'll get it.'

'When?' she demands.

I think about the energy I used travelling to Scotland and back, and all the bottles of blood I burned through while I was researching the bond. There's none left in the fridge, so I've been managing on red wine and denial. Drake must be able to feel that through the bond, stretching it the same way as the fire burning under my skin stretches it. He'll be here any day now, and he always comes bearing gifts.

'Soon,' I say. 'You'll get more money soon.'

'Okay,' Mina says, nodding to herself thoughtfully, all business now.

'What?'

'I might have an idea.'

'About getting into Solis Invicti HQ?' I say. 'And back out again with the blood?'

'Yes,' she says. 'Potentially.'

Excitement fizzes through me. If we can get in there and find Khalyed, get his blood, and get away without getting caught, then I can solve this whole burning-to-death issue without having to involve Drake at all.

'Really?' I say, unwilling to believe it.

'Really.'

'Mina, I could kiss you.'

'About time I got some action.' She gives me a teasing

smile. 'Do you have any idea how hard I've been working for you?'

I smile back. 'I do. And I appreciate it. And thank you. So what's the plan?'

'I'm not a hundred percent just yet,' she says. 'I need to check some plans, but give me some time to work things out and I'll be back soon with a proper scheme. And a sizeable invoice, of course. Make sure you're ready to settle it, one way or another.' She winks filthily then turns to leave.

'Come on, Mina. Surely you can tell me some...' I say, but she's already rushed out of the balcony doors and into the night.

If I had any blood left, I'd be tempted to follow her at super-speed, but that's not an option. I guess I'll just have to wait until she's ready to share.

13

'HAPPY MAY DAY, Valentine.'

'You're not in Oxford anymore, Drake,' I say, letting him into Tabitha's apartment. 'The North doesn't care about your quaint little southern traditions. It's too busy working for a living.'

'Am I to gather from your chippy attitude that you're going to be supporting yourself from now on instead of living off the bags of blood and cash with which I supply you?'

'Not likely. I'm a southern girl, Drake. Hand over the goods.'

He passes me his bag and sits down on Tabitha's shiny new sofa as I unpack the blood bottles into the fridge.

'You're in a good mood,' he observes. 'Why might that be, I wonder?'

'None of your business,' I say, shutting that subject right down.

I don't want to tell him about my trip to Scotland, or my hopes for a cure, or that if Mina is unsuccessful, I'm planning to wangle the location of Khalyed's blood from him by whatever means necessary. At the moment, I'm just

102

enjoying the idea that this might all be over soon, and it's not just about the staying-alive thing. The fact that I have to kiss Drake to get healed is making my feelings towards him more complicated than they already were, and that's saying something. For once, I wish this could just be easy. I wish I could be allowed to feel what I feel without mitigation.

I can feel Drake's eyes on me as I move around the kitchen, and I don't hate it. The truth is, I've missed him. However awkward things are between us, however many people he's killed, and whatever the circumstances are, it isn't changing the way my body reacts to him. Just having him in the same room as me is enough to notch up my heart rate. He must be able to hear that, and if I can feel the physical pull of the bond between us, urging me closer to him, then it must be even stronger for him.

'Why are you so early?' I ask, trying to ignore the urge to rush across the room and throw myself into his arms. 'I wasn't expecting you for another couple of weeks.'

'You needed me,' he replies simply.

'Excuse me?'

'You know I can feel when something's wrong through the bond. You're hurting. You're weaker. The bond feels thinner somehow too, like the tether that holds me to you is getting weaker.'

'Maybe it is,' I suggest, although the strength of my desire to move closer to him tells me otherwise.

'Or maybe you've done something to burn through your energy and your blood supply, because you're too stubborn to keep yourself out of danger.'

There's nothing I can say to that without revealing more than I want to, so I just stare at him placidly and wait for him to continue.

'You're infuriating,' he says.

'I am, aren't I?' I grin at him.

'But this is a *very* good mood,' he goes on. 'You haven't told me to fuck off once since I walked in the door.'

'Are you trying to make me?' I ask as I join him on the sofa.

'No. I'm wondering what it would take to get you to give me a tour of your new flat. The bedroom, in particular.'

I shouldn't have been so friendly. I shouldn't even have let him sit down, and I definitely shouldn't have sat down next to him. Instead, I should have insisted on the regulation peck on the lips, then turfed him out into the street like it did last time. But I'm just so damned cheerful this afternoon. There's an anti-serum in the works, Mina's working on a plan, the sun is shining outside, and here's Drake – all tousled hair, soft lips and dangerous eyes – sitting on my shiny new sofa in my shiny new flat, and somehow it feels like I've stepped into another life where this could be normal. Natural, even. In this moment, I can no longer remember why I'm resisting the urge to pull him closer.

'Killian—'

That's all the invitation he needs. He reaches across the sofa, hooks an arm around my hips and pulls me straight into his lap.

'Do you know how long I have been waiting,' he says, running his fingers through my hair, 'to hear you say my name again?'

It's about four months, by my count, but I forget to answer him when his fingertips touch that spot at the back of my neck that drives me wild, the spot that only he has ever been able to find. The best I can manage in the circumstances is, 'Unnhhh.'

'Do you know how many times this year I've dreamed that you might whisper my name?' His other hand is on my hips now, pulling me closer. 'Or moan it. Or scream it,' he says softly, and honestly, I don't think it'll be long before

I'm doing exactly that.

No.

I can't let this happen. I can't let myself get swept up in the thrill of his touch when there's still so much at stake. But then he touches that magic spot again and I decide that maybe I can handle just a *little* thrilling.

'Scent marks,' I say, trying to think rationally despite the overwhelming distractions of his touch, 'they only get left from full-on kissing on the mouth, right?'

'I don't know,' Drake murmurs, his gaze flicking from my eyes to my lips to my throat, and lower. 'Do you want to find out?'

'For science?' I suggest, as if that explanation would fool anybody.

'For science,' he agrees, then he leans forward and kisses me on the side of my neck, just below my ear. 'You know,' he murmurs, his lips moving gently against my skin as he kisses his way down to my collarbone, 'if this works, then I can think of any number of places I could kiss you that won't leave a mark. Kiss and—' He scrapes my skin with his teeth. '—more.'

'No biting,' I say.

If he drinks from me, the bad blood in my veins will get into his, and I won't be able to heal him like he can heal me.

'No biting,' he murmurs, his lips against my neck. 'No kissing on the mouth. And no scent marks.'

But our experiment is already a failure. My lips haven't even touched his, or any part of him, and our mingled scents are filling the air.

'Shit.'

'I didn't know that could happen,' he says, pulling back so we can look each other in the eye. He seems troubled. 'I didn't mean to—'

'Fuck it,' I say, then I shift position so I'm straddling his lap, take his face in my hands and press my mouth to his. The moment our lips touch, I feel myself healing, but I'm not stopping there. If it's too late to stop the scent mark, then we might as well enjoy ourselves. All this self-denial… Well, I've abstained long enough.

Drake seems to agree. He certainly doesn't give me a chance to change my mind. Instead, he cradles the back of my head in his hands and, teasing at just the right spot with his fingertips, kisses me exactly the way I need him to: deeply, slowly, and possessively. Before I know what's happening, my top's on the floor, my fingers are digging into his naked shoulders, and I'm moaning and grinding against him in slow strokes that mimic the movement of his mouth on mine.

'Bedroom,' he says, breaking away for a moment. 'Where?'

I wave in the right general direction, then capture his bottom lip between my teeth and nibble it. He moans and the vibration of it through his body threatens to send me over the edge. I want him to feel as precarious as I do, so I release his lip and turn my attention to his neck. When my teeth touch his skin, playfully at first, then harder, though not hard enough to break the skin, he jerks in my arms.

'Bedroom,' he demands. 'Now.' Then he scoops me up in his arms and walks across the flat while I cling to him, legs wrapped around his body, kissing his neck every step of the way.

'You're killing me, Valentine,' he moans, throwing open the bedroom door, then he backs towards the bed and sits us down on the edge. One bonus about being on the run: I haven't got enough possessions to have created my usual minefield on the way to the bed. The path is clear and easy. 'How quickly can you be naked?' he asks.

'You want to rush this?' I tease, my mouth back at his

neck.

'Yes,' he says. 'No. I don't know. Just don't stop.'

I'm not intending to, but hearing the edge of desperation in his voice, I slow things down. The kisses are lighter now, the touch of my teeth just a whisper on his skin. He groans, and I can feel how much he wants this. How much he wants me. He tears off my bra – the only one I own, or owned I guess, but who cares? – then he's ripping at my fly in a way that suggests he's too distracted to realise that until we shift positions, it'll be hard to get any more naked than we are right now.

Killian Drake is stupid when he's horny. Fortunately, his fingers are not.

I roll onto the bed on my back, dragging him with me, and by the time my hands reach for his belt, he already has my jeans off and is starting on my knickers. I'm trying to pull his belt loose, but it's difficult to concentrate when his biteable, half-naked body is inches from my face and his fingers are doing something incredible between my legs. In the end, I give up and let him have at it. I've got one leg hooked around his waist, another pinned to the bed at the ankle with his free hand, and my knickers have gone the same way as my bra.

There's no point in fighting it. Killian Drake is going to do whatever he wants to me, and I'm going to let him. But it turns out that what he wants to do is pure torture. He strokes. He coaxes. He teases. And then, just when I think I've had enough, he lightens off the pressure in a way that has me wriggling my hips, trying in vain to bring him closer again.

'Look at me,' he whispers, and it's only then that I realise I have my eyes closed. When I meet his gaze, he's not hiding his silver anymore. His eyes are a constellation of silver stars in darkness. His pale cheeks are flushed. His lips are red from my bites and kisses. Looking at him like this, watching him revel in what he's making me feel... It might be the most deliberate sex I've ever had, and it's definitely working for me.

'I can't wait,' I moan mere seconds later, squeezing my eyes shut against the sensation. 'I'm going to—'

Then he takes his fingers away. I open my eyes again so I can aim properly when I thump him, then stop dead. He's staring at me with an intensity I've never seen in him before.

He whispers, 'Look at me.'

I do.

He whispers, 'Say my name.'

'Killian,' I whisper back, and he groans.

'Again,' he says.

But his clever fingers are back where they belong and this time when I say, 'Killian,' I'm moaning.

'Again,' he says.

Then he can't talk anymore because his mouth is where his fingers were a minute ago, and now I'm screaming, 'Killian, Killian, *Killian*,' as I break apart beneath him, just like he wants me to. I have never been so obedient in my life, and especially not for him, but if this is what happens when I am, then I might try doing it more often.

'Valentine,' he whispers, with one last, possessive lick. '*My* Valentine.'

I'll probably take issue with that later, but right now I am in no state to argue.

I'm expecting a breather when he lets go of my ankle, but then he's kissing his way up my body, slowly and skilfully, and suddenly I'm ready for more. Like, right now.

I divest him of his trousers with a messy combination of hands and feet, pushing them down his legs and off, and his underwear follows quickly afterwards. But he stops me before I can pull him on top of me.

'We're not rushing this,' he says.

'Oh, so now you've decided?' I say, impatient. 'What if I want to rush?'

'If you want to be in control, then be my guest.'

He asked for it.

I sit up, push him onto his back and say, 'Stay.'

Then I swing one leg over his and hold myself there for a moment, crouching over him, watching the desire build in his eyes. Now it's my turn to torture him. He doesn't know what I'm going to do, and it's thrilling to watch his excitement as he tries to work out my next move. I haven't made up my own mind until I shift down the bed a little and watch his eyes go wide with disbelief.

'You can't,' he groans. 'It's too much. You'll ruin me.'

'Well, when you put it like that...'

How can I resist?

When I take him into my mouth, he yells so loudly that if I had any neighbours on this floor, he'd be disturbing them. His body is shaking before I even start to move my lips, and by the time my tongue gets into the mix the bed is shaking too. Who knew that the great Killian Drake could be so easily disarmed?

'Valentine, please,' he gasps. 'I want you.'

I show him mercy, just this once, and release him. Not for long, though. He put me in control, and that's where I'm staying.

He watches me with big, bright eyes as I crawl my way slowly up his body, then I plant a trail of kisses along his collarbone – gently – and wrap a hand around the back of his neck – roughly – to pull him up into a seated position. When he realises what I have in mind, his breath gets shaky and I hear his heartbeat notch up a gear.

I straddle him again, but this time there's nothing between us, and I know that just one quick tip of my hips would bring us thudding together. But I want to draw this moment out, because I can see what it's doing to him. I can chart the escalation of his need in the look in his eyes, in the set of his jaw, in the way his fingertips are gripping into the flesh of my thighs.

'Don't make me beg,' he whispers.

I've just decided that I like the sound of Killian Drake begging, quite a lot, when he slides a hand between my legs and touches me in a way that makes me impatient too. I decide to grant him a reprieve. I catch his mouth with mine, then our bodies are slipping together like puzzle pieces in an explosion of sensation that shocks my mouth away from his, just for a second, before I claim it again. In that moment, I claim the rest of him, too, every part of him. If only for tonight, wrapped in the scent of my mark, he is truly mine. If only for tonight, I can pretend that being with Killian Drake is an unmitigated pleasure that I am allowed to enjoy.

Then we climax, and the world turns upside down.

I've had some pretty awesome orgasms in my time – some on my own, some in company – so I don't want you to think that I'm some starstruck newbie when I say that I have never felt a release so electric, so cathartic, so *sensational*, in my entire life. I don't think I've ever screamed so loud, either, and I'm not alone.

For a moment after we fall apart and lie next to each other on the bed, I can't do anything but stare up at the ceiling and *feel*. My mouth is dry, my feet are tingling, and I can't feel my face.

It takes a few minutes before he says, 'I… That was… Wow.'

'Holy shit,' I whisper.

'You too, then?'

'What *was* that?' I ask. 'Was it the bond?'

'I don't know,' he says, pulling me lazily back into his arms. 'But I was right: you've thoroughly ruined me.'

He presses a kiss into my hair, trails his lips down my cheek, then nuzzles that magic spot at the back of my neck, sending pleasant shivers down my spine. Killian fucking Drake is snuggling me. If you'd told me a year ago that we would end up here... It makes no sense. I can't explain it, and with our scent marks swirling around in the air, I can't be sure how I really feel about it, either. I need to think this over, to work out what just happened and what it means for us – for me – but it feels as though my mind has been wiped clean and I can't seem to access rational thought.

I don't mean to fall asleep.

I shouldn't get comfortable with Drake in my bed for a whole host of reasons, not least of which is the fact that if any of the Silver who are searching for me happen to find us here – me with my silver lips and both of us with our scent marks – they'll put two and two together and realise that Drake has silvered for me. Then we're both dead. But with the post-coital glow and Drake's warm body wrapped around me, I've fallen asleep before I even realise there's a danger I might.

14

WHEN I WAKE up, it's morning. I guess life-changing sex is tiring, because we slept right through.

Struck by an unusually domestic urge, I slip out of bed without waking Drake and pad into the kitchen naked to get the coffee machine going. It doesn't feel like a day for clothes.

That's when I see the note taped to the balcony window.

Didn't want to interrupt, but thought you should know asap: the SI plan is a bust. It won't work. Sorry. Ask him again. M.

My good mood vanishes in the blink of an eye.

If Mina can't get into the Solis Invicti building to get a sample of Khalyed's blood, then unless I can get Drake's stash from him, Tabitha can't make me a cure, and I'm going to die, which means Drake is going to die too.

I feel sick.

I shouldn't have let myself fall into bed with Drake, and I certainly can't let whatever this is continue. If I keep pulling him back to me, I'm going to kill him.

Just like Winta.

I turn off the coffee machine without taking any steps to

112

make an actual drink – the urge towards domesticity has vanished along with my good mood – then slip back into bed to enjoy the last few moments I have in Drake's arms before the bubble bursts. It's not long before he's awake and looking for a repeat performance, if it's even possible for us to repeat what happened last night. I can feel his fingertips creeping their way down my back, around my hip, across my belly and—

I catch his wrist before it can go any further, then roll over to face him.

'Good morning, my Valentine.'

'I'm not *your* Valentine,' I say, surprised by how much the words hurt. 'I'm not your anything.'

'You're grumpy in the mornings,' he says, his eyes twinkling with silver and mischief. 'I can fix that.'

Regardless of everything I've resolved upon, it's difficult to stay grumpy in the face of his charm. He's leaning in towards me, his lips just a breath away. His fingertips are on my thigh now, slowly making their way upwards, and his touch has me remembering everything we did last night: every taste, every sensation, every moment in the sublime, timeless ecstasy of—

'No! No more kisses,' I say, pressing a finger to his lips to push him away. 'No more anything. No more scent marking.'

'There must be something I can do for you that won't mark you,' he says, running his hand down my side in a way that makes me shiver.

'You could give me Khalyed's blood,' I suggest, already knowing what his answer will be.

'No, I can't. Come on, Valentine,' he says cajolingly. 'Don't kill the mood by asking for things you know I'm going to refuse.'

'I need it,' I insist.

'No, you don't.'

'Yes, I do.'

'Why are you picking a fight? Look, even if I still had it – which I don't – I still wouldn't give it to you. It's too dangerous.'

'What?' I ask, feeling my last shred of hope disintegrate between my fingertips. 'Why don't you have it?'

'The Invicti needed it. You don't.' He pulls me back against his body, trying to distract me with other things he can make me need instead. 'I'm taking care of it. Now let me take care of you.'

Shit.

The Invicti have every last bit of Khalyed's blood. The only thing that can save my – and Drake's – life is currently in the hands of the very people who want me dead.

Shit shit *shit*.

'No more marking,' I say, unwrapping his arms from around my body as I pull away. 'You have to go.'

'Or I could stay,' he says with a seductive smile.

'No, you can't.' Despite my misery, I laugh at his persistence. 'We can't just keep renewing the mark over and over. You have to go back to your life eventually.'

'No, I don't.'

'Yes, you do. You're the Baron of Oxford.'

'I don't have to be,' he says softly. 'This could be my life. With you.'

That gives me pause, and not in a good way. I might have been fantasising about exactly this yesterday, but back then it was nothing but fantasy, a fantasy in which I was already cured. But Mina can't get Khalyed's blood, and Drake doesn't have it, so I need to face facts: I have no cure for what's killing me. Drake will die if I can't break the bond, and my only hope of doing that is by putting some space between us, like the manuscript said.

I could tell him that I'm dying. Given that my impending death means we're *both* dying, I probably should tell him, but the words get stuck in my throat. All I can think is: this is my fault. I'm the one who planned to kill the Primus. I'm the one who actually killed Winta. I'm the one who fucked the whole thing up, got Khalyed's blood in my veins, and in the process doomed the both of us.

However much I *should*, I just can't bear to tell Drake what I've done. I can imagine a hundred different ways he might react, and they all make me hate myself a little bit more. Call me a coward – you'd be right to – but I just can't face it, not from him. I'm going to clear up my own mess or die trying.

I have to push him away so I don't take him down with me.

'I'm on the run,' I say. 'You can't stay with me.'

'I could just… disappear. We could run together.'

The Invicti are searching for me, my evil ex-girlfriend's brother and her own evil ex-girlfriend both want to kill me, and I'm being burned alive from the inside by a mad scientist's blood serum, but none of that scares me as much as that one word: together.

Just the two of us, from now until forever.

My forever is so much shorter than his. I'm already shaking my head and getting out of bed, taking the sheet with me.

'So, what?' he says. 'You're going to run away from me, too? You know I can always find you, Valentine.'

'This was a mistake,' I say.

For a moment, he says nothing at all. He just looks at me, shocked.

'I can't believe this. I thought…' He turns his back to me and sits up on the side of the bed with his head in his hands. 'No. I don't know why I thought that. You're never going to stop denying that this thing between us is real, are you?' He grabs his clothes from where I threw them on the floor last night and starts pulling them back on.

'This thing between us is not a thing, Drake. It can't happen.'

He turns to face me. 'It *is* happening, whether you like it or not.'

While Drake's standing there shirtless with his unbuttoned trousers and his gloriously messy hair, it's hard to deny it, but I'm going to try anyway.

'Only until we find a cure for Khalyed's serum,' I say, 'and you're working on that, right?'

'Well, you're not giving me much incentive, are you?'

'Seriously? You'd rather have me under your control than have me be well?'

He stares at me for a moment, non-plussed. 'How can you say that?'

'Come on, Drake,' I say, fabricating wildly. 'I've always been trouble for you, and I always will be. We're too different. There's too much history behind us, and too much shit ahead. The sex is okay, sure—'

'*Okay*?' Oh, he is angry now. 'Are you serious? *Okay*?'

'—but this is never going to work.'

He's staring at me again.

'You're not joking, are you?' he says. 'I can't believe this. You really just expect me to walk away? After *that*?'

Yes. He has to, because I'm not sure I can anymore.

'If I were you,' I say, 'after everything I've done, I would have walked away months ago.'

'Then you'd be a coward.' He moves towards me and takes my cheek in the palm of his hand. 'Don't throw this away for my sake. I'm not afraid of what's coming, Valentine. I'll be there with you when it does. You know that I—'

I can't let this go on. Whatever I feel, whatever I want, I have no cure, and so I have nothing to offer him but death.

'I don't want you to be,' I say, hardening my tone. 'I'm not responsible for how you feel, Drake, and when I try to tell you this gently, you don't listen, so let me be blunt: whatever it is that you think you feel for me, whatever you think makes us special, I don't feel the same way. To me, this is just sex. Nothing more. I have to rely on you right now, so I will, but the moment I'm cured, this is over. You will never see me again, and the sooner you understand that, the better.'

I swear I see a little piece of him break away. He stares at me for another long moment in disbelief, then he gathers the rest of his clothes, pulls on his shoes, and walks right out of the flat, closing the door gently behind him.

That feels like a bad sign. If he'd just been angry, he would have slammed it, but this is something different. I will never be able to wash those words away. I will never be able to take them back. Maybe they will be the thing that breaks the bond. I should be happy, but in this moment, as selfish as it is, I wish I didn't have to die alone.

15

SINCE TABITHA'S APARTMENT is the penthouse, I don't have any neighbours on my floor. I do, however, have a neighbour in the building next door. Our balconies are side-by-side, too far apart for a human to step across comfortably, but close enough that we've occasionally waved and said a quick good morning or, more commonly for me, good evening. I am not a morning person at the best of times, and now is certainly not that.

I'm not totally sure where the time goes, or how the blood in my fridge disappears so quickly, but apparently I'm back to moping and – surprise, surprise – I'm doing it with booze. In those circumstances, I can't be too clear about when Faith and I become friends, but it happens. I can't even remember asking her name, but apparently she knows me as Ophelia, which is a relief. I could so easily have slipped up and given her my real name.

'You love those Bloody Marys, huh?' she asks one night as we sit out on our respective balconies, enjoying the first properly warm night of the year.

'Tomato juice has all sorts of vitamins in it,' I say, knocking back what is in fact a Valentine's Massacre. I shouldn't be drinking blood so openly around a human, but like I said, things are a little fuzzy these days. 'Vitamins counteract the alcohol, you know. This is actually a *healthy* drink.'

'Yeah, right,' she scoffs. 'About as healthy as my quadruple gin and tonic.'

Faith is cute as a button, with generous curves, long curly hair the colour of straw and a heart-shaped face that predisposes you to be friendly to her. By all accounts, it's an image that's been paying her way for some time; until recently she was a sex worker, though she seems very young to me, and now she's in a relationship with a married guy she refers to only as Mr P. He rents the flat, which is even more glamorous than Tabitha's, and keeps her in champagne and diamonds. It's an arrangement that seems to work for her, for the time being, but she's realistic about its longevity. The guy is obviously a dick, and I don't like the way he talks to her, but she knows this, and she also knows I'm right next door in case she needs me. I've told her I'm a black belt in jiu jitsu, which is a complete lie, but at least it'll make her more willing to come to me for help.

If I'm not too smashed, that is.

'By the amount you're drinking, I'm guessing you still haven't heard from him,' she says.

'Not since the beginning of the month. I think I've properly pissed him off this time.'

Yes, I told Faith about Drake. Not the details, of course, but I had to tell her something. Turns out I'd left the balcony door open, so she heard us screaming at each other that night, then screaming at each other again in a less friendly way the following morning. Since Mina hasn't reappeared since then either – probably worried I'm going to make her find another way to break into Solis Invicti HQ – Faith is basically the only person I have to talk to.

'Well, at least you're not relying on him for your allowance,' says Faith. I haven't told her about the bags of cash Drake brings me. She thinks I'm a remote-working coder, which is a laugh given that I don't even have a phone, much less a computer, but it seemed like an easy lie. 'When Mr P stops coming around, I worry.'

'When was the last time?'

'Five weeks now. Apparently he's been on holiday with his wife, but I don't know. Seems like maybe we're coming to the end of the line.'

'Are you sad about that?' I ask.

She shrugs and sloshes a little of her drink over the brim. I don't see the spill so much as I hear it pattering down onto the marble that floors her balcony. It's a grander than Tabitha's, which is a rather brutalist creation of concrete and iron, whereas Faith's larger terrace wouldn't look out of place in Rome, with its curving stone balusters and ornate carvings. I'm sitting on an old plastic chair, whereas Faith is on some kind of fancy wooden lounger. She has patio heaters; I have blankets. You get the idea.

'Have you got somewhere else to go?' I ask.

'Always,' she laughs. 'I don't spend everything he gives me, you know. I have more than enough to get out of here and start over. I thought maybe nursing school, actually.'

'Yeah?'

'Yeah. It's what my mum used to do.'

This is the first time Faith's even mentioned her family before, so the reference takes me by surprise. It also suggests she's in a more reflective mood than I can navigate sensitively in my current state. I'm not exactly Captain Compassion at the best of times, and a drunk Jack Valentine is a careless Jack Valentine. In the circumstances, the best I can do is keep my mouth shut and let her talk.

'We didn't see her much when we were kids,' she says.

'She worked all the hours, partly so we could have the things we wanted, and partly because she loved it. Messy work, but fulfilling, she said. And I thought, well, I know about messy work. Maybe it's not that different. Nursing's mostly less dangerous, and it might not pay as well, but I've got some in the bank, and maybe there's more than one way of getting paid. So I'd like to give it a try, at least.'

'You going to stay around here?' I ask.

'Maybe. Maybe I'll move down south and get a fresh start. I've done a bit of googling, and I like the sound of Oxford.'

I shudder involuntarily.

'You've got a history there?' she asks, seeing my reaction.

'The worst. But there are a lot of hospitals there, lots of research stuff too, I guess, with the universities.'

'Exactly. Are you planning to head back one day?'

'Nope,' I say, then I down the rest of my drink. 'Nothing there for me anymore.'

'Well, maybe you could visit.'

I say, 'Maybe,' in a way that makes it clear that the likelihood of my ever going back to Oxford is exceedingly low, then I hear a knock at the door and drag myself out of my chair.

'Door,' I say to Faith by way of explanation.

'Same time tomorrow?' she asks.

'Probably.'

It's not much of a goodbye, but I'm rolling drunk at this point, and it's all I can manage. She waves, and I go to answer the door, but whoever was knocking has already left. There's an envelope on the doorstep with no address on the front, not even my name. It's only then that I realise it's a bit late for deliveries.

Maybe I should pause to consider whether the letter is actually intended for me, given whose flat I'm staying in, but its delivery method is clandestine enough that I don't give any alternatives a second thought. I rip into the envelope immediately. Someone's found me, I think. Adewale Ladipo, or Yolande Leclercq, or maybe even Benedict. Either way, it feels like it can only be bad news.

I'm right about that, but not for the reasons I first suspected. Instead of a death threat or a demand for surrender or any other of the myriad things I thought the envelope might contain, instead it holds a single sheet of letter paper – thick grade, fancy texture – with a few lines' worth of ornate ink handwriting. I should recognise the hand, but I only realise it's from Tabitha when I see her initial signed at the bottom.

I don't have any good news for you, hen. I'm sorry, but it's getting worse. The infected cells have multiplied twofold since your last blood sample. We're running out of time. You need to find the final ingredient for me. Do it fast, and burn this letter. The friend who's delivering this is discreet, but still. ~ T

I sent her another blood sample just after Drake's last visit, as we'd agreed before I left Scotland. I collected it myself, which I can't pretend was anything like as clinical and professional as it would have been if Tabitha had extracted it – to be honest, I used a knife and an empty spice jar and a lot of bad aim – but we couldn't risk meeting in person, so I wrapped the package up tight, enclosing it in multiple layers of thick plastic and duct tape, chucked it in the postbox and hoped for the best. It's been so long since I sent it that I was starting to think it must have got lost in the post, but I guess it took her a while to analyse it, or to get someone to bring her note here, or to be certain enough that she was right to be willing to give me such crappy news.

Not that it's really news at all. I expected this, I tell myself as I crumple to the floor on the doormat in a drunken mess. I knew the end was nigh. I guess I was still hoping, even in the face of all the evidence, that between me and Tabitha and Mina, we might find another way. But it's time to accept the reality of the situation: it's too late for me. The best I can do is try to break the bond before it's too late for Drake as well.

16

I MUST HAVE passed out on the doormat, because when I wake up I'm greeted by the smell of burned coir matting directly in my nostrils. Turns out I did as Tabitha requested and set her letter on fire, but for some unfathomable reason I decided the doormat was a safe place to do that, then planted my face directly into the smouldering ashy mess for my little drunky snooze. Classy, I know.

It takes me a moment to work out that the acrid smell is actually not the thing that has woken me up. Instead, it's the front door pushing against my shoulder. Slowly, I am sliding backwards across the wooden flooring as the door swings open.

'What the—?'

The voice is a woman's. I look up and see a punky crop of platinum blond hair. For a moment I panic, thinking that it's Leclercq and she's cut her hair short, but then I see the woman's face. It takes me a moment to recognise her without her ridiculous staircase hat.

'*L'Escalier?*' I say, squinting up at her from the floor.

'Oh. Um. Hello.'

Back when Tabitha and I were still together, we met

L'Escalier on a night out to the local blood bar in Oxford. She's a performance artist who dresses like she's just walked off a Tim Burton set, with a signature top hat whose brim is circled by a tiny lacquered staircase. If you'd asked me ten minutes ago which of our mutual acquaintances was least likely to end up with a key to Tabitha's hideout, L'Escalier wouldn't even have been on my list, because honestly I'd forgotten she existed. Apparently Tabitha hadn't.

'I wasn't expecting anyone to be here,' she says.

'Ditto,' I reply.

She looks a little scared. It's possible that I'm glaring. Maybe that's unfair, but I'm shocked to see her, and imagine what would have happened if she'd walked in while Drake was here? Bad enough that she's walked in to find me like this. It makes me feel small and pathetic, but my hostile mood has nothing to do with Tabitha. Nothing at all.

I climb to my feet as gracefully as I can, which is a big ask since one of my legs still seems to be asleep, and pull myself up to my full height. I'm still several inches shorter than L'Escalier. That does not improve my mood.

'Does Tabitha know you're here?' I ask, even more brusquely than I intended, which was pretty brusque to start with. Maybe I've inhaled some of the coir soot, or maybe days of overindulgence have just ruined my throat along with the rest of me, but either way my voice has gone raspy and threatening. It's enough to make L'Escalier's eyes widen a little.

'No,' she says fearfully. 'Not exactly.' Then the shock of finding my hungover body blocking the doorway wears off and she squares up to me, hands on my fists. 'Does she know *you're* here?' she says combatively. Then adds with just a hint of anxiety, 'I thought you broke up.'

'Oh, don't worry, we did.'

'Then why are you here?'

'Why are *you* here?'

We face off against each other for a few long seconds, neither of us willing to make the first admission.

'Okay, let's sort this out right now, shall we?' says L'Escalier, then she whips out her phone and starts a video call before I realise what's happening. I guess I'm still a little fuzzy.

'Petunia?' says a familiar Glaswegian accent on the other end of the call. 'Is everything okay? I was expecting you here an hour ago.'

'*Petunia?*' I say, incredulously. With a name like Petunia, no wonder she had to create a ridiculous alter-ego like L'Escalier.

'Who's that?' says Tabitha.

L'Escalier – or Petunia, I should say – swivels the phone so Tabitha can see me.

'Oh,' Tabitha says. 'Bugger.'

'I think your girlfriend got her wires crossed and went to the wrong address, Tabs,' I say.

'Jack, I can explain. The thing is—'

'You don't need to explain anything to her,' says Petunia, swivelling the phone back around so she can look at Tabitha herself. 'You broke up with her, didn't you?'

'Yes,' says Tabitha.

'Then why is she here?' Petunia demands.

'Er…'

Petunia softens in the face of Tabitha's obvious panic. There's something in her eyes that makes me wonder just how serious the two of them are about each other, because it looks to me like Petunia is ready to go all in.

'I know this thing with us is new,' she says to Tabitha, 'and you can tell me to fuck off if you want, but I feel like this could be going somewhere real, and yet here you are harbouring a fugitive who also happens to be your ex, so I sort of feel like I deserve more than *er.*'

'Um,' I say, feeling like a third wheel. Petunia glares at me, but I soldier on. 'Hi. So, look, this is my fault. You obviously know I had a bit of trouble with the Invicti, and then I started having trouble with another thing that I thought maybe Tabby could help me with—'

'So you decided to drag her into this?' Petunia says, rounding on me. 'Haven't you fucked with her enough?'

'Petunia...' Tabitha says on the other end of the call.

'No, she's right,' I say. 'Tabby and I have talked about it, and I've apologised—'

'Well I'm sure that made it all better,' Petunia says scathingly.

'And obviously that can't make up for what I did,' I continue, 'but Tabs was still kind enough to offer to help. So maybe you two can talk this through, and I can go somewhere else until you're done.'

'Maybe to the shower,' Petunia suggests.

I think she's just being rude until I catch a glimpse of myself in the mirror that hangs by the door. I have black soot spread over half of my face, and some of it has congealed in clumps at the edges of my eye and mouth. There's blood in the mess too, so I guess the fire may not have been properly extinguished when I face-planted into it. Thankfully, the blood I drank in my faux Bloody Marys last night seems to have healed my face, but I can't say I'm happy about Tabitha and her new squeeze seeing me looking like a half-burned corpse.

No wonder Petunia was so unimpressed. Well, maybe there are other reasons too, but best not to dwell.

By the time I get out of the shower, freshly scrubbed and dressed in loungewear so I look less like a dangerous fugitive and more like a totally non-threatening ex-girlfriend, Tabitha and Petunia are giggling at each other through the video chat, so I guess they've sorted out their differences.

'Oh,' Petunia says when I discreetly clear my throat. 'You're back, are you?'

Apparently she is not a fan. In the circumstances, I can't really blame her.

'Did you get my note, Jack?' Tabitha says on the other end of the phone. Reluctantly, Petunia turns it towards me.

'Got it, burnt it, fell asleep with my face on it. How much have you told Petunia?' I say, glancing at her as I do so.

'About the favour I'm doing you?' Tabitha says. 'Nothing.'

'Good,' I say. Then I add to Petunia, 'No offence.'

'None taken,' she says. 'It's bad enough you've got Tabitha mixed up in your nonsense. You can leave me right out of it. In fact...' Petunia hands me the phone and heads for the door. 'I'll be back in half an hour. And Jack?'

'Yeah?'

'She's doing you a favour.' Petunia points a finger at me. 'Don't be a dick.'

'All right,' I say, holding my hands up defensively.

'And don't go through my phone!' she yells a moment before she slams the door behind her, loudly enough that I'm pretty sure Faith will have heard it next door.

'So,' I say when I'm alone with virtual Tabitha.

'So,' she replies.

'You and Little Miss Staircase Hat.'

'Don't call her that,' Tabitha says, but she's smiling. 'She's actually very talented.'

'I'm sure,' I reply in a tone of voice that reminds me of Mina.

'I like her,' Tabitha says simply.

'I'm happy for you.'

'Jack.'

'No, seriously. I am. It doesn't matter what I think, I

know, but I'd like you to be happy. Let's face it, we were kind of crap for each other. And crappy to each other.'

'Kind of. But there were good times too.'

I laugh. 'More than a few.'

We smile at each other for a moment, and it feels like we're drawing a line under the past year. We met, we dated, we fell into bed, we betrayed each other in horrible and torturous ways, and now we're in a neutral territory where we can be something like friends. It's strange, because Tabitha and I have never been just friends to each other, but I think I like it.

'We should talk about your prognosis,' says Tabitha.

'Are you sure this is a safe way to do it?'

'No one's watching my phone or Petunia's. Honestly, Jack, I think most people would assume I'd be the last person you'd come to for help.'

'That's fair.' I exhale heavily, remembering the feelings of hopelessness that sent me face-first into the doormat last night. 'How long have I got?'

'The rate that I'm seeing the cells multiply? A month or two, maybe, if you drink a lot of blood, you keep up with your secret healing treatment, and you get lucky.'

'Shit.'

It's worse than I thought, and it puts me in a hell of a predicament. Drake's due to visit in another week to heal me, and that would buy me some time before I burn to a crisp from the inside out, but if I let him heal me then it'll close the distance between us, and so minimise the chances of breaking the bond and saving his life, all assuming that my plan to break the bond is actually sound. It's a long shot, but what choice do I have?

I may not succeed in breaking the bond, but I have to try.

'But I've got everything ready in the lab for the cure,' Tabitha says. 'All you need to do is bring me a sample of Dr

Khalyed's blood.'

'I'm really grateful for your help,' I say, trying to convey to her how much I mean it. 'You didn't have to do this for me, particularly not after everything, so thank you. And I'm really glad we had a chance to talk again, to clear the air. It was pretty good, you and me, before it went bad.'

'What are you on about?' she says. 'Why are you talking like—' Her face falls. 'You can't get it, can you?'

'No,' I say. 'I'm sorry, Tabby, but it's over. The Invicti have Khalyed and all his blood.'

'Damn,' she winces. 'I'm sorry, too, hen, but maybe this is for the best.' For a moment I'm a little taken aback by that, because what the fuck? But then she carries on and I realise she's not actually talking about me dying after all. 'Maybe the best thing you can do is turn yourself in. I know the formula Dr Castell has been working on is slightly different from mine, but you can give him my notes. I'll give everything to you and they'll be able to mix you up a cure.'

Which is actually a pretty good plan, assuming I can get them to cure me before they put me in a box. Unfortunately, given my past encounters with the Invicti, I have no faith at all that that's what would happen. Imagine if I ran into Benedict before anyone else. He'd lock me up and throw away the key, no questions asked, no protests heeded, and then Drake and I would both be dead in a matter of weeks.

I'll consider it as a last resort, but it's not going to be my next step. No, my next step will be breaking the bond. That's priority one.

'So I'm guessing you're not keen on the idea of asking them for the blood yourself?' I ask.

'It's not that,' she says. 'It's just that I already know they wouldn't trust me with it. Dr Khalyed's blood is dangerous stuff, and I burned a lot of bridges on my way out.'

'Not as many as I did.' I laugh, then I ask in an offhand

way, 'I don't suppose you know of any way to break a bond, do you?'

'A bond? What, you mean a Silver bond? Why would you —?' Unfortunately, Tabitha is pretty good at jumping to the right conclusions. 'Oh, Jack. Tell me he didn't.'

'I wish I could.'

'That's how you've been healing,' she says.

'Yes.'

'And you're trying to save him by breaking the bond.'

'Look, I know you don't like him much, but—'

'You can't, hen,' she says, her eyes full of pity.

'But I found this old document that said the bond could be broken if I put enough space between us.'

'Old as in old English?'

'I guess.'

'Then you're talking about the Hardwicke manuscript,' she says.

'Am I?'

'I think so. I was looking into it while I was studying haematopsychosis and I'm sure I have a copy...' She rustles around for a few seconds, the camera panning wildly, then her face comes back into the centre of the screen. 'Here it is: *Yif that the lengthe bitwene the tweye encresseth in espace and in understondynge the bondemark mot strecche and at mooste destresse breke.*'

'Yes!' I say. 'That one. So how do I do it?'

'Jack, *bondemark* doesn't mean the Silver bond.'

I feel like she's just slapped me through the phone.

'What?' I say stupidly.

'I know you might not want to believe me, particularly given my track record when it comes to the baron, but it's true: the *bondemark* is a different Silver phenomenon entirely, something that frankly I think is apocryphal. I'm sorry, but as far as I know, there's no way to break a bond once it's made, not without killing someone.'

I groan. 'Double shit.'

I pushed Drake away for nothing. I said all those awful things for nothing. We could have been spending the past few weeks enjoying each other and instead... nothing.

'But I tell you what, hen,' Tabitha says. 'When you do get this cure sorted and come out on the other side – and you will, because you always land on your feet – I'd love to take some more blood samples to see if I can study the effect that the bond has on—'

'No, Tabby,' I say, struggling to push off the wave of exhaustion that's threatening to drag me under. Maybe it's the hangover, or the bad blood, or the fugitive thing, or the range of increasingly shitty options for my future life or lack thereof, but I'm ready to go back to sleep, in a bed this time. 'No more tests. Look, L'Escal— Petunia has a key, right?'

'Yes. Sorry, I forgot about that.'

'No, it's fine. My point is that she can let herself back in to get her phone, so I can go back to bed, right?'

'From what I heard, hen, you weren't in bed to start with.'

'Yes, well, impending death and all that. It makes me thirsty.'

'That's not going to help with the replication, Jack,' she says gently. 'You might be taking in human blood in those lethal drinks of yours, but you're also drinking your own Silver blood, I'd guess, and we don't know what effect that's going to have on you with the mutated serum in it. Plus, combining it all with alcohol is only going to wreck your body and increase its need for blood, speeding the whole process up. You're cutting your time shorter every time you drink one of those things.'

'You were more fun when we were dating,' I say.

'And you were more healthy,' she replies. 'You need to look after yourself, for his sake if not yours.'

'I was trying to,' I whisper.

'I know, but there's nothing you can do about the bond. I'm sorry. If he lov—'

'Don't say it!'

Tabitha rolls her eyes at me and says, 'I can't believe you're still such a commitment-phobe. He's silvered. You know what that means. You've got the proof you always wanted.'

'But I wanted it from you, Tabs,' I say quietly.

'It wasn't meant to be me,' she replies, just as softly. 'It was always going to be him. I think we all knew that, it just took us a while to work it through. I've accepted it, and he clearly has. When are you going to?'

It's a perfectly legitimate question that I don't want to answer, so instead I fake a yawn and say, 'I'm really tired.'

'Sure you are,' she says, clearly unconvinced.

'I actually am, but I also don't want to talk about this.'

'You'd better go and run away from it then,' she says teasingly. 'Go on, go hide under the covers. But you don't have much more time for that, hen. I'd make the most of it if I were you.'

'Yeah, yeah.'

'And I'm here when you need me,' she adds with a smile. 'Just say the word, and I'll send you all that I have on the cure.'

'Thank you, Tabby,' I say. 'Really, thank you.'

'You're welcome. And play nice with Petunia.'

That feels like the least I can do for Tabitha, so instead of crawling back into bed where I long to be, I manage to keep myself awake until Petunia comes back for her phone.

But not a minute longer.

17

KILLIAN DRAKE IS late.

It's been well over a month now, and I'm so weak I'm starting to wonder if one day I'll just never wake up. The fire in my veins is a constant burn of throbbing heat, searing pain down my limbs and collecting to an inferno in my stomach. I keep drinking cold water, thinking that it'll bring my temperature down, but then I feel it boiling up inside of me and sweating out through my pores. Soon enough, I won't be able to contain the heat any longer, and then *poof*, I'll go up in smoke like Matthew Felton, like Winta did on the rooftop that night in the memory I've been desperately trying to suppress for five and a half months.

Drake must know all of this. He can feel it through the bond, he said, the way it gets stretched thinner when I'm starting to fall apart, and I am definitely falling apart now. So why isn't he following the pull of the bond to my side when he knows that I need him? Either something's wrong, or he's trying to teach me a lesson. I wouldn't put it past Drake to be that petty. After all, I was a bit of a dick the last time I saw him. Okay, a lot of a dick. But he's going to have to get over it because if I don't get him to heal me soon then we're both dead.

Unfortunately, the pull of the bond doesn't work both ways. Drake's the one who's silvered, so he can follow it to me, but I haven't silvered for him, so I can't use it to track him at all, which leaves me with no way of knowing where he is. So I'll just have to search, like anyone else.

Before I can get started, Mina finds me passed out on the sofa.

'You look like hell warmed up,' she says. 'Have you been mixing your drinks again?'

'Five weeks, Mina,' I say.

'Since you saw the baron?'

I nod, because I can't get up the energy to speak. I can't get up the energy to do much at all. I'm still wearing the clothes I fell asleep in last night, and even though that isn't exactly a rare occurrence for me at the best of times, I feel as though my skin is crawling with grubbiness today. In fact, now I think about it, I might have been wearing these clothes the day before yesterday too. Maybe even the day before that. I can't really remember, and that feels like a bad sign.

'Shit.' Mina looks at me with concern as my eyes start to close. 'We've got to sort you out.'

If I were at full strength, I'd make some sarky comment about how her kisses will do nothing for me, but instead I just croak, 'How?'

'I don't know,' she says, exasperated. 'I'm not your bloody nursemaid. I'm a sexy, ball-busting, arse-kicking P.I.! Why do you keep putting me in this position, Jack? And you're *never* naked anymore. Honestly, I'm starting to wonder what's in this for me. I mean, bloody hell.'

I just look up at her, unable to do much more.

She stares at me for a moment, then takes a deep breath and lets it out slowly.

'Well,' she says, 'I suppose we can't get the bad blood out

of you, given the toxicity and all, but maybe we can dilute it a bit. When did you last drink blood?'

I shrug. It's been a few days, I know that much. I've only got one bottle left in the fridge from the stash Drake brought me, and I've been saving it until I'm really desperate. It occurs to me then that maybe I've saved it a little too long.

'Right, then,' Mina says, heading for the door. 'Be right back.'

When she returns, I'm asleep on the sofa.

'Wake up!' she yells in my face.

I blink at her groggily. She looks all floaty and blurry, like an impressionist painting in violent shades of black and red.

'Drink this.'

She shoves something into my hand. When I do nothing, she helps me raise it to my lips and drink. I'm not really thirsty, but I finish the bottle and she replaces it with another, and another, until I'm strong enough to take them from the cooler myself.

Five bottles, I drink. Five bottles, and I still feel punch drunk, but at least I'm fully conscious.

'Better?' she asks.

I flex my fingers and sit up straighter, testing my strength. 'A bit.'

'Thank fuck for that. Now, about the baron. Where is he?'

'Back at the mansion, I assume. Don't you know?'

'No,' she says. 'He's not there. Hasn't been for a while now.'

'How long is a while, Mina?' I ask. I'm getting a bad feeling about this.

'A few weeks. Maybe five. Actually, now that I think about it, he left pretty much right after you saw him last.'

Oh, god. I've really done it this time. I've driven him away for good.

'Why didn't you tell me?' I ask.

'You didn't tell me to watch him. You told me to watch the others.'

'I thought it was obvious.'

'Why would it be? Come on, he's silvered for you. You have the bond. He'll find you. It's not like he's going to leave you to suffer, is he?' There's a pause during which I can only assume that Mina is considering the state in which she just found me. 'Not on purpose, anyway.'

'Hmm,' I murmur, noncommittally.

'Jack,' Mina says. 'What did you do?'

'Nothing.'

'Jack, I know that look. It's the same look you had on your face when you told me that you and the Invicti were having, and I quote, "a minor disagreement".'

'Well, let's just say that Drake and I had a minor disagreement too.'

'How minor?'

I wince. 'It's possible that I told him he was okay in bed.'

'*Okay?* You said he was *okay* in bed? Jesus Christ, then no wonder. If you told me that, I'd be sulking too.'

'Sulking enough to let us both die?'

'You're not dead yet, Jack. You can suffer a little while longer.'

'A very little while,' I say, gauging the burning under my skin. It won't be long now.

Mina is unsympathetic. She just says, 'Then the question becomes: if Baron Drake was trying to piss you off, where would he go?'

With that little prod, my brain finally jumps to a conclusion it should have reached days ago. The first time Drake and I ended up in bed together, I did a runner the next morning and, by way of retaliation, he promptly fucked off for an extended sexcation with his ex-girlfriend. I might not have literally run away from him this time, but I did practically chuck him out, and I definitely hurt his feelings. It makes sense that he'd react in the same way.

'Europe,' I say. 'He'll be in Europe with Carlotta Arden.'

'The drop-dead gorgeous half-French half-Argentinian film star sexpot he was engaged to?'

I groan. 'Yes.'

'Oh, Jack.' She's laughing at me. Even at a time like this, she's bloody laughing. 'You're lucky he'd literally die if he didn't kiss you again, because if I was swanning around on the continent with naked-times access to Carlotta motherfucking Arden whenever I wanted, then I would never, ever come back. Ever. And after you told him he was *okay in bed*… Is that true, by the way?'

'I really don't see how that's any of your business, Mina.'

'Well, I'm guessing that you want me to help you track down the baron, yes?'

'Obviously.'

'Then I think it's pretty fucking relevant information. Wouldn't you agree?'

'No.'

'And if I refuse to help *unless* you tell me? I could just leave you here on the sofa to lapse back into unconsciousness, if you prefer.'

'Fine!' I relent, but only because I could really do with another bottle of blood about now, and Mina's holding the cooler hostage. 'No, Killian Drake is not just *okay* in bed. He is… I'm too fucked up right now to come up with the words to describe how good he is in bed. But he's definitely better than okay. Are you happy?'

'Happi-*er*,' she says. 'But if I found someone who was dynamite in the sack and also happened to be head over heels in lo—'

'Don't, Mina!'

'Well, fine, you get my point. But just in case you don't,

it's that you're an idiot.'

'Yes, thank you, I'm aware that I've played this badly. Now can I have another bottle, please, or what?'

She hands me a bottle and I drink it down. It's not enough.

'I need another,' I say.

'Explain yourself first, and you can have the rest,' she says.

I groan. 'Mina...'

'Why have you been fighting him so hard?'

'I told you I didn't want to talk about Drake.'

'Yes, but now I'm blackmailing you,' she says, crossing her arms over the cooler, 'so you basically have to.'

'Lots of reasons,' I say. 'How about this one: I'm dying, which Tabitha says is happening much more quickly than I thought, and she also says the plan I had for breaking the bond is bullshit—'

'I could have told you that,' Mina says, but I just carry on talking.

'—and since you apparently can't get hold of Khalyed's blood—'

'Which I notice you also haven't magically managed to do.'

'No, and I'm not getting at you, but the point is that we can't make the cure without it, and since we can't get it from the Invicti, and they also have Drake's stash, we have nothing. I'll probably be dead before we can find him, which means he'll be dead too. What about that situation screams romance to you?'

'I'm not hearing reasons,' she says. 'I'm hearing you avoiding the question.'

'Fine, here are some reasons: we have a shitty history, we're in this weird place of forced intimacy where we have to kiss each other to heal me whether we actually want to or not, the power imbalances are all over the place, and, oh, he's a serial murderer.'

'Okay, now give me a *good* reason.'

'Those are good reasons.'

'Yeah, but I want the real one.'

From now until forever ~ W

'I killed her for him,' I whisper.

Mina gives me a hard look for a moment, then says, 'So because you killed your sire and first love for the baron then, even though he's silvered for you, you're not allowed to be with him and be happy about it – even though you *definitely* want to, whatever you say – because instead you have to spend the rest of your life being crushed by guilt for what you did?'

'Something like that,' I mumble.

'Oh, boo-fucking-hoo,' she yells dismissively. 'Get over it. If you hadn't killed her, then you know he would have done it for you. And it's not like she didn't deserve it.'

'Mina!'

'In fact, from what I heard, if you hadn't let her bite you all those years ago and turn you Silver, giving her the blood she needed to escape that cell in his basement, then she would have gone the same way as Elise Santiago twenty years ago, and tens or maybe hundreds of humans would still be alive. Plus, none of this shit would be happening. You wouldn't even be Silver, just some boring middle-aged human with a bunch of kids and bad credit, and the baron would probably be off fucking his way around Europe instead of... Actually, maybe it's not that different after all.'

'You're not helping.'

'Maybe I'm not trying to.' She grins. 'But I fancy a holiday, so are we off to Europe, or what? If you feel like evening the score, then we can fuck our way from country to country, too.'

'Are you proposing that we fuck each other, or other

people?'

Mina shrugs. 'I'm easy.'

'I know. And no thanks.'

'To other people, or…?'

'To the whole plan,' I say.

'It's just sex, Jack.'

'*Just sex.*' I laugh dismissively, because that's what I used to think about Drake. Our first night together was supposed to be the only night, just a way to get him out of my system so the sexual tension would stop interfering with my life, but oh no. He went and silvered for me, and suddenly there were feelings involved. *Just sex.* That's what I said to him the last time I saw him, when I broke him and sent him away. If I'd been honest with myself for once instead of hiding behind my fear, maybe things would be different now. *Just sex.* What a joke. 'It's never just sex, Mina.'

'Not with the baron, sure, but that's because he loves—'

'Ah-ah-ah!' I say, covering my ears. 'We are not talking about that right now. Or ever, in fact.'

'Deny it all you like, but it won't make it any less true.'

'I thought you were trying to seduce me,' I say grumpily.

'I am,' she says, and she sounds genuinely surprised that I think there's any conflict between her wanting to jump my bones and her bringing up the fact that Drake… feels things. 'I don't see what that has to do with anything. I told you: it's just sex. We've been here before, haven't we? With me, you know it'll never be anything other than sex.'

'I'm not well.'

'I'm asking you to take your clothes off and lie down for a bit, not run a marathon. Who knows? It might even make you feel better.'

The weird thing is, part of me agrees with her. I don't know if it's the loneliness talking, or the fact that Drake's healing kisses have confused the feelings of wellness and

141

arousal in my brain, but it actually sounds like a good idea. Besides, I know from experience that Mina is dynamite in the sack. She should be; she's certainly put in the hours learning her craft.

But she isn't him.

Turns out that I haven't just ruined Drake. He's ruined me too.

'No,' I say.

'No sex, no Europe, or no to everything?' Mina asks, hedging her bets.

'Definitely no sex, and no Europe yet. We're getting ahead of ourselves. Look, we can't waste time running aimlessly around the continent unless we have some kind of confirmation that Drake's actually there.'

'And how are you going to get that?'

'I'm not going to get anything. *You're* going to call him.'

'Bollocks to that. I'm a wanted criminal in Oxford, Jack.'

'Not as wanted as I am,' I say.

'Braggart.'

'Come on, Mina. I'd do it if I could, but the call could be tracked if I make it from here, and I'm not strong enough to go super-speed running at the moment. You are, though, and there are still a couple of bottles of blood left in the cooler. You could down them, run a hundred miles or so, find a payphone, make the call, then run back here, all before I could manage to get my boots on.'

'Jack—'

'Please.'

'Fine,' she says with a groan. 'I'll call the mansion.'

'No, you don't have to do that. Here,' I say, grabbing a pen and notebook from the side table. I scribble down a number, tear off the paper and hand it to her.

'Did you just give me Baron Drake's private mobile number?' She's staring down at the paper she's holding like it's a grenade. 'A number that, apparently, you know by heart?'

'Don't make a big deal out of it, Mina.'

'If I take a look through the rest of that notebook, am I going to find a load of love hearts with "Mr and Mrs Baron Drake" written all over them?'

'Just drink your blood,' I say, shoving a couples of bottles at her, 'then go and make the call, will you?'

'I'm going, I'm going.' She shoves the paper in her pocket, then necks the blood, one bottle after another, and heads for the door. 'But Jack?' she says, turning just before she leaves. 'Just so you know, you've got it bad.'

I'm starting to think she might be right.

And it's only going to get worse.

18

YOU MAY HAVE realised this already, but patience isn't a virtue that comes easily to me. I'm bad at waiting. Normally, I'd fix myself a drink and go to sit out on the balcony to distract myself from everything that's going on in my head, but I think if I drank another Massacre right now it might kill me, so instead I just go and sit out on the balcony. I'm hoping to see Faith, but she isn't there, which makes the whole exercise feel a little pointless.

I'm about to turn around and go back inside when I notice the curtains. Faith decorated her flat herself, she told me, in neutral tones of the lightest pink and cream. I'm not much for interior design, so I mostly blanked on her rhapsodic descriptions of carpets and cushions and drapes, letting the words flow over me without really listening at all, but I do remember her saying that she would die before she decorated with red. Too aggressive, or something. Now, though, the bottom of the curtain billowing out through the balcony door, which is standing slightly open, is a deep shade of blood red.

I should make a plan. I should call the police, or get out of here, or both. I should definitely stop and think, at the very least, but I don't do any of those things. Instead, I leap the distance between our two balconies on shaky legs and go to check it out myself.

I can tell before I've cleared the gap that the stain is blood. I can smell it even before I get close enough to see the way it's soaked its way up the drapes like melted wax up a candle wick. Faith is just inside the door, lying on her back in the same clothes she was wearing last night, the glass she was drinking from smashed on the floor a few inches from her open hand.

Fuck.

I know better than to approach, but apparently my brain isn't running my body right now because before I know what's happening, I'm kneeling on the floor in a pool of Faith's blood, hauling her into my arms, desperately searching for signs of life that I know won't be there.

'Faith!' I yell. 'Wake up!'

Unsurprisingly, she does not. Her eyes are open and lifeless, staring straight up at me, though it must be hours since she was last capable of seeing anything at all. I stroke her hair back from her face and take her hand in my own. Strange that we haven't actually touched before this moment, even though we've shared so much time together. Her skin is cold, cold, cold. There are bruises around her wrists and a patch of hair behind her ear has been ripped out by the roots, but that's not the worst of it. Just under the place where the hair is missing, there's a bloody and unmistakable bite mark.

A Silver did this.

I should have heard it. Maybe, if I hadn't been so blood-deprived, I would have. And I certainly should have smelled it. The blood is starting to rot in the warmth of the day, and it's a heady aroma that tickles my salivary glands at the same time as it turns my stomach. But, lingering over it all like oil floating on water, there is the unmistakable scent of a Silver violence mark.

I'm not picking up any other Silver scent, though in this state I'm not sure my nose is up to much anyway, but there is one further clue: there, on the side table by Faith's formerly-cream sofa, there's an empty glass bottle of a shape that's horribly familiar. There's even still a little red liquid congealed in the bottom and, on the neck, a clear brownish-red stain of a thumbprint. I'm almost certain just from looking at the bottle that it's from the stash Drake brought me last month, but just to be sure, I ease Faith carefully out of my lap and back onto the floor, take a crumpled receipt from a bag on the floor and press my bloody thumb against it. When I hold the receipt up against the bottle neck to compare the two prints, they match.

Oh god oh god oh god.

Did I do this?

Of course, that's the moment Mina chooses to return. She must have followed my scent over here from Tabitha's apartment, because she's standing on Faith's terrace with a look on her face that says I have a lot of explaining to do.

'She's dead,' I say hopelessly.

'Yeah, I can see that. What did you do?'

'I'm not sure.'

'Bloody hell,' Mina says, then she's picking her way inside, stepping around the blood. I've spread it about a bit. I have no idea how I'm going to get out of here without leaving a trail. 'But this blood is old, Jack,' she says, sniffing.

'It must have happened last night.'

'What do you mean *must have*? Don't you know?'

'No! But I think that's one of my bottles, and look,' I say, holding the paper with my fingerprint on it up to the bottle neck again. 'This is my print. I must have left it behind, but I don't remember coming here.'

'You were thirsty,' Mina says flatly. 'You ran out of blood.'

'I guess. I don't know.'

'Well, I don't smell anyone's scent but yours and hers in here.'

'I know,' I groan.

Mina looks around at the place and sighs. 'You're a messy eater, you know that?'

'Jesus, Mina. I've never drunk human blood from the vein. Never, ever.'

'Until now.'

'I don't know... I can't believe I'd do this. Not to Faith. I knew her. We were friends. I'm not a—'

I was going to say I'm not a killer, but of course, I am. Maybe I've got a taste for it now. Maybe Drake was right when he warned me about crossing that line. Maybe there really is no coming back.

'Go back next door,' Mina says. 'I'll tidy this up.'

'What do you mean *tidy up*?'

'Come on, Jack. You were in the Seekers. I'd think you'd know well enough what I meant. I'm going to make it look like nothing ever happened.'

'That is *not* what we did.'

'Isn't it?'

'No! We worked with the police to make sure the Silver were brought to justice for their crimes against humans.'

Mina laughs incredulously. 'Yeah, sure you did. It wasn't all a massive cover up operation funded by the Primus *at all*. I must have imagined that part.'

'Mina—'

'Do you want me to clean up this crime scene for you, or are you going to hang around leaving even more prints for the police to find?'

'I didn't—'

'Go pack. I'll be ten minutes, then we're out of here. We'll deal with the chit chat later, all right?'

'Fine.'

'I think what you meant to say was, "Thank you, Mina. You're the best, Mina. I promise not to murder any more people on your watch, Mina."'

And maybe I should be more appreciative, it's true, but the moment I hear her say *murder* my stomach turns and I think I'm going to be sick. I wish now that I hadn't drunk all that blood. And if it was on top of what was in Faith's veins last night…

'Oh god,' I mutter, holding my hand over my mouth.

'Just go!' Mina yells, pointing to the terrace. 'Out, now! Before you make any more mess.'

She doesn't have to tell me twice. The blast of fresh air as I cross from one balcony to the other helps to clear my nausea a little, but when I get back to Tabitha's flat my legs are shaking, and by the time I've chucked my bloody clothes in a bin bag and dragged myself into the shower, my hands are shaking too. Mina's back before I've got myself under control. She walks into the bathroom without knocking and scares me half to death.

'Mina!' I yell. 'I'm naked!'

'Finally,' she says, 'but I'm covered in blood and bleach right now, and we're in a rush, so maybe later. You could budge over though.' She's already taking her own clothes off.

'Is a little privacy really too much to ask?'

'When your neighbour's dead in her flat and the police could be here any minute? Yes. Yes, it is. If you don't want company then hurry up and get out so I can get in. You've got two minutes before we're out the door.'

'What did you do?' I ask, shuffling out of the shower and

grabbing my towel as discreetly as possible.

'I tidied up,' she says simply.

'But—'

'Pack now, talk later.'

I dress. I pack. I make it look like I was never there. Mina showers and comes out of the bathroom wearing my spare jeans and T-shirt – both comically big on her – then adds her own clothes to the bin bag. She carries that, I carry my duffel bag, and we both leave together through the front door. I lock it up tight, then post my keys through the letterbox.

Goodbye, lovely apartment. Goodbye, sanctuary. Goodbye, sanity.

Hello, downward spiral.

19

MINA AND I keep moving, walking through the city streets as though we know where we're going. We lob the bag containing our bloody clothes into a large commercial bin at the back of a local supermarket that we find on our way.

'Where to?' I ask.

'What, so now *I'm* supposed to be masterminding this disaster?'

'You seem to be doing all right so far.'

'Better than you,' she sneers.

'My point exactly.'

She thinks for a moment, then says, 'Train station. Hop to the next city down the line. Hotel. Then we'll talk.'

I nod. We walk. She buys tickets with cash and we sit in separate carriages. When the train pulls in, we wait until we're through the forecourt before we reconvene in a cab outside. It takes us to a hotel that no one would choose to stay in unless all the city's park benches were already taken, but it's loud and anonymous and cheap enough that Mina has enough cash to cover us until this evening. I didn't think rooms by the hour were a thing outside of seedy nineties fiction, but apparently I was wrong. We pay for five and make our way to the first floor through dark corridors that reek of piss and mould. The key grates in the lock, the door sticks so badly that I have to put my shoulder to it to pry it open, and once we're inside there is absolutely nothing that I'm comfortable touching. Frankly, I'm a little scared to breathe.

'How do you even know about this place?' I ask Mina when the door is safely locked behind us with a concerning number of bolts and chains.

'I've got a contact.'

'A contact?'

'It's not as shady as it sounds. I used to do a bit of location scouting for a production company, and we used this place a few times.'

'So they know you here?'

'Of course not.' She looks affronted. 'I'm not an idiot. Unlike you, I have a little discretion. I don't, for instance, go around leaving my fingerprints at a murder, then return to the scene of the crime and wade right through the blood so I can leave nice, clear footprints too. Now sit down and explain yourself,' she adds, pointing to a ratty armchair covered in stains I'd rather not identify.

'I'm not sitting on that.'

'Then pick a spot, because you need to sit somewhere before you collapse.'

She's not wrong; until now the adrenaline has kept me rocking along well enough, but now that we've stopped I can feel the exhaustion creeping into my limbs. I feel like an invalid, because I guess I am.

I look around and assess my options. There's a double bed with a velour bedspread and matching headboard that look as though they've been there since the eighties, the aforementioned armchair, or the floor, which is formed from a sticky brown substance that might once have been carpet.

In the end, I strip the covers off the bed and sit on the sheet underneath, which at least looks clean. I just hope there are no bedbugs.

'Right,' Mina says, plonking herself down beside me. 'Talk.'

'I'm not sure what else I can tell you that I haven't already.'

'From the beginning,' she says. 'How did you end up in her flat?'

'I went out onto the balcony while I was waiting for you to get back. I saw that there was blood on the bottom of her curtain. I went over there. She was on the floor. Then I saw the bottle with the print, checked it against mine, and then you walked in.'

'And you're sure you didn't just take that bottle over there with you?'

'Yes,' I say impatiently.

'And you didn't leave it while you were visiting?'

'Because I routinely go and visit human acquaintances and take my own drinks?'

'I don't know what you get up to in your spare time,' Mina says in a tone that implies that whatever I do, it's probably kinky.

'No, Mina,' I say. 'I didn't leave the bottle when I was visiting. I'd never been in her place before today.'

'As far as you remember.'

'As far as I remember,' I admit.

'Which is a fucking problem,' Mina says. 'I've made it look like an accident – she got drunk, dropped the glass, fell on it, bled out – but everything I saw in that apartment points to you being the one who did this.'

I drop my head into my hands and try to find a reason that she's wrong, but beyond my gut feeling and the fact I don't remember doing it, there's nothing. Counting against me is the violence mark, the bottle, the fingerprint, the bite mark, and the fact that I can't remember a thing about last night. I think I went out to the balcony to chat with Faith, because I usually do, but I don't remember it actually happening. I can't remember going to bed, but I'm pretty sure I've been sleeping on the sofa these days anyway, so that doesn't mean anything. Khalyed's blood has been chewing away at my memory in the same way that it's chewing away at the rest of me, and there are so many bites missing that I can't arrange what's left into a coherent narrative.

'What if I got a taste for it?' I whisper.

'For what?' Mina asks. 'Human blood? You mean the stuff you've been drinking for twenty years?'

'Maybe the bottles Winta gave me were different. The blood was fresh, single origin, not mixed source like the bottles we get from Solomon College. Maybe it's changed me.'

'Bollocks,' Mina scoffs. 'I've drunk from the vein, Jack. Trust me: it's messy, and it's awkward, and it doesn't taste any different from the mixed stuff. It's really not that great.'

'Then what if the same thing that happened to Khalyed is happening to me?' I ask, voicing a secret fear I've been nursing since I left Faith's apartment.

'What are you talking about?'

'Didn't I tell you the whole story?' I ask, no longer able to remember. 'Khalyed's serum, the thing that's bonded to his blood and is currently trying to burn me to death, it made him act... weird.'

'Weird how?' Mina asks.

'Apparently it put him into a sort of trance state, and he started biting Silver and drinking their blood without even realising he was doing it.'

'But Silver,' Mina clarifies. 'Not humans.'

'Maybe it's affecting me differently. We've already proved

that drinking a fuckton of human blood can dilute the effects of the poison, at least for a while. Maybe my body is trying to increase the dilution, only it's happening without me realising it.'

'Like you're some kind of vampire zombie?'

I shrug.

'Then why is it only happening now?' she asks. 'Where are the rest of the bodies?'

'It's only just got this bad. It's been too long since I saw Drake. Unless... Fuck.'

A horrible thought has just occurred to me.

'Explain,' says Mina.

'I had other neighbours.'

Louise.

Mr Inman.

'Jack,' Mina says. 'Please tell me you haven't left a trail of bodies across the fucking country. You were supposed to be in hiding!'

'I don't know, Mina!' I yell. 'Just let me think.'

I'm wracking my brains, desperately trying to remember what state I was in when my previous two neighbours died. With Louise, I was definitely day-drinking. Could I have drunk-walked my way over to her place and killed her? Possibly. But I wasn't hitting the Massacres when I was in Scotland. I was barely even drinking blood, because I didn't have much of a supply with me. But – oh god – maybe that was the problem. Maybe I needed blood and...

But I was in control back then. I wasn't losing time. Surely I couldn't have found my way inside Mr Inman's locked house, murdered him, and found my way back out again without even noticing I was doing it. Unless I did it in my sleep?

'I don't know,' I say. 'I don't think so. Louise died from a heroin overdose, the police said. And Mr Inman was an old alcoholic. I don't think their deaths were suspicious.'

'I'll check,' Mina says, pulling out her phone to run a few quick searches. 'There's nothing jumping out,' she says after a few moments. 'I'll keep digging, but in the meantime we need to make a plan. Whatever else is going on with you, we need to find the baron, and quickly.'

'I thought you were going to call him?' I say.

This morning feels like a month ago now given all that's happened since.

'He didn't pick up, but I did a little tracing, and I tracked the cell towers his phone was pinging from.'

'What? How?' Even in the Seekers, with all the access we had, tracking phones was a bitch unless the circumstances were life or death. Sometimes it took *weeks* to get the data.

'I've got awesome hacker contacts. They're the best.'

'And very illegal.'

'What do you care about illegal? You just did a murder. Correction: *another* murder. Possibly three.'

I groan.

'So, where are we heading?' I ask, trying to contain my rising panic. 'France? Spain? Italy?'

'None of the above. He's still in Oxford.'

'Oxford? You mean, the first place everyone who wants to kill me will be looking?'

'Yup. There.'

'Fuck.'

'I'm not exactly thrilled about it either. I left a trail of broken hearts in my wake,' she says dramatically.

'You left a trail of debts as long as my arm, you mean.'

'Those too.'

'Maybe it's better if you stay behind,' I say. It'll be enough of a problem trying to remain stealthy on my own, but with Mina in the mix too...

'You're joking, right? You can't go on your own, not in

this state. I'm coming with you.'

'Mina, you don't have to—'

'Yes I do. You need to be supervised at all times in case you decide to run off and murder someone else.'

Oh, god.

'Was it really me?' I ask as the nausea sweeps through me again. 'Did I really kill my friend?'

'I don't know, Jack, but we're going to find the baron and get you well, then we'll get to the bottom of it. Give me half an hour to pack and get my car and I'll meet you outside. And do not – I repeat, do *not* – leave this room until then.'

20

BACK TO OXFORD we go.

By the time we pull up outside Mina's old place, it's dark and it's cold and it's pissing it down with rain. Somehow, that feels appropriate.

Mina and I have spent most of the car ride debating the wisdom of her choice of accommodation. I think it's a fucking stupid idea for us to hole up in the first place anyone would come looking for her, but she insists that everyone who might have wanted to find her will already have checked there, and anyway, since the bank has repossessed the property, it'll be securely locked up and a decent option for staying under the radar. When we arrive and see the damaged plywood panels covering what used to be the door and ground-floor windows to her office, my sense of vindication is short-lived. Despite the fact that the place was obviously being used as a crack den until recently, Mina's enthusiasm is undiminished.

She declares it, 'Perfect!' before stashing the car in the garage and dragging me inside after her.

Let me tell you, it is far from perfect. There are some unexpectedly pleasant surprises, like the fact that the water is still on and whoever was squatting here was lucid enough to use the bathroom for a toilet instead of the rest of the upstairs flat, but there are also less pleasant ones, like the rats' nest in the kitchen and the charming new fire pit in the middle of the office. It's a miracle the whole place hasn't burned to the ground.

'No,' I say. 'And aren't you supposed to be some kind of anal-retentive germaphobe? You were all preachy about my old flat being a mess just because there were a few empty pizza boxes and some empty blood bottles and Eric my pet rat, and yet you're willing to stay in *this*?'

'Desperate times,' she says. 'We don't have a choice. You did.'

'I'd rather sleep outside.'

'Really?' Mina asks, putting her bags down inside the door. 'Because that is literally your only other option.'

'There must be other vacant places.'

'Not ones we've scouted. Not ones that are unoccupied. Not ones we know no one will be coming back to anytime soon. And besides, you've gone wobbly again.'

Irritatingly, she's right. It was a long drive and my adrenaline was spiking most of the way, which appears to have burned a lot of energy, and all that blood I drank earlier feels like it's no longer helping. I'm struggling to stay upright. Mina drags over a chair from the remnants of her old desk and has me sit.

'Here,' she says, offering me a bottle from her refilled cooler, but I wave it away.

'I'm not thirsty,' I say.

'You must be. Look at you. You're falling over.'

'I'm not. I just feel sick and tired.'

'You could have slept in the car,' she says.

'I really couldn't,' I say, staring through the dirty floorboards and back in time to the moment that I scooped

Faith up into my arms and felt the finality of her dead weight. 'I can't stop seeing her. I can't believe I did that to her. I just can't.'

'It's late, and you need to sleep,' Mina says.

She's not really listening. Instead, her attention is on the bottle in her hands as she fiddles with the lid. She's not understanding what I'm trying to say, so I say it again.

'I can't sleep. I can't eat. I just can't.'

Every time I close my eyes, all I can see is Faith, and then her face melds into another one I know better, one whose contours haunted my dreams for twenty years. Their deaths are blurring into one in my mind, until I almost have myself convinced that I saw Faith die, just like I saw Winta disintegrate into dust in my arms. The weight of their deaths is different, the way they felt in my hands and in my heart, but in my memory they have blurred into a single terrible event that's looping back and forth out of my control.

'Jack!' Mina yells, snapping her fingers in front of my face. 'Drink this.'

'I told you, I'm not—'

'And I told you to drink it,' she says, shoving the bottle at me. 'Don't make me pour it down your throat for you. You're not that weak.'

I sigh and take the bottle. I drink. I blink, then I open my eyes to see the afternoon sunshine pouring through the windows. I'm suddenly upstairs in what used to be Mina's bedroom, but is now devoid of bed. Instead, I'm lying on the floor on a blow-up mattress, tucked inside a sleeping bag that smells of mould. Mina is sitting in an armchair across the room at the top of the stairs that lead down to her office.

'Did I pass out?' I ask.

'Sort of,' she says.

She throws me a bottle of blood and I catch it easily, far more easily than I would have done last night. In the time it takes me to pop the lid and take my first gulp, I've put two and two together.

'You *drugged* me?' I ask, horrified.

'It seemed like the only way to get you to sleep. No offence, Jack, but you were a fucking mess.'

'Without my knowledge? Christ, Mina, how could you? You know what Winta did to me.'

'Not in detail, actually. You've been strangely reluctant to talk about your relationship with the psychopathic ex-girlfriend who you ended up murdering. Can't imagine why that might be.'

The fact that she's being flippant just makes me more furious.

'This is such a fucking violation,' I say, throwing back the sleeping bag and getting to my feet. 'I thought I could trust you, and then you go and pull something like this? How exactly did you expect me to feel about that?'

'Better,' she says, eyeing me significantly. 'And you do, don't you?'

She's bloody right, but I'm not going to admit that to her.

'And you can trust me, Jack,' she goes on, standing up to face me. 'Sure, maybe I don't always do things the proper way, respecting your trauma and your fragile feelings and all that bullshit, but you're feeling better, so why are you complaining? It's not like you would have been much use if I hadn't drugged you, and we've got shit to do.'

'Not cool,' I say, pointing a finger at her and handing back the bottle of blood. A little sloshes onto her suede boots, which was actually an accident, but it brings me spiteful joy nonetheless. 'Pull that shit again and we're done.'

'Done with what, exactly?' She pushes the bottle back at me, sloshing more onto my leather jacket, which I suppose is only fair. 'You mean this arrangement of yours where I get to endanger myself in order to save your life, in exchange for nothing at all?'

'I'm paying you,' I say.

'No, *Baron Drake* is paying me, or at least he was, until he pissed off and left you with nothing: no healing, no blood, and no fucking money. Your credit ran out days ago, so I'm doing this out of the kindness of my black little heart, and there's not much left in there, so don't push your luck.'

'Fine,' I say, because she's right. An apology is probably in order, but we're nose-to-nose now and I can't seem to make myself back down.

'Fine!' she yells in my face. Then she adds, at a more modest volume, 'So are we having make-up sex, or what?'

Even in the middle of a crisis, Mina is always Mina.

'No,' I say, finally stepping away with the bottle. Mina smiles smugly at me as she watches me drink it, knowing she's won, the tricky minx. 'At least tell me you've been doing something useful while I've been sleeping off your fucking Silver roofies.'

'Yeah, but I didn't want to give you bad news when we were getting along so well.'

I groan. 'How is it possible for there to be *more* bad news?'

'I've been doing some digging on those cases. Your neighbour who died from the drug overdose, and your other neighbour who died from old age and alcohol? Well, they didn't.'

I was half expecting it, but it's still a shock.

'Then what did they die from?' I ask. 'I heard the police talking in Louise's flat. They said it was heroin.'

'It was, a bit,' Mina concedes. 'And the old guy was probably sped on his way by the alcohol too, but mostly what killed them was the bites on their necks.'

'*Bites*?'

'Bites,' Mina confirms.

161

'Which the police missed *how* exactly?'

'I guess they didn't look too closely when they saw the needle. From the crime scene photos I've managed to dig up, they weren't like the last one. The bites were clean, with no blood at the scenes, and I guess it might have been easy to miss a bite on the first one since she had her hair down.'

Mina passes me her laptop and I take it with me to the air mattress so I can sit and look through all her open tabs, so many that the sheer number makes me anxious at first sight. They're not the only open windows, either: there are photos, PDFs, video files, basically everything the police have related to the two investigations. I probably don't want to know how she got them.

When I've had a chance to flick through and absorb the basics, there's one detail that's still screaming at me.

'No blood at all?' I ask her.

'I haven't managed to get my hands on the post mortem reports yet, but those bites look *dry*, and I'm not seeing blood in the crime scene photos. Are you?'

'No.'

Which doesn't make any sense at all.

If the evidence points that way, I'm willing to accept the fact that I might have killed Faith in some sort of Khalyed-blood-induced zombie state. I've even willing to entertain the idea that she might have been my third unintended victim. However, I'm not willing contemplate the suggestion that, in such an uncontrolled state, I would have been able to drain Louise and Mr Inman of every drop of their blood, neatly, and leaving so little evidence that the police wouldn't have immediately recognised that Louise had been the victim of an attack.

'That doesn't sound right,' I say. 'There's a *lot* of blood in a person. Is it even possible to drink that much at once?'

'You tell me. You must have drunk at least eight bottles

yesterday.'

'Yeah, but they're small bottles, so that was less than three litres. There's nearly double that in the average person, but I don't think I could have drunk any more than I did yesterday.'

'Because Khalyed's blood is taking up space in your veins?'

'I don't know. Maybe.'

'But the doctor said it's been multiplying over time, right?' Mina says, flopping back down into her armchair as she thinks. 'So maybe with the first two, you had space to drink all of it, but with this last one, you didn't? Maybe that explains why the last scene was so messy?'

'But why weren't the first two?' I ask, passing the laptop back over to her. 'Look at the photos, Mina. There's nothing out of place. If it wasn't for the bite marks and the complete exsanguination, I'd think they'd been staged to look like accidents.'

'Maybe they were.'

'Look, either I wasn't in control of my body, in which case there would be more mess, or I was in control of my body, in which case I would remember it, but I don't, so I can't have done this.'

'Maybe someone's been cleaning up after you?' Mina suggests, grasping at straws.

'Who? Unless you've got something you want to tell me, then I just don't think I could have killed Louise and Mr Inman, and if I didn't kill them, maybe I didn't kill Faith either.'

Now I'm the one grasping at straws, I know, but I have to believe I didn't do this. Whatever's in my blood, and whatever I did to Winta, I am not a serial killer. I can't be.

'Then who did?' Mina asks. 'You were the only Silver in the area, Jack. Even in the state you've been in, you would have noticed the same scent popping up wherever you went, and there was no scent in Faith's place except yours and hers. You've got to admit, it's a bit suspicious that these murders are following you around the country.'

'Unless someone's trying to frame me,' I say.

Mina gives me the same look I used to get from Deputy Boyd when I rolled in an hour late for work. It makes me a little nostalgic.

'Seriously, Mina,' I go on, because I'm on a roll now. 'It wouldn't be the first time. It's what I thought Winta was trying to do with the dead students. She left the last one at the house in Jericho to frame Leclercq, but then I got stuck in the middle of it.'

'Winta's dead,' Mina says. 'Remember?'

'But Leclercq helped her kill those students. And, might I add, they were all drained of their blood completely – bone dry – not just with bites, but by using tubing to decant their blood into bottles. Holy shit, Mina, this is it. It's not me. It's Leclercq.'

'But *why*, Jack? She threatened to kill *you*, not a bunch of random humans who happened to live next door to you.'

'To try to draw attention to my location? To move me on to a new one, maybe? Or just to piss me off. I don't know, but it fits, Mina. It all fits.'

'You know Leclercq's scent,' she points out.

I can tell from the look on her face that she still doesn't believe me. I'm going to have to prove it.

'I'll find evidence,' I say. 'She thinks she's some kind of master stealth ninja or something, but she's not perfect, and she's not as good as me. Laptop,' I say, gesturing for Mina to gimme.

'Nope.'

'Mina—'

'You can play detective tomorrow. This evening, we're

going to find the baron and get you healed.' She snaps the laptop shut, stows it away in her bag and throws me a towel of questionable provenance. 'But first, you need a shower.'

'I'm not using this,' I say, holding the towel at arm's length.

'Well you're not seeing the baron with blood under your fingernails either, so tough shit.'

I look at my hands and see that she's right: there's dark brown still crusted around my cuticles. I thought I'd been pretty thorough yesterday, but I was rushing and panicked and I obviously hadn't done a very good job.

'Is there coffee?' I ask Mina.

'There can be,' she says, hefting her bag onto her shoulder. 'Fifteen minutes?'

'Deal.'

Mina goes to get coffee – taking the laptop with her, as though I can't be trusted with it – and I take the questionable towel into the bathroom, lock the door behind me and shower in freezing cold water by torchlight. I think I'm doing pretty well with the whole awful experience until a spider the size of my face tries to drop in on me. I vow then that even if it means turning myself in to the Invicti, I am not staying in this place another night.

21

I WAIT UNTIL dark before I leave Mina's and head up to Summertown on foot. It would make sense to drive, because that way at least I wouldn't be strolling through the city, leaving my scent wafting behind me for any passing Silver to pick up the trail, but a cab feels conspicuous and Mina is out in her car. I wanted to do this on my own, and the only way I could slip away without her following me was by leaving while she was out fetching more bottles of blood. I think I've got away with it until I hear familiar footsteps behind me as I crouch in the bushes outside Drake's mansion.

'So what's the plan?' Mina asks. 'You just going to hang out in the flowerbeds until midnight, or what?'

'Get down!' I whisper, dragging her down beside me. 'He's got a cameras and guards and everything on this place.'

'But you want him to know you're here, don't you?' she says, making no effort to moderate her volume.

'Yes, but I don't want everyone else to! Just be quiet, would you? I'm trying to think.'

'You don't have a plan, then.'

'Of course I have a plan. I'm just trying to work out how to put it into action.'

Mina humphs sceptically. I can't blame her. I do not, in fact, have a plan, but then I see a familiar face appear on guard at Drake's front door, and I'm right back on track.

I gesture for Mina to stay where she is, then creep my way carefully through the bushes at the front of the house and into the flowerbeds at the side. It's a good thing spring is springing all over the place, or I'd never have enough plant cover to get this close. Finally, I get near enough that if I speak quietly, no one else will hear but my target. She's bleached her pixie cut and dyed it red since last year, but otherwise she's just the same as always: tall, muscular, and always on duty.

'Psst,' I whisper. 'Kulika.'

'Yes, Jack, I know you're there,' she says softly. Her lips barely move as she speaks, and her eyes are fixed dead ahead. 'Remarkably, my years of experience as an elite bodyguard have trained me to the point where I can detect the sound of clumsy bastards pissing about in the gravel six feet away from me.'

'Then why didn't you acknowledge me?' I whisper.

'Because I'm not the only guard here, you idiot. The other one will loop back this way in thirty seconds, so bugger off, will you? I'll meet you on the roof of the new bar at four am.'

'Is he here?' I whisper, conscious of the burning that's been growing in my veins throughout the day. I could really do with seeing Drake now. Like, *right now*.

But Kulika doesn't respond. Instead, she fixes her grey eyes on the guy coming around the corner, a huge bald goon whose name is Cosmo or Hugo or something equally incongruous that I've forgotten. He's never been a big fan of mine. I bet he'd salivate at the chance to turn me in to the

Invicti, so reluctantly I disappear back into the bushes and drag Mina back out to the street as fast as I can. I hope she managed to get more blood before she followed me here, because if I have to wait until four, I'm going to need it.

This time, I persuade Mina to stay behind. She's loaded me up with blood and is fairly confident that I'm not about to go on a killing spree across Oxford, confident enough to give me an hour at least. I have a feeling that she's going to be watching the clock, so I'd better make sure I do the same.

Being looked after by Mina is a strange experience that I reflect upon as I walk along the High Street to Oxford's only open blood bar. She's not the most nurturing person in the world, and yet she's been looking after me in a way that gives every indication that she does, in fact, care. If it was just about following me around in Oxford, then maybe I could chalk it up to her desire to stop me from leading the Invicti back to her, but that explanation doesn't account for her concern for my wellbeing, or the coffee she fetches me, or the new pillow I found in my sleeping bag this evening. For someone so resolutely determined to fly solo, she's been treating me like a copilot. We've been side-by-side for so much of what's happened over the past few months that it feels strange to be heading to the club without her.

I can't help but see the contrast to the relationship I had with Winta, who made me her subordinate rather than her partner. If we had worked together as easily as I do with Mina, maybe none of this would be happening. Maybe we would have ended up in Vancouver together after all. So many maybes. So many things that could have gone differently to land us in a better place than this.

Just the two of us, from now until forever ~ W

But there's no point to any of it, because here we are, one of us dead and the other dying, and I just have to deal with it.

And so: the blood bar.

The place is spread over multiple floors with various levels of exclusivity – this bit for Silver only, this bit for VIPs, this bit for *Silver* VIPs – but, importantly, it has a roof terrace. That means I can just do a quick check to make sure no one else is around, then clamber right up the side of the building to the meeting spot. I guess that's one of the reasons Kulika chose the place, the other likely being that with so many Silver frequenting this place on a nightly basis, my scent's going to get lost in the crowd.

The roof terrace is dark when I reach it, though the ambient light from the street lamps and moonlight makes it easy enough to pick out the chairs, tables, patio heaters and incongruous hot tub arrayed around the space. I haven't been here since the last time I saw Carlotta Arden, Drake's ex. I met with her to arrange what I thought was to be my and Winta's getaway to Argentina, but was apparently just a misdirection for Leclercq.

I wonder if Leclercq ever used those tickets. I wonder if she got as far as Buenos Aires before she realised she was on her own, or if she waited in vain at the airport for Winta to arrive. I wonder if she ever doubted Winta's intentions. She should have. I should have, long before that night on the rooftop.

Rooftops. I fucking hate rooftops.

Then there's a soft *thump* behind me and I turn to see that my visitor has just joined me, jumping straight up from the street.

'Kulika,' I say, looking around to make sure she's alone. 'Thanks for coming.'

'You shouldn't be here, Jack.'

She looks as anxious as I am as she crosses the terrace to stand at my side. She's still wearing her work clothes – black cargo trousers, black vest, muscular arms out – though I'm not sure she ever wears anything else. Stick a pair of fingerless gloves on her and she could just as easily be in the gym, which is where she spends all her time when she's not working.

'Do you know where he is?' I ask.

'The baron?'

'Yes.'

'No.'

'I thought you were supposed to be his guard?'

'I am, but he's been cagey about his movements since New Year's. Can't imagine why that might have been. Can you?'

She raises her eyebrows at me emphatically, obviously unhappy to have been kept out of the loop. As Drake's right-hand woman and number one bodyguard, I guess I can understand that. She's clearly worked out where he was going, and she's pissed off at being excluded from his forays to visit me.

'So you've got no clue where he is?' I ask, avoiding her judgemental glare.

'To be perfectly honest, I thought he'd decided to stay with you.'

'No. I haven't seen him since the morning of the second of May.'

'Well. That's not good.' Now she sounds worried, and that makes me worried.

'You haven't seen him?'

'Not since he left on May first. He didn't say when he'd be back, just that I should look after things while he was gone.'

'Kulika!' I say, suddenly angry. 'Why didn't you look for him?'

'Because I thought looking for him would mean looking for you, and he absolutely, expressly forbade me to do that.

Besides, it's not like this is the first time he's disappeared. I'm his head of security, not his mother.'

'You're talking about the Europe trip.'

'I'm talking about the time I thought he'd eloped with Carlotta Arden.' As she says this, she watches my face for a reaction. I try to control it, but apparently I do a shit job, because now she's smirking at me.

'What?' I ask, defensive.

'Just confirming a hunch.'

'Look, I really need to find him.'

'Grand gesture time, is it?' she asks. 'It must be serious if you sent him running back to that prima donna.'

'So you think he's with Carlotta?'

'If he's not with you, then who else would he be with?'

'Then why is his phone still at the mansion?'

Kulika goes still and I realise I've told her something she didn't already know.

'It is?' she asks.

'Accordingly to the tower data, yeah.'

'Well, that's really not good.' She drops down into a nearby chair, far too low for her long limbs, though she doesn't relax her posture one bit. She's poised, curled. Worried.

Then she pulls out her phone and makes a call.

'Yeah, Hugo?' she says. 'I want you to go into the baron's office and pull open the top right-hand drawer of his desk. No, he won't. It's me asking, Hugo. I just want you to tell me whether his phone is in there. Okay.'

There's a long pause as, presumably, Hugo makes his way into Drake's office. I can't hear what he says on the other end of the line – Kulika's better at controlling the volume of her phone than I am, apparently – but I hear him say something before Kulika thanks him and hangs up.

'It's in his desk, isn't it?' I ask.

'Yes,' she says. 'He sometimes puts it there to charge when he's working. I found it on the bar in his office on Valentine's Day this year and guessed he might have left it behind deliberately while he went to see you.' She pauses. 'He did go to see you, right?'

'He did,' I confess. 'A couple of other times too.'

'Well, he wouldn't have wanted his phone tracked, then.'

'But he took it to Europe when he went with Carlotta last year,' I say. 'He wouldn't have any reason to ditch it when he was with her.'

'Which means wherever he is,' Kulika says, looking more worried by the second, 'he didn't have time to collect his phone. He must have gone there straight from his last visit with you.'

'That's a pretty sudden holiday,' I say.

I know we didn't part on the best of terms, but running off without bothering to pack, or even to collect his personal phone from his office, seems an extreme reaction for someone who's pretty rational about most things. I know I hurt his feelings, but I didn't remove his common sense.

'There's another possibility, other than Ms Arden,' Kulika says.

'What?'

'The Solis Invicti.'

My rising feeling of dread is starting to pool in my stomach like acid. Between that and the itchy burning in my arms, my desperation to find Drake is like a siren blaring in my brain.

'You think they have him?' I ask.

'Jack, these discussions he's been having with the Primus... They're not going well.'

'But he hasn't done anything wrong.'

'He hasn't done much right, either, from their point of view. You know he's always done his own thing, and he and the Primus have always been more friends than anything else, but now that the Seekers have disbanded and the Invicti have Dr Khalyed—'

'That's true, then? They took him back to London?'

'Oh, yeah,' Kulika says emphatically. 'And somehow they found out about— Well, I guess the baron must have told you about the, um...'

'All those people he killed?'

'All those *serial murderers*, Jack.'

'And if he murdered a series of serial murderers, what does that make him, Kulika?'

She gives an irritated tut and says, 'Semantics. The point is, the Invicti weren't pleased.'

As the Baron of Oxford, Drake's been in something of a privileged position up until now. His role put him in charge of the most important city in the country barring London, from a Silver perspective, because Oxford has Solomon College and, until recently, the Seekers. That put him on a level with the Secundus in terms of status in the Silver hierarchy, and made him as close to a peer to the Primus as anyone gets. But now, with all this pro- and anti-reveal infighting, the frontiers between the worlds of the Silver and humans are starting to get messy. If Drake can't keep the Primus on side, then despite their long friendship, he could be first against the wall.

It's enough to make me panic.

'Do you think Drake is even safe with them? How worried should I be, here? If the Invicti have it in for him—'

'It's not the Invicti you have to worry about. In Solis Invicti HQ, it's all about the Primus.'

'Okay, so how does he feel about what Drake's done?' I ask.

'The Primus's whole life has been a series of moral maths problems, so he probably doesn't give a shit – probably would have done the same himself, even, given how many people those Silver had been killing – but he'll have to pretend to condemn the baron in order to save face. I don't think the baron will be in any danger, at least not for the time being, but that could change at any time. I don't like the idea of him being with the Invicti while they work out their power struggles.'

'Because he could get caught in the middle.'

'Right. You remember the vote. You know there's a pro-revelation upswing. You know how precarious things are. In the current climate, any move against the Silver to protect humans is going to look bad, and that's what the baron did when he killed those scabs.' She pauses for a moment, then adds, 'It was the right thing to do, though.'

'Is murder *ever* the right thing to do?' I ask, but I'm not thinking about Drake anymore.

'When it prevents multiple more murders of people less able to protect themselves? Isn't that a no-brainer, Jack? Come on,' she says, sounding as exhausted as I feel. 'Don't pretend you wouldn't have done the same yourself, because you did, and we all know it. You fucked up, but you made it right. He did the same. You're walking the same path, the two of you. I wish you'd stop making it so fucking difficult for him.'

'I'm not trying to.'

'You could've fooled me,' she says, and she's angry now. 'If you'd chosen right in the first place then none of this would have happened. You can't pretend this isn't entirely your fault.'

'I'm not trying to do that either,' I say, sitting down on the chair next to hers so I can say quietly the things I can hardly bear to say aloud. 'I know I fucked up, Kulika. Okay? I fucked up. I was working through some shit, and I did it badly. I was a twat. I was an idiot over Winta and, worse,

I've carried on being an idiot about Drake all this time, but I'm trying to make it right. I just need your help. Please.'

She looks into my eyes for a few long seconds, gauging my sincerity, then tips her head slightly to the side in a gesture I can't decipher. Either she's decided to trust me, or she's decided to string me along a bit. Who knows which.

'If the Invicti do have him,' she says, 'then they haven't told me, which is a bad sign.'

'But we don't *know* they have him. We need to find out, one way or another. Can you call them?'

She clasps her hands together under her chin into one big fist, flexing her jaw as she thinks. After a moment, she slaps her hands down onto her thighs and says, 'No. Here's what we're going to do. I'm going to call Ms Arden and make sure Baron Drake isn't with her in Italy, then I'm going to call every other person I can think of and see if he's with them.'

'Subtly,' I add. 'We don't want anyone to know he's AWOL.'

'Of course subtly. What did you think I was going to do? I'm not a fucking wrecking ball like you, Jack. Give me some credit.' Maybe I should feel insulted, but she's right. I'm not good at subtlety. 'In the meantime,' she goes on, 'you're going to go over to Solomon College and speak to Dr Castell.'

'Ed's in Oxford? I thought he went back up to London with the Invicti.'

'He's back and forth,' she says in an uncertain tone that makes me suspect she's even more out of the loop than I thought she was. 'Anyway, I'm sure he's more likely to talk to you than he is to me.'

'Are you?'

'Yes.' She grimaces.

'Why, exactly?' I ask. Judging by her expression, there's something between the two of them that I don't know about.

JOSIE JAFFREY

'You know his girlfriend?' she says.

I remember the brunette I met in the college bar a year or so ago. I haven't seen much of her since – she came to the ill-fated opening of Crimson, but that's about it – and we haven't spoken enough that I'd say that I *know* her.

'Know of her,' I say. 'Carrie, right?'

'Right.' Kulika looks miserable. 'Up until about eighteen months ago, she was my girlfriend.'

Oh.

I knew Kulika was gay, but I wouldn't have thought that Carrie was her type, or that Kulika was hers, for that matter. I guess I know Carrie even less well that I thought.

'I took it badly,' Kulika rushes on. 'I can see that now, and I apologised, but I'm not Dr Castell's favourite person, so if anyone's going to approach him, it should probably be you. If they're keeping the baron prisoner, then they're unlikely to tell me about it, but maybe Ed would talk to you.'

'I'm not so sure about that. If this is our best strategy for approaching the Invicti, then maybe we should think again.'

'He's probably not even with them. We're probably making a big deal over nothing,' Kulika says, but I can see that internally her security training disagrees. She's not in denial exactly; she knows that there's something wrong, but she's trying to stay calm, and to keep me calm. It almost works, until she adds, 'He's probably off with Ms Arden and just forgot to call.'

'Does that sound like him?' I ask.

She doesn't answer me. Instead, she says, 'Well, where do you think he is?'

'I think the Invicti have him, but not for the reasons you think. I think they've got him locked down because they want to draw me out, to get me to turn myself in.'

'That seems a bit heavy-handed. No offence, Jack, but I'm not sure they care that much about you. I don't think they'd

176

do that.'

'Cam wouldn't, I know. The others... I'm not so sure. I did try to kill the Primus, after all.'

'And you think they've taken that as a personal offence?'

'Exactly.'

I've been considering this while we've been talking, and I've come to some conclusions. Firstly, if Drake were anywhere he was free to call from, he would have let Kulika know he was okay. She's basically his deputy. He'd be stupid not to, and Drake is many things, but he is not stupid. Secondly, whoever snatched him likely did so very soon after he left Tabitha's place. Given her connections to the Invicti, it's not beyond the realms of possibility that they know about her secret hideout, however well she thinks she's hidden it. Thirdly, imprisoning Drake in order to get to me is just the kind of creepy psychological tactic that I'd expect from one member of the Invicti in particular. It feels like Benedict's brand of sadism.

And then, of course, there's Adewale.

'Cam warned me about Winta's brother,' I say.

'Adewale Ladipo?'

'Yeah. He's not happy.'

'You think he's behind this?'

'I killed his sister.'

'Well,' Kulika concedes, 'there is that. Maybe you shouldn't be the one to go to Solomon College after all.'

'No, I'm going,' I insist. I have to do something, because otherwise my anxiety over Drake is going to eat me up and make me even more useless than I already am. 'But if you don't hear back from me by the end of the day, maybe you could come looking.'

'Maybe you could give me a reason to.'

'I care about him, Kulika.'

She makes an unconvinced *huh* noise.

'I'll die without him,' I say, with complete truthfulness.

I don't think she knows that I'm poisoned with Khalyed's blood – she hasn't said anything about it, and surely she would have if she knew – so I can only imagine how she's going to take that comment. Her face is so hard to read that I can't tell if she understands that I mean it literally rather than as an expression of emotion. Either way, she scans my face for sincerity again, and she's convinced.

'Call me by midday,' she says, then she gets up from her seat, nods goodbye and leaves me alone on the rooftop before I have a chance to feel bad about misleading her.

I guess I'm going back to Solomon College. Otherwise known as: home.

22

THE SUN IS just starting to creep over the horizon as I make my way unsteadily through the winding, ancient streets of Oxford to Solomon College. It should feel like a homecoming, but it feels more like a walk of shame. Maybe that's because the only other times I've rolled down this street this early in the day have been when I was coming back from the pub, or maybe it's because I'm about to break in uninvited, but either way I'm feeling shifty. When I hear a footstep behind me, I jump a foot in the air.

'I heard you were looking for Dr Castell.'

I whirl around to see a tall man looking down at me. He's dressed oddly in a hoodie, trainers and jeans – not oddly for most people, granted, but oddly for him – so it takes me a moment to recognise him.

'Boyd?' I whisper. 'Is that you under there?'

'Hello, Jacqueline.'

'Boyd!'

I hurl myself at him and throw my arms around his neck. For a second, he's very still, and I wonder if I've crossed a line, but then his arms go around my back, wrapping me up in his solid dependability, and he holds me close.

'You shouldn't be here,' he whispers into my hair.

'Are you okay?' I ask, pulling out of the hug so I can get a good look at him. 'I had Mina looking for you, but she said you'd gone off-grid.'

'Mina? You mean Mina *Parchek*?' he says, his lip rolling in disgust. Ah, there's the Boyd I know and love. 'Jacqueline, please. Tell me you didn't.'

'We're not sleeping together!' I say quickly. 'She's just helping me hide out.'

'Yes, that's what I was afraid of. What in the world makes you think that you can trust Mina Parchek, of all people?'

'What makes you think she can't?' Mina asks, stepping around the corner. Clearly my hour has expired and she's decided to come looking for me. I should have heard her coming, but I was so distracted by Boyd's sudden appearance that I haven't been paying attention.

'Number one,' he says, counting on his fingers, 'you lie to us all the time.'

'When you were the Seekers, yeah, ' she says, 'but it doesn't count if you're only lying to the law.'

'Number two,' Boyd continues, 'you're an unscrupulous mercenary who only cares about money.'

'Jack's been paying me pretty well, though.'

'And number three, you're probably only helping Jacqueline because you're a sexual deviant who's obsessed with undressing her.'

'Is that a bad thing?' Mina asks, and it's not a joke. She seems genuinely confused.

I sigh.

'No,' Mina says to me, 'really. Since when is that a bad thing? It's not like I'm trying to get you to do anything you don't want to do anyway. I'm just sort of… encouraging you, in case you're in the mood. That's all.'

'Harassing her, you mean,' says Boyd, ever the prude.

'It's fine, Mina,' I say. 'I don't mind.'

And really, I don't. Maybe I should, but Mina's never been anything other than straight and direct with me, and that's refreshing in its own way. She propositions me, I roll my eyes, and we move on. It's just how it's always been with us. I could judge Mina at face value, like Boyd, or I could look at the way she's grafted for me and nursed me over the past couple of months, and appreciate that she's more than she appears. Underneath all the jokes and innuendos, Mina really does care for me. Maybe even loves me, just a bit.

'How did you know I was looking for Ed?' I ask Boyd. 'I literally just came from… Were you eavesdropping, Deputy?'

'It's just Boyd now, Jacqueline. Why am I not surprised that you wait for me to lose my job before using my proper title?'

'I feel like now you've finally earned it.'

'Not Captain, though?' he teases.

'Don't push your luck.'

'Awww, you guys,' Mina says with feigned emotion. 'Standing in the middle of Oxford chatting away about old times like Jack isn't the most wanted Silver fugitive in the world. So cute.'

'She's right,' I say. 'We shouldn't be hanging around in the open. I need to go and see Ed.'

'Then you're in the wrong place,' Boyd says.

'But Kulika said—'

'Kulika's information is out of date. He's in London, Jacqueline, and he's not coming back.'

'Can we get off the street, please?' Mina interrupts, looking up and down the quiet lane as though she's expecting someone to jump out at any second. Given that they've both managed to do exactly that, maybe it's not such an irrational fear.

'I know a place we can go,' says Boyd.

'One that's open at ridiculous o'clock in the morning?' I ask.

He just smiles and motions for us to follow him. Mina looks at me sceptically, but she tags along anyway as Boyd leads us away from the college, down a series of slowly lightening streets and into an alley I didn't even know was there. I thought I'd been to every corner of the city during my two decades' residence, but apparently I was wrong. I've never seen this tight passage, nor the heavy door sitting at its end. It looks like one of the old college entrances, all ancient wood and black iron studs, but there's no signage and the key Boyd pulls out of his pocket is so huge that it must be hundreds of years old.

'Where are we?' I whisper, because the setting seems to call for hush.

'You'll see,' Boyd replies with a smile as he inserts the key.

I'm not sure I like cryptic Boyd. It's not like him to be anything other than open and direct and, usually, grumpy. I don't recognise this version of him. It's as though now that he's been freed from the obligations of his role as our deputy, he's also shrugged off the starchy persona that came with that role. In the hidden alleys of early morning Oxford, his eyes glint with mischief and his expression is graced with a shadow of a smile. Despite all that he's lost, he looks happy.

The door swings open silently and Boyd ushers me and Mina inside ahead of him. It's not what I was expecting at all. Instead of the worn stone and wooden beams I associate with college interiors, the room we've entered is strangely clinical. There's a small entrance hall with a table and a bowl filled with various keyrings, as though many people are using this as their home, but the room is small and contains nothing else except a wide concrete staircase that leads us down from the door into darkness. The handrails are metal painted bright blue; the concrete steps are edged with striped hazard tape; the walls are plaster painted glossy grey. It feels like we're in a hospital basement, a complete contrast to the ancient building this appears to be on the outside. It smells of bleach.

'I don't like it,' Mina says.

She's right; the vibe in here is weird. But it's Boyd, and however much of a dick he might sometimes be, he's a good guy. I'm sure I can trust him. He wouldn't lure me away into some kind of underground lair just to turn me over to the Invicti. Would he?

'Look, Boyd,' I say. 'If you want us to go down there, you're going to have to do a little explaining first.'

A light flicks on at the bottom of the stairs and a familiar voice rises out of the stairwell.

'Jack? I don't fucking believe it!' Then the person-sized teddy bear that is my old drinking buddy and one-time colleague Raul comes bounding up the staircase, sweeps me up into a hug and swings me around in a circle. 'It's really you! What are you doing here?'

He's grinning so widely that I can't help smiling back, and just like that my anxiety about the situation evaporates. There's the slimmest of possibilities that Boyd might decide to hand me over to what he would consider the proper authorities – he's always been a stickler for the rules – but there's no way in hell that Raul would ever betray me.

'Hello, mate. It's good to see you,' I say, with feeling.

I expected him to be drowning his sorrows at the bottom of a bottle, but here he is with Boyd, stone-cold sober and looking like he's been hitting the gym. I swear his arms didn't use to be that muscular.

'What's going on here?' I say to the two of them. 'Are you running some kind of underground fight club, or what?'

'Not quite,' Raul chuckles. 'Come on down and I'll show you around. If that's okay with you, Chief?' he adds, looking to Boyd.

Boyd nods at Raul with a gentle smile and I understand that he's still in charge, but whatever his role is here exactly, it's made him softer than he was as deputy of the Seekers. That desperate, grasping edge has gone out of his bearing. As deputy of the Seekers, he was always trying to prove himself and climb higher. As chief of whatever this is, he's at peace. Suddenly he's wearing his authority like a benevolent father instead of an irritated drill sergeant, but I can't imagine what could have caused such a dramatic change. I guess I'm about to find out.

The four of us head down the staircase, Boyd and Raul in front while Mina and I follow along behind. It feels endless. There must be hundreds and hundreds of steps, so many that I find myself holding onto the handrail to keep my balance, which doesn't do much to assuage my dizziness, but does make Mina cast concerned looks in my direction. I wave her off. At the bottom of the stairs, there's a metal blast door with a keypad and fingerprint scanner. Mina raises her eyebrows at me, questioning whether we really want to go inside what looks like some kind of prison, but I just shrug back. We've come this far, and I'm curious.

While we wait for Boyd to deal with the locks, there's a clicking noise above our heads, and a moment later a mist of something sprays down over us like perfume. It stings my eyes.

'What the fuck?' I say, blinking it away.

'Sorry,' Boyd says. 'I should have warned you. It's on a sensor to douse everyone who comes in and out.'

'Like decontamination or something?' Mina asks.

'Should we be worried?' I ask.

'No, nothing like that,' Boyd says, finally swinging the

metal door open. 'I'll explain later, but right now there's somewhere I have to be. Come on through.'

Given the lengthy build-up, I'm expecting some grand reveal on the other side of the door, but there's nothing except a long, boring, grey corridor that turns off into several other long, boring, grey corridors.

Boyd heads off along one, saying, 'I'll meet you all in the refectory when you're done,' and Raul, Mina and I take another that runs parallel to it.

We walk. And walk. And walk some more, passing nondescript metal door after nondescript metal door, but we don't stop.

'If I'd known we were walking a bloody marathon then I would have worn different shoes,' Mina says.

'We can go super-speed if you like,' Raul offers.

'No thanks,' I reply, already feeling the heat in my veins increasing. I can't afford to burn through the small amount of good blood still left in my veins that's there diluting the bad shit, but I don't want to tell Raul about that, at least not yet, so instead I say, 'I want to get a feel for the place, and that's easier if we go slow.'

He doesn't ask questions, so I guess he accepts my explanation, and it isn't much longer before the corridor lets out into a wide open space decorated in the same uninspiring shades of grey. It looks like an underground garage, only cleaner and with better lighting.

'The assembly hall,' Raul says.

'How many people exactly do you need to assemble?' I ask, because the place is huge. You'd be able to accommodate a hundred easily, two hundred comfortably, and maybe as many as four hundred if they didn't mind getting a little cosy.

'A few,' Raul answers cryptically.

Mina's been quiet up until now, taking in our surroundings

with a critical eye, but it seems like she's had her fill of that.

'All right,' she says. 'What the fuck is this place? Where are we?'

'Underneath Solomon College,' says Raul.

Then he opens a set of double doors in the middle of the assembly hall's longest wall so we can see for ourselves.

I notice that Mina's mouth has dropped open and realise that mine has done the same. I thought the assembly hall was huge, but I was wrong. The room beyond the door is *huge*. It looks like a mix between an ancient cathedral and a dwarven mountain hall, all stone and grandeur, with lines of pews and painted walls and a vaulted ceiling that sweeps so high above us that it feels ludicrous this far underground. I guess anything's possible with super-strength and solid engineering.

'We're under the college?' I ask.

'Yup,' Raul replies.

I step into the echoing, pillared hall, pacing into its centre as I turn in circles, looking up at the ceiling. It's so far away from me that it feels like I'm looking up at the stars, but I can still clearly see the painted panels between the dark vaulted beams that partition the wood into diamond-shaped slices. They're intricate and beautiful and horribly disturbing. There's light coming from somewhere, illuminating figures with shining eyes biting the necks of what look like humans, and hooded figures stripped naked to the waist beneath their robes with blood on their chests and candles in their hands, and so many configurations of blood-smeared bodies that it's hard to tell exactly which are about sex, which are killing feeds, and which are something in between the two. The only thing I can say for certain is that every single one is intended to be dark, except the massive multi-pointed star-shaped panel in the centre of the ceiling, where all the arches converge. The image there is entirely different: a single sunlit figure, arms spread wide, expression beatific, with cherubic golden curls and a face so beautiful that if I were standing anywhere else I might mistake him for a representation of a saint or an angel. But I recognise the cold, ice-blue eyes of the Primus, and I know that I'm standing in the temple of a demon instead.

'But... I've never seen this before,' I say. 'How is this beneath the college and no one knows it exists?'

'They know,' says Ellie, coming up behind us. 'They've just decided to forget.'

'Ellie!' I say, surprised and happy to see her. 'You're here too?'

'Yup. Quentin, Rolf and Cheryl are around as well,' she says, naming the rest of her old team from the Seekers.

'What about the others?' I ask, but she just shakes her head.

'They've all gone to the Invicti,' Raul explains. 'Or to the other barons. They don't want to carry on with the work.'

'Fuck 'em,' says Ellie, with uncharacteristic impropriety. 'More space for us.'

And there's certainly a lot of that. If the assembly hall was built to hold hundreds, this place was built to hold thousands. I leave the others in the centre of the room and drift out to the edges, where painted stories line the walls in a tapestry of frescos that feels like a narrative. It starts by the door with a single blond-haired man who must be Solomon, though he seems less other-worldly in this image than he does in the painting on the ceiling. As the story flows on around the walls, he's joined by other figures. There's some kind of exchange or joining of hands with a woman who's picked out entirely in silver leaf, and from that point onwards his eyes glint with the same shining material every time he appears. There's biting and blood and fighting as he makes his way through the world, and dark figures begin to follow him along the wall like the ghosts of those he's bitten before. I come to realise that this is a story about the origins of vampirism, but I don't understand what the ghostly figures mean, because I don't recognise them from any mythology I've ever heard or read. By the time I reach the back wall, climbing a few steps onto a raised platform where a stone altar sits, there are so many wraiths surrounding Solomon's image that it's hard to make out anything else in the background at all. Then, in any explosion of gold leaf centred behind the altar, the Primus seems to eclipse them all.

'Creepy, huh?' Mina says, coming to join me.

'Very,' I agree. 'What does it mean?'

'That wall? Fuck knows. Something that happened so long ago we've all forgotten it, I guess. This wall, though,' she says, pointing to the side of the hall I haven't explored yet, 'is about how he became Silver, then turned the first of us, then over here is how he became the Silver "god king" apparently.'

'I thought that bit by the door was how he became Silver,' I say, pointing back at the scene where the silver woman has taken his hand.

'Maybe they're two versions of the same story. I don't know. Things get fuzzy over the millennia. Some of the stories are just fucking weird.'

I move to get a closer look at Solomon in gold behind the altar, and I stumble a little over my own feet.

'Jack,' Mina says softly, but it's a warning. 'You're going wobbly again.'

I want to deny it, but she's right. The burning is starting to ramp up to the point where I can no longer ignore it, hardly the best time for a Silver history lesson. And anyway, the mural's giving me the creeps. The more I look at it, the more unsettling I find the ghosts trailing in Solomon's wake.

I let Mina lead me back to the centre of the room, where Raul and Ellie are waiting.

'Why would anyone choose to forget something like this?' I ask them, gesturing at the glinting splendour that surrounds us.

'It's the Temple of Solomon,' Raul says, as though it's strange that I don't already know. 'They did bad shit here.'

'Really bad stuff,' Ellie adds.

'Blood sacrifice?' I ask. 'That kind of bad shit?'

'Worse,' Raul says.

'If you don't know, then you don't want to know,' says Ellie. 'We don't use this place for the work we do, but the complex we do use was built out from it as a bomb shelter back in the day. All it needed was a little expanding and rewiring and redecorating, which was easy as pie at super-speed, and here we all are. State of the art bunker, right under Solomon College.'

'You keep talking about "the work" like it's some big secret,' Mina says, 'but what exactly *are* you all doing down here?'

'What we've always done,' says Ellie. 'Catching scabs and putting them out of harm's way.'

'And all this is being financed how, exactly?' Mina says, squinting at Ellie in full-on P.I. mode.

'By a generous Silver benefactor who believes in our mission.'

'You mean Drake,' I say.

It's not hard to jump to that conclusion. First, there was that night under the bridge, when he finally confessed that he'd silvered for me, and he offered to keep the Seekers funded if I wanted him to. Second, there was the way he kept reassuring me that he was taking care of everything back in Oxford. Apparently, this is how he did it.

'I absolutely did not say that Baron Drake had anything to

do with this operation,' Ellie says, but she's never been able to lie to me. She's actually blushing.

'It's definitely Drake,' I say to Mina, who nods back as though to say, *Of course it is.*

'So you're still the Seekers,' I say, 'only you've gone underground?'

'Pretty much, but we're not calling ourselves that,' says Ellie.

'Then what *are* you calling yourselves?'

'We don't have a name, but mostly I think of us as the Dregs.' Raul laughs, but it sounds a little bitter. 'You know, because we're the ones that got left behind.'

Which explains the bitterness. Cam and Naia were inducted into the Solis Invicti, and maybe the others didn't even apply, but Boyd and Raul would probably have been rejected if they had; Boyd because of the image problem that came with his previous role as our deputy – too toxic to touch right now – and Raul because of his drug problems – toxic in an entirely different and more literal sense. He was only just getting clean at the end of last year, and the last time I saw him, his sobriety was tenuous.

Then I left him too.

'I didn't mean to abandon you, Raul,' I say. 'Aren't you kind of glad I did, though? You know how badly I fucked up.'

'Yeah, we do,' he says.

Then a terrible thought strikes me. 'You haven't brought me down here to box me, have you?'

'Don't be silly,' Ellie laughs. 'Of course not. Imagine you thinking that.'

'Yeah, imagine,' Mina parrots her, mockingly.

'Be nice,' I whisper.

Ellie looks down her nose at Mina. Mina looks up her nose at Ellie. Those two have never liked each other. Ellie's too prissy for Mina, and Mina's too sleazy for Ellie. For some reason, they both seem okay with me.

'But you do know what I did, right?' I say to Ellie and Raul, just to be sure.

'You mean about the Primus?' says Ellie. 'Of course.'

'And the blood tests Ed ran?'

Ellie and Raul exchange a confused look, and I know I still have some explaining to do. It makes sense that they're in the dark about the blood. Ed would have reported the contents of my blood sample to the Invicti, so doubtless they all think that I killed those students at the end of last year, but with Boyd and the others out here on their own, disconnected from the rest of the Silver hierarchy, they'd have no one to tell them about my other supposed crimes. As if the big one isn't enough.

'Later, then,' I say. 'I'll tell you everything.'

'Okay,' says Raul with a shrug, as though he doesn't really care either way.

'Just to be clear, though,' I say, struggling to understand their friendliness in the context of my past actions, 'you do know that I stole Khalyed's blood from Drake's basement and tried to use it to kill the Primus? Him,' I say, pointing up at the massive portrait of the vampire god emblazoned above our heads.

'Yes,' Ellie and Raul say together.

'And then I used it to kill Winta instead.'

'Yes,' they say again.

'And you don't have anything to say about that? No questions, or comments, or feelings?'

'You've always been anti-establishment, Jack,' Ellie says dismissively. 'It was hardly a surprise. And anyway, it's not as though you followed through with it. You did the right thing in the end.'

'The right...' I'm struggling for words, because I can't

believe how blasé she's being about this. 'I'm a murderer, Ellie.'

'Oh, big deal,' she says. 'Hands up anyone here who *isn't*.'

I look from her, to Mina, to Raul, and their hands stay resolutely stuck by their sides. I knew about Raul – it was an accident last year after someone poisoned him – but the others are a surprise.

'There we go, then,' she says. 'Now can we move on? There's loads more to show you. You're going to love this place, I just know it.'

The others leave the hall with Ellie, but I can't help myself from trailing behind to stare back at the grandeur of Solomon's temple. Hundreds of feet above my head, I swear his eyes are following me as I go.

23

ELLIE AND RAUL are so excited about giving the big tour that I don't feel I can cut it short, even when my feet start dragging and the burning sensation travels up my arms and throat into my mouth. In the end, after we've seen the computer suite and the dorms and the meeting rooms and the gym and the library, and Ellie threatens to drag us off to see yet more offices, Mina puts her foot down on my behalf.

'I'm tired, I'm hungry and I'm wearing the wrong shoes for this walking tour shit. Refectory, now.'

Ellie gives her a dirty look, but that fades when she glances my way. Apparently I'm looking as bad as I'm feeling, because there's no more pissing about. I'm sitting at a table within three minutes with a bottle of blood in front of me.

'We get it from the college supply,' Raul reassures me, which makes me wonder if he knows more about Winta's student murder bottles than he let on. He's one of those quiet ones you have to watch, because sometimes he hears more than you think.

'If we're under the college,' I say as I sip from my bottle, 'aren't you worried that the Silver up top will be able to hear you down here?'

'Through five layers of soundproofing and lead lining?' says someone from the table behind ours. 'I don't think so.'

The woman speaking is in her forties with short, thick brown hair. And she's human.

'*Angie*?' I say, confused and a little horrified to see the Seekers' old maintenance chief in this place. I turn to Raul and whisper, 'What is a… Not one of *us* doing here?'

'She knows,' Raul says simply. 'They all know.'

'Excuse me?'

'I know about the vampire thing,' Angie says, as though she's bored by the subject. 'They told me.'

'And you don't care?'

'Don't really see why I should.'

'We drink human blood.'

'From what I hear,' she says, turning in her chair to face me, 'you get it in bottles, and you stop the others from getting it any other way, which is fine by me. Now, I've been waiting here quarter of an hour for you lot to show up, so is someone going to help me lift that bloody girder in the boiler room, or am I going to have to get Faizan to do it?'

'Faiz is here too?' I ask Raul.

'Yup, and Meera too. All the old crew.'

Faizan Malik used to be our long-suffering police liaison, a Silver embedded in the ranks, but when everything went tits up he got sacked from the force, and then from the Seekers. Meera's his wife. She used to be a lawyer and now, after a cookery course that transformed her food from inedible to sublime, she's a full-time chef. Or at least she was when I last saw her.

'What's Meera doing here?' I ask.

'Mostly trying to make sure we all eat our greens,' Raul smiles fondly. 'Some legal stuff too, but she's probably in the kitchen now. It's hard to keep her out of it.'

'The girder,' Angie reminds us with a stern look that sends Ellie popping up from her chair.

'I'll do it,' she says, and the two of them go off to sort out whatever needs sorting out.

Boyd joins us a moment later, and he's not alone. He's holding the hand of a tall, beautiful East Asian woman who's dressed like a librarian, probably because she is one. She has a satchel over her shoulder, a clipboard in one hand, and Boyd's hand in the other.

'You remember Mildred?' he says, then he smiles at her like she's the centre of his world. Maybe this is the answer to the changes I've noticed in Boyd: Mildred Chen.

I should have expected her to be here. She first met Boyd on a case we were working last year, then they got together and things got a little messy because, like Angie, Mildred is human. Boyd got caught up in the same poisoning incident as Raul and bit Mildred while he was under the influence, which nearly killed her, but Tabitha managed to help her before she went the same way as Raul's victim. I'd thought that would be the end of their relationship, but looking at them now, it's clear that it just brought them closer together. They both take seats at the table opposite me and Mina, but they keep on holding hands, as though they're scared to let go. It's strange to see Boyd like this, and touching, but it makes me worry that the weight of his happiness is riding on someone so fragile and mortal. There's no way that's going to end well.

Mildred and I say hello, and I introduce Mina, who's looking around her with open suspicion. I can't imagine she likes being trapped underground like this and under someone else's control. These aren't her people, they're mine, and she doesn't trust them any more than she trusts anyone else. Even in my weakened state, I can feel discomfort radiating from her body. But still, she stays.

'What do you think of the place?' Boyd asks me.

'It's very grey,' I reply, and he laughs.

He *laughs*.

The old Boyd would have given me *that look* and chastised me for my disrespectful tone, but apparently the new Boyd likes my half-arsed sass.

'It's reckless to have a bunch of humans locked down here with you,' Mina observes. 'Closed environment, limited escape routes, concentrated scents. Seems like a recipe for disaster to me.'

'We're not animals, Ms Parchek,' Boyd says coldly. 'If you think you'll have trouble controlling yourself, Raul can escort you to the exit.'

But Mina doesn't move, she just crosses her arms over her chest, slumps back in her chair and cuts a glance at me. I know it's not herself she's worried about. She thinks I'm going to go vamp-zombie and start killing people, just like she thinks I killed Faith and Louise and Mr Inman.

'Dr Castell,' she says to Boyd. 'Where is he?'

'In London, Ms Parchek. Like I said.'

'And your so-called secret benefactor,' she asks, glaring daggers at him the whole time. 'If he's financing this whole thing, then you must know where he is. You wouldn't lose track of your bank card, right?'

From the way Boyd flinches – just a little before he catches himself – I guess they have no idea where Drake is either. We're in the same boat here: everyone's looking for Drake, no one knows where he is, and none of us are in a position to ask the Invicti a straight question.

'All right,' I say. 'Let's get some shit out of the way, shall we? I tried to kill the Primus, and I did kill Winta. A bunch of people are unhappy about that, mostly Yolande Leclercq and Adewale Ladipo and the rest of the Invicti, but I have to imagine that the Primus isn't exactly thrilled about it either.

So why do you not seem to care?'

'We're not the Invicti, Jacqueline,' Boyd says softly. 'We were all there when everything started falling apart around us. You tried to warn us that something was wrong, but we didn't listen in time, and then the Seekers were disbanded... I don't know. Maybe it's just that I feel guilty for not backing you up sooner, but at least you tried to do something to fix it. It was the wrong thing, and it was stupid and dangerous, and it escalated a situation that really didn't need escalating any further—'

'Feels like you're losing your thread a bit here, Deputy,' I say.

I was enjoying the feeling of Boyd being on my side for once, but that old scolding tone is creeping back into his voice. I guess no one changes overnight.

'Well, it was stupid,' he says, bringing his rant back under control. 'But she was your sire, and I suppose I understand why you followed her so blindly.'

Compassion and sympathy from Boyd. I never thought I'd see the day. It makes me wonder about his own sire, but Boyd's always been very tight-lipped about his past. Maybe there's a reason for that.

'Winta and Leclercq were the ones who killed the students last year,' I say. 'Did you know?'

'I wasn't sure,' Boyd says. 'Baron Drake confirmed it for us.'

'Exactly how much has he told you?' Mina asks, probing.

'Exactly how much has Jack told *you*?' Boyd asks her in return.

They stare at each other for a moment, neither of them prepared to be the first to lay their cards out. In the end, it's Mildred who intervenes.

'Ronald and I know about your blood test results,' she says softly. 'Raul and the others don't, but they won't care.

You're safe here, Jack.'

'What blood test results?' Raul says, looking between us quizzically.

'Cam took a sample of my blood before... Well, everything. Turns out Winta had been giving me bottles of the dead students' blood to drink, so their DNA was in the sample Cam took.'

'So the Invicti think you killed the students?' Raul asks.

'Yep.'

'But you didn't.'

'Nope.'

'All right then.'

I look at Raul, at Boyd, at Mildred, and I can't quite believe what I'm hearing.

'So that's it?' I say. 'You just don't care?'

'What would you prefer?' Boyd asks. 'Were you expecting recriminations, or punishment, or anger?'

'I... Yes.'

'Then maybe your guilt is overwhelming your common sense,' he declares. 'Look at it this way: from our point of view, all you did was take out a scab, which is what we're in the business of doing ourselves. Perhaps there were some wrong turns along the way, but you ended up in the right place eventually. We know you, Jacqueline. Our benefactor appears to be on your side, and we are too. So the party line is: you're ours, we're not letting the Invicti have you, and that's that.'

Maybe it's the exhaustion, or the fact that I'm dying, but I'm getting a bit emotional about the sincerity in Boyd's eyes. Raul is looking at me in the same way, as though I'm an errant sheep being welcomed back into the flock. After having spent so many months running, feeling like I'd never belong anywhere ever again, it's a little overwhelming. It also makes me feel terribly guilty about all the secrets I'm still keeping. Not only do the Dregs appear to be on Team Jack, they're also my old colleagues and friends, and they've let us into their secret underground lair. That has to count for something. Abruptly, I decide that they've earned some trust. Maybe they could even help.

'I need to find Drake,' I say, 'as soon as possible, and I think the Invicti have him. I was looking for Ed because I thought he might be able to tell me where he is.'

'What does Ms Yadav think?' Boyd asks, referring to Kulika by her surname.

'She's making some calls to check, but she agrees it's the most likely scenario,' I say. 'Oh, shit. What's the time?'

Boyd points up at the clock on the wall behind me and I turn to see that we're already well into the morning.

'I promised I'd call her,' I say. 'She thinks I've been trying to infiltrate the college.'

'No calls,' says Mina. 'Too traceable.'

'Agreed,' says Boyd, 'but we can get a message to her that you're safe with us.'

'She knows about you too?' I ask.

'She knows we exist, but not where we are,' Boyd says. I must look put out by that, because he adds, 'She is the baron's deputy, after all.'

That absolutely makes sense, but at the same time it makes me furious. All this time I've been trying to work out what's been going on back here in Oxford, and Drake's been building a secret underground rebel base with all my old friends without even telling me. I know he was only trying to keep me safe by keeping me out of the loop – just like I have been by keeping my imminent death secret from him – but it still feels like a betrayal. And now I'm thinking about Drake again, regretting everything I said the last time I saw him, and wondering if it's my fault that he's missing. Yes, back then I still thought that breaking the bond was a possibility.

And yes, I thought I was protecting him by keeping my distance. But given what I know now, everything I've done since I left Oxford feels so pointless. I could have spent the last months of my life in the arms of the man I... kind of like, and instead I'm trying to rescue him from the people who snatched him while I was pushing him away.

Assuming, that is, that he isn't just off with Carlotta again.

'I'm still finding this place a little hard to believe,' Mina says, looking around the refectory sceptically. 'Solomon College has been here forever, so I guess the temple makes sense, but the bunker? How does no one know about that? And how did you expand it without them realising you were doing construction right beneath their feet?'

'It was always need-to-know,' Boyd says. 'And the expansion work has been going on for years. People have learned to treat it as background noise.'

'For *years*?'

'The captain was more farsighted than me. She wanted a safe harbour in case we ever needed it, but we kept it quiet. I knew, the captain knew, the baron knew, and that's about it.'

'But the Primus must know,' Mina says. 'It's right under *his* college.'

'Oxford hasn't been truly his for centuries, Ms Parchek.'

Mina seems personally offended that she didn't know about the bunker. Given her propensity for sniffing out secrets, I can understand why it might rile her. I'm as shocked as she is, particularly given that I was living on top of all this for two decades without ever realising it was there, but I'm also starting to feel more than a little woozy. To use Mina's phrase, I'm going a bit wobbly, and their increasingly-heated discussion is fading in and out of focus in time with the pulsing burn in my veins.

'I think you underestimate the baron,' Boyd is saying.

'Oh yeah?' says Mina. 'Well, if you knew everything I did

about—'

'Jack?' Raul says, cutting across their bickering. 'Are you okay? You don't look— Whoa.'

That's the last thing I hear before my head hits the concrete.

24

WHEN I WAKE up, I'm in a bed I don't recognise. That's becoming such a regular occurrence that it barely fazes me at all this time. There are fluorescent lights in the ceiling, a blue curtain around the bed on a rail, and the blanket on the bed is paper thin. My first thought is: hospital. Then I remember where I was when I passed out, and I know that can't be right.

'Hello?' I croak, pulling myself up to a sitting position with more effort than seems reasonable.

The curtain shoots back along its rail to reveal an efficient-looking woman in scrubs and a doctor's coat. Mildred's hot on her heels.

'Oh good,' Mildred says when she sees me sitting up. 'We were starting to worry. I'll go and get Ronald.'

While she's out of the room, the doctor listens to my heart and my pulse, then takes my blood pressure.

'Do you feel dizzy often?' she asks, looking at her watch as she checks my pulse again.

'At the moment, yes,' I reply.

'And nausea?'

'Sometimes.'

'You hit your head when you fell, and the bruise is still visible. Have you noticed that you're healing more slowly than usual?'

'Yes.'

'But you've been drinking plenty of blood?'

'Yes.'

'Then is there something you want to tell me?' she asks, looking at my stomach in a significant way. 'Is it possible that you might be pregnant?'

The dizziness, the nausea, the thirst, the slow healing... It's so inconceivable that it takes me a moment to process what she's said, and when I do, I laugh.

'It's not what you think,' I say. 'I'm not... I'm definitely not *that*.'

'Okay...'

'The thing is, I'm dying.'

She looks puzzled. 'You're Silver.'

'I'm infected with Dr Jay Khalyed's blood.'

From the way she flinches, I guess she's heard of him.

'I didn't cut my head when I fell, did I?' I ask as the implications belatedly occur to me. 'Because if I bled and someone else touched the—'

'No,' says the doctor with a smile, though I can't help but notice that she's taken a step away from my bed. 'Just a bad bump.'

'Jacqueline,' Boyd says, pulling the curtain aside further as he hurries in. 'You're all right.'

'Just a bump,' I say.

'Just a *bump*? You passed out, just after you'd drunk a bottle of blood. Can you explain that? Because it makes no logical sense to me.'

I can understand why he's freaking out. Vampires who drink blood usually feel better, not worse, but I guess I'm getting to the point where there's no room in my body for anything that isn't Khalyed's rapidly-replicating cells. Apparently, my dilution technique is failing, hard.

'I think maybe it's time you told me what's going on,' Boyd says.

Mina barges him out of the way and says, 'We're getting out of here, Jack. Now.'

'Ms Parchek—'

'No, *former* Deputy Boyd, we're going. You can't help her, and you don't know where the baron is, so just stay out of our way, all right?'

'She's blood poisoned,' the doctor says to Boyd, ignoring Mina's objections. 'Dr Khalyed's. I'm not sure how she's still alive, but I can't imagine she'll stay that way for long. I'm sorry, Chief.'

'Snitch,' I say to the doctor, but she just shrugs and leaves us to it.

'Jacqueline—'

'Look, Deputy,' I interrupt him, because I can't cope with the prospect of an emotional Boyd, on top of everything else. 'It happened. It sucks. But the only hope I have of curing myself is by finding Khalyed, who we think is with the Invicti, and we all want to find Drake, who's probably with the Invicti too. The way I see it, all roads lead to the Invicti, so I guess I'm going to London.'

Painfully, I extract my burning limbs from under the threadbare blanket and swivel so my feet are on the floor. There are shooting pains in my joints now, screaming with heat with every movement, and I feel like I'm about to cry. Instead, I push away the agony and push myself to my feet. At least, I try to, but my legs aren't strong enough to hold me up.

My head hits the floor.

Thunk.

When I open my eyes, I'm in the bed again.

'Stay,' Mina says, pointing a finger at me. 'I'm going to the Invicti, and you're staying here.'

'Bollocks am I,' I say, trying to sit up, but apparently I can't even do that anymore.

Then Boyd and Mina are staring at me with identical wide-eyed expressions, and Boyd is yelling, 'Doctor!' in a panic.

'What?' I croak.

The doctor pushes aside the curtain, takes one look at my face and says, 'Blood transfusion. Now.'

'Will someone please tell me what's going on?' I ask.

Boyd points at the wall beside me, where a mirror sits over a small hand washing sink, and I see why they're all so frantic. On the curve of my left cheekbone, just below the outside edge of my eye, a coin-sized piece of skin is glowing red hot. I touch it with my fingertips and, although I don't feel the burn during the contact, when I take them away they're glowing too.

'Tabitha,' I say to Mina. 'Call Tabitha.'

'I can't call her,' Mina says. 'I can't fucking call anyone down here.'

'You mean Dr Ross?' the doctor asks. She's prepping a transfusion at super-speed with a nurse at her side, but she slows down to ask me the question.

'Yes,' I say.

'She's treating you?'

'Sort of.'

'We can reach her.' The doctor turns to the nurse and says, 'Get the laptop from my desk.' Within seconds she has the thing open to some kind of VPN-encrypted emergency consult application and Tabitha's face is right there on the screen.

'Dr Nguyen?' Tabitha says, then the doctor tips the laptop to show Tabitha my face. 'Oh no.'

'Transfusion?' Dr Nguyen asks her.

'It won't do any good unless you drain her first,' Tabitha says, and the doctor baulks. 'Get into a hazmat suit first. You don't want to touch her blood,' Tabitha goes on, 'but draining is the only thing I can think of that might save her life.'

'Do it!' Boyd orders her.

'You'll need glass receptacles,' Tabitha says as the doctor bustles around the room, throwing the curtain fully open so I can see the rest of the space for the first time. I assumed I was in some kind of sickbay, but it's more like a science lab with a bed in one corner. I feel like a specimen.

'Glass?' the doctor asks as she pulls on a plastic suit.

'The serum melts through plastic,' Tabitha says. 'Glass tubing, glass syringes, metal needle should be fine. How are you doing, hen?' she asks me.

It's all I can do to say, 'Hot.'

And god, I am burning up. It feels like there are flames licking up my arms and the sheets on the bed are starting to turn a toasty golden shade of brown where they touch my skin. If I blew out a lungful of air all at once, I think I'd be breathing fire.

'Everyone back! I'm starting the draw,' the doctor says, reaching for my arm, but she drops it as soon as the needle pierces the vein. 'Oh my god,' she says, looking at the melted gloves of her suit.

She's not managed to do anything more than stick the open syringe into my arm, but apparently my blood is hot enough to burn through the valves inside it because it's rushing out of my body now, through the outer case of the syringe and into a glass tank the doctor's put on the floor beside the bed. When it leaves my vein, the blood is burning orange red, but as it pools in the tank, it turns black around the edges as it cools, like lava cooling into rock. The blood doesn't harden though, it keeps sloshing in the tank, threatening to splash back up and onto the people gathered around my bed, and then who knows what would happen? I try to warn them, but I have no energy left to say a single word.

Then things go a little blurry, and I miss the rest of the procedure. When the world clicks back into focus, there's fresh blood in my veins and the old stuff is being sealed away in the tank by Dr Nguyen on the other side of the room. Mina and Boyd are no longer here, though I don't remember them leaving. There's a clock on the wall that has to be wrong, because there's no way I was out for ten hours.

'Jack?' Tabitha says from the laptop screen that's now resting on the table beside my bed. 'How are you feeling?'

'Alive,' I say. 'Less burny.'

She breathes out. 'Good.'

The background behind her is wobbling all over the place, and she's out of breath, so either she's on the move, or she was more worried than I thought.

'What time is it?' I ask her.

'Three pm.'

'Jesus.'

'You needed the rest, hen,' Tabitha says. 'What your body just went through—'

'How long will it give me?' I ask.

'I don't know,' she says sadly. 'Not long. Dr Nguyen's drained the blood from your veins, but the reality is that by now Dr Khalyed's cells are embedded in every part of your body, and they're not going to stop replicating. At the speed things are accelerating, it might give you a couple of weeks, or as little as a couple of days. It's not linear, so I'm having a hard time predicting anything, particularly since you should never have survived the first infection.'

'But couldn't we just keep draining me and refilling me?'

I ask, confused because this seems like the obvious solution. 'Couldn't that work for a while, at least?'

'It's too risky,' she says, shaking her head. 'I wouldn't even have suggested it in the first place if it hadn't been life or death. The problem is that draining you not only removes a lot of Dr Khalyed's cells, it also removes the normal blood you're trying to use to dilute them. I'm worried that if we drain you again, you'll be left with nothing but Dr Khalyed's cells inside you, and then—'

'*Poof*,' I say, making an exploding gesture with my hands.

'Exactly.'

'So this is my last shot?' I ask. 'One time reprieve?'

'Maybe,' she says. 'Unless the baron can heal—'

'He's gone, Tabby,' I say. 'We think the Invicti have him, along with Khalyed.'

'Jack…'

Tabitha looks like she's close to tears, and I realise she thinks I'm not going to pull through this. But I can't accept that. I won't accept it.

'I'm going to find him,' I say to her, swinging my legs out of bed. This time, they hold my weight. 'And Khalyed.'

'But Jack, you can't—'

'Yes, I can,' I say.

I locate my boots and jacket beside the bed and pull them on – thankfully my jeans and T-shirt are unstained – then I'm up and off.

'Ms Valentine…' Dr Nguyen says as I make my way to the door.

'Thank you for your help, doctor,' I say to her. 'I'm leaving now.'

But when I open the door, there's a guard waiting in the corridor on the other side, blocking my path.

'Ms Valentine, the chief would like you to stay here, please,' he says.

I look him up and down, noting that he's human, which seems a poor choice for restraining a Silver, even if I am a little impaired right now. In fact, I should probably be insulted.

'No, thanks,' I say, gently but firmly moving past him.

Unfortunately, Boyd has somehow been notified that I'm trying to leave and has appeared at super-speed before I've had a chance to get more than halfway down the corridor.

'Jacqueline, wait,' he says.

'Places to be, Boyd.'

'Then you'll want to go in the other direction. You're heading towards the boiler room.'

Shit.

I turn myself around and walk up the corridor past Boyd and the guard, avoiding eye contact with both.

'Feeling better, then?' Boyd asks, falling into step beside me.

'Yes, thanks.'

'Going straight out to pick a fight with the Invicti?'

'Looks like it. Where's Mina?'

'She's having lunch in the refectory. Do you want me to take you there?'

'No,' I say. 'Better that I do this on my own.' Then I push through the double doors at the end of the corridor and into a T-junction I don't know how to navigate.

'Left,' Boyd says, and I follow the direction. 'You know,' he goes on, 'now that the Solis Invicti are all back in London, we could keep you safe here, Jacqueline. Safer than you'd be out there, anyway. We can offer you that. The baron would want me to offer you that.'

'But he's not here, Boyd, and I need to find him.'

'Then you'll want to turn right through this door,' he says.

Beyond the door is another boring, grey corridor — seriously, how do they keep track of their directions in this place when there are no signs and every single doorway looks the same? – but the background noise is louder here, with voices and footsteps and laughter, as though we're approaching a busier part of the complex. I keep walking, going at a decent pace now, and Boyd keeps trailing along at my side.

'If you're determined to break into Solis Invicti HQ all by yourself,' he says, 'then you could at least let us help to prepare you.'

'And how are you going to do that, exactly? Despite what you might have seen in the cinema, Deputy, the stuff that happens in training montages takes more than two and a half minutes in real life. I don't have time. Thanks, but no thanks.'

'Not even if I can help you camouflage your scent?'

I stop walking and turn to face Boyd, looking up into his dark eyes suspiciously. 'If you're playing me—'

'Remember the mist sprayers on the entrance door?' he says. 'That's what they do. They're designed to make us invisible to other Silver as we move in and out of this place, so no one can pick up a scent and follow it back here. There are other decoys installed in the alley.'

'I don't believe you.'

'Then you weren't paying attention.'

That, at least, is true. When we arrived, I'd been so distracted by the danger of the situation and the strangeness of the location and, frankly, the incapacity of my body, that I didn't think to analyse the effect of the mist at the time.

'How?' I ask. 'It's impossible.'

'Nearly impossible,' Boyd corrects me. 'If you remember, it's been done before.'

I wince and say, 'You didn't.'

'Yes,' Boyd replies. 'We did. You remember the Dealer.'

'Yeah,' I say, hands on hips now, striking what passes for

my defensive pose. 'Remarkably, after everything that bastard put me through, I haven't forgotten him.'

The Dealer was a serial scab murderer. It's been a year since we finally dealt with him – no pun intended – after a killing career spanning a horrific number of human deaths, not to mention some targeted aggression that I took extremely personally. When someone tries to kill me, repeatedly, it tends to piss me off.

But Boyd isn't mentioning him just to stir up bad memories. The unique thing about the Dealer, or one of them at least, is that he worked out how to mask his scent so he could disguise himself as someone entirely different, even when he was around people who knew him well. Before he resurfaced last year, I hadn't thought that such a thing was possible. He'd even managed to fool Cam's nose, which I'm pretty sure hasn't happened before or since.

'We can mask your scent,' Boyd says. 'We worked out how.'

'Who's "we"?' I ask.

'Raul.'

'What? No.'

I'm not trying to impugn Raul here, but although my old drinking-buddy has plenty of wonderful qualities, he's definitely not a scientist. He knew a bunch of them though, back in his drug-taking days. Which gives me a bad feeling.

'Oh no,' I say. 'He didn't come up with this by himself, did he?'

'No. He had help. Apparently he was trying to cover up his continuing drug habit while he was working with us in the Seekers—' Boyd clears his throat, obviously offended by the lack of respect that showed. '—so he asked a friend of a friend, and they delivered the Dealer's old notes.'

'They?' I ask, because I need to know the worst of it.

My suspicions are confirmed when Boyd says, 'Matthew

Felton had them. He passed them on to Raul before the... incident.'

'You mean the incident where Winta used Khalyed's blood to turn Felton into a Roman candle?'

'Jacqueline,' he says reprovingly. 'I was trying to avoid being explicit.'

'Not for my sake, I hope,' I say. 'Of all the murders Winta committed, it's the only one I approve of. Even more so now I know that Felton was chummy with the Dealer.'

Boyd looks uncomfortable at that admission, but I'm not going to take it back. Felton was a rat, and he deserved to burn. Maybe what's happening to me right now is karma catching up with me for the fact that I set him on fire myself a couple of times, but I'm not going to change my mind about how moral that was. The world is a better place without Matthew Felton in it.

'My point is that we can help you,' Boyd says. 'Just give me an hour.'

I consider it. It might not seem like much to ask, but if the worst case scenario is that I only have a couple of days left, delaying for even one hour is a sacrifice I might come to regret.

'How long do you think it'll take the Invicti to sniff you out if you *don't* mask your scent?' he asks.

He's right; it's worth the delay.

'An hour,' I say. 'And then I'm going, on my own.'

'Done.'

25

BY THE TIME we get back to the refectory, Boyd has gathered the troops by radio. It's old-fashioned, but he tells me it's the best thing for communicating when everyone's down here, then he goes into serious gadgetry detail that's of absolutely no interest to anyone except himself. Boyd might be a new man, but apparently he's retained his passion for electronics.

Everyone sitting around the refectory's central table turns to face us as we enter the room. Mina's there, and Raul, and Ellie with her old team, and Faiz and Meera, but there are three faces I wasn't expecting to see: Kulika, Tabitha and Petunia.

'So the whole gang's here?' I ask, though now everyone's gathered together like this, I feel the absences in the room keenly. A lot of the old gang is missing, including Ed and Naia and, of course, Cam.

'We want to help,' Kulika says.

'You mean you want Drake back,' I reply.

Everyone knows that Kulika hates it when he leaves her in charge. She wants to do her job then go to the gym and piss about with the weights to her heart's content. She has no interest in being the acting baron.

'Of course I want him back,' she says. 'Have you seen the state of this?' Then she flexes one arm and prods at what seems to me to be an outrageously muscular bicep, but apparently it disappoints her. 'I'm missing out on my reps.'

She performs this little piece in a lighthearted way, but she doesn't quite mask the anxiety in her eyes as she does it, at least not from me. She's trying to downplay her concern for the benefit of the others, but we both know this isn't about her weightlifting regime. She's worried about Drake. She doesn't need to give me the news from her morning's calls, because I can read it on her face, but she does it anyway.

'No one's heard from him,' she says as Boyd and I join them all at the table. 'And Ms Arden isn't even in Europe, she's in Oxfordshire. She'll be back to overseeing the blood bar from next week.'

'So we're all agreed that the Invicti have him?' I ask.

A few people nod, and Boyd says, 'It seems like the likeliest option.'

Mina's got her arms crossed over her chest again, radiating vitriol at everyone around the table like a muzzled pitbull. I already suspected that her silence wasn't going to last, but she breaks it rather spectacularly by standing from her chair so abruptly that it falls over backwards and clatters onto the concrete behind her.

'Of course the Invicti have him!' she says. 'And Khalyed. So why are we all sitting around here like a bunch of un-fisted Muppets instead of getting our arses up to London to bust into Solis Invicti HQ, fuck up the Invicti, get the guys out, save Jack's life and live happily ever after?'

'Because the chances of us fucking them up before they fuck us up are vanishingly small?' I suggest. 'Sit down, Mina.'

'Jack—'

'We've got time,' I reassure her, though I'm feeling pretty insecure about that myself. On the other side of the table, Tabitha's looking uncomfortable too, but she doesn't contradict me. 'Mina, remember how you said you had a terrible idea about sneaking into Solis Invicti HQ to get Khalyed's blood?'

'The one I decided would be a suicide mission?' she says.

'Yes, that one. I need to know the details.'

'No, you don't,' she says, then she rights her chair, sits back down and crosses her arms again.

'Why do I get the feeling I'm not going to like this?' Kulika asks.

'Because it relies on us doing something very stupid,' Mina answers her. 'I worked out how to get us inside, but since the Invicti are bound to pick up on scents that don't belong there – particularly Jack's, given what she did – there's just no way to get us back out again without being caught.'

'We can help with that,' Boyd says.

'How?' Mina asks combatively.

'Forget about getting me back out for now,' I say. 'How sure are you that you can get me in?'

'I'd say the odds are about are fifty-fifty. Maybe thirty-seventy. Actually, with you in the state you are, I'd say twenty-eighty.'

'You're not filling me with confidence here,' says Boyd.

'Do you want to hear the plan or not?' Mina says, on the defensive now.

'Yes,' I say.

Mina gets up out of her chair again, more calmly this time, and says, 'Give me ten minutes. I need to fetch someone.'

'Who?' I ask.

'Just a contact of mine,' she says evasively. 'I'm not telling you who it is unless and until they agree to come back here with me. Just give me ten minutes and someone to guide me in and out of this maze, and we'll see.'

'I'll take you,' Quentin volunteers, getting to his feet.

'Great,' Mina says. 'I'll go with Purple Mohawk here.'

'Just to be clear,' I say. 'This plan of yours is for one, right? Because I'm doing this on my own.'

There's a small chorus of protests from the fightier members of the squad – mostly Mina – but I don't give them a chance to get going.

'It'll be easier with one of me,' I say, shouting them down. 'Sneaking in on my own is one thing, but sneaking in en masse is never going to work.'

'Then send someone who's not falling over,' says Raul. 'I'll go.'

'I know the building,' I say.

Well, I sort of know it. A bit. At least I did before Leclercq blew it up, so as long as they rebuilt it the same, I should be fine.

'I know it better,' Boyd says, which is probably true.

'You know it has to be me,' I say, looking at Mina and Tabitha.

They know about the bond. They know I need to get to Drake as soon as possible, so that means it has to be me who does this. I'd just rather that the others didn't know why.

'She's right,' Tabitha says.

But Raul won't let it go. 'Why?' he asks.

I try to come up with a good excuse, but I've got nothing, so instead I go with a revelation that I'm sure will make them all want to get rid of me.

'There's something else you should know.' I tell them about Louise, and Mr Inman, and Faith, and Khalyed's vamp-zombie state, while Mina looks on and scowls. 'So the thing is, I might be a serial killer, and I might be killing humans. You've got a lot of those down here with you, so it's not safe for me to be here too.'

'That sounds like more of a reason to keep you here than let you go, Jacqueline,' Boyd say. 'If you stay here, then we can make sure you aren't dangerous, instead of letting you loose on the world with potentially catastrophic consequences. Maybe Dr Ross could keep you under observation.'

'But I might have killed a bunch of humans,' I say plaintively. 'You should be throwing me out.'

'But you can't remember it?' Meera asks.

'No,' I say.

'If you had, then you would remember it. I don't believe you've killed any humans at all.'

'Neither does she,' Mina says.

'Mina!'

She ignores me and says to the others, 'She thinks Yolande Leclercq is framing her.'

Meera nods as though this makes perfect sense.

'That fits,' says Raul. 'And anyway, even if you did kill those people, then you did it under the influence of Dr Khalyed's blood. It wasn't you, Jack. You don't deserve to be punished for something you had no control over. You don't have to sacrifice yourself like this.' Then he reaches over the table to take my hand and says, 'It's not your fault.'

I guess this all hits a little close to home for Raul, given what happened to his friend Rachael when he got poisoned himself. I appreciate his sympathy, I really do, but right now it's working against me. I don't have time for this, but I don't know what else to say to persuade them all that this is the right move.

In the end, it's not me who does the persuading.

'Jack should be the one to go,' Tabitha says sadly. 'If this all goes wrong, then Dr Khalyed's blood will kill her within the next few weeks anyway. It won't make much difference to her if the Invicti capture her or kill her or box her, because at this point, she has nothing left to lose.'

Mina winces on my behalf, but I don't hold it against Tabitha, who's looking at me apologetically. She's not only right, but this is the perfect excuse to offer the others.

'This is Jack's fight,' she adds. 'We should let her do this herself if she wants to.'

No one has anything to say to counter that, so I guess it's settled.

'I'm leaving as soon as I can,' I say to them all, 'so Mina, go get your secret contact, and everyone else, give me what you've got. If you have an idea that could help, I want to hear it.'

Quentin leads Mina out of the refectory, but not before she gives me a dirty look as she leaves. She knows why I have to do this myself, but she's still not happy about it.

Then Boyd says, 'Scent masking,' and nods at Raul.

'I'll get you a pack of pills and a portable spray,' says Raul, then he leaves the refectory too.

'The spray covers your existing scent,' Boyd says, 'and the pills inhibit scent production for an hour or so at a time, so if you're careful, you'll only have to spray yourself once.'

'Excuse me?' says Tabitha from the other side of the table. 'You've worked out a way to mask and inhibit our scents? How?'

'Not the time, Tabby,' I say. 'Talk about it when I'm gone. What else can you give me?'

'What exactly is your plan here?' Petunia asks me. 'You're not going to try to kill the Primus again, are you? Because that didn't go so well the last time.'

'No, he's safe for now,' I say petulantly.

'Well, that's a relief,' she replies, then she mumbles sarcastically, 'I'm sure the idea of a twenty-year-turned Silver coming after him was a super serious concern.'

'Petunia,' Tabitha says with gentle reproach, nudging her with her elbow.

'Why is she here?' I ask Tabitha.

I'm not trying to start a fight, but I've got limited time and limited patience for someone I'm not sure I trust.

Then Petunia says, reluctantly, 'I'm booked to do a gig at Solis Invicti HQ tonight with a few other performers. Tabitha thought I could get some information for you while I was there.'

'Or maybe you could smuggle Jack inside,' Tabitha suggests. 'If she's wearing the masking spray...'

'Where are you performing?' I ask.

'Big show in the grand hall,' Petunia replies.

'Where's that?'

'I thought you said you knew the building?'

Petunia is really starting to get on my nerves.

'It takes up most of the ground floor,' says Boyd. 'It's the lobby, really, but it's an impressive one. They use it for events.'

'So you don't have to go through the security barriers to get to it?' I ask.

'No,' Boyd says.

'Then Petunia wouldn't be smuggling me anywhere,' I point out. 'I'd still be in the public area.'

'Which is exactly why they hold their larger events there,' says Boyd.

'But maybe it could be a distraction?' Tabitha suggests. 'Maybe you could time your break in with the start of the show, or maybe Petunia could kick up a fuss or something to cover your entrance?'

'Maybe,' Boyd says dubiously. 'It would help if we knew where you needed to get to.'

'The basement, probably,' says Tabitha. 'That's where the boxes and holding cells are. The labs, too. You'd need to use the lifts to access them, though. That's the only way in or out.'

'That doesn't sound like it would be compliant with fire safety laws,' says Rolf, Ellie's partner. Sometimes I forget he's German, and then he says something like that and makes it impossible to forget. Now that Boyd's become Mr Laid Back, I suppose Rolf has to fill the role of Head Pedant.

'I think secret underground lairs get a pass on building compliance,' I say. 'For instance, I bet this place isn't exactly up to code.'

'I don't think the captain would have told the city council about the building works,' says Boyd, shiftily.

'My point exactly. So how do I get to the lifts?'

'Schematics,' Faiz says, tapping frantically on a large tablet he's holding across his lap. When he finds what he's looking for, he lays the tablet flat on the table in front of me and leans over to show me a bunch of charts that seem confusingly busy, so overlaid with lines and arrows that they bear little resemblance to the floor plans I was expecting him to show me.

'What am I looking at?' I ask.

'This is the ground floor,' says Faiz. 'Entrance here, security barriers here, lifts way back here opposite the security station.'

'So what you're saying is that someone on the ground floor has eyes on the lift at all times?' I ask.

'I'm afraid so.'

'Fuck.'

'So you're not getting in that way,' Boyd says. 'But maybe there's another access point you can use?'

'Ummm...' says Faiz, flicking from one schematic to the next. 'The problem is, every floor has those sealed floor-to-ceiling windows that don't open, and I'm pretty sure they'll be reinforced too, given that it's the Invicti who are using the building, so I'm not sure that there *is* another access point.'

'Maybe you can convince someone to let you in?' Tabitha suggests. 'Maybe if you pretend that you're there for the show like Petunia, then you could, I don't know, seduce one of the guards?'

'You want me to seduce one of the Solis Invicti?' I ask. 'Even on my best day, Tabs, I can barely get any of them except Cam to tolerate me, let alone—'

Mina slams the refectory door open and comes back to join us at the table. I can't help but notice that she's alone.

'Well?' I ask.

'Sounds like you've figured out that you're not going to be able to talk your way in there,' she says, 'and you're too weak to fight your way in, even if you weren't going up against a bunch of elite supernatural soldiers.'

'So basically, you're telling me I'm fucked.'

'Not necessarily. I had the idea that maybe you could hack your way in there.'

'Mina,' I say, exasperated, 'you know I don't know how to do that.'

'No, but we both know someone who does.'

She turns back to the door as though she's expecting a dramatic entrance. Unfortunately, whoever's on the other side of the door doesn't seem to have anticipated her intent. But, now that I'm focussing on that spot, I can hear voices filtering through from the corridor outside. There are two men in conversation somewhere beyond the door. I can't make out the words exactly, but the voices sound familiar, and the tone of their giggling suggests that whomever Mina's brought with her has become pleasantly distracted.

'We don't have all day, here!' Mina yells, then there's an abrupt exchange of goodbyes and the refectory door swings open once more, less violently this time.

'Frank?'

'Hiya, Jack!'

Frank the Hacker is a short redhead with a delicate build and impish features that always make me think of Peter Pan. He used to be our computer guy back before the Seekers started laying people off, and I've wondered from time to time what he's been doing since then. Apparently, he's been working for Mina.

'So this is how you got Drake's cell tower data so quickly?' I say to her.

She taps the side of her nose in that sleazy way of hers and says, 'Got to protect my sources.'

'That's me!' says Frank, smiling as he gives me a jaunty salute and takes a seat at the table. 'I hear you need a digital skeleton key.'

'A what, now?' I say.

'A way to get through a digitally-locked door.'

I turn to Mina, not entirely understanding. 'Is that what I need?'

'Yes,' she says, grabbing the tablet from Faiz and scrolling to a different schematic. 'You remember the party at Solis Invicti HQ at New Year's?'

'Yes.' I'm hardly likely to forget it, given that it was the worst night of my life.

'And you know the rooftop terrace they had on that building, up until Leclercq made it go kablooey?'

'Yes.'

'Well, they've rebuilt it, but they've made some alterations.'

She brings up a photo on her phone and zooms in, then turns it so I can see the screen. Instead of the terrace taking up the entirety of the flat roof, as it once did, half the floor is now built on, with big glass doors that lead out into a manicured and gravelled garden. Beyond the glass, I can even see an indoor swimming pool.

A pool. On a roof. In England.

Bonkers.

'The floor below is now the Primus's penthouse,' Mina says, pointing to what used to be the Solis Invicti's gym. I always thought it was a waste of that view. Turns out, the Primus agreed. 'And the top floor is his private space too. It's connected to the penthouse by a private stairwell, and the penthouse is connected to the rest of the building by the central lift shaft, so all you have to do is get through these doors here,' she says, pointing to the big glass doors on the roof, 'and then you're in.'

'It can't be that simple,' I say.

'Oh, it's not,' says Frank. 'There are cameras, and biometric locking mechanisms, and lasers, and all the cool stuff you see in spy movies.'

'Then how do we get past those?'

'It's pretty easy when you're the person who installed them.' Frank grins, then pulls a small black box out of his pocket and puts it on the table. 'This is the access key. You just hold it close to the panel on the door, and it'll hook up to the locking mechanism wirelessly to unlock the door. And take this.' He hands me a basic mobile phone. 'My number's programmed in there. It's all secure, I promise. When you get to the door, *before* you use the key, just give me a call and I'll remote in to divert the other systems. What time do you think you'll arrive?'

'I don't know,' I say, knowing that I can't afford to hang around long, but also knowing that I can't waste energy by travelling at super speed. I'll have to travel by conventional means, which will take time. 'What time's your show, Petunia?'

'Eight.'

'I'll do it then, when everyone will be gathered in the lobby. Hopefully then I'll be able to take the lift all the way down to the basements without interruption.'

'Here and here are your best bets,' Faiz says, pulling up schematics of the lower floors on Faiz's tablet. 'This spot looks like the easiest access to the boxes, and here are the holding cells.'

'They'll be guarded,' says Boyd.

'Then I'll fight if I have to,' I say.

Mina snorts in a way that suggests her confidence in my current fighting strength is limited.

'We have some stuff in the armoury that might help,' Quentin says.

'Like?' I ask.

'Some of those tranquilliser darts the Invicti developed last year. You know, the ones that knocked out you and the baron.'

'What?' I ask, confused. 'How? I thought the Invicti had gathered them all back in?'

'They did.' Quentin smiles sheepishly. 'But when it became clear at New Year's that they had no intention of recruiting all of us from the Seekers, I took the opportunity to gather some back out again.'

'You sneaky bastard,' I say, but I'm impressed. Quentin's never really struck me as the proactive type, so I find it strangely heart-warming to hear that he's directed his bitterness into vengeful theft.

'There are only a few,' he cautions, 'so you'll have to be careful with how you use them, but they might be enough.'

'I'll go fetch them,' says Ellie. 'You'll need a gun for them, and some blood capsules too, and the other essentials. You know what? I'll just pack you a bag.'

'Great,' I say as she leaves the room, 'then I just need to work out transport.'

'I'm driving you,' says Mina.

'It might make more sense for me to travel with Petunia

and her troupe,' I say.

However distasteful the idea might be on a personal level, travelling with other Silver is a good way to mask my approach.

'I'm driving you,' Mina repeats. 'The troupe will be getting there too early, so you'll have to hang around, which means there'll be more chances for the Invicti to sniff you out. So I'll drop you a few streets away and you can building-hop from there.'

'It'll burn more blood.'

'Then we'll load you up well.'

I hesitate, because I'm not sure what that will do to the rate of replication, but Mina forestalls my objections by saying, 'Even if you went with Petunia, you'd still have to climb up to the roof somehow, which would burn plenty. Instead, we can get you up the lift of one of the nearby buildings so you skip the climb, then you can use the blood you would have burned climbing to jump across instead. It'll end up the same, and it'll be a safer approach.'

'She's right,' Boyd says. 'You don't want to scale the Solis Invicti building anyway.'

'They have sensors,' Frank adds.

'Okay, then,' I say. 'I guess I'm jumping. Do I have to worry about sensors on the roof?'

'No,' says Frank. 'Not in the garden, but there are patrols every fifteen minutes or so, so you'll have to avoid those. And remember: call me *before* you use the electronic key on the door.'

'What'll happen if I don't?'

'You'll set off all the alarms and back up systems, and some of those have a sting in the tail, so I just wouldn't. Okay?'

'Okay.'

I dread to think what Frank means by a "sting". I guess I'd

better not find out.

'So you're all set?' Boyd asks.

'I think so,' I say. 'And, you know, thank you. Everyone.' I look around the table, feeling a bit overwhelmed at the way these disparate friends and acquaintances have come together to try to save my arse, even when it means defying the Invicti and the Primus himself. 'I really appreciate it.'

'You're welcome, hen,' says Tabitha. 'I'll be getting everything ready here for when you come back. Just bring me Dr Khalyed's blood, and I'll do the rest.'

She's putting on a brave face, pretending she thinks I'll make it, but we were together for too long for her to hide her sadness from me. She thinks I'm a dead woman. I don't disagree, but I'm still going to try, for Drake's sake.

'I'll turn the volume up for the show,' says Petunia. 'And we've got some pyrotechnics at the start. Hopefully that should mask any noise you make.'

Then Raul and Ellie return with the supplies, all packed away in a small black backpack that looks like it's designed for stealth. It doesn't really go with my leather jacket, but I shrug it on anyway while Raul shows me how to apply the scent-masking spray.

'Do it at the last minute if you can,' he says. 'Then you can make it last longer.'

'Thank you,' I say.

He pulls me into one of his wonderful hugs, and that seems to break the seal. Now everyone wants to hug me, which I'm okay with when it comes from Tabitha and the old Seekers, but being hugged by Petunia is a little weird. Kulika just waves, which is a relief.

'Ten minutes then,' says Mina. She's also avoiding a hug, which feels just as weird. 'Out front. I'll go fetch the car.'

26

ONCE EVERYONE HAS dispersed, Frank walks me out to the entrance. Apparently he can remember the way after just one trip into this labyrinth, which I find staggering, but it's not that surprising given how his mind works. If he can navigate code like a wizard, no wonder he's not phased by a few samey corridors.

'You could get in a shitload of trouble for this,' I say as we walk.

'I doubt it,' he replies.

'You're breaking into the Primus's penthouse.'

'Yes, but he knows that I could also break into any number of *other* secret locations, so as long as you don't cause too much trouble—' He gives me a sharp look. 'You're not going to try to kill him again, are you?'

'No!' Why does everyone keep asking me that? 'I'm planning to avoid him entirely. He should be down at the show watching Petunia and her mates.'

'Then everything should be hunky-dory. He likes me,' Frank says, then he adds, 'I get the feeling he likes you, too.'

'Why do you say that?'

'Because if he didn't, I've got to imagine you'd be dead

by now.'

'Yeah, right.' I laugh. 'He'd have to find me first.'

'Jack, please. I might be freelancing now, but Mina's not my only client. If the Primus had wanted me to track you down, don't you think I could have done it? Do you have any idea of the kind of tracing technology that's available these days if your budget and your skills are infinite? Unless you've been hiding in a box for five months – and knowing you, I bet you weren't – then I'd happily bet you a million, billion pounds that I would have been able to find you. But he never asked.'

I remember Cam saying something similar about how he could track my scent, and I wonder if the Primus would really have been unaware of that, or of Frank's skills. For that matter, wouldn't the Invicti have been aware of both of their abilities too? Which begs the question: why wouldn't they be using them?

'Why not?' I ask.

'Oh, don't sound so offended,' Frank says. 'I'm sure you're a very scary little fugitive. It's just that he has other things to worry about right now.'

'Like what?'

'Come on, Jack. You wouldn't trust me if I went spilling all my clients' secrets to anyone who asked, would you? When you have a world of information at your fingertips,' he says, wiggling his fingers in the air, 'you have to learn to be discreet.'

I'm desperate to know what the Primus has going on at the moment that's important enough to ignore me trying to murder him, but Frank clearly isn't going to tell me. Still, he has given me new information: whatever reason the Primus might have for holding Drake, it's not to lure me in. Now I'm worried that it's about something else entirely, like the fact that he's been using Khalyed's blood to kill the scabs who were boxed in his basement. That would also explain why Khalyed and Drake were both whisked away at around the same time.

Which raises another horrifying possibility: maybe the Primus didn't need to use Frank or Cam to track me down because he already knew where I was. And, if that's true, maybe he used Drake's last visit to me as the perfect opportunity to snatch him while he was alone, away from Kulika and his guards, and probably distracted enough by our fight to be vulnerable.

Maybe this has never been about catching me at all. Maybe it's always been about catching Drake.

Shit.

It fits. Honestly, I was a little surprised that the Invicti were taking so long to find me. Sure, I've been hiding as well as Mina and I know how, but that will never be as well as the *Invicti* know how, and the Primus has the kind of reach that you can't even measure, so it was inevitable that they'd catch up with me sooner or later. I thought I might get away with it for a few weeks, or maybe a month, but I was hoping that would be long enough for me or Drake to find a solution. Five months on the run, though?

Of course they knew where I was. Any newbie Silver would have been able to track me given that much time. I hadn't even left the country, beyond my quick trip to Scotland. Staying put seemed like a necessity at the time, firstly so I could stay close to Drake, and later because I didn't have the strength to run, but now it seems like insanity. I should have run further. I should have hidden harder. But now the Primus has Drake and Khalyed, I'm still dying from blood poisoning, and either I'm going vamp-zombie and killing humans or Leclercq is trying to make me believe I am.

Because of course she would have found a way to track

me too.

'I've been an idiot,' I say out loud.

Frank blinks at me quizzically for a second then asks, 'About what? Because I can think of a few options.'

'About everything. Hey, can you look into something for me?' I ask.

'Sure,' he says cheerfully. 'What do you need?'

I tell him about Faith and Mr Inman and Louise, and about the files Mina found. 'I haven't had time to go through them properly, but nothing jumped out at me, and I'm wondering if there's anything Mina missed,' I say.

'What are you expecting to find?'

'I don't know. Something that points to the person who did this. Ideally something that proves it couldn't have been me. Phone tower data for other Silver in the area. Security camera footage. Licence plate recognition systems. I don't know.'

'That's a lot of possibilities to explore,' he says. 'It'll take time.'

'Whatever time you can give me, I'd be really grateful for it.'

'Okay, but can it wait until tomorrow?' he asks. 'Because the thing is, I just met someone, and he invited me to a thing tonight, and I'll totally be available until you're safely in and out of Solis Invicti HQ tonight, but after that I'd really like to go party. Only if your other thing isn't urgent, though.'

I can't really object. Frank is a sort-of friend, but more of a former colleague than anything else. I like him, and I think he likes me or he wouldn't be helping at all, but everything he's done for me up until now has been for money and, with Drake MIA, I don't have any more to offer him. He's already putting his neck on the line for me tonight, and he's doing it for free. The extra work I'm asking him to do now is a pure favour, so although digging up this information feels pretty fucking urgent to me, I can't expect to get it immediately. Besides, I'll be away in London for the rest of the evening and, assuming that I even survive, I won't be able to catch up with Frank until tomorrow anyway.

So I say, 'Tomorrow would be good, if you can manage it.'

'First thing,' he promises.

We've reached the exit now, and Frank presses the release button beside the door at the bottom of the endless staircase that leads back up to daylight.

'Oh, dear,' Frank says, patting his pockets with a concern that seems forced. 'I've left my, um, key fob thing back in the refectory. You'll be fine the rest of the way on your own, right?'

'Sure,' I say.

'Call me later, okay? I'll be ready and waiting at eight.'

He's already halfway back along the corridor, waving over his shoulder. I'd bet a million, billion pounds that he's off to find whoever invited him to that party earlier. After all, it's hours until eight o'clock. He's got time to kill.

Alone at the bottom of the stairs, I pass through the mist of scent-masking spray and start to climb alone. Unfortunately, that takes a while at normal speed, so I'm soon overtaken by someone going far faster. Unfortunately again, they slow down to chat.

'Jack,' says Kulika. 'Do you want a lift?'

'I'd love a lift, but apparently they didn't bother to install one.'

'No, I mean...' She mimes picking me up and carrying me.

'Absolutely not,' I say. 'I do have some shreds of dignity left.'

'You're about a tenth of the way there.'

'Fine,' I say. Yes, I have some vestiges of dignity

remaining, but I also have some vestiges of common sense, and that is a *lot* of stairs when I need to preserve my energy for jumping buildings tonight. 'But over the shoulder, not like you're carrying me across the threshold on our wedding night, okay?'

In the end, Kulika zips to the top so quickly that the whole thing takes less than a second, and by the time she sets me down, Mina hasn't even arrived in her car to pick me up.

'You said the discussions Drake has been having with the Primus weren't going well,' I say as we wait in the alley. 'What exactly has he told you?'

Kulika shrugs. 'Not much by way of detail.'

'Then given me the broad picture.'

'I don't know,' she says, furrowing her brow as she thinks. 'It's a vibe more than it is anything else, you know? The way he was when he left those meetings just made me worry. He was frustrated, angry even.'

'About what?'

'I'm not sure. They were talking about a lot of things: the dead boxed Silver, what to do with Dr Khalyed, the pro-reveal movement, the vote, the whole governing structure of the Silver, your stupid bloody assassination attempt… They covered a lot of ground, but the baron didn't let me in on all of it. He could have been upset about the Primus's reaction to one of those things, or all of them, or none of them. I can't tell you. Why?'

I shake my head, frustrated by the possibilities. 'I know I said that maybe Drake had been taken to lure me out of hiding, but I don't think it's about that anymore.'

'No shit.' Kulika laughs. 'The Great Jack Valentine thinks something *isn't* about her? Let me alert the media.'

'Yes, all right, settle down. The point is that I've got some information suggesting that the Primus doesn't really care about the whole assassination attempt thing after all.'

'So your big theory is a bust.'

'Apparently,' I admit ill-naturedly. 'Which means that if the Invicti really do have Drake, then they must have taken him for another reason. It might help if I knew what that reason was.'

Kulika thinks for a moment, stretching her neck muscles as she does so. I can hear her vertebrae cracking.

'If I had to guess,' she says after a few seconds, 'I'd say it was about the pro- and anti-reveal issue, which sort of ties into the killing-Silver-in-the-basement problem. You have to understand that most of the Silver aren't like you, Jack.'

'If this is going to be an insult, you can save it,' I cut in.

'No, I mean they don't see humans as being on the same level as them. Most of their arguments for coming out are some variation on the idea that that they shouldn't have to hide, or stop themselves from drinking from the vein. They think humanity owes them whatever they want to take from it, just because they can.'

'You sound like Drake,' I say, and to my surprise I realise I'm smiling.

'Yeah, I'm probably paraphrasing him. We talked about that kind of thing a lot.'

'For a serial killer, he's strangely moral.'

Kulika's smiling now too. For a moment, we stand there next to each other on the kerb at the end of the alley, both lost in our own recollections.

'You really do care about him, don't you?' Kulika says.

'Of course I do.'

'Well, you're bad at showing it.'

'What a shocking revelation,' I say. 'The Great Jack Valentine is guarded with her emotions. Who would have guessed?'

'And she uses sarcasm to cover up for it,' Kulika says wryly. 'Are you in love with him?'

233

The question makes me squirm, so instead of answering her, I say, 'I don't want to talk about this with you.'

'Then will you talk about it with him?'

'If I find him,' I say. 'Maybe.'

'Jack—'

'Okay fine yes,' I say in a rush. 'But I've got a heavily-guarded fortress to break into, and I'm literally dying second by second, so can we just drop it now, please?'

'If he's got himself into trouble with the Invicti,' she says, 'you know it's either because he was trying to protect humanity from scab Silver, or because he was trying to protect you.'

'I know. I'm trying to do the same for him.'

'Okay, then,' she says.

'We're okay?'

'We're okay. Bring him back, though, will you?'

'I'm going to try my best. But Kulika, if I don't make it —'

'Don't be an idiot,' she interrupts. 'After all, since when is the Great Jack Valentine anything less than annoyingly lucky?'

'Since always?'

'You can do this, Jack,' she says. 'And if you can't, all you have to do is call. Phone.'

She holds out her hand and I pass her the burner phone Frank gave me. She programs her number into the memory and passes it back.

'I'll come running,' she says. 'Literally.'

'Thank you.'

'I'd do anything for him, you know,' she says, and the confession is little more than a whisper. 'Don't make me regret trusting you with this on your own. If you need me, you bloody well call.'

Mina interrupts us by pulling up beside us, throwing the

passenger door open and telling me to get in. This would have been more dramatic had she been driving something other than a Fiat 500, but I do as she says. When she peels away, with more acceleration than I consider strictly necessary, Kulika is still standing at the kerb. She watches us all the way until we're out of sight, turning the corner onto the High Street, but I swear I feel the pressure of her gaze following me.

Drake and I will both die if I fail tonight. I can't let her down.

27

'THIS IS IT?' I ask as Mina pulls into an underground car park in central London.

'This is it.'

She cruises around in circles for a while before finding the right numbered bay and parking up. This building houses offices that are used in part by one of Mina's many contacts, and they've given her access to the parking space and the lift up to the roof, for a price, no doubt. Whatever that price is, she hasn't made any mention of passing it on to me. Maybe she's running a tab.

We're here sooner than expected – the traffic was light – so we have about half an hour to kill before it's time for me to head up top and start jumping. That gives me a chance to climb into the back seat and cover myself in the scent-masking spray. I'm worried it's going to gas us out of the car, but it's in a spray bottle rather than an aerosol, and it smells of nothing at all. I might as well be splashing water around. It's a bit awkward having to strip to my underwear in the back of the car, but Mina is uncharacteristically courteous during the process. It's not until the very end of the application, when I'm down to my bra on top but otherwise fully dressed once more, that I catch her eyes on me.

'Do you want a hand with that?' she asks, looking at me in the rearview mirror as I struggle to cover my back.

'I can manage.'

'Bollocks you can.'

I'd like to snap back that she's just looking for an excuse to take my clothes off, but she isn't acting that way, and I really do need help reaching that one spot in the very centre of my back, so I acquiesce with bad grace and let her join me in the back seat.

'Just here,' I say, pointing to the bit I can't reach. 'Raul said I need to cover every inch of skin.'

Which is why my hair is now damp and plastered to my scalp. The formula seems to dry pretty quickly on skin, but I had to put extra on my head to get through to my roots, and now it's a mess. Luckily, Ellie has packed me a beanie hat – every burglar's must-have accessory – that will cover the worst of it.

When Mina's coated the parts I couldn't reach, she helps me gather my hair into a bun and tidy the whole lot away under the cap, so now only a few damp curls are escaping around my ears. I'm just thinking I've got away with being in such close proximity with her while partly undressed, when she lets her touch linger pointedly behind my ear as she tucks away a loose strand of hair. I can feel her breath on my skin. She leans forward to press her lips against my neck.

'Mina,' I say, warning her off.

'You could die up there, Jack,' she says. 'What's the harm in one last tumble?'

'I don't have time.'

'You'd be surprised how little you might need.'

I catch her hand at my neck and turn to face her, and it's only then that I notice she's not pissing about. She looks unsettled, upset even. I realise that she doesn't think I'm coming back, and this is her way of saying goodbye.

'I'm going to find him,' I say. 'Both of them: Drake and Khalyed. This isn't going to end here. You'll have plenty of time to make indecent propositions to me tomorrow, and the day after, and the day after that. You don't have to blow through them all now.'

'Then you don't have to blow through all your rejections, either.'

I'm not expecting her to lean in, so I don't dodge the kiss. I don't kiss her back, but I do wait a moment before I push her away. I don't know why I let it happen. Maybe as a thank you, for everything she's done for me. Maybe because, despite what I said a second ago, I don't think I'm going to be coming back from this either, so I might as well give her a proper goodbye. Mostly though, it would just be too awkward to reject her outright, and I don't have the energy for it.

'I've got to go,' I say, then I pull my top on over my head and slip into my leather jacket.

The letter from Winta is still in my pocket – I can hear it crinkling – and it fills me with trepidation. Another rooftop chase in the darkness, another betrayal, another brush with death. I pull the tranquilliser darts out of my backpack and load the first couple into the chamber of the gun, then flip up the back of my jacket and stuff it down the waistband of my jeans. I'm not comfortable with guns, but I can probably manage a point and shoot like this one. Hopefully I won't need more than two shots, because I definitely can't reload in a hurry.

'There's something else you should know,' Mina says.

She's been watching me prepare myself step by step, never taking her eyes off me, but it's not desire or disappointment in her eyes. She's afraid for me, and she doesn't want me to go. That's why, at first, I assume she's just trying to delay me.

'I'll be fine,' I say dismissively. 'I've got to go.'

'No, look,' she says, then she reaches into the boot to grab her laptop and cracks it open. After a couple of clicks, she shows me the screen. 'This is a picture of your friend Louise that arrived in my inbox this evening. It's why I was late with the car, and I was in two minds about whether or not to show you at all when your head needs to be on what you're doing tonight, but... You see the marks, right?'

Now I know there's something to look for, the bruises aren't hard to make out. There are several on each side of her neck, long and clumped together in the shape of someone's hands tightening around her throat.

'I finally got a copy of the post mortem report earlier today,' Mina goes on, 'and it says the bruising is peri-mortem.'

'So it happened during the struggle that killed her?'

'Likely. According to the post mortem, she injected herself – or was injected – with heroin, which knocked her out, then someone strangled her and drained her blood.'

'Oh god,' I say. 'That would explain why there was no blood at the scene.'

'Right. They drained it all and bottled it to sell.'

Supposedly, drinking the blood of humans who are high on various drugs can give the Silver a high themselves. Back in the Seekers, we'd occasionally see scab murders where a Silver decided to test this concept for themselves, either by purchasing drugs and ambushing an oblivious human with them, or by tracking down a human who was already using and draining them.

Spoiler: it's bullshit. There's a reason that there's a market for drugs designed specifically for the Silver, and it's that regular human drugs do fuck all to us. They do even less when they're already part-metabolised by a human body, and less again when they're combined with copious amounts of blood. The whole urban legend is the result of some seriously magical thinking and a deficit of common sense, but it just won't seem to go away. The worst of it is that some particularly cynical but enterprising Silver are always spreading the story around so they can create a market for bottled secondhand-drug-filled blood that they know will have absolutely no effect at all on their customers, but will earn them a quick fortune. Drug users are easy pickings for Silver like that, and there isn't exactly an ombudsman that scammed customers can complain to when they don't get the high they're expecting, so it's win-win for the dealers.

Louise's death looks like another case of idiocy guided by either avarice or mythology, but that can't be the only thing going on here. There must be a reason it happened in the flat next to mine. That can't be pure coincidence.

'What about Faith and Mr Inman?' I ask, looking for the connection.

'I still haven't got their post mortem reports, but I took another look at their crime scene photos, and I'm seeing similar bruises. They're harder to see on Faith, because of all of the blood, but my guess is that maybe something went wrong – an interruption, or a struggle – that meant the attacker had to leave before draining her, and he made a mess on the way out.'

'*He*?' I ask. 'So you're ready to accept that it wasn't me?'

'From the size of the bruises, the pathologist thinks the attacker must have been a man. So yeah, your hands are small enough to put you in the clear.'

I'm off the hook. I didn't kill my friend or my neighbours.

'What a fucking relief,' I say.

'What? That there's a Silver scab out there with big, manly hands who's following you around, murdering your neighbours and draining their blood?'

'Better some scab with manly hands than me.'

'But it means you're wrong with your theory, too,' she says. 'It can't be Leclercq doing this.'

'It could be the Invicti, though. Probably Benedict.'

'But why?'

'Maybe he got bored while he was stalking Drake. I don't know. Maybe I can find out while I'm in there. The point is that it wasn't me.'

Mina's found exactly what I was looking for. When I call him in a bit, I'll be able to tell Frank to call off the search. That thought reminds me of my schedule, and I check the clock on the dashboard to see that I only have a few minutes left to get upstairs and get moving.

'Mina, you're a gem,' I say, kissing her quickly on the cheek. 'I've got to go, but can you keep trying for those post mortem reports? I bet there are drugs in Mr Inman and Faith's blood, and I want to see if there's anything else we can use to narrow down the suspects.'

'Sure,' she says, but she looks more worried than I expect her to be. 'It's not like I have anything else to do while you're out invading Solis Invicti HQ and probably dying in the process.'

'I'm not invading. I'm quickly sneaking in and out, and I've got a load of toys to help me do it,' I say, patting the backpack before shrugging it on. 'I'll be back within the hour, and if I'm not, you can come in after me. Okay?'

'Okay.'

'Then I'll see you in an hour,' I say with confidence that I don't feel, then I leave her in the garage and head for the lift.

Turns out, Mina's concerns are not misplaced. The first part of the plan goes as smooth as you like – key in access code, press button for roof, then jump jump jump all the way to the

Primus's roof terrace, powered by the blood I drank on the journey – but when I reach the big double doors to the swimming pool, everything starts to go wrong.

Frank isn't picking up his phone. I paused on top of the adjacent building before jumping over here, watching until the last patrol passed by before making the final jump to the door. I've now been ringing Frank constantly for ten minutes, and if I hang around here much longer then not only will the distraction of the show's grand opening downstairs be over, but the patrol will also be coming around again. I can hear the speakers blasting out many floors below – Petunia wasn't lying when she said she could make it *loud* – but the volume is starting to reach its peak and I have to imagine the fireworks will be over soon. I know Frank said to wait for him, but I have a limited window and I don't have the energy to keep jumping back and forth until he finally decides to pick up the phone, so if I'm going to do this – and I *have* to do this – then I need to move now.

It's stupid and it's reckless but what choice do I have?

With so little left to lose, it feels like a no-brainer. I'm right about that, in the sense that it's a decision someone with no brain might have made, but I don't entirely realise that until I press the electronic key against the lock as directed, pull the door open and step inside. At which point my entire body begins to jerk and spasm, throwing me to the floor under what feels like a carpet of bees, but is actually an electrified net of some sadistic design. I guess this is the sting in the tail that Frank was talking about, but it would have helped if he'd been a bit more explicit.

Granted, he told me not to use the key without calling him, but my thinking was that since the lock released and the door opened, the infiltration had obviously worked, so maybe he'd already done what he needed to do without speaking to me. I don't think that's an unreasonable assumption. My current self hates my former self for making it – as I lie here on the floor being electrocuted into unconsciousness – but it's not *unreasonable*.

Really, all of this is Frank's fault.

I'm about to pass out when a pair of fancy shiny shoes comes into view and the terrible buzzing finally stops.

The Primus is looking down at me, hands on his hips holding his suit jacket open. From this angle, with his cold blue eyes floating so high above me, it's easy to see his resemblance to the godlike portrait on the ceiling of his temple.

I groan involuntarily. I've bitten my tongue while I was being fried and it stings like a bastard.

'Ms Valentine,' he says with an irritated sigh. 'Have you thought this through?'

'No,' I rasp out. 'Not really.'

'You do know that the minute my Tertius finds you here, he's going to kill you. I don't currently have any reason to stop him.'

'I wouldn't be here if I wasn't desperate,' I say, still immobile on the floor. The words come out broken and gasping and kind of slurred. 'I need to see him. Please.'

'See whom, Ms Valentine?'

'You know *whom*.'

'I have my suspicions. I imagine that you're referring to my Baron of Oxford, correct?'

'He's not *your* baron.' I try to snap the words out, but instead I'm just drooling blood onto the floor.

'Centuries of tradition would beg to differ. But am I to understand that you prefer to think of him as *your* baron, Ms Valentine? What a fascinating reversal.'

'No. What are you talking about?'

I'm too fried to follow his train of thought. In fact, I think I might pass out after all.

Amazingly, the Primus takes pity and lifts the net off me, throwing it into a heap in by the door as though it's made of gossamer instead of thick copper so heavy that its weight has to be intended as part of the trap. Unfortunately, even once relieved of it, I still can't seem to stand up. The Primus walks away, heading downstairs to his penthouse, and at first I think: *This is where he calls Benedict and puts at end to this futile mission once and for all.* But only a second or two after I hear his footsteps going downstairs, I hear them coming right back up again, and then he's propping me up and holding a bottle of blood to my lips.

If you'd told me last month that not only would Mina be nursing me back to health, but that the *Primus* would be doing it as well... It's a shocker, is what it is.

'Better?' he asks once I've drained the bottle.

'Yes, thank you.'

And I am. I can sit up on my own, even get to my feet and shuffle along like an invalid. It's embarrassing, but not as embarrassing as lying on the floor like a lemon.

'You're welcome,' he says. 'Perhaps you'd like to join me downstairs, where we can sit more comfortably?'

I wasn't expecting the charm offensive, and I don't trust it, particularly given that I not only tried to kill him that one time, but I also just broke into his home and should be far from welcome. I can only imagine that his hospitality is intended to put me off balance, but why? If he wanted me under his control, all he had to do was leave me on the floor to slip into a coma. Either he was doing me a kindness by reviving me – unlikely in the circumstances – or I need to be conscious for whatever he wants to happen next, which is a far from comforting thought. Maybe he wants information. Maybe he wants my loyalty. Or maybe he just wants to watch me squirm. One thing is for certain: I can't let my guard down just because, for the moment, he seems friendly.

I follow him down the curving glass and metal staircase – far too slippery and shiny for my current state – until the penthouse opens up beneath us, and then I have to take a moment to steady myself because the place is obscene. And I mean *obscene*. The open space I can see takes up about half of the area of the floor, and it's a building with a sizeable footprint, so we're talking serious square footage. One corner forms a high-tech kitchen that I'm sure sees no use at all, another is the dining area for said kitchen, which could comfortably seat twenty, the third is filled with comfy-looking sofas and an open fire – an *open fire*, in a modern penthouse apartment, as though that's a perfectly normal thing to have in the middle of the city on the god-knows-what floor – and the final corner is filled with towering bookcases that remind me of the library in the cartoon version of Beauty and the Beast. And yes, there is a rolling ladder. Of course there is because, like I said, the place is obscene.

Who needs this much space and this much stuff and this much grandeur, topped off with an indoor swimming pool on the top floor? Only a man who thinks he's a vampire king and, sometimes, a god.

Obscene.

When I've gathered my chin back off the floor and struggled my way down the remaining stairs, the Primus directs me to an irritatingly inviting loveseat in the massive sunken seating area. I have to navigate a couple more steps to reach it, which nearly ends in disaster, and I end up falling into the seat more than sitting in it. Once I'm safely ensconced in squishy comfort, I want nothing more than to close my eyes and sleep for a year, but I'm here for a reason and the Primus clearly isn't done talking yet. He takes a seat in the armchair across from my loveseat and leans forwards with his elbows resting on his knees, giving me an appraising look.

'I'm here for Drake,' I say, before he can start the interrogation.

'Oh yes,' he says. 'The baron. When I referred to your fascinating reversal earlier, you realise I was simply surprised by your abrupt transfer of affections.'

I did not realise. In fact, I'm still struggling to follow him.

'When we last met at New Year – while you were trying to murder me, if I remember correctly – you were very firmly attached to Ms Ladipo,' he goes on, 'and yet only minutes later, she apparently died by your hand. Baron Drake would have me believe that you took such action to protect me, and he is prepared to swear to that as the only witness to the event, but we both know that isn't quite the truth, don't we, Ms Valentine?'

'Do you want me to apologise?'

'Not particularly. I am curious, though. When I suggested that you rethink your affiliations to Ms Ladipo, I didn't think you'd take such drastic and immediate action.'

I don't want to talk about this. I've been hoping that the burning I've been feeling in my veins since I got here was just the after-effects of the electrocution, and in a way I suppose it is, since that probably sped the process up, but the fire is creeping up on me and I don't have time to sit around raking over ancient history.

'I need to see him,' I say. 'Please. I'm begging you. You can box me if you want – I don't care – just please, let me see him first.'

'I have little interest in locking you up,' he says, brushing invisible lint from his knee.

'But I tried to kill you.'

I shouldn't be arguing, but old habits die hard. Harder than the rest of me, apparently.

'And are you planning on doing so again?' he asks.

'No.'

'A happy conclusion for us both, then. Believe me, if I imprisoned every Silver who had tried to murder me, there would not be enough boxes in the world to contain them all. Besides, I find you rather entertaining.'

'*Entertaining*?'

'I mean no disrespect. But perhaps I begin to understand Baron Drake's fascination with you. Or should I say: obsession?'

'Then will you let me see him?' I ask, for the third time, now with added desperation. 'I'll do whatever you want, just please—'

'Whatever I want? A dangerous offer, Ms Valentine, when you are apparently unfamiliar with my appetites.'

'I don't care. Will you just let me see him?'

'If it were within my power, then yes, I probably would,' he says, and it sounds as though this surprises even him. 'But the point is moot: he's not here.'

If I had the energy, I would scream.

'Then where is he?'

'I'm not his keeper.'

I think I'm going to cry. I came all this way, I took all these risks, and he's not even here. Unless...

'I don't believe you,' I say. 'He has to be here.'

'What possible reason would I have to lie to you?' the Primus asks, his tone one of fascinated interest rather than offence. He's staring at me, his ice-cold eyes glinting. I can see him trying to get inside my head. He wants to discover how I work.

'You took him to lure me here,' I say, because my brain is frazzled and my first theory is the only thing that comes to mind.

'For what purpose, Ms Valentine? As I've already told you, I have no interest in your confinement.'

'But the Invicti—'

'Have no particular reason to believe that Baron Drake would be suitable as bait for you. They tell me there was some liaison between the two of you between our first meeting and our last, but as far as they're concerned, you're just another of the baron's many flings. And that is all you are, is it not? Unless there's something more to it...' He raises an eyebrow, inviting disclosures that I refuse to give.

'No,' I say. 'Of course not.'

'Well, then,' he replies, but there's a glint in his eye that says he knows I'm lying.

He *knows*. I'm not sure how he worked it out, but he knows about the bond. For fuck's sake. Can anything else go wrong today?

'And you're not pissed off with Drake?' I ask.

'About what?' He smiles with bemusement.

'About him killing a bunch of boxed Silver, or defending me?'

'No. Should I be?'

'No.'

'Then I'm surprised you raised the subject. And if you will excuse me for saying so, Ms Valentine, you don't look entirely well.'

'Yeah, no shit. I've just been electrocuted.'

'No, it's something more than that.'

Now we're getting into seriously dangerous territory. If the Primus has worked out that Drake has silvered for me – and I'm terrified that he's done exactly that – then confessing to this me-dying-from-poisoned-blood situation could seriously jeopardise Drake's safety. If he wanted Drake gone, the Primus could just let me die. But on the other hand, we're both going to die anyway without Khalyed's blood, which I'm clearly not going to be able to retrieve myself at this point. Time is running out.

What do I have to lose?

'When I killed Winta,' I say, 'the syringe broke and cut my hand.'

'So you're dying,' he says, without needing any further explanation.

'Yes. I have someone who can make a cure—'

He raises an eyebrow at that, so I think he's guessed who.

'—but I need a clean sample of Dr Jay Khalyed's blood to do that, and I don't have one. I'm hoping you do, and that you'll give it to me, because otherwise I have maybe a couple of weeks left if I'm lucky. Probably less after your electric net.'

So there it is. Everything's out on the table. I've entreated the vampire god for benevolence, and I await his prophecy.

For a few seconds, he does nothing but look me directly in the eyes. It's disconcerting, but maybe that's the point. When he finally snaps out of it, he does so with an abruptness that makes me jump. His gaze is so hypnotising, I think I nearly fell asleep for a moment there.

'I propose an exchange,' he says.

'Wuh?'

'I have a problem that perhaps you might help me solve,' he says. 'Two of my Invicti seem to have absconded, and I'd like you to help me find them.'

'*Seem*?' I ask. 'Don't you know?'

'Ha,' he laughs, but condescendingly, as though he's indulging a favourite child. 'Despite what you might have been led to believe, I am not omniscient, Ms Valentine.'

Omniscient.

The word again conjures up the temple beneath Solomon College, the giant portrait on the soaring ceiling, the cold blue eyes that followed me around the room, and that are watching me now in person.

'No,' he says. 'My Invicti are, of course, free to leave my

service should they so desire, at any time they wish. They are not prisoners here. However, I suspect that these two have taken something of mine with them, and I would like it back.'

'What?'

'Later,' he says. 'First, we should discuss terms.'

'I don't know why you think I'll be able to find them if you can't,' I say, and I can't help but notice that I've started slurring again. I guess one bottle of blood wasn't enough to counteract the frying.

'Because I can't be seen to interfere,' he says. 'I do, in fact, already know where they are. A mutual friend tracked them down. He's on his way up to brief you, in fact.'

'A mutual...'

The lift pings at the far end of the floor, in a part of the penthouse that's walled off from view behind the dining area. I look in that direction, but I'm moving with strange slowness, as though I'm turning in treacle, and by the time my target comes into view I can make out the blurry figure of a tall, blond-haired angel lolloping in my direction, and that's about it. I blink a few times to try to clear my vision, but it doesn't help, and I finally realise I'm in trouble.

What did he put in that blood?

'Cam,' I breathe, then I pass out in the loveseat.

For fuck's sake. It's becoming an irritatingly frequent habit.

28

WHEN I COME back to consciousness, it takes me a moment to orient myself. As it turns out, I'm still in the Primus's penthouse, lying on his sofa with my head in Cam's lap, wrapped up in a blanket so thick and cosy that I'm tempted to pretend I'm still asleep. That isn't the only reason to pretend unconsciousness, of course; I'm deep in the lair of the enemy and should be coming up with a plan to escape, though somehow the call of the blanket feels more urgent right now.

The pretending-to-sleep trick doesn't work with the Silver, though. They hear my pulse notch up before I ever open my eyes.

'Welcome back, Ms Valentine,' the Primus says. He's sitting in an armchair on the other side of the coffee table, his elbows resting on its arms and his hands steepled under his chin like a supervillain. 'I trust you had a pleasant nap.'

I try to sit up too quickly, and the room starts spinning. Cam catches me before I fall down again.

'You bastard,' I splutter. 'You drugged me.' Though it comes out more like *Oobagutoodugee*, so maybe it's not a surprise that neither of them seems to understand me.

'Easy, Jack,' Cam says, holding a bottle of warm blood to my lips.

He helps me finish the bottle, and by that point I'm strong enough to sit up unaided. I take the blanket with me, because although the blood in my veins feels like it's boiling, my skin is unaccountably cold.

'You drugged me,' I say to the Primus, with more clarity this time.

'You appeared to be in need of the rest,' he replies.

'You *drugged* me. Why does everyone keep doing that?'

'I can't speak for anyone else, but for my own part, I did it in order to avoid having you encounter those members of my Invicti with whom you are less than friendly.'

'And you couldn't just have asked?' I say, furious now. 'Does no one just *ask* anymore?'

'When the individual concerned is possibly hostile? No.'

Well, fair enough, I suppose. 'It's still a shitty thing to do,' I say.

'For which I apologise. And now, perhaps you need a stronger drink.' He gets to his feet and crosses the room – I hesitate to call it a "room" because it's more like an aircraft hangar – to the kitchen. There's some clanking, but I'm too tired to turn my neck to watch, so instead I rest my head on Cam's shoulder and let myself relax into his familiar scent.

'You should have come sooner,' he whispers, pulling me into a hug.

'You know why I couldn't,' I whisper back.

'So you've let yourself get right up to death's door before asking for help? Actually, I don't know why I'm surprised. That sounds like exactly what you'd do. Why do you smell of… nothing at all?'

'Secret.'

I hear a faint buzz of static, then a tinny voice coming from too far away for me to make out the words. Cam sits up to attention, shrugging me from his shoulder, and I realise he's wearing an earpiece.

'Yes, sir,' he says, pressing a button on his shirt cuff as he speaks. Casual Cam is wearing a long-sleeved, dark, smart shirt. I never thought I'd see the day, but apparently he's willing to make any number of sacrifices to be in the Invicti. 'I'll look into it,' he says, then he turns to me and says, 'I think you've got a friend on the roof.'

Mina. Fuck.

'I promised I'd be in and out in under an hour,' I say.

'Ambitious,' says the Primus, returning to the sofa with a mug, which he puts down on the coffee table next to me. It's steaming liberally and it smells like chocolatey, sugary, bloody heaven. 'For you, Ms Valentine. No drugs, I promise, unless you count cocoa.'

I try to get up to go to Mina's rescue, but my legs aren't quite there yet.

'I'll deal with it,' says Cam, getting to his feet. 'You drink. Who exactly am I expecting up there?'

'Mina.' I wince.

'Mina *Parchek*?' he says, horrified. Cam and I worked a lot of cases together during which Mina not only failed to cooperate, but often actively disrupted our investigations, so I can understand his consternation. 'Please tell me you're not sleeping with her again.'

'Cam!' I cut my eyes to the Primus, urging Cam to shut up.

'You are, aren't you?' he whispers, as though the Primus won't still be able to hear every word.

'That is absolutely none of your business—'

'Oh god.'

'—but no, I'm not.'

I can hear thumping on the glass doors upstairs now. It sounds like Mina is trying to break her way inside, but either she's unwilling to push her luck quite that far or the glass is Silver-proofed, because I don't hear any shattering. I can, however, hear a muffled voice screaming, 'Give her back, you bastards!'

'Just go and let her in, will you?' I say to Cam.

'I'd rather he didn't,' the Primus says. 'But I will explain to Ms Parchek that you are well and will be leaving the premises in, oh, say fifteen minutes' time?'

'Yes, sir,' Cam says. 'Thank you, sir.'

'Then I'll leave the two of you to catch up,' he says. 'If you have any further need of me, I'll be upstairs.'

I wait until he's gone to say, '*Yes, sir*,' mimicking Cam childishly. '*Thank you, sir.*'

'Jack!' Cam glances up the staircase and gestures for me to hush. 'He is the *Primus*.'

'I'm aware. Are you really so in awe of him that you told him about me and Drake?'

'What? No! Of course not. I haven't told anyone,' he says, lowering his voice to a whisper. 'And I wouldn't. You know that, Jack. I promised.'

'Well, he's found out from someone, and you're the only one of the Invicti who knows about it.'

Cam shrugs. 'He probably worked it out for himself. You and the baron do tend to get a little...' He makes a weird fluttery gesture with his hands that I can't interpret.

'A bit *what*?'

'A bit, you know. Fizzy. He probably picked up on that. He's the Primus. He has the power.'

'*Fuck.*'

I put my head in my hands then reach for my bloody hot chocolate, because I need the strength. After one slurp, I feel refreshed. After two, I feel strong. After three, I start to wonder if maybe the Primus was lying about not drugging the stuff because I feel pretty fucking amazing.

I squint at the mug suspiciously and Cam says, 'It's just blood and hot chocolate. I'd smell it if there was anything else in there.'

'Hmm.' I'm not convinced, but I drain it anyway.

'Your secret's safe with me,' Cam says. 'And with the Primus.'

'Really?' I scoff. 'You don't think he'll abuse that knowledge, just like he abuses every other privilege he has?'

'Jack. Be realistic. You tried to kill him, and you're sitting here in his private penthouse on his private sofa with a cup of blood and hot chocolate in your hands that he made for you himself. Even if he doesn't always play fair, I'd say this time it's working in your favour. Wouldn't you?'

'I guess I looked too pitiful to victimise.'

Cam shakes his head and sits back. 'You don't understand: no one gets to come to the Primus's private rooms. I've never been here. I'd bet money that not even Drew has sat on this sofa before, and he's the Secundus.'

'Well. I—' I don't know if that makes my situation better or worse, but I know I don't like it. 'What am I supposed to take from that?'

'I don't know,' Cam says. 'He's fonder of Baron Drake than the others would like him to be. Maybe he likes you too.'

'Because I'm Drake's pet?'

'Because you're you,' Cam nudges me gently with his shoulder, then he looks me over, and doesn't seem to like what he sees. 'You're still not looking great. Is that why you're here? Are you turning yourself in so Ed can help you?'

'No,' I say. 'Sort of. Why? Can he?'

'Um.' I can tell from Cam's face that the news isn't going to be good. 'Ed hasn't been working on a cure for Dr Jay's blood, Jack. He's been working on a cure for the first generation serum, the one that Kayode Ladipo took. And he's found it.'

'He has?'

'Yep. Dr Kay's in the middle of his first course of treatment right now. By the end of the month, he'll be good as new.'

'Then surely that means he'll be able to cure me too?' I say, hope making my voice rise.

Cam looks down at his hands.

'I guess not,' I say.

'He says there's something weird about Dr Jay's blood, that it's messed with the second generation serum and turned it into something new.' That tallies with what Tabitha told me. 'He needs to analyse a pure sample of Dr Jay's blood to create a cure for you.'

'Look, that's partly why I'm here,' I say. 'I don't need to bother Ed, because I've got someone who can make me a cure. I just need Khalyed's blood, and I need Drake. I thought maybe you guys had locked him up in your basement.'

'What?' Cam looks beyond confused. 'He's missing too? Why would you think we have him?'

'I wouldn't put it past Benedict. It would be a good way to draw me out of hiding, get me to bust into Solis Invicti HQ to bust Drake out, and save him the trouble of finding me himself. But the Primus says I'm wrong.'

'Jack,' he says, giving me a frank look. 'You think I'd let Ben kidnap the baron to lure you out, when I could have found you at any time?'

'You would have turned me in to *Benedict*?' I say, horrified.

'No! But I would have at least tracked you down to warn you about it.'

'Wait,' I say. My brain has finally caught up with

something he said earlier. 'What do you mean *too*? Who else is missing?'

'Dr Jay Khalyed.'

'What?' Now I'm really panicking. 'I thought Khalyed was in your basement too. But Ed must have some of his blood samples, and if he could just give me a few, or just one would do it, then—'

'About that...' Cam says, rubbing at the back of his neck. 'Remember when I came to warn you about Adewale Ladipo? Well, I don't know if it has anything to do with Baron Drake's disappearance, but Ed is pretty sure Adewale's the one who's taken all the samples of Dr Jay's blood from our lab, and it looks like he also took Dr Jay out of Baron Drake's basement.'

It takes several long seconds for me to process this. I've burned a couple of my last precious hours breaking into Solis Invicti HQ, and neither Drake nor Khalyed nor any of Khalyed's blood is here. I'm going to leave empty-handed.

'Why would Adewale do that?' I ask. 'If his father's cured...'

'Adewale's father was Dr Jay's closest friend in the world,' Cam says softly. He looks as though he's going to cry. 'After what Dr Jay did to Kayode Ladipo, he doesn't want to be cured. He thinks he's nothing but a danger to us all. He wants to be destroyed, along with all trace of the lethal blood in his veins. We think Adewale and Alistair are going to do it for him.'

No.

If all the samples from Drake's mansion are gone, and all the samples from Ed's lab are gone, and Khalyed himself is gone...

There'll be no hope of a cure, ever.

'That's not actually possible, though, is it?' I ask. 'They can't destroy the blood. That's what makes it so deadly.'

'Ed's worried that Alistair might have found a way to make it happen. It would explain why Adewale took all the blood samples from the lab.'

'For testing?' I ask hopefully. 'The development process will take a while though, right?'

'They've had a while,' Cam says.

Fuck.

Fuck fuckity fucking fuck fuck.

There are not enough fucks in the world for how fucked I am.

And Drake. Oh god, Drake.

Then I remember the exchange the Primus promised me, and I get a horrible sinking feeling.

'The Primus said I could have Khalyed's blood if I helped him track down a couple of rogue Invicti,' I say. 'He's talking about Adewale and Alistair, isn't he?'

'Yes.'

'So he's not actually intending to help me at all.'

'No.'

'He just expects me to go out and help myself.'

'Yes.'

'You know what? That's a really wanky, pretentious, *I'm an omnipotent and benevolent deity who believes in free will* kind of bullshit trick to pull.'

Cam just shrugs, which I take as tacit agreement.

'So are you going to help me get them back?' I ask.

'No,' he says shamefacedly, 'but I think I know where they've gone.'

'You're really not going to come with me?' I ask incredulously.

'I can't, Jack. I'm sorry.'

From which I gather that he's been ordered not to help me. The Primus has a lot to answer for. Seriously, spare me from immortal Silver bastards with a god complex. Here I am, literally dying on my feet, and instead of helping me to save my life and the life of the man I... sometimes fancy, he's not only making me do all the work, he's forbidding my best friend from helping me.

Well, I'll show him. If he wants to be a manipulative, supercilious control freak then he can go fuck himself. I can manage just fine on my own.

Priority one: find Khalyed and make the cure.

Priority two: find Drake and live happily ever after.

I mean— Jesus Christ, where did that come from? Forget I even thought that. What was in that hot chocolate?

When I walk upstairs to let myself out of the glass doors and onto the roof, the sun is setting outside, sending shafts of warm yellow, orange and pink light into the indoor pool. The Primus is doing laps. While I'm crossing the room from the stairwell to the doors, he reaches the wall and hauls himself out of the water, turning to sit on the edge in one smooth movement that's so graceful it feels balletic. As he turns, drops of water spray away and make rainbows of the evening light, spreading out in arcs of colour from his pale body like light refracting through crystal. He is poised and beautiful and terrifying; more than human, more than Silver, more otherworldly than any living creature I have ever seen. Behind the glass of the penthouse, he's like distilled sunshine. In that moment, I can understand why some of the Silver still worship him as their god.

And he's staring straight at me.

'I'll see you again soon, Ms Valentine,' he says, and his words have the heft of prophecy. I find them oddly comforting, because despite the burning in my blood and the pain in my limbs, he speaks with such authority that I have no doubt that he's right.

I will find Khalyed. I will find a cure. I will find Drake.

And I will see the Primus again when this is over, so we

JOSIE JAFFREY

can settle the score.

260

29

WHEN I GET back to the garage where I left Mina, not only is she gone, but her car is too. I check the burner phone Frank gave me – some fucking good that did me – and she's sent me a message.

Primus ordered me back to Oxford on pain of death. Sorry. You're on your own. Good luck.

For someone who's apparently so fond of me and Drake, it's weird how much the Primus wants me to fail. Maybe this is a test to see how well I can perform under pressure, or maybe he's just a god playing with me like I'm a chess piece he can control at his whim, impersonally curious to see what will happen next. Whatever the reason for this ridiculous set up, I'm determined to beat it. I'm feeling stronger than I have any right to feel after being thoroughly zapped by his stupid booby trap, and hopefully I'll be feeling even better within the hour.

The location Cam gave me isn't far away. It's so close, in fact, that I could speed-run there in less than a minute, but I'm trying to conserve my energy, so I pull my wallet out of my backpack full of toys and take the tube instead. Not many of the machines take cash anymore, but I can't leave a trail by using a card – from what I've heard, Alistair's good enough to track them – so I take the time to find one that takes my coins, then bomb along the London Underground, crossing the river and travelling so far south that I'm out of the gentrified, fancy beard-wearing, cronut-eating suburbs into the parts of the city that are too grotty to be worth redeveloping. The houses here are a mix of new concrete high-rises and damp old terraces, all painted a sooty grey from the traffic that proliferates along the capital's main rail and road arteries. I'm heading to one of the miscellaneous mid-height buildings: box-shaped, four storeys, sealed windows, bars across the glass, tucked down a series of side streets so filled with rubbish that they reek in the burgeoning summer heat. I don't want to be here, but apparently no one else does either, so my journey through the lamplit streets is uneventful.

Cam told me he picked up a scent in this area earlier today, then he tracked down property records that show a lease of this building to A Jameson Ltd, so here I am to break in to Alistair and Adewale's not-so-secret hideaway, my second break-and-enter of the day. Hopefully this one will be more successful than the first.

The front door is locked. Not surprising really, but irritating. Every delay makes my skin itch a little more. It's not as bad I as expected it to be by this stage, but I can still feel the burn.

I consider breaking the glass, but I want to make a quiet entry – if Cam's right and Adewale and Alistair are inside, then even if they are a couple of floors down like he says, they'll easily hear me if I start smashing windows – and the lock on the front door looks impregnable. Instead, I slide around the side of the building, quite literally in some places because the alley is packed with vehicles and junk, and find an access ramp that leads down to a garage roller door. It's padlocked down to a metal loop in the concrete, but that's easy enough to break with even a modest application of Silver strength. Then all that remains is to lift the roller door as smoothly and quietly as I can, and slip inside.

At which point my carefully-laid plans go to shit, for the umpteenth time today. Suffice it to say that whoever's been maintaining this building has been doing a shit job of greasing the runners of the garage door because the whole thing screeches and creaks like a car crash at the tiniest bit of pressure. At that point I think, *Fuck it*, and just charge inside. I'm all in anyway, so why bother with stealth?

Turns out, I needn't have worried. I'm expecting to be greeted by two furious Invicti on the defensive, but instead there's just a concrete loading bay filled with old pallets and abandoned packaging. I guess this must have been a warehouse once upon a time, but now it's mostly empty. There's water standing in the corners of the room and the whole place smells of mould and neglect. It's the same story on the upper floors, which I search and find empty except for a few bits of broken office furniture and some mildewed carpet, and the lower ground floor, which is much like the loading bay where I came in. Things only get interesting on the very bottom floor, where a brand new electronic lock has been installed on an otherwise boring orange door at the bottom of the stairwell. It's too sophisticated for me to pick, so I call Frank, but he still doesn't pick up. I hope the party he's at is worth it, because he's going to get an earful when I get home.

Brute force it is.

I pull the forgotten tranquilliser gun out of my backpack and use the butt to smash the lock's keypad to smithereens. This makes me feel better, but doesn't actually open the door. I'm stumped for a moment, then I decide to slam my shoulder into the door next to the lock and just see what happens. To my surprise, the door opens, so widely and so quickly that I end up flat on my face on the floor beyond. It takes me a second or two to pick myself up again, which is the same amount of time that it takes me to realise that the door unlocked because someone opened it, not because of my door-breaking skills. The thing is made from fortified metal several inches thick, whereas I am a poisoned Silver with rapidly-diminishing strength. A padlock is one thing, but a blast door is quite another.

'Hello,' says the man who is now holding the door open for me.

It takes me a while to recognise him, because he doesn't look the same as when I saw him in his box. Not at all. Back then, his skin was bleached to a sandy brown and threaded with green veins full of rotten blood, his cheeks were sunken into his face and his eyes were glued shut with bloody tears. When he finally opened them, the intelligence behind them was feral and sharp, causing him to snap his teeth and growl at us for several long moments before his self-control returned. Now, he is nothing but control. His skin is still paler than its natural shade, but the blood running in his veins looks like a normal colour. Whatever else Adewale Ladipo has been doing to Khalyed, he's been treating him well. If it wasn't for the fact that he's still wearing his old lab coat and suit, I'm not sure I'd recognise him at all.

'Dr Khalyed?' I ask cautiously. I'm not going to forget the way he lunged and snarled at me the last time I saw him.

'Ah,' he says pleasantly. 'The blood thief. My eyes were not up to much at the time, but I recognise your voice.'

'You remember that?'

'Parts of me do. Come in, why don't you?'

He ushers me into the room and lets the door swing shut behind us with an ominous *clunk*. There's a beep, and then I see the keypad on the inside of the door.

'Is that locked now?' I ask, starting to panic.

'Oh, yes,' he says unconcernedly.

Okay, now I'm really panicking. I know I'm already infected and at death's door anyway, but the thought of being stuck in what turns out to be a twelve-foot-square concrete box with a blood-hungry Silver is slightly terrifying. Khalyed doesn't look very scary, though, and he becomes even less so as he offers me the cell's single plastic chair – which I refuse – while he rambles gently on.

'They wouldn't like to think that I could open it on my own,' he says, 'but they were a little careless with the code when they thought I wasn't able to hear and... Well. Sweet boys, but they do occasionally let themselves get distracted by their bickering.'

'*Sweet boys?*' I repeat incredulously. 'They've got you trapped down here in a cell and you think they're *sweet boys?*'

'They're only trying to help, you know. Oh,' he cocks his ear towards the door, 'here they are now.'

There's an earsplitting screech and a crash of metal and masonry, and the door falls inwards. I have to jump out of the way to avoid having it hit me.

'You could have knocked,' Khalyed chastises gently. 'I would have let you in.'

'What are you doing here?'

This is directed at me by Adewale, and his tone is not friendly. When Cam was warning me about him, I just waved away his concerns, but now that we're sharing the same air again I abruptly remember how imposing he is in person. It takes me right back to the moment he cornered me at Drake's mansion last year, when it felt as through he was spring-loaded. Now, oddly, he seems to have mellowed.

'What am *I* doing here?' I ask. 'What are *you* doing here with Dr Khalyed? You know the Primus is looking for him, right?'

'And he sent you to find us?' Adewale asks sceptically, then he walks past me as though I am irrelevant and joins his friend Alistair, who's helping Khalyed sit down in the chair.

'You got it?' Khalyed croaks.

It's only then that I see how frail he still is. He was hiding it well, but it looks as though he's even more wobbly that I am.

'We've got it,' Alistair says gently, then he crouches down at Khalyed's feet and opens the small ice chest he carried in with him.

'Got what?' I ask.

They all ignore me. Honestly, it's a bit insulting. When you go to the trouble of breaking into someone's secret underground lair, you really expect a bit more attention. When I went to the Dregs' hideout, I got a tour. When I tried to break into the Primus's, I got a whole electric net routine, and a bloody hot chocolate to boot. Here, I'm not even getting a second glance.

'And you're sure it'll work?' Khalyed asks Alistair.

'We're sure, Dr Jay,' Adewale says.

'We already sorted the rest,' says Alistair.

Khalyed sighs and relaxes back in his chair as though the weight of a hundred years has just been lifted from his shoulders, saying, 'You're good lads.'

'I don't forget my promises,' says Adewale.

Khalyed reaches out and takes Adewale's hand in his then squeezes it firmly, conveying some meaning that I don't understand. Then Alistair lifts a syringe from the cooler and I start to get an inkling.

'Hey, wait—' I say, but the needle is already in Khalyed's arm, the plunger depressed, the load delivered.

'If you came to steal more of his blood,' Adewale says, his eyes never leaving Khalyed's face, 'then you're too late.'

'What did you do?' I ask, horrified.

Khalyed smiles at Alistair and Adewale in turn. His skin is turning pink, then orange, then there's a pop of flame so hot it burns white, and in the blink of an eye Khalyed is nothing but ashes and memories.

'It's what he wanted,' says Adewale.

I'm left gaping at the piles of ash on the chair, on the floor, in Adewale's hand, unable to believe what's just happened.

I missed my window. He was right there, with all the blood I needed for a cure pumping around his veins, and now it's gone along with the rest of Khalyed. It's all gone.

It happened so quickly.

'What?' I ask, struggling to come up with much else.

'He lived that way a long time, Ms Valentine,' says Alistair, quietly gathering the ashes into an urn he takes out of the cooler. 'He didnae want to live any more, nor did he want his blood to be used as a weapon.'

'Again,' Adewale chips in.

'So I made a cure, of sorts, that pushes the serum over the edge and makes it kind of burn itself out. You saw for yourself: he didnae suffer, it was over so quick.'

'I was keeping a promise to an old friend,' Adewale says when he sees me gaping.

'The other samples?' I ask, finally finding my words.

'You mean the blood the Invicti and Baron Drake both extracted from Dr Jay?' says Alistair. 'He wanted it all to be destroyed. He wanted it to be over. He didnae set out to make a poison when he made the stuff all those years ago, and before he said his goodbyes he wanted to know his legacy would die with him.'

'But, you see, it didn't,' I say snappily, 'because I've got it inside me, and by killing Khalyed, you effectively just killed me. So, thanks for that.'

'What?' Alistair says.

'Maybe that was your intention though, right?' I ask, rounding on Adewale. Now that the shock has worn off, the words are building up behind my teeth and pouring out in a relentless, vitriolic stream. 'I get it: you want me dead. Join the fucking club. And sure, I killed Winta, but you do know she was no angel, right? She killed people. A bunch of people. I'm sorry it happened the way it did and I'd be lying if I said I didn't wake myself up screaming some nights with nightmares about how she died – how *I killed her* – but I didn't feel like I had a choice in that moment, and I'm not going to apologise for making the one I did. And, by the way, if you'd bothered to wait a second, or even ask why I was here, then I would have told you that I have a cure lined up, actually, not that you probably give a flying fuck about my life, but did you ever even try to save Khalyed's instead of just sending him up in smoke?'

'He didn't want a cure,' Alistair says, but he's looking worried. 'You're... infected?'

He takes a step backwards, and I mark him down as the coward of this duo. I take a step forwards to match his, and he's now stuck in the corner, so he'll have to go past me to leave this room. I'm not actually planning to do anything about that – I'm angry, but I'm not stupid enough to forget that I'm in no state to be fighting – but I enjoy the way his eyes widen, just a little, as though I've made him think twice about his assessment of me.

'I'm not looking for revenge, Ms Valentine,' Adewale says, stepping between the two of us. 'In fact, I'm grateful.'

'*Grateful?*'

'I knew my sister,' he says. 'I loved her, but I knew what she was.'

'Then why didn't you tell me?' I ask desperately. I'm feeling hopeless and I want to blame someone else, anyone else, for what happened on that rooftop. 'Back when you came to see me last year, you told me she wanted Khalyed's blood to cure your father, not to use as a weapon. You didn't tell me what she'd done. If you'd told me—'

'You wouldn't have believed me,' he says, 'any more than you believed me about the other things I told you that day. I told you that I only wanted to protect her from herself, and that was true. I wanted to bring her in before she could do any more harm, perhaps even find a way to heal her, so she wouldn't feel the need to feed the way she did. But if that hadn't worked, I would have killed her myself.'

'Your own sister?' I whisper.

'She made me what I am, Ms Valentine, just as she made you, but neither of us has to follow the path she led us down. We can choose to be different. I made that choice, and I would not have compromised my morality for her. Better her death than the deaths of hundreds of others. So yes, I'm grateful that you spared me the necessity of killing my sister and my sire.'

'You've got a funny way of showing it,' I say.

He might not be looking for revenge, but I'm feeling pretty vengeful myself right now.

I'm dead. They've killed us: me and Drake and all hopes of our future. I think it's that last thing that pisses me off the most.

'Where's Drake?' I ask.

The two of them exchange a confused look.

'*Baron* Drake?' Alistair asks. 'He's missing?'

'You already told me you knew he took Khalyed's blood. I guess that pissed you off and you decided to teach him a lesson, so you snatched him and stashed him... in another room somewhere?' I ask speculatively, but I didn't see any more doors on this floor, and the looks on their faces are making me concerned. Neither of them seems to know what

I'm talking about. 'You don't have him here?'

'We don't have him at all,' says Adewale.

'And I'm just supposed to believe you?'

'Yes. Why would I lie about that? Dr Jay gave his blood to the baron willingly. He knew what he intended to do with it and considered it a good cause. It was only later, when he'd had a chance to imagine what would happen if it got into the wrong hands, that he began to regret that decision.'

'He held no ill will towards the baron,' Alistair says, driving the point home.

'Then maybe you took him to get back at me?' I suggest to Adewale.

He just shakes his head in confusion while Alistair says, 'Why?'

They don't know. They really don't know.

Abruptly, I am exhausted. I turn my back on them and the ashy little cell, and start climbing back up the stairs, but the going is slow. Now that I know there's no hope at all, I might as well take my time. Wherever Drake is, I can't help either of us now.

It's over.

30

I HAVE MAYBE a day and a half left, if I'm unlucky, and I don't know what to do with it. I know what I'd *like* to do, but I can't find Drake, so that's out, which leaves me at a loose end with nowhere to go.

This is the kind of thing I should really have planned in advance. It's one of those questions people ask each other at three in the morning when even the late-opening pubs are starting to close up and half of the group you came out drinking with has either bailed for home or passed out under the table: *If you only had a few hours left to live, what would you do with them?*

I haven't given it much thought, and I'm too tired to think about it now. In the end, I hop back on the tube and get the last train from London Paddington back to Oxford. It feels right to end this where it started, even if it means wasting time with travelling. I make the most of it by calling Mina on the way on the burner phone.

'Total failure in every respect,' I say when she picks up. 'Khalyed's dead, his blood is all destroyed, and I can't find Drake. I'm fucked.'

'Hello to you, too,' she says.

'I'm *dying*, Mina.'

She's either unwilling or unable to discuss that, because instead of giving me any reaction at all, she says, 'What happened at the fancy pants Solis Invicti building?'

I groan. I don't want to relieve my humiliation in detail, so I give her the short version: 'Got trapped by an electrified net, passed out, chatted with the Primus, passed out again, chatted with Cam, found Khalyed with Adewale, watched Khalyed go up in smoke, caught the train home. I'll be back in an hour.'

'Eventful night.'

'And completely pointless.'

'Did you say electrified net?'

'Yeah, bloody Frank,' I say. 'He told me to call him at eight when I was at the doors with the electronic key, and I called and called and he didn't answer, so I used the key, stepped inside, then got frazzled.'

'He didn't answer?' Mina says, sounding worried. 'That's not like him.'

'He said he was going to a party or something. I guess he decided that it was more important than me not dying.'

'That's not like him,' she says again. 'And after you left, I found his bag in the refectory. He must have left it there by accident, which *is* exactly like him, I know.' Frank is the world's most forgetful computer genius. 'But he never came back to collect it, and that isn't. Something's wrong.'

'He's only been gone a few hours,' I say reasonably. 'Maybe he just decided to collect it later.'

'It's got his laptop in it, Jack.'

'Okay,' I agree. 'Something's wrong.'

Frank not picking up the phone when I called was weird, but I haven't dwelt on it too much because, in case you haven't been paying attention, I've been a little busy this evening. But Frank would never – and I mean *never* – leave behind his laptop for more than five minutes at a time. He'd forget it, sure, but he has a near-symbiotic relationship with the thing, so he'd realise it was missing almost immediately and make sure he retrieved it. If his laptop is still in the refectory at the Dregs' hideout, then that's because Frank has somehow been physically prevented from going and getting it.

'What do you know about the party he was going to?' Mina asks.

'Not much.' I'm desperately trying to remember what he said exactly, but my famously-photographic memory only does images, not words. 'He'd met someone just before he arrived at the meeting earlier, and they invited him. He was chatting to someone outside the refectory.'

'You think a Dreg invited him?'

'It must have been. He was inside the complex when it happened and when I last saw Frank, he pretended he was on his way back to the refectory to fetch his keys, but I'm pretty sure he was heading off to find whoever invited him. We need a list of everyone who has access to that facility.'

'On it,' she says. 'I'll call you back.'

She does, eventually, but not until I've nervously chewed my way through all the remaining blood capsules in my backpack. The way the night – well, morning now – is going, I think I'll need all the energy I can get.

I pick up on the first ring.

'Well?'

'There's something you need to see,' she says. 'Check your messages.'

She's sent through a photo, but because this burner phone is some kind of antiquated, limited network piece of shit, it takes a million years to download. When it finally does, I say, 'Shitting fuck.'

'It's him, isn't it?' says Mina's tinny voice on the other

end of the line.

I hold the phone back up to my ear and ask, 'What was his name? Do you remember?'

'It's listed as Harry Carmichael on the systems here, but when he introduced himself to us he said his name was—'

'Mikey,' I finish. 'That sneaky little shit.'

'I told you he had a weird vibe.'

'You called it,' I admit.

In the photo Mina's sent me, he still has the same average brown hair and eyes I recognise from when he moved into Louise's old apartment earlier this year, but the flamboyant clothes and fingernails are gone. Instead, he's wearing plain dark fatigues with no adornment at all. It's like Mina said: when we first met, he was peacocking.

Well, it didn't work. I see him now.

'So the Dregs have a mole,' I say. 'Have you told them?'

'They're out looking for him now. But whatever he was trying to do by stopping Frank from disarming the Solis Invicti building for you, it must have backfired, right? You're here.'

'But when he invited Frank to that party, we hadn't even made the break-in plan yet,' I point out.

'So he's taken Frank for another reason.'

'Maybe related to the reason he moved in next door to me?' I suggest. 'I suppose he wasn't there by accident.'

'I doubt it. Remember how I said the bruises on Louise's neck were made by a man?'

'Oh shit.' After everything that's happened in the past few hours, I'd forgotten all about Louise and Faith and Mr Inman. 'That explains why I didn't pick up on a recurring scent, and why there was none except mine in Faith's apartment: Mikey was wearing the Dregs' scent-masking spray.'

'That would be my guess. And if he really is the Silver

whose hands match the prints on your neighbours' necks,' Mina says, 'then whatever he wants Frank for, it's not going to be good. The other post mortem reports came through.'

'And?'

'Their necks were both bruised. They were both injected with drugs – cocaine and opioids – but there was a broken needle in Faith's carotid. Looks like something went wrong when he was trying to drain her, and the needle snapped.'

'Hence the blood at the scene,' I say.

'Right.'

Poor Faith. If she hadn't had the misfortune to be living next door to me, she'd still be alive and well and living on her sugar daddy's millions.

'Mikey said something about a basement party room,' I say, remembering his invitation to me and Mina the night we met him. 'A soundproofed place by the river. Remember?'

'And?' Mina says. 'It was probably just a line to try to get you to…'

'Yeah, exactly: to what? None of this makes any sense.'

'Yet. I'll pull up everything I can find on him and see if I can make any connections, but honestly it's going to be harder without Frank's help.'

'All right. I'll be there in half an hour, forty-five minutes tops. Get Boyd and the others to help.'

'Jack, you know I don't play well with others.'

'I learned. You can too.'

'Fine,' she says like a petulant teenager, and then she hangs up and leaves me to finish my nervous train journey alone.

I'm out of the train station and rushing through town on foot – at a normal human speed, but a quick one – when the burner phone rings in my pocket.

'I'm on Park End Street,' I say breathlessly. 'I'll be at the door in five minutes. Ten tops.'

'Oh, I doubt that!' says the voice on the other end of the phone, which is definitely not Mina's. It's also incongruously cheerful.

'Mikey,' I say.

'I've got your friend!' He's talking so loudly that I have to hold the phone away from my face to avoid blowing out my eardrums.

There are only two people who have this number. One of them is Mina, who I know is safe with Boyd and the others right now, and the other has been missing since early this evening. It doesn't take a genius to work out whom he's referring to.

'Is Frank okay?' I ask. 'Can I speak to him?'

'Oh, right: I've got *two* of your friends!'

My stomach drops.

'Who's the other one?' I ask, but I already know.

'Tall, dark *and* handsome! We might disagree about a lot of things – because let's be honest, those boring black outfits you and the others wear are a complete snooze, and you wouldn't catch me *dead* in that rank leather jacket of yours – but I have to say, *Ophelia*, at least you have good taste in men, only of course this one actually isn't yours, is he? Well, not anymore obviously, since I have him chained up in my basement, but I mean, he never even was to begin with, and that's just a really shitty way to behave, you know? Do you not have any respect at all?'

I don't follow most of this, but I can just about tease out his central point.

'Are you telling me you have Drake?' I ask.

'*Drake*,' he says mockingly. 'This is exactly what I'm talking about, you know? The nerve, the gumption, the absolute fucking gall of you to be behaving like you have the right to call him that, or to call him anything at all! You know what? I've had it!'

The line goes dead, and I realise he's hung up on me, leaving me mostly in the dark. I gather that he has both Frank and Drake locked up in a basement somewhere, but as to the rest of his conversation, I'm pretty much clueless.

I stare at the phone for a second, then hit redial.

'What?' Mina answers. She sounds harried, and I can hear her footsteps echoing as she walks.

'I just got a very strange call from our kidnapper,' I say. 'I think he has Drake as well as Frank, and he's got Frank's phone.'

'Shit. I'd offer to do something clever to trace it, but without Frank—'

'We're fucked,' I finish for her. 'He mentioned a basement, so I guess we were on the right track with that. Did you manage to find any properties that would fit?'

'Nope.'

'Great. And I have no idea why he would have snatched Drake, so there's another mystery. I suppose he must have worked out that Drake was visiting me, because he said something about my taste in men—'

'Historically appalling,' Mina chimes in. 'I'd stick to women if I were you.'

'—but he seemed to be pissed off with me about it. I don't know. Maybe he has a crush on Drake. And Frank.'

'Maybe he's building some kind of Silver sex dungeon,' Mina suggests, and I wish she hadn't. 'I'm on my way to see a couple of the Dregs who were friendly with him. Give me two minutes and I'll call you back.'

I keep walking through the city centre as I wait for her call. There aren't many cars left on the road, but the night buses are running, ferrying a few tired passengers from street lamp to street lamp on their way home from late jobs, or off to work at early jobs. Oxford might be a small city, but some part of it is always awake.

Two minutes later, to the second, the phone rings again.

'Detour to the blood bar,' Mina says. 'Go speak to Carlotta Arden. She should be there.'

'Carlotta? What's she got to do with this?'

'Looks like this Mikey is some kind of deranged fan of hers. Apparently her security team had to get involved, and they've looked into him. She might be able to give you some info on possible locations.'

'You think Carlotta's the reason this is happening?'

'Well, you did sort of steal her fiancé, and some of these uber fans go off the deep end when shit like that happens. You're the Victor Laszlo to her Rick Blaine, you know?'

'I'm the who to her what?' I say, bewildered.

'Millennials,' she mutters. 'You're the Angelina Jolie to her Jennifer Aniston. He could be pissed off with you on her behalf, is what I'm saying.'

Oh no.

'Pissed off enough to hurt Drake?' I ask.

'Maybe,' Mina says thoughtfully. 'I don't know, though. Taking down a few humans is one thing, but the baron? Now that all Khalyed's blood is gone, I don't think it would be that easy to kill Baron Drake. And why would Mikey want to hurt him, anyway?'

'Well, if he thinks I stole Drake from Carlotta, then surely he'll be even more pissed off with Drake than he is with me. After all, *I* wasn't engaged to her. Drake's the one who committed to her and then broke it off. I don't owe her anything.'

'Oh, Jack,' Mina says. 'How little you understand fandom's rampant misogyny. You're the other woman. You're the vicious harpy who lured the poor, innocent, helpless baron away from poor, innocent, helpless Carlotta. It's always the woman's fault. Haven't you worked that out by now?'

'So you think he's doing this to get to me?'

'Likely, yes.'

Then there's a shove between my shoulder blades, accompanied by the acrid scent of Silver violence, and I sail directly into the path of an oncoming bus.

I'm not sure how exactly, but part of me – the edge of my boot, I think – gets hooked under the front bumper and, coupled with the forward momentum of the bus, it drags me down onto the tarmac and under the double-decker monstrosity. I feel the pop as the bones in my spine separate with the force of it, but worse is the crushing pressure as the bloody bus rolls over my legs. It doesn't stop until every one of its six tyres has made contact with some part of my battered body, leaving me a broken mess in the road behind it.

I lift my head and groan, looking up the pavement to see if I can spot whichever bastard did this to me, but there's no one in sight and no scent I recognise in the air. No matter. Given the lovely conversation I had recently with Mikey the Superfan, I've got a pretty good idea.

Thank god its stupid o'clock in the morning on a week night, and thank god I ate all those blood capsules on the train, because otherwise it would be impossible to slip away, and that's exactly what I do, using the last of my energy to drag myself out of the road and down a nearby alley, where I plaster myself against the wall in an attempt to stay out of sight. By the time the bus driver has rushed out of his seat and into the road, I'm nowhere to be seen. He'll find no trace of me except my smashed phone, the sole of my favourite boot – rest in peace – and the smear of blood I've surely left on the tarmac.

My deadly, infected blood.

Oh, shit.

But when I look down at myself to see how much I'm leaking, there doesn't seem to be any blood on me at all. My clothes are scuffed and ripped and, now that I look closely, the sole of my other boot is half hanging off, but there isn't a spot of blood on me, and I can't smell any either. I tentatively explore my face with my fingertips, expecting to find a bleeding and broken nose or, at the very least, a case of serious road rash, but there's nothing at all.

Even for the Silver, that's not right. It's not right at all.

I was flattened by a *bus*. I should be bleeding, but although the burning in my veins is now bordering on agonising, and I feel so exhausted that I'm not sure I'll be able to walk more than a few steps before falling over, that's just the poison taking over. All of the actual injuries I suffered have healed, apparently before I could even bleed.

I'm distracted from this mystery when I hear footsteps coming from the far end of the alley, and I brace myself for Mikey's finishing move. But then I realise the footsteps have the unmistakable ring of stiletto heels and, while I'm sure that's a look the flamboyant Mikey could pull off, I didn't hear that sound before he shoved me into the road. In fact, the figure that emerges out of the shadows is more slight, more feminine and entirely more understated than the bastard superfan.

'Carlotta?' I say by way of greeting. 'I was just coming to look for you.'

'What a coincidence,' she says with a devastating smile. 'I was looking for you, too. I caught the scent of Silver violence from the roof terrace of the bar and came to see who needed rescuing, and from whom. But your attacker seems to have disappeared, and apparently you're not in such bad shape after all.'

She leans up against the wall, hitching her hip and crossing her arms over her chest in a way that makes her cleavage extremely obvious. If I wasn't so fucked up right now, I'd be taking it as a come on, but she is dead wrong about me not being in bad shape. I'm at the stage where standing is becoming hard work. Frankly, breathing is starting to feel a bit of a chore too, so now I'm leaning against the wall too, and I can only imagine the effect when I do it is far from seductive.

When my only response is to prop myself up and wheeze, she asks, 'Why were you looking for me?'

'Thought you might know where Harry Carmichael is,' I say, not without difficulty. At this point, every word is costing me. If I don't get some blood into my system soon, things are going to go downhill very fast.

'But *chère* Jacquéline, you look terrible. Here,' she says, putting my arm around her shoulders. She smells of libraries and cigarettes and something delicious buried underneath it all. 'Come with me and we can get you some blood.'

'Mikey?' I ask. Well, it's not so much a question as a word, but she gets the idea.

'We'll talk later. But first, let me take you back to the bar. We need to feed you. You can't carry on like this.'

She gestures at me, up and down, apparently unable to put my discomposure into words. Maybe that's the kindest way, given that I am now drooling onto my jeans.

'Okay,' I agree, and I let her half lead and half carry me back to the club. I don't have the energy to argue.

When we arrive, Carlotta walks me past the front door – dark and shuttered now – to an unmarked entrance a little further along the street. It's so nondescript that I can't remember ever noticing it was there before. When she inserts a key and opens the door, there's just a narrow staircase on the other side leading downwards into what appears to be a cellar.

'The landlord's flat,' Carlotta explains. '*My* flat, now. The beer cellar is at the front here, and my living space takes up the rest.'

Apparently living underground is trending at the moment, even in damp and mouldy Oxford, though as Carlotta helps me down the stairs, I note that her place is a lot more welcoming than the Dregs'. There's a brick floor in the part of the cellar that houses the kegs and gas canisters for the pumps upstairs, but it's well kept and dry, with bright lighting and none of the fustiness I was expecting. On the other side of the room are two doors. Carlotta opens one with a key, but the second has no lock, so I guess it leads up to the bar upstairs.

'This way, *chère*,' she says, ushering me into the darkness ahead of her.

There's enough light coming from the cellar behind me to guide my first few steps, so initially it doesn't seem strange that she hasn't turned on the light inside the flat. It's only when the door shuts behind me, locking me in the darkness, that I realise I'm in trouble. My eyes don't have time to adjust before something sharp hits me in the neck, and then it's lights out.

Again.

Maybe for the last time.

31

WHEN I OPEN my eyes – which was a possibility rather than a certainty at this stage, so I'm counting it as a win – I'm in a dank little stone cell I don't recognise, handcuffed to the wall opposite someone I recognise very well indeed.

'Hello, Valentine,' he says.

Drake's chained up across the room about eight feet away – too far away to touch – and he looks so beaten up that I guess his handcuffs are about as necessary as mine. I say handcuffs, but actually our hands are sunk into solid lumps of metal that are themselves sunk into the wall, as though the whole kaboodle has been melted around our hands. I don't know how that's possible, but there's no give at all and however much I strain, the metal isn't moving an inch. We're both lying on our sides on the stone floor with our hands tethered behind us, neither of us able to lift our heads. It's a bit pathetic, really.

'Hello, Killian,' I breathe.

'Fancy seeing you here,' he whispers back.

'I was trying to rescue you.'

'And how's that going?'

'Not quite according to plan,' I admit.

'You actually had a plan? Knowing you, I thought you'd just bust in half-cocked and mess everything up.'

'Yeah. Well. Surprise,' I croak. But he's right: I really should have thought things through before I'd willingly let Carlotta carry me back to her place. I'm not sure where we are now, but I'm sure she's the reason we're both here. 'I'm sorry.'

'I'm not. I'm glad you came,' he says, then he smiles at me in a way that suggests he expects it to be the last time he can.

Despite the dire circumstances, and the fact that we're both probably about to die, I can't help but smile back. When I imagined my last hours on earth, I imagined spending them with him, and although this isn't quite what I had in mind – he's wearing far too many clothes for that – at least it's something. Just being this close to him, I'm overwhelmed by an irrational sense of relief and calm, as though his mere presence has soothed the bees buzzing in my veins. I thought I'd never see him again, but here he is. I might not be close enough to touch him, but here he is. I look into his eyes across the space between us, and I see constellations of stars shining just for me.

'When we last saw each other…' Even this brief reminder of our activities during his last visit makes something flip in my stomach. 'I thought I'd driven you away.'

'As if you could. In any case, I've learned to judge your feelings by your actions rather than your words.' I'm just thinking about how unexpectedly sweet this sentiment is when he ruins it by adding, 'Since your words are mostly profane, I don't have much choice.'

I was all ready to get heartfelt with him and now he's making jokes. The bastard.

It reminds me of the last time I let myself be drawn into a sentimental exchange with Drake in a life-or-death situation, and then the situation ended up not being quite as terminal as expected, and I ended up feeling like an idiot. I won't let that happen again now. Next time I spill my guts to him, I'm going to make damn sure neither of us will live to be embarrassed by it later.

'If you're not going to say anything helpful, then just be quiet and let me think,' I say. 'I'll come up with something.'

But by the time Carlotta comes into the room a minute later, my mind is full of pain and nothing else. I don't know if it's the torturous proximity of Drake and the healing kisses that are just out of my reach, or if it's the fact that I got hit by a fucking bus, but the burning is so bad now that it's all I can do not to scream. I'm so distracted that it takes me a few seconds to realise that Carlotta's not alone.

'Leclercq?' I say, not sure I can trust my eyes.

'Hello, *Jacky*,' she says, using Winta's pet name for me, the one I always hated. 'Or should I say, goodbye?'

'You're working with Yolande Leclercq?' I try to yell at Carlotta, but it comes out as a whisper. 'What the hell?'

Perhaps I shouldn't be surprised. It explains the papery odour I noticed on her skin earlier and, after all, it was Carlotta who helped Winta with our decoy escape plan. I knew she was at least acquainted with Leclercq, probably better acquainted with her than she was with Winta. I just never imagined that Carlotta would be harbouring any hard feelings towards me, particularly given that she'd always been a bit Mina-ish around me, always hoping for nakedness and never taking my rebuffs with ill humour. Apparently, though, she has been nursing a grudge.

'I'm sorry about this, *cher* Baron,' she says to Drake. 'I really am. But you understand I have a reputation to uphold. Carlotta Arden is not the type of person who finally takes a fiancé – after many, *many* offers – only to have that fiancé run off and silver for a scruffy little Seeker with all the fashion sense of a drowned capybara.'

'Hey!' I croak.

'Don't take it personally, Jacquéline. You know I find you intriguing, but you have to think about how it would look to other people. I am irresistible, and that means that anyone who can resist me cannot exist. You understand?'

'Oh, I understand, Carlotta,' Drake says. 'I knew were vain, but I never realised you were such a narcissist.'

She laughs, tossing her hair over her shoulder with careless charm, and I remember why I used to have her pictures on my wall. She's right: she is irresistible.

'Baron Drake is calling *me* a narcissist?' she says. 'Well, you would know, *cher*.'

'And *you*,' Leclercq says to me. 'You have been taking an irritatingly long time to die.'

'Sorry?' I say.

I don't mean it as an apology, but as an expression of serious affront. She takes it the wrong way, of course.

'You should be,' she says. 'Five months. *Five months* I've been waiting for you to go up in smoke.'

'Knock, knock!' a cheerful voice says outside the door, then Mikey's in the room too. He's back in his colourful gear again, though I'm not sure who he's peacocking for today.

Now it's three-to-two, and two of us are dying and chained to the walls, so I'd be lying if I said the odds were anything other than dismal.

'You pushed me in front of a bus,' I croak at him.

'Just to take the edge off!' he trills back. 'I thought it was all over for you when you went up to London, but somehow – amazingly – you came back from the brink *again*, just like you did over and over while I was trailing you around the country, and when I saw you walking down the street just now looking totally fine, I thought I couldn't have you tracking us down before you were properly ready to explode, and then it came to me in a flash: bus!'

'And my neighbours?'

'Yeah, well, you were taking so long to weaken and I was getting bored, and then I heard about this thing from a friend of a friend, who's kind of not a friend but a *friend*, if you know what I mean?'

I do not know what he means.

'But anyway, he told me about how you can kind of filter drugs through human blood by giving the drugs to the human then draining them, and it's supposed to give you the same thrill you'd get if you were human yourself, and I thought it would be fun to try, and he said that if you drank the stuff with special combinations at particular points in the, um, *friendship*, then shit could get pretty exciting, so I thought why the hell not? It sounded like fun! And if it had worked, and if that last one hadn't struggled so hard and ruined everything, it would have been pretty awesome, wouldn't it? I mean, can you *imagine*?'

At the moment, all I'm imagining is poor Faith bleeding out on her apartment floor with no one there beside her except this idiot, who has clearly been blessed with more power than brains. This is why you're supposed to have an official Casting ceremony to turn someone Silver, and why the Primus is so picky about who he approves to get turned. If he wasn't, the world would be swarming with Silver whose strength far surpasses their intelligence, like Mikey here. His transformation must have been off the books, because although he looks great, he doesn't half talk some shit.

Even at the best of times, I find Mikey's circuitous chat exhausting. Right now, it is excruciating. Apparently, the others agree.

'Shut up, Mikey,' Leclercq says.

He zips his lips and steps backwards, letting Leclercq

have the floor. This is obviously her show.

'I have to tell you,' she says, 'I was pretty fucking irritated when I found out you were getting healed. I expected you to burn up soon enough, but every time Mikey got in touch to say it was nearly time for the end game, there'd be another call saying you—' she points at Drake '—had been to visit, and suddenly Jacky was entirely recovered. Carlotta knew about the bond, of course, but we thought its healing power was apocryphal. It took us a while to realise that the only way to stop you from recovering over and over again was to separate the two of you, and once we did, it worked like a charm.' She laughs, and it is a bitter sound. 'Now you're going to feel what it's like to burn alive from the inside, just like Winta did, and I'm going to watch, just like you did. That feels like justice to me.'

'How did you even know where I was?' I ask.

I can't understand how they found me so quickly. I thought I'd been doing so well to cover my tracks, but apparently they knew where I was all this time, and had only been keeping their distance because they were waiting for Khalyed's blood to kill me. But I took precautions. They didn't have Cam's scent-tracking abilities, or Frank's skill with technology, so unless I'm missing something, it shouldn't have been possible for them to find me.

'You love that stupid leather jacket, don't you, Jacky?' Leclercq says. 'You take it everywhere with you. You think I didn't notice that when we were all living together in our uneasy little threesome? All I had to do was wait for you to shower so I could plant a little bug, and from that point on, I always knew where you were. Just in case you got any bright ideas.'

Oh shit.

I'm kicking myself for not figuring it out sooner. After all, this isn't the first time someone's stuck a tracker in the pocket of my leather jacket. Mina was the one who tagged me previously, and if you believe her then she was only doing it to keep an eye on the Seekers so she could avoid them during her less-than-reputable assignments, but that was largely innocuous. This is something different. Leclercq had access to all of my stuff when we were crammed into that little house in Jericho together with Winta. I should have suspected she'd pull something like this, even back then. We'd never liked each other.

Well, the tracker isn't the only thing in my jacket.

'She was double-crossing you, you know,' I rasp out. 'She was going to run away with me and leave you behind.'

'Bullshit.'

'Her letter's in my pocket, right here,' I say, nodding down at my jacket. 'Read it for yourself.'

Leclercq snatches the letter so quickly that I barely see her move, scans it quickly, shoots me a look of pure hatred, then turns and abruptly leaves the room. Carlotta looks at me in confusion for a moment, then says, 'Stay here,' to Mikey and hurries out after her.

That leaves me and Drake alone with Mikey.

'Frank?' I ask him.

'The computer nerd? He's fine!' says Mikey. 'We only needed him to get us in here. Once we're done and dusted – Ha! Excuse the pun! – I'll totally let him go, okay?'

'And where is *here*, exactly?'

'The Seekers dungeon under Solomon College,' Drake says.

I blink.

'What dungeon?'

'They sealed it all up tight, then added some digital locks to be extra sure no one could get in, but they didn't count on the people breaking in having the guy who programmed the locks in the first place!' Mikey says cheerfully. 'They designed this room so it's airtight, you know? You can fill it with water from up there—' He points to a round hole in the corner of the ceiling. '—and it'll stay filled until someone pulls the plug, and not just water either! You can use oil or gas or acid – can you *imagine*? – or basically anything you like!'

'And what are you planning to use?' I say, a little afraid to ask, but needing the answer nonetheless.

'Epoxy resin!' Mikey says gleefully.

I consider this for a second, but I've got nothing.

'I think you're going to need to explain that one.'

'Okay, so actually, this is really fucking cool, and when you hear it you're going to be all *what an awesomely creepy idea* and *that's so spooky serial killer man I wish I'd thought of it* because – and I'm being totally open with you here and probably telling you too much, but whatever – that's what they said to me when I told them about my idea!'

'*Your* idea?' Drake asks. 'So we have you to blame for this?'

'Partly, but really, I can't take all the credit, because those ladies are *amazing* and Carlotta... I mean, couldn't you just *die* for her? Well, you're going to, I suppose – what a laugh! – but they came up with a lot of the details to make it work, like using this place, but what I was thinking is: Pompeii, you know?'

'Pompeii,' I repeat uncomprehendingly.

'Pompeii! You know how there were all those people in Pompeii who got covered in the hot ash, and they were vaporised on the spot, but the ash took like impressions of their bodies and so when archaeologists came along thousands of years later they could take casts of the holes left behind in the ash and see the shape of where the person or dog or whatever had been when they died?'

'Yes...'

'Well! I thought that when you go up in flames, you're going to get vaporised and ashed and that sort of created this amazing connection in my brain, and I thought about Pompeii, but the whole problem with that is that firstly, they had to break the hole apart a bit to take the impressions so they lost the last traces of people in the process, you know, and then secondly, you wouldn't be able to see the whole vaporising thing happen – and I know Yolande is *dying* to watch you die – so I thought what can I find that will kind of suspend and freeze like plaster but be see through and I was watching this video on my socials about updating your kitchen work surfaces and it came to me in a flash, like: epoxy resin! And if we're feeling dramatic, we can even put some bits of glitter in it so your deaths can be encased in twinkling perfection for eternity! Wouldn't that be *awesome*?'

I can't think of anything worse. Dying is bad enough. Dying with Drake is awful. But dying in *glitter*? I can feel my top lip curling of its own volition.

Mikey, however, doesn't seem to think it's weird to expect us to get excited about our own deaths.

'I don't mean to be negative,' Drake says, 'but wouldn't you need a substantial quantity of epoxy resin to fill this room?'

I'm not sure where he's going with this, but Mikey's clearly the weak link in this little threesome, and there's a twinkle in Drake's eye that says he has a plan.

'Yeah,' I croak, backing him up. 'This cell might look small, but it would cost a fortune to fill with resin.'

'Aw, man!' Mikey clearly hasn't thought about this in any kind of detail.

'And,' Drake says, 'if I might mention an additional concern, doesn't it take some time to dry?'

'Oh, not at all!' Mikey insists. 'It's like the stuff they use on my nails, and you can cure it with UV light, and then it dries in like thirty seconds flat, like so fast you wouldn't *believe* it!'

'In small quantities,' Drake points out.

Mikey looks utterly deflated. 'You think it'll take longer than thirty seconds?'

'Um, yes,' I say.

'Quite a lot longer,' Drake adds.

'Aw, *man*! That's the whole reason I wanted to come to this place!' Mikey looks so befuddled that I start to feel a little sorry for him, but then he gets a bright idea and his face lights up in a way that fills me with dread. 'Then I just need a smaller container, right? In which case, I have this mate who does princess cosplay and she does this killer Snow White bit with a perspex coffin and wouldn't that be *perfect*? Because if I filled the whole room with resin then we'd have to come in and sort of cut you out later and that sounds like a lot of hard work if I'm honest, but if you're already wrapped up tight in a box when it happens then you're, like, already *portable*! Oh my god, I am a fucking genius!'

'Sure you are,' I say, trying and failing to keep the sarcasm out of my tone. He doesn't notice, but Drake does, and he shoots me a wry look.

'Hey, so I guess that means I need a little more time to get everything ready so I can get the box and the resin and the glitter—'

Oh god. I was hoping he'd forgotten about the glitter.

'—so how long are you actually going to last?' He directs this at me. 'Three hours? Four hours?'

Drake widens his eyes at me, and maybe we've finally hit the same wavelength, because I get his point immediately.

'Oh, not long,' I say weakly. 'An hour, tops, I think.'

'No!' Mikey wails. 'I need longer! I can't pull together a fucking work of art from resin and plastic and twinkly joy in an hour! You've been taking bloody ages up until now, so can't you just... slow things down a bit?' he pleads.

'Well,' I say, 'maybe if you loosened Drake's handcuffs a little then he could reach far enough across the room to heal me—'

'No!' Mikey interrupts. 'No, no, no, because can you imagine how disappointed Carlotta would be in me if I loosened it too much and I let him go and she never got to see him go up in flames and I am *not* going to let that happen! But!' He holds a manicured nail up dramatically. They must be acrylics, because there's no way he could have been wearing them last night when he snatched Frank; they don't fit with the bland Dregs persona I saw in his file photo. 'Maybe,' he lowers his voice, 'I could give you a couple of these? Not enough to break free, just one each, and maybe that would buy me the time I need to get everything set up nicely?'

He pulls a pack of blood capsules out of his pocket. I see Drake's gaze narrow and flicker in a way that suggests he's trying to conceal his satisfaction, so I guess this was his aim.

I play it cool, saying, 'That might work.'

'All right, then!' says Mikey, then he tosses a capsule at each of us.

Neither of us manages to catch them, because we're both still lying weakly on the ground with our hands behind our backs, but they're close enough that we could worm our way to them and suck them down without too much effort.

'Not a word, though, right?' He points at each of us in turn. 'You don't tell Carlotta about this, because... because we never had this discussion, I never gave you these pills and – you know what, actually? – I was never even here!'

'She knows you were here, Mikey,' I groan. The man is so stupid it almost beggars belief.

As if on cue, I hear stilettoed footsteps on stone outside in the corridor. Drake has somehow already disappeared his blood capsule about his person – I know he hasn't swallowed it, because if he had then he would be looking better instead of worse, which is how he actually looks – so I follow his lead and shuffle around a little so that my capsule is hidden under the spread of my unbound hair by the time Carlotta and Leclercq come back into the room.

They make a striking couple, striking enough that it makes me wonder. There's Carlotta with her dark hair and her light brown skin and impeccable taste, then Leclercq with her platinum hair and pale skin and taste so boring I have literally never noticed what she's wearing – for the record, tonight it's black jeans and a black T-shirt. They're about the same height, and if you ignore Leclercq's relatively plain features, side by side they look a little like negatives of each other.

'You're not the only one who got a letter,' Leclercq says, pushing past Mikey.

She holds a piece of paper in front of my face so I can read it. It's as well worn as my own letter from Winta and says basically the same thing, only now I'm the one being left behind and it's Leclercq who'll be meeting up with Winta later for their happily ever after, in New Zealand rather than Vancouver, but the premise is the same.

Just the two of us, from now until forever ~ W

It's all the same.

She was going to set us each up in separate cities and have us each believe that we were the only one. Us and who knows how many more, scattered around the globe.

A girl in every port.

'Unlike you,' Leclercq says, snatching the letter back, 'I wasn't naïve enough to actually believe it. Unlike you, I *knew* her. I knew she would always want more than just me, and I accepted that. I accepted *her*. She was hungry for everything she could get from life, and I loved her for it, even if I thought you were so far beneath her you could only see the bottom of her shoes. I *loved* her. You never understood her. You never deserved her. And you chose him —' she points a sharp finger at Drake '—a petty, narrow-minded, vindictive little man, over her.'

She spits in my face, then turns around and kicks Drake in the chest. I hear a snap that reverberates through my soul, then Drake grunts and a mouthful of blood spills through his lips onto the stone.

'Don't you *dare* touch him again!' I scream with a snarl, trying and failing to push myself up to a sitting position. 'I will kill you. I will *kill you*.'

'Calm down, Jacky. You'll do yourself an injury.' Leclercq is laughing. *Laughing*. My rage could boil metal. 'Very soon there won't be anything left of him to touch, anyway. That's how the bond works, isn't it? So I get to watch you go up in flames, and Carlotta gets to watch him do the same.'

'Double feature!' Mikey chips in from the doorway. 'In glitter!'

'Shut up, Mikey,' I snap.

Then Leclercq kicks me in the chest too, twice, with a series of sickening crunches that leave me screaming as bones break and heal in a second.

But I'm not bleeding. It makes no sense at all, but I am still not bleeding.

'Mikey, go get everything you need,' Carlotta says. 'Be back in three hours.'

'Four,' he says.

Carlotta's beautiful face darkens and I think she's going to snap at him, but then Mikey gives her a look that's all puppy-dog eyes and says, 'I want it to be *perfect*, for you, queen! Please, just an extra hour, and I promise I'll have everything ready for you!'

Her expression softens. She smiles indulgently, then she kisses him on the cheek, leaving a red lipstick moue behind on his skin.

'Go on then, *chèrie*. They'll last until then. But not a minute longer, now.'

'I promise!' Mikey says, then he gives us all a little wave and hurries off along the corridor and into the darkness.

'You know he's a fucking idiot, right?' I ask when he's gone. 'You know he can't really freeze our deaths in epoxy resin?'

'Of course he can't,' Carlotta says, 'but he's so excited about it, is he not? And he amuses me.'

'Then why are we even in this dungeon?'

Drake sighs and says, 'Because this is where Winta was held.'

'You mean this is where she was *tortured*,' says Leclercq.

'She... what?' I ask.

This is news to me. I knew Winta had been held in a cell in Drake's basement, because that's where I found her on the night she made me Silver, but Drake had only just caught her. Before that, she'd been on the run. At least, that's what she'd told me.

'When?' I ask.

'Before you even knew her,' Leclercq says. 'When she was a child. A *child*.'

'*What*? Why?'

'Because her parents are sadistic, evil bastards,' Leclercq spits.

That doesn't track. Cam told me that Adinde, Winta's mother, was his best friend once upon a time. I can't believe he would be friends with anyone who would torture a child.

'Because she was uncontrollable,' Drake says. 'They couldn't stop her from biting humans, and they needed somewhere to keep her that she couldn't break out of. It's a

296

problem sometimes, with the young ones.'

I knew that Winta had been born Silver to Silver parents rather than turned, like I was, but I've never thought about what that might mean in practice. Silver children aren't common – the captain's daughter is the only one I know of, but I've never even met her – so I haven't had much occasion to consider the dangers of combining the Silver appetite for human blood with a child's lack of impulse control. I can see how it might be an issue with strong-willed children, and Winta was nothing if not strong-willed.

'They left her in here alone,' Leclercq says, letting her anger show. 'They starved her of blood.'

'Because she would have broken out otherwise,' Drake says, but he's talking to me, not Leclercq.

'But that's not all they did, is it?' Leclercq insists. 'They used this cell to punish her it every way it can be used to torture the Silver. They tried to burn and beat and fry and drown it out of her, and when that didn't work, they did it again, and when she finally broke out, they wondered why she wanted to bite and kill and murder the Silver who had thrown her in here. What a fucking mystery.'

'She never told me,' I say, feeling even sicker than before.

'Of course she didn't,' Leclercq says. 'You were one of them. But *you* knew all about it, didn't you, *Baron*?' She sneers his title like an insult.

'Afterwards? Yes,' he admits. 'During? No.'

'You expect me to believe that? You expect me to believe that *anything* that happened to the Silver in this city under your control would be without your knowledge and approval?'

'She was under the care of her parents. I didn't know—'

'You *should* have known! You should have at least checked to make sure she was safe, and now you're going to pay for that. You're both going to pay.'

a

She turns and ushers Carlotta out of the doorway ahead of her. I can't help but notice that Carlotta has been very quiet through all of this. Mikey and Leclercq might be having the time of their lives, but Carlotta is not entirely on board.

'I'm sorry, *mes chers*,' she says before Leclercq hurries her on her way.

Leclercq remains in the doorway for a moment, fiddling with something on the wall outside the door. There's some ominous clanking and the sound of metal groaning within the walls, then a ratcheting click that I don't like at all.

'What are you going to do?' I ask her.

'Only what they did to her,' Leclercq says lightly. 'It'll take a little time for the tank to fill up. You've got about twenty minutes if you want to say your goodbyes. I'd make the most of them if I were you, because they're all you're going to get.'

Then she slams the door behind her and leaves us in the dark.

32

MY NIGHT VISION isn't great at the best of times, not for one of the Silver, at least. Now, blood-starved and on the brink of death, and with not even the slightest hint of ambient light, I can see so little that I might as well not bother having my eyes open at all, so I let them close.

'No, you don't,' says Drake from across the room, who can clearly see better than me. 'I've only just got you back. You're not just going to lie down and give up on me.'

'We're chained to opposite walls in the cell where we will both shortly be tortured and die,' I say. 'In what world do you *have me back*? And I'm just resting my eyes.'

'No, you're not.'

'I can't see anything anyway.'

'Well, I can see you,' he says, and something in his voice has changed. 'I see you, Valentine. I never thought I would again.'

'Yes, nice of them to let us die together,' I say, because I have to ruin the mood somehow. He sounds serious and reflective, and if I let him go on like this then he's going to say something that I don't want to hear, that I can't let myself hear, not now, when he's so close, and so far away. I think if I did, I might break.

And I can't break.

'If we're under the college, then we must be close to where the Dregs are,' I say. 'They must know about this place. Maybe if we shout then they'll hear us and—'

'No,' Drake interrupts. 'We're not deep enough. There's a lot of earth between us and them, and they don't know about these dungeons. Almost no one still alive knows about these dungeons, and those who do wouldn't want to admit that knowledge. Nothing good ever happened down here.'

'And what exactly *did* happen down here, Drake?' I ask. 'Cam told me Winta's parents were scared of her, but he said that was because she'd gone feral and turned into a Biter, not because she wanted revenge for...' I can't bring myself to repeat what she was subjected to, so I just say, 'That.'

'Later,' he says. 'Right now, we need to get out of here. If I give you my blood capsule and you take it along with yours, you might be able to break through your restraints.'

'No, I won't. You should take them.'

'I'm not sure it would be enough,' he says, 'even for me. They drugged me.'

'Is that how they snatched you?' I ask the darkness.

Drake laughs, which feels incongruous when I can't see his face, but then I realise he's embarrassed.

'I was a little distracted when I left your apartment,' he says, 'understandably, I think. And Leclercq appears to have acquired or replicated a small supply of the Invicti's tranquilliser darts.'

'The ones that you're basically allergic to?' I ask, horrified. 'The ones that nearly killed you last year?'

'Yes, those. They used a smaller dose, but the effect was much the same. Then they used it again. I'm not sure how long I've been here.'

'Nearly six weeks,' I say.

'Six *weeks*? Oh, no.' He's not panicking, because Killian Drake doesn't panic, but the tone of his voice is edging in that direction. 'You haven't been healed in—'

'Which is why you need to be the one who takes the capsules. Now can we please stop wasting time and get on with it?'

'All right,' he says, all business now. 'Throw yours over here.'

'Oh, because that's so easy? *How,* Drake? My hands are stuck in the wall, just like yours.'

'Use your mouth, then. Come on, Valentine,' he says, his voice soft. 'We both know you're good at that.'

One good thing about this burning alive thing: my blood is already practically boiling, so he won't notice how that comment has raised my temperature. And, since we're in the dark, he won't be able to see me blush, so that's another plus. The major drawback, of course, is that I can't see the blood capsule I hid under my hair anymore, and even when I do finally track it down with a mixture of luck and earnest wriggling, I can't be sure of my aim when I'm ready to chuck it his way.

'Shay shumshing,' I garble around the capsule I'm now holding in my front teeth.

'Over here, Sean Connery,' Drake replies.

Then I spit the capsule as far as I can in the direction of his voice. Too far, as it turns out, because I hear it ping off the wall and fall back to the floor somewhere between the two of us.

'Fuck,' I say. 'Can you see where it went?'

'It's down by your feet.'

'*Fuck.*'

'Can you get your boots off?'

'Maybe.'

And, as it turns out, I can. I wasn't expecting there to be

an upside to being run over by a bus, but the tarmac has shredded so much of the leather that I manage to toe off first one boot, then the other. The socks are trickier, but with a bit of writhing about I manage to get one foot free so I'll be able to pick the capsule up between my toes. Good thing that Drake has a minor foot fetish. Bad thing that I've been wearing the same socks since that last shower at Mina's old place.

'Where is it?' I ask.

'Left a bit,' he directs me. 'Down a bit.'

This hotter/colder process goes on for an excruciatingly long time, so long that I'm starting to think our twenty minutes must already be up, but finally my toes close around the capsule. I straighten my leg and hurl it in Drake's direction.

'Got it?' I ask.

There's some scrabbling around in the darkness, then Drake says, 'Not exactly.'

'Can you see it, at least?'

'Yes. It's about an inch away from the farthest point I can reach.'

'Shit. Is one capsule enough to get you free?'

I hear him swallow, then there are a lot of grunting noises that make me think of happier times and wish for different circumstances.

Eventually, he says, 'No.'

'So we're stuck here.'

'So it appears.'

'Until we die.'

'Perhaps not. Ms Leclercq said they were filling the tank, which suggests they're planning to start by filling the cell with water. If we get lucky, maybe the pill will float in the right direction when they turn on the tap.'

'That's a big if.'

'Hmm.'

I want to scream. Hell, the place is soundproofed, so I may as well let rip.

'What was that in aid of?' Drake asks when I'm done.

'This is all your fault, you know,' I say. 'Why even build a cell like this in the first place?'

'For the worst of the worst. Back when I founded the Seekers—'

'*You* founded them?'

'How do you think I became Baron of Oxford? I had a good idea and I ran with it. The Primus let me.'

'Huh. And your good idea was to torture the Silver in a dungeon?'

'The concept of a dungeon didn't really exist back then, not in the way you're thinking of it. There were oubliettes, which weren't that dissimilar from the boxes we use now, but nothing like this. And these cells weren't intended for torture, they were just somewhere to keep people who couldn't be contained anywhere else while we decided what to do with them.'

'So you used this cell to torture the Silver so you could work out how to imprison them indefinitely?'

'Not exactly. We used it to torture ourselves.'

I'm not sure I've heard him correctly.

'What?' I ask.

'We were trying to find a way to make the Silver less harmful, so we could effectively neuter the ones who couldn't or wouldn't be controlled. So we tested and tested, but we were the guinea pigs.'

'*We*?'

'Me and a few others.' He adds quietly, 'Gone now.'

'Dead?'

'Yes,' he says. 'Two went scab. I had to take them down, with the assistance of the Seekers. Two suicides.'

'Oh, god.'

'As I said, nothing good ever happened down here. After that, I put an end to it and sealed the place up.'

'Until Winta,' I say.

For a while, he doesn't say anything at all. I wonder if he's just going to ignore my implied question entirely, but then he takes a deep breath and says, 'Yes.'

'What happened?'

'There was a doctor that the Ladipos trusted. They asked if they could use the space down here to contain Winta while the doctor worked with her, and I agreed. These cells had long fallen out of use, and the Ladipos were concerned for the doctor's safety. None of us realised that he had his own agenda. He repeated our tests, more or less without deviation, because he was convinced our error lay in the test subjects we used. He thought that the same methods that unbalanced previously balanced Silver would balance those he considered unbalanced.'

'So he tortured Winta.'

'Yes.'

'With her parents' approval.'

'From her perspective, yes. From theirs, they put their trust in the wrong doctor. They ended it when they found out what exactly was being done to her, but by then it was too late. If anything, it cemented her desire to bite.'

'And her desire for revenge.'

'Which I suppose is finally being fulfilled,' he says darkly.

'So at least this place was good for something then, right?'

He doesn't laugh, but then it wasn't a very good joke.

'It served its purpose, even back then,' he says. He sounds as though his thoughts are a long way away. 'We learned how to drain and box the Silver, but we never learned how to hold our kind without harming them at the same time. And when the so-called crime they're being punished for is just an accident, or it happens because someone goes looking for the kind of justice the Seekers can't give them... It doesn't seem fair for us to hurt people for that, does it?'

I think of Gabriella de Palma, and of Raul, and I wonder how many other Silver were boxed and damaged over the centuries in similar circumstances.

'But the Primus will have his rules,' he goes on, 'and I have to follow them, or pretend to at least. And then there are the others.'

'The Biters,' I say.

'Some Biters, some more twisted than that. The ones like Charles Legrange.'

Legrange was a suspect in the May Day murder that Gabriella committed last year. He'd been killing humans and dropping their bodies into the middle of public events for shits and giggles. He's a monster, but the Invicti have him under lock and key now in one of their boxes in London. If he'd gone to Drake's basement, he'd be dead by now, and no one would have missed him.

'We both know there are people who can't be redeemed,' he continues, 'and they're the same Silver whose sentences are long enough that they're almost guaranteed to come out of a box worse than they went in. It would be kinder to kill them, but the majority are so old that even the most brutal and thorough approaches to murder wouldn't have any effect.'

'And then Khalyed came along.'

For a while, he doesn't say anything at all. When he finally does speak, his voice is quiet, but filled with conviction. 'It was the lesser of so many evils. It's cleaner.'

'Does that make it better?' I ask, not sure I know the answer myself.

'For whom?' Drake replies.

I can't answer that either.

'Wait a minute,' I say, because there's a hole in the middle of this logic. 'If you're letting the Gabriella de Palmas go after a few months or less, and you're killing the Charles Legranges, then who exactly is boxed up in your basement right now?'

'No one,' he says softly. 'No one at all.'

'You mean—'

'We're out of time,' he interrupts. 'They've opened the tap.'

He's right; there's a rushing sound above our heads as the tank opens, then I hear water pouring into the corner of the room. A second later, my side is wet. It's coming in fast.

'Drake…' I say. 'The capsule.'

'Nearly,' he says, straining. 'Nearly there… Got it!'

I hear the screech of twisting metal, then Drake says, 'It's stuck.'

'This is a lot of fucking water, Drake. Hurry up!'

'I am hurrying,' he replies, 'but this isn't ordinary iron. I'm going as fast as I can.'

'Go faster!'

The water is halfway over my body now, and I'm having to twist my neck to hold my face clear of it.

'It's going to take a little longer,' he says, grunting. 'But I'm coming for you. I promise.'

'You bastard!'

The water is covering most of my face now, and it's rising quickly.

'Deep breath, Valentine!'

Then I'm underwater.

It is… not fun.

The Silver don't technically need to breathe to live, but our bodies want to. When they can't, they fight for air the same way a human would. It's a reflex you can train yourself out of with serious practice, or so I've been told, but I've never seen the need. Now, as my lungs fill with water for the third time, making me feel like I'm drowning over and over again, I have ample opportunity to regret my choices.

The more I drown, the more I struggle, and therefore the more my body burns as it consumes the non-Khalyed blood in my system, concentrating his poison in my veins. Pretty soon, we're not going to have to worry about the water, because the heat under my skin is going to evaporate the lot. Maybe Mikey would have been all right with his resin after all.

Then something touches me on the cheek. At first I flinch, imagining countless horrors that Leclercq could have thrown in here with us, but then the touch turns into a caress and I realise that it's Drake, and he's free. His hands trace their way along my arms to the point at which my wrists disappear into the wall. I'm expecting him to try to yank me free, but instead I feel a series of impacts as he pummels at the wall on either side of the metal tether. He's trying to free the metal from the wall, rather than freeing me from the metal. This is probably for the best, because trying to pull me out would probably just shred my hands, and I could do without any more injuries right now.

I leave him to his work and carry on drowning, because there's not much else I can do. The pain has my full attention.

It's not until I feel the water rushing past me that I realise Drake's pulled me clear from the wall. It felt like it took hours for him to free me, but it must have been only seconds, because by the time he helps me swim up to the top of the cell – with the unwieldy metal block still clamping my hands behind my back – there's still some air up here. I can't tell how much, because my eyes are giving me nothing but black, but I'm grateful that there's any at all. I cough out the water from my lungs, then gulp the air down hungrily, along with the dark spicy scent of the man treading water beside me.

Let me tell you, it is a heady remedy. I feel a little light-headed, and not just from the multiple drownings or the fire in my veins. Then his lips meet mine in the darkness, and I'm ready to go nuclear.

'Valentine,' he whispers as our scents swirl around us. 'I thought you didn't care.'

'Then you're an idiot.'

About as much of an idiot as I've been, I guess.

Our scent marks are concentrated in the small, dark space in a way that makes the call of his body to mine practically irresistible. I can feel the healing mojo doing its work in my veins as Drake deepens the kiss, which is reassuring given Tabitha's dire predictions about its continued effectiveness, but that isn't what takes my focus. Instead, my thoughts are cascading through everything I want to do to Drake, and have him do to me. I want him so badly that, even in these extreme circumstances, for a moment I consider whether it would be possible to take my clothes off underwater with my hands tied behind my back. I go so far as to try it, with zero success, before snapping back to reality.

'Not now,' I say, trying to push him away, which is a challenge while I'm bobbing around like this. I say *bobbing*, but I'm mostly trying not to sink while Drake fights the weight of the metal pulling me down. 'We have to get out of here.'

My head brushes against the ceiling as the water level rises. We're out of time, and we're still not out of the woods. Although the blood in my veins is cooler than it was, it is not a normal temperature by any measure. The longer I have to keep struggling in the water, the more of my precious remaining blood energy I'm going to burn, and the hotter I'm going to get.

'I'm going to try the door,' Drake says, still holding me close. 'I need you to keep kicking so you'll stay up here in the air until I get back. All right?'

'All right,' I say, more because we have no choice than because I think it's remotely feasible.

Drake kisses me once more, then his supporting hands disappear, followed by a splash as he dives down to the door. I start kicking upwards, but I can already feel I'm not going to last long. Drake's healing kiss has sorted out the dead cells in my blood – the ashy ones Tabitha showed me on her microscope – but what I need is new blood to drink, and I have none. Without it, I have no energy left to power feats of super-strength, and either this metal around my hands is really, really heavy, or I'm in worse shape than I thought.

I keep it up for about five seconds, and then I sink like a rock, despite kicking as hard as I can. Time to get busy drowning again.

There's a muffled thumping as water fills my lungs. It takes me longer than it should to work out that the noise is Drake trying to break down the door, but the tone of the sound remains constant, and the water isn't going anywhere, so I guess he's not having much success.

After a period of time that feels interminable, but is probably only a matter of seconds, an arm goes around my waist and I'm tugged back up to the surface.

'Breathe!' Drake shouts at me. 'Breathe, Valentine!'

I try to comply, but it's easier said than done. There's only a couple of inches of air left. It's while I'm spitting up water and trying to grab one last lungful that a memory hits me hard.

'Plug,' I splutter. 'Mikey said there was a plug!'

Then the last of the air is gone and I have to concentrate on drowning again.

This isn't the first time I've been tortured, but it is

definitely the worst. Everything is black, but the world behind my eyelids is burning red. I can only tell which way is down because the metal block has pulled my hands to the floor, tethering me to the bottom of the cell, though my body is trying to rise up to where the air once was. There is nothing in my lungs now except water, but my body keeps trying to expel it in round after round of agonising spasms that only succeed in filling them more thoroughly. Leclercq must be planning on draining the cell eventually, because she made it clear that she has more than one kind of torture in store for us, but that's not particularly reassuring right now when every second feels like an hour. If Drake doesn't manage to pull the plug soon, I'm not sure I'll make it to torture method number two.

There's a noise like a vacuum unsealing. I think it must be the plug giving way, but nothing happens for several long seconds. Then I feel the force of a current and slowly, very slowly, the metal block starts to move along the stone. By the time the water finally releases me into a spluttering mess on the floor – which is not a comfortable landing when I have a large metal block directly underneath my back and no free hands to break my fall – I have drowned more times than I can count.

I am never, ever going swimming again.

'I've got you,' Drake whispers, and I feel his arms around me, pulling me upright and into the soggy comfort of his embrace.

'What happened?' I gasp, trying to catch my breath. 'Did they pull the plug?'

'No, I smashed it in with my restraints.'

'I thought they were still in the wall?'

'No,' he says. 'One of my hands didn't come away clean.'

'Drake—'

'No time. I'm fine. We have to go.'

'Are they watching?' I ask.

I didn't see a camera or a window before the lights went out, but that doesn't mean there isn't hidden surveillance in this cell.

'I don't think so. I can't hear any electronics in here, and the observation windows have been bricked up,' Drake says.

I'll have to take his word for it, because it's still darker than night in here.

'But why bother torturing us if they don't get to watch?' I ask. 'Who are they doing it for?'

'They don't want to watch us weaken,' he says softly. 'They just want to weaken us so they can watch us die. I suggest we get out of here before that becomes a reality. I'm going to try and free your hands.'

I feel his fingertips on my wrists, then he says, 'Oh.'

It's only a little noise, barely more than a sigh, but his defeated tone makes my stomach drop.

'What is it?' I ask, frantically twisting in an attempt to see my hands over my shoulder or under my arms, which is impossible not only because I'm not that flexible, but also because it remains pitch dark in here, to me at least. 'Are my hands fucked? Is the metal stuck or something?'

'In a manner of speaking. Stay still.'

'In *what* manner of speaking?'

'I'm going to need some tools to get you free, but we have a more immediate problem.'

'What?'

'There's something melted into the metal beside your wrist,' he says. 'It looks like it's stuck into your vein, but it disappears into the block so I'm not sure. I think it's a thermometer.'

'A *what*?'

'I suspect they're keeping track of the heat in your blood.'

'But you just healed me,' I say, freaking out. 'They're

311

going to see that the temperature's dropped a bit and work out—'

'Then there's no point in leaving quietly, is there? I'm going to pull out the thermometer, then we're going to smash our way out of here.'

'Through the door?'

'I've already tried the door. It opens inwards and I can't force it. We're going for the old observation window. Hang on.'

'No,' I say. 'If the thermometer really is in my vein, then it's got my blood on it, and you know what that'll do to you if you touch it.'

'And if it's feeding data to them wirelessly, then it might have a tracker function, and then they'll be able to follow you wherever we go. It has to come out.'

He doesn't wait for me to argue further. Instead, there's a screech of metal, I feel a tug and an unpleasant wrenching pain, and for a moment there are stars in front of my eyes despite the darkness. Drake holds me by the shoulders, stopping me from falling back to the floor.

'Thermometer. Broken now, damn,' he says, then his tone changes. 'You're not bleeding. Why aren't you bleeding?'

There's no time to get into that mystery. That thing was *definitely* in my vein, but whatever the reason is for the lack of blood, it can't be good. I'm feeling worse with every moment, and if I can't even drain Khalyed's blood out of me anymore, then I can't see how we have any hope at all.

I can't tell him that, though. Not until I know for sure.

'I guess it was just pressed against my skin,' I say. 'So, are we getting out of here, or what?'

33

IT DOESN'T TAKE long for Drake to use his metal-bound hand to smash his way through the brickwork covering the old observation window, and then through the window itself. Suddenly, there is ambient light. The dimly-lit corridor is so bright in comparison to the darkness of the cell that my eyes start watering in response.

Drake's just clearing out the glass so we can both squeeze out when a faint blue glow starts pulsing on and off. At first, I think it's something to do with my eyes acclimatising, or that the drowning or bad blood is having some effect on my vision, but then I turn to see the thermometer on the ground where Drake left it. As it turns out, it wasn't so broken after all.

'Drake,' I say, pointing at the blue light that's flashing on and off at the tip of the device. 'I think we're in trouble.'

Then I hear a noise: a door opening or shutting, maybe. It sounds like it's a long way off right now, but with Silver speed, that means nothing.

'There are locked gates for them to get through between here and there,' he says, hoisting me out through the window. 'It'll buy us a few seconds.'

I land on my side in the corridor in a manner that is less than graceful, then struggle up to my feet, dragging the block with me. Drake is already standing beside me, and for a moment the sight of him takes my breath away, which honestly I could do without right now. I've seen him naked, obviously, but now he's barefoot in dark trousers and a shirt that not only has a few buttons missing, but is also soaking wet, slightly see-through and clinging to every inch of his chest. It's really not the time, but I don't have words for how good his hair looks when it's damp and pushed over his forehead like it is, and his lips are still wet and...

Then I notice blood in the water at our feet, and for the first time I see just how injured he is. The hand that he managed to free looks all right, but the one that's still half-encased in metal is a mess, and it's dripping onto the floor. In small spots the skin on the back of his hand is bared, but for the most part there are sharp ribbons and shards circling around his palm and stabbing into his flesh. It makes me a little sick to look at. He needs to drink some blood to heal it up, and he needs to do it quickly. Then he takes a step and I see that his bare feet are also bleeding from where he's landed on the broken window glass. Mine, of course, are mysteriously fine.

'Shit,' I say.

But we have no time to spare tending to his wounds, because the footsteps are getting steadily closer. They're not hurrying yet, probably because they haven't yet realised that we're free, but they're going to work it out soon enough, and then we'll be really fucked.

'Come on,' I say, moving off along the stone corridor.

'Wrong way!' Drake whispers, pulling me in the other direction. 'The exit's this way.'

'Which is exactly where they're coming from,' I whisper back. 'I don't know about you, but I'm not in any condition to fight right now, and I don't want to get shoved back in that cell to be covered in glitter by one of your ex-girlfriend's brainless fans. Isn't there another way out?'

He thinks for a moment, which is too long for me when those footsteps are coming ever closer, so I shove him along the corridor with my shoulder and start running. He falls into step beside me, both of us too blood-starved to go faster than human speed. That's going to be a problem, because our captors aren't similarly impaired. Though they're taking their time getting to the cell, they could search this whole complex in seconds if they're well-fed enough, so whatever we're going to do, we're going to have to do it quickly. *Very* quickly.

The stone corridor is long, with cell doors lined up at regular intervals along both sides. None of them is occupied. I'm not keeping count, but there must be a hundred of them at least. It's more than a little chilling. By the time we reach the end of the corridor, the light from the lamp outside our cell is mostly gone. As Drake leads me around a corner into another corridor, I'm back to being in the dark. He has to hold my arm to stop me from running into the walls, and the detritus that's built up on the paving stones over decades of misuse is not only stabbing into my feet with every step, but also making me trip up more often that I'd like. With our captors bound to discover our absence any second, the whole escape feels like an exercise in futility.

Until.

Drake pulls me to a stop.

I'm about to ask why when I hear a noise.

Back in the corridor we've just left, there's a tinkle of glass and a small, tremulous voice says, 'Uh-oh.'

It's Mikey. I'm expecting him to come after us – our footprints won't be hard to follow – but instead I hear him swear up a storm, mutter, 'She's going to kill me,' then walk back the way he came, his footsteps retreating slowly along the corridor. Apparently he's in no hurry to tell Carlotta what's happened.

Once he's far enough away, Drake starts pulling me along the corridor again, past empty cell after empty cell.

'Where are we going?' I whisper.

'The old baths,' he murmurs back.

'There are baths down here?'

'Yes. We needed them so we could wash off the blood after… After.' Probably best to avoid thinking too hard about that, I decide. 'There's a pool fed by a spring, and a drain that should take us out into the river.'

I groan. 'No more water.'

But he says, 'It's the only other way out,' so I guess I'm going to be swimming again sooner than I expected.

Unfortunately, when we finally reach the old baths, there have been some changes. Instead of the basic medieval facilities I'm expecting, there's a large room with a line of open lockers, a couple of cupboard-like changing rooms, a series of toilet stalls and, in a separate cubicle in the corner, a retro avocado bathroom suite. I can see all of this because there is also an overhead bulb, which Drake has turned on with a click, leaving blood on the pull cord. I don't see a drain, but I see something better. In one of the lockers, Drake's jacket is hanging beside the backpack I took with me on my spectacularly unsuccessful infiltration mission. Carlotta must have thrown them in here to keep them out of the way. This is good news because hooray backpack, but bad news because it suggests they might actually be using this side of the complex too, and not just the cells.

We'd better hurry.

'Check the other lockers,' I say to Drake, then I watch impatiently over his shoulder as he leafs through moth-ridden old clothes and pulls two blister packs of blood capsules from the inner pocket of his jacket.

Thank the lord.

'Never leave home without them,' he says with a smile.

He pops and swallows the first pack in one mouthful. It's enough concentrated blood to run several marathons at super speed, but Drake's so battered that he can barely heal himself up and release his hand from the remaining metal restraint before he's out of energy. If Leclercq and Carlotta have been feeding him at all during his captivity, then it has barely been enough to keep him alive. They will pay for that, I swear.

But first, I need to get out of my own restraints.

'I can feed them to you,' Drake offers, holding out the second pack. The words make my insides dance in a way I'd rather not describe in too much detail, but I know it's not going to work.

'I'm too far gone,' I say. 'I'll take a couple, but you take the rest.'

'What are you talking about?'

'I mean it won't do any good. My veins are too full of Khalyed's blood, so I'm never going to be strong enough to break myself out. I need you to do it for me.'

He gives me a look that tells me we're going to be discussing this later – if there is a later – then he puts a few capsules to one side, swallows the rest, and gets to work on my hands.

It is excruciating. He does his best to break me out cleanly, but there's a world of difference between forcing your own hands out of a substance, pushing evenly from the inside, and trying to dig someone else's out. Inevitably, it pinches. The sharper points of the metal squeeze and puncture and twist in a way that has me biting my lip to keep myself from crying out in pain. When he peels the last mangled piece away from my hands and they are finally released from behind my back, I'm expecting to see blood everywhere.

There is none.

I turn my hands over, looking at the pristine and unbroken skin. Drake is staring.

'What's going on?' he asks, half awed and half afraid.

'Later,' I say, hoping that either I'll have an explanation by then, or we'll both be dead so it won't matter. 'Pass me those pills.'

I swallow the last few capsules and feel very marginally better, but the burning is reaching a peak that I don't think I'll be able to quench, no matter how many capsules I swallow or how much blood I drink. In the circumstances, maybe it's strange that I'm even bothering with this futile escape at all. If Drake wasn't here with me then I probably wouldn't have made the attempt, but if we can get out of here, and if we can do it with a few hours to spare before we both go up in flames, then perhaps we can spend our final moments in exactly the way I had hoped we might. It's not a particularly lofty ambition, but if there's a possibility that I can end my days in bed with the man I'm... slightly fond of, then it's a possibility I will fight tooth and nail to manifest.

'Right, we need to make ourselves invisible,' I say, at the same time as Drake says, 'I need to make a call.'

We both stare at each other for a second, then Drake says, 'Invisible?' at the same time as I say, 'You've got a *phone*?'

'You're not the only one with a burner,' he says, pulling an ancient flip phone out of his jacket pocket. 'Not much signal this far underground.'

'So, my plan, then?'

He dials a number then holds the phone to his ear. The call fails. He tries again. Same result.

'Try your phone,' he suggests.

I so, shooting off quick messages to Mina and Kulika, but they don't send.

'I'll try messaging too,' he says. 'Maybe we'll get through eventually.'

'And in the meantime, my plan, yes?'

He makes a third call.

'You were all judgey about me not having a plan earlier, and now that I do have a plan, you won't even listen to it. Make up your damn mind.'

'One sec.' He holds up a finger, not meeting my eye as he makes a fourth call.

'Drake,' I say, getting irritated now. 'Our time is extremely limited. Mikey could be back any minute with Leclercq and Carlotta. Stop pissing about. I may not be a master strategist, but I've actually got a plan and you don't, so we're doing mine.'

He sighs and flicks the phone shut. 'Your plan is to go invisible. That's not a plan, it's a fantasy. I can only assume you have a head wound.'

'Just listen, will you?' I say. 'The only way out of here is the way we came in, but they're back that way, right?'

'I would assume so. There's a control room on the floor above this one, and we'd have to walk right past it to get to the exit.'

'Okay, then. But, we also know that Mikey knows we're out, and he's going to have to tell them sooner or later, so if they're not on their way down here already they will be very soon. Right?'

'Again, I can only assume—'

'Great. Now what's off in that direction?' I ask, pointing along the corridor away from the cells.

'Store rooms,' he says. 'Sleeping quarters. It's a dead end.'

'But we could have gone that way, right? So here's the plan: we go and leave some footprints heading off in that direction. Then we come back here – carefully stepping only in the footprints we've already made – then we wash ourselves clean, apply a load of this to make ourselves invisible to their noses,' I say, holding up the scent-masking spray I've just located in my backpack, 'then hide in this room while they go running past. Then we slip back into the corridor while they're in the dead end, run out past the cells and make a break for freedom.'

'And if they spot us?' he asks. 'I'm not sure that I'll be able to run far at super-speed, particularly not if I'm carrying you, and I don't imagine you'll be moving very fast otherwise.'

'Aha,' I say, rootling around in my backpack once more. 'But I have this.' I pull out the tranquilliser gun, still loaded with the two shots I put in it before I walked into Solis Invicti HQ. 'It should buy us some time at least.'

'But—'

'No buts. No time to argue. Move.'

And, to Drake's credit, he does. We leave our trail of footprints, we return to the baths, we get the blood cleaned off his hands and feet, and then... Well, then things get a little more heated.

'How do we do this?' he asks, holding the bottle of scent-masking spray.

'Quickly,' I say. 'We have to cover every inch of skin.' Then, without thinking too much about it, I unbutton his wet shirt and push it off his shoulders.

The moment my hands touch his skin I realise what a terrible idea this was. I haven't been this close to Drake since he left Tabitha's apartment all those weeks ago, and with the heat already thrumming in my veins, the touch of his skin is like a match to a flame. Not for the first time, I feel like I'm about to combust.

'Valentine,' he whispers, leaning down to rest his forehead against mine. 'No time.'

'Yes.' I clear my throat. 'Right. The time. People chasing us. Uh-huh.'

With some effort, I shake myself back into action and give his upper body a thorough spraying. I have to turn away as he shucks his trousers and coats his lower half, because otherwise I'm worried I might do something I'll regret. Then it's my turn. I hop into one of the changing rooms and cover myself thoroughly in the scent mask. This whole spraying process has taken less than a minute, which is a pretty impressive feat given that we're moving at human speed.

But we're not quite done yet. That spot in the middle of my back is still giving me trouble. I have to step out of the changing room in my bra to get Drake to reach it for me – there's no getting at it any other way – but when his fingertips touch my skin, it undoes me entirely.

'Remember Sir Percival's party?' he whispers. Then he trails his fingers up from the centre of my back to the nape of my neck, to the spot that makes me go *unh*.

I go, 'Unh.'

'That backless gown you wore just to torment me.'

'Drake…' I say in a warning tone. If he carries on like this then he's going to set off our scent marks, which will entirely defeat the purpose of the scent mask. 'This is not the time.'

'And that's not my name,' he whispers back. Then he leans in to kiss my neck, but stops abruptly just before his lips touch my skin. 'You don't smell like yourself. You don't smell like… anyone.'

'Exactly!' I say triumphantly.

That's when I start to believe, for the very first time, that my plan might actually work, and we might really get out of here. In the same moment, I feel a thud in the side of my neck and realise I've left the loaded tranquilliser gun in the locker on the other side of the room. We've let ourselves get distracted, and in the meantime Mikey has snuck up on us. I should never have touched Drake's skin. I should never have let him touch mine. I've always known he'd be my downfall.

Really, I only have myself to blame.

34

WHEN I WAKE up, I'm warm and comfortable and wrapped in something that smells *incredible*. My eyes snap open. I'm wrapped in Killian bloody Drake, and we're crammed together tight in Mikey's bloody perspex box.

I groan.

I'm lying on my side with Drake's bare chest pressed up against my back. My head is pillowed on his arm and my nose is practically pressed against the perspex, so I don't think there's going to be much wiggle room for changing position. I do, however, have a clear view of the new cell in which our soon-to-be coffin has been placed: it's just like the last one, only the observation window is still intact and the light from out in the corridor is spilling into the cell, so at least I can see this time. Our box is on top of some kind of stone plinth or table, putting us level with the observation window.

I turn my head, trying to look at Drake, but there's not enough space in here for me to turn to face him. I can just see the edge of his cheekbone in my peripheral vision, and then I have to stop straining because even that small effort makes my vision fill with black spots. My veins are burning so much that I want to scream. Then Drake lays his hand across my bare stomach – I'm still only wearing my bra on top – and the pain somehow eases.

'Welcome back,' he says from behind me. 'You'll be pleased to hear that Mikey's gone to get the glitter.'

'Oh, good,' I croak. 'At least our deaths will be appropriately fabulous.'

I must have been out a while, because the scent mask has worn off. All I can smell is iron and spice and every bad thing I wish I'd had the time to do to Drake before Mikey caught up with us. Oh, the indignity of being captured by *Mikey*, of all people.

'Are you hurt?' I ask. 'Did he knock you out too? If he's hit you with another of those tranquilliser darts then are you going to—'

'No. I'm fine,' Drake says. 'He didn't shoot me.'

'Then how did he overpower you?'

'He didn't have to,' he says, as though the answer should be blindingly obvious. 'He had you.'

'So you just climbed in here?'

He clears his throat.

'You're an idiot,' I say.

'So I've been told. Earlier today, in fact. By you.'

'Well, I wasn't wrong. Where are Leclercq and Carlotta?' I ask.

He points over my shoulder at the observation window where, intermittently, I can see the two of them passing to and fro behind the glass. I don't like their busyness, or what it might herald.

'Wave,' he says.

'No, thanks.' I drop my voice to a whisper, in case they can hear. 'So much for my plan, then.'

'It was a good plan, Jack.'

'Just Jack now, is it?'

'Would you prefer *my Valentine*?'

I smile without meaning to, but thankfully he can't see my face. 'If by some miracle we ever make it out of here, then maybe,' I say brusquely. 'Speaking of which, can you break us out of this thing?'

'No. Believe me, I've tried, but there was some skirmishing after you were hit, and I lost what little blood I had left in my veins in the process. Three to one doesn't seem very fair to me, particularly when one has been imprisoned for months on end, but I got the impression that they're not very interested in sportsmanship.'

'Says the man who murdered a bunch of incapacitated, boxed-up Silver.'

'Divine retribution, is it?' There's a small pause, then he says, 'Can I ask: what is that smell?'

Even if I wasn't in the process of going critical from the blood poisoning, then my cheeks would still be burning. We are very close together, in fact we couldn't get much closer, and the only ventilation in this box is from the small hole above my ear through which Mikey is doubtless intending to gild me with glitter. The air is thick, and I'm suddenly very self conscious about that. If I can smell Drake as strongly as I can, then I must be reeking.

'Oh, right, apologies for not showering so I'd be daisy-fresh when I came to rescue you,' I say defensively. 'Weirdly, I was in a bit of a hurry. And also,' I say, looking down at my shirt suspiciously, 'I fell into some bin bags at the back of a Chinese takeaway. There might have been fish.'

'No, not that. The water took care of that. I was talking about…'

He pulls me even closer, nuzzling into my neck, and I wonder if maybe it's not so important that we find a way out of this torture device right this very second, even if we do have an audience.

Then he ruins the moment by drawing back abruptly and saying, 'Have you been with the Primus?'

'When you say *been with*—'

'Jesus *Christ*. Why would you do that? Are you trying to torture me?'

'No, I didn't. I mean, I was at his penthouse. I was trying to find you and I thought you might be boxed up in his basement.'

'So you screwed him for information?'

'No! Of course not! I just *asked*.'

'Then why do you smell like him?'

'Because,' I say irritably. 'I was in his penthouse, like I said.'

'And between the water and the scent-masking spray, there should be no trace of him left on you. So I'm going to ask you this just once: if you weren't trying to torture me, then why did you drink the Primus's blood?'

'I didn't! Why would I— Oh, wait.'

I'm thinking about the hot chocolate the Primus made me in his penthouse, and about how I felt afterwards, refreshed to a degree that shouldn't have been possible given how much of Khalyed's blood was infecting mine.

That bastard just cannot stop drugging me without my consent.

'It's possible,' I admit. 'He gave me a blood-based drink.'

'No,' Drake says. Suddenly, his tone is so dark it's frightening. Part of me wishes I could see his face so I could better gauge his mood, and part of me is glad I can't. 'He can't do this. Not to you. Not now.'

'Do what? When?'

'Winta is dead,' Drake says. 'Your sire is dead.'

'Yes, I'm aware. Thanks for the reminder, though.'

'Now that she's gone, he's trying to claim you.'

'What?' This isn't something I've heard of before, but it sounds more than a little out there. 'How does that work?'

'It doesn't, not really. It's symbolic. If your sire dies and you drink enough of another Silver's blood then – in the eyes of the other Silver, at least – they become your new sire. You belong to them.'

'*What?* But why? I didn't consent to that. And why would he do that when he knows you—' I manage to catch myself just before I say the dangerous word. 'Um, he knows about the silvering thing.'

Drake goes deadly still behind me.

'How?'

'I didn't tell him!' I say quickly. 'But I'm pretty sure he's worked it out. Cam too.'

'Damn.'

'Good thing we're about to die anyway, right?'

'Are we?' he asks softly. 'I did wonder. You said that drinking blood wouldn't do you any good, and even though I healed you earlier, you're not entirely better, are you?'

'No. I don't think I'm going to make it through this. I'm sorry.'

'Don't be sorry,' he says, pressing a kiss to my neck. 'Just tell me what's going on.'

'We're stuck in a reinforced plastic box about to get drowned in glitter,' I say. 'I think I'm allowed to be sorry about that. Hang on a minute.' A thought has just occurred to me. 'I've drunk your blood. Doesn't that make you my sire now?'

'No. You haven't bitten me since your sire died.'

'Oh.'

Because we were trying to avoid haematopsychosis, and to avoid spreading Khalyed's poison, like responsible kinky vampires. If I'd known we'd end up here, maybe I would have just enjoyed myself while I had the chance.

'I'm getting really bored with all this old Silver lore,' I say. 'Between the bonds and the claiming and the healing mojo, it's becoming really tiresome.'

'Tiresome?' Drake whispers, then he puts his hand on my hip and pulls me back against him so I can feel exactly what my proximity is doing to him. He said he didn't have any blood left in his body, but apparently he's found some. 'The bond is not tiresome, Valentine. It's everything. It's the blood in my veins and the beat of my heart and the pull between the two of us, dragging me closer to you every second, whispering that you're mine.'

As he speaks, his breath brushes over my cheek. I shudder, and there go our scent marks, filling the perspex coffin with dark spice and sexual tension.

'You're mine,' he says again.

When he whispers those words to me, I want them to be true. I am aching for them to be true. The rational part of me says only cavemen think possessing their partner is sexy, but the rest of me is on fire, and not just from the bad blood in my veins.

I try to fight my desire anyway.

The problem with being stuck in this box is that it puts his mouth right by my ear, so he can whisper all his terrible promises, and right by the nape of my neck, so he can kiss the spot that makes me go wild, and neither of those things feels appropriate when we're stuck in a display case in the middle of a torture chamber. It also makes me really fucking angry, because I don't want to go out like this, pinned in this frustrating position where what I want is so close – too close, really – and yet so impossible to manoeuvre towards a satisfyingly screamy conclusion.

Seriously, I am pissed off.

'Is this thing bolted down?' I ask.

'Why?' he asks, kissing my neck again. 'What exactly did

you have in mind?'

'Rock,' I say.

The kissing abruptly ceases. 'What?'

'*Rock*,' I say.

I start moving my weight back and forth as much as is possible in the confined space. Drake gets the idea after a moment and joins in, and with the two of us moving simultaneously, the box finally starts to shift. Which is just as well, because – as I'm sure you can imagine – the motion we're replicating to get the stupid perspex coffin towards the edge of the stupid plinth is doing absolutely nothing for my sexual frustration. Drake seems to be enjoying himself, though.

'I'm not sure how much more of this I can take,' he groans.

Then the coffin finally rolls. For a moment, I'm face down with Drake on top of me while the box balances on the edge of the plinth, then the whole thing topples onto the ground, tipping as it does so, leaving me on my back on top of Drake. There's a large shard of perspex missing from the box right in front of my face, cracked and snapped away during the fall, but that's it. The rest of the box stays intact.

Bugger.

From the noise filtering through the glass of the observation window, I would guess that our tumble hasn't got unnoticed. One of the women raises her voice – I can't tell who, because it's muffled, but I would bet on it being Leclercq – and then there's the jingle of keys at the door.

'I have a plan,' I whisper.

I explain myself quickly and quietly while the door is being unlocked. By the time the unlocker reaches us – Mikey, going by the scent – both of us are pretending to be knocked out.

'Er, Carlotta?' he calls. 'I think… I think we might be too

329

late.'

'*What?*' yells a voice I recognise as Leclercq's. 'What do you mean, *too late*?'

'I mean, they're not moving,' Mikey replies.

'Are they breathing? Can you hear a pulse?'

'Err…'

'Oh, forget it.' Leclercq lowers her voice to a normal pitch as she enters the room. 'I'll check them. But I swear, Mikey, if you've fucked this up by insisting on your stupid glitter…'

Drake and I are both pretty far gone at this point, and we're controlling our respiration, so she's going to have to work hard to find a pulse or hear us breathing.

I wait until she gets close. Really, really close. Until I can feel her breath on my face. Then I open my eyes.

'You're not dead, then,' she says.

'No,' I say. 'But you are.'

Then I thrust one hand up through the hole in the perspex and drive it right into her open mouth. Whatever weird healing my body is doing at the moment to stop me from bleeding, it doesn't work when Leclercq's teeth are embedded in my knuckles. As I pointed out to Drake a few moments ago, I am a person-shaped poison syringe. Khalyed's blood is now so concentrated in my veins that it only takes the tiniest drop for Leclercq to go up in smoke. This isn't a slow, drawn-out process like it was with Winta. Leclercq is a new Silver. One second she's there, and the next she's nothing but ash on the floor. And in my face, and my hair, and a little in my mouth too, which is something I'd rather not think about ever again.

I splutter.

'Good plan,' Drake says.

'Yeah, well, I may not be a master strategist, but I have fucked up blood and a belly full of rage.'

'Good enough.'

He sounds a little out of breath, which isn't surprising given that I am still lying on top of him, but it reminds me we should probably do something about getting out of this box. There's no sign of Mikey or Carlotta, so I'm guessing they've decided to abandon ship. After all, it was Leclercq's show. They were just along for the ride.

Drake and I roll the coffin onto its side again and, now that there's a weakness in one side, between the two of us we manage to push our way free.

That, of course, is the moment the cavalry arrives.

35

ELLIE'S FIRST THROUGH the door, yelling, 'Oh my god. Are you all right?'

'Do we look all right?' I groan.

'You look... a bit scandalous, actually.'

She's not entirely wrong. I've ended up in Drake's arms on the floor in my jeans and bra, and he's just wearing his trousers. The unfair part is that we haven't had a chance to do anything remotely scandalous yet, however much I might have been leaning in that direction.

'Miss St John,' Drake says. 'Your timing is... impeccable.'

Boyd and Raul are in the room now too, with Faiz and Kulika close behind.

'He means appalling,' I say. 'Your timing's appalling. Seriously, they torture us for however long—'

'Two days,' Raul supplies.

'—two days,' I continue, 'and you wait until we've just got ourselves free to— Wait. Two *days*?'

'I only just got your text message, Jack,' says Kulika. 'And yours, Baron. My apologies.'

Drake waves away her contrition.

'We're underground,' I say. 'How did you receive them at all?'

'We found these in the alley up top,' Kulika says, holding out our burner phones. They've been smashed into several barely-connected pieces. 'Yours?'

'Yes,' Drake says.

'Carlotta and Mikey?' I ask Kulika.

'Gone. Quentin and Rolf are following their scent.'

'Maybe they took the phones with them when they ran and didn't realise the messages were waiting to send until they got up top,' I suggest.

'Or perhaps Carlotta took them above ground precisely *because* she realised the messages were waiting to send,' Drake replies.

'You mean she wanted us to get rescued?'

'Carlotta's feelings about me are… conflicted. More conflicted than I realised, apparently.'

He pushes himself up onto his knees and helps me up alongside him, but standing feels like a big ask right now.

'Blood,' Kulika orders.

Raul produces a cooler and hands us each a bottle. I swig it back, for all the good it does. I feel marginally better, but the only thing that really steadies me is Drake's hand on my bare back.

'How about some clothes, too?' I ask.

I'm feeling more than a little self-conscious now that everyone's crowding into the tiny cell, but the issue isn't so much the partial nudity as it is the way they're all staring at me and Drake.

'Jack!' Mina barges into the cell, pushing the others out of her way. 'What the fuck? You disappeared.'

'What's she doing here?' Drake asks.

'Helping,' Mina says defensively. 'Trying to stop her dying, and killing you in the process. The words I think you're looking for are *thank you.*'

'Mina!' I say, incensed that she's talking so openly about the bond in front of a bunch of people who don't know about it. 'A little discretion, please?'

'You're kidding, right?' Mina says, then she looks at Drake and says, 'Isn't she?'

Drake smiles ruefully at me and says, 'Valentine, I think they already know.' Then he cups my chin with his fingers and strokes along my bottom lip with his thumb.

Shit.

He healed me with a kiss when we were escaping from the first cell. My lips will be their usual post-healing silver, and everyone in the room has seen them. That's why they're all shuffling their feet and smirking. The scent marks probably aren't helping with that, either.

They know about the bond.

What a clusterfuck.

'So,' Kulika says, crossing her arms over her chest, 'you two are finally doing this, then?'

'Um…' I say.

'Clothes, Kulika,' Drake says. 'If you wouldn't mind.'

She leaves, muttering as she goes.

'Yes, let's give them some space for a moment, shall we?' Boyd says, clearing his throat. 'Everyone out.'

By the time Kulika returns with something for us to wear, everyone except Mina has left the room. She must have moved at super-speed, because she's gone for less than a minute, but the boiler suits she hands us look like they've come from the Dregs' hide out.

'Thank you,' Drake says to Kulika. 'Please go and search the rest of the tunnels.'

'My backpack was down here,' I say. 'With the tranquilliser gun. If Carlotta and Mikey have gone off with it —' Then I realise that, in all the desperate confusion of our time underground, I've forgotten something important. 'Oh, god. Frank. Mikey took Frank. Have you found him?'

'I found him,' Mina says. 'He's fine.'

'Sir,' Kulika says, 'I should take you to get checked out. If you could just—'

'Give us a moment,' he says.

Kulika doesn't move.

'You have your orders, Ms Yadav,' he adds. His tone is light, but it's clear that he is not prepared to be argued with. 'In the meantime, we will call if we need you, but I assure you I am perfectly capable of getting dressed by myself.'

With bad grace, Kulika says, 'Yes, sir,' then turns on her heel and walks out of the room to search the complex.

Mina, however, seems to be going nowhere.

'I don't need any help putting my clothes on either,' I say to her. 'So, you know, bye.'

'Just as well,' she says. 'I'm better at taking clothes off than putting them on anyway.' But she shows absolutely no sign of leaving.

'Mina,' I sigh. 'What is it?'

'You never turned up at the lair—'

'Lair?' Drake says quizzically.

'The Dregs' place,' I supply.

'—and I thought you'd just given up,' Mina continues, 'or I thought maybe I'd offended you with that kiss—'

'You *kissed* her?' Drake says. His voice is so quiet and calm that I know he's trying to control himself. 'You dared to kiss *my*—'

'Whoa, hold on there, Baron,' Mina interrupts. 'Firstly, I think we have bigger things to worry about right now. Secondly, yes, but only once. And thirdly, what are you going to do about it while you're sitting there on the floor, all beaten up and blood-starved?'

'More than you might imagine, Ms Parchek,' he says

threateningly.

'Children,' I say. 'Please. It's been a very, very long day. Can you just get to the point, Mina?'

'The point is… Are we okay?'

I give her my most tolerant and reassuring smile. 'We're okay, Mina. And thank you. But right now, I'd really like to put some clothes on and get out of here. Okay?'

'Okay.' She smiles.

Mina doesn't smile often, at least not in a non-leering way, so I take this as the compliment it is. Apparently, the two of us have become close enough over the past few months that she no longer feels the need to sexualise every single comment she throws my way. We are… friends. It's nice, even if it will be short-lived.

She leaves the room and finally – *finally* – Drake and I are alone, unbound, and face to face. Unfortunately, I don't have the energy to do much about it. Despite what I said to Mina, I am barely strong enough to dress myself, but I get the boiler suit on with Drake's help.

'By the way,' he says as he zips me up, 'if you let Mina Parchek touch you again, I will have to kill her.'

I laugh, but he's not joking.

'I don't belong to you, Drake,' I say.

'The scent mark on your skin says otherwise. Face it, Valentine: you're mine.'

'The scent mark only says I'm yours for twenty-four hours,' I say.

'Right. Then another twenty-four, and another, and another. The clock restarts every time you kiss me, and twenty-four hours is a long time when you're wrapped in my scent.' He leans in close, letting his lips hover just over my cheek. 'Do you really think you can resist the temptation to take another taste?'

We both know the answer to that. I have always had

crummy willpower.

He takes my hesitation as permission, and lifts me up to sit on the now-vacant stone plinth. He's standing between my legs, his chest pressed against mine, leaning in to kiss me.

But.

'Drake, wait,' I say, pulling back.

'I've waited, Valentine. I've waited for months. After everything we've just been through, are you really going to keep pushing me away? When are you finally going to admit that this thing between us...' He leans in again to rest his cheek against mine and pauses there for a moment as our mingled scents fill the air around us. We don't even need to kiss and we're renewing the mark, claiming each other again and again. 'It's real.'

'It's too much,' I whisper.

'You think I'm not scared, too?' he says. 'You think I'm not absolutely fucking terrified? I've silvered for you. You know what that means.'

'Don't say it.'

'I won't,' he says sadly. 'But I feel it all the same.'

And that's a problem. It's not just that everyone knows about it now, or that I don't want the kind of immediate commitment it implies. It's a problem because I'm *dying*, literally right now, and I'm going to take him with me, whether I want to or not. Maybe he still thinks his kisses will be enough to save me, but they will never be enough. Nothing will.

It's time for my own confession.

'It's getting worse,' I whisper.

'What is?' he whispers back.

'The burning in my veins.'

'Then let me heal you again,' he says.

'You can't.'

He just looks at me, his expression fearful.

'Every time you heal me,' I say, 'the pain comes back quicker. Tabitha looked at my blood, and the bad cells are multiplying inside me. We need Khalyed's blood to make a cure, but we don't have it, and I don't suppose you have any extra vials stashed around the place, do you?'

'They're all gone,' he says. 'The Invicti took them away to be destroyed, but we can get more. They moved Dr Khalyed to the London facility, but—'

'No. He's gone, too.' I tell him about what Adewale and Alistair did. 'Without Khalyed's blood,' I say, 'we can't make an antidote for the poison that's killing me, and my time's nearly up. Tabitha only gave me a couple of weeks to live, maximum, and that was days ago, so between the torture and the electrocution and the tranquilliser and the getting run over by a bus—'

'You were genuinely run over by a bus? I thought that was a joke.'

'Mikey's fault. What I'm trying to say is that everything that's happened over the past few days will only have sped up the timetable. In the next day or so, it'll get bad enough that you're not to going to be able to heal me at all anymore, and when that happens, we're both going to die. Unless…'

'Unless what?'

'Unless we find a way to break the bond.'

I swear I see the colour drain from his cheeks, but I push on anyway. He needs to hear all of this, now that we're free. He needs to know everything I know, so he knows all his options. I might not have been able to save him on my own, but maybe he'll be able to save himself in the time we have left.

'I found a manuscript that said something about distance making the bond stretch and break. Tabitha says I'm reading it wrong, but maybe—'

'*That's* why you pushed me away so hard the last time I came to see you?' he says. 'You think you can stop me from lov—'

'Don't say it!'

'No,' he says, taking my face in his hands. 'You need to hear this: I love you.'

I groan.

'That's not the reaction I was hoping for, I admit,' he says, letting his hands fall. 'But I suppose it's the one I was expecting.'

'Look, I don't want to hurt you. And, however irritating I might find you, I actually don't want you to die either.'

'You can't break the bond, Valentine. It just… is. Nothing you can say or do will ever change that. You can try to ignore it, or actively fight against it, or you could finally accept it and enjoy what we have for what little time we still have together. So what's it going to be?'

That's the moment Boyd chooses to come back into the cell. Honestly, it's a welcome reprieve.

'I'm sorry to interrupt,' he says, 'but Dr Ross is demanding that Jacqueline has a health check. I can't delay her much longer.'

He's barely finished speaking when Tabitha bustles past him and into the cell.

'Oh my god, hen, look at you,' she says, ignoring Drake entirely as she puts her medical bag down beside me on the plinth and opens it up. 'You're too pale.'

'Dr Ross,' Drake says by way of greeting.

'Baron,' she replies with a small nod.

Apparently, they have reached a strained detente.

Drake perches on the plinth on my other side while Tabitha turns her attention back to her bag, pulling out glass syringes and needles and a stethoscope. You wouldn't think a Silver doctor would need one, given how good our hearing is, but apparently I'm weak enough that my pulse needs amplification. She slips the earpieces into her ears and moves to unzip my boiler suit, but Drake stops her hand and does it for her, taking the chest piece and holding it against my heart.

My eye roll is eloquent, but neither of them seems to notice it, so I bat Drake's hand away and hold the chest piece myself.

'How are you feeling?' Tabitha asks me as she puts the stethoscope away. 'Is the burning worse?'

'Yes.'

Now that the drama is over and I'm no longer distracted by the primal urge to stay alive, or the immediate desire to jump Drake's bones, the burning is consuming me.

'How bad is it?' she asks, her forehead furrowing in concern.

'Pretty bad.'

Her forehead furrows some more.

'Mina told me about Dr Khalyed,' she says as she takes my temperature and my pulse and fiddles around with a load of other instruments I don't understand. 'I'll try to find a way around it. I'm not giving up on you yet. If only I had Dr Castell's notes, maybe I could do something with those.'

'Call him,' Drake says. 'Ask him to come and assist you, on my authority.'

'You're not worried about the Invicti finding you?' Tabitha asks me, looking alarmed.

'No,' I say. 'Apparently Leclercq was the only person who hated me enough to bother doing something about it, and she's dead now, so I guess I can come out of hiding.'

'All right, then,' she says. 'I'll call. In the meantime, I'm going to take some blood,' she says, pulling on a couple of pairs of latex gloves in lieu of the usual hazmat suit. I'm half expecting the syringe to come up empty given all the weird shit that's happened since the bus hit me, but there's my blood, glinting darkly in the tube. 'I won't be able to tell you much until I get it under a microscope,' she says, 'but for the moment you should rest and drink plenty of blood.'

'We should get you back to the Dregs' lair, as you call it,' Drake says as Tabitha packs her bag away. 'You'll be safe there.'

'Can't we just go home?' I ask.

'Home?'

'Your home, I mean,' I say quietly, finally giving in and asking for what I really want. 'I'm sick of being underground.'

Drake smiles and kisses the top of my head. 'Home it is,' he says.

Then he carries me out into the light of day and into Boyd's waiting car. I'm asleep before we're even halfway to Summertown.

36

I WAKE UP while Drake is putting me into bed. It's not his bed, though, which is both surprising and disappointing.

'Where are we?' I ask.

'Guest suite,' he says softly. 'Go back to sleep.'

'Oh. Okay.'

He pulls the covers up over my boiler suit – aptly named, because I am *boiling* – and sits in an armchair by the window.

'Don't you have somewhere else you'd rather be?' I ask. 'I mean, you should probably get your affairs in order.'

It's not that I want him to go, but I also don't want to keep him here if he has better things to do than watch me sleep.

'No,' he says. 'I'm staying right here.'

But when I wake in the middle of the night, he's gone.

To my surprise, I'm actually feeling a bit better. Maybe it's the fact that I finally got some sleep that wasn't chemically assisted – I haven't done that since before I left Tabitha's flat – but I don't trust it. For all I know, I'm only feeling better because my temperature is equalising as I get closer to burning up, or something. Still, I'm well enough to pull myself out of bed, chug down a bottle of blood from the room's convenient mini-fridge, and drag myself through the shower.

When I come out of the bathroom wrapped in a towel, Drake's back.

'You should be resting,' he says.

But he's been through the shower too, and his damp hair is begging for my fingers to run through it. He's still barefoot, wearing black jeans and a shirt that has too many – and simultaneously not enough – buttons undone. I feel a little lightheaded, and I don't think it's from the poison.

With eyes as dark as Drake's, it's hard to tell whether or not his pupils are dilated. Until, that is, he stops hiding his silver. Then I can see just how large his pupils are, ringed in a corona of starry silver.

He says, 'You need to rest,' but he still takes a step closer.

'If we only have a few hours left,' I say, taking a step myself, 'then I don't want to spend them in bed.'

'Don't you?' His eyes are twinkling at me.

'Not asleep, anyway.'

He takes one more step to close the gap, then his fingertips are hovering over my cheek, willing me to lean into him. He smells like copper, and spice, and sanctuary.

'Are you sure?' he asks.

'Are *you*? You only have as long as I do.'

'Oh, I'm sure,' he says.

Then my arms are around his neck, my hands are in his hair, his lips are on mine, and our scent marks are whirling around us in a mixture so powerful and intoxicating and so *right* that I can't believe how many times I've managed to say no to him. He is irresistible.

'Not here, though,' he says against my mouth.

Then he lifts my feet off the ground, wraps my legs around his hips and starts moving towards the door, kissing me all the way. Apparently he fuelled up on blood during the day, and I could not be happier to see him back to full strength. He's going to need it.

'Your room?' I ask, breathlessly.

'Sort of.'

I hope he's cleared the guards out from the upper floors of the mansion, because we are neither quiet nor discreet as we push each other into walls and furniture on our way from the guest suite to his rooms upstairs. My towel gets lost somewhere along the first corridor, and though I don't have a conscious memory of removing his shirt, Drake is down to his jeans. Maybe I'd give a shit about my potentially-not-private nudity in normal circumstances, but if I'm dying tonight then does it really matter who sees my naked arse? Let them get an eyeful, for all I care. As long as Drake doesn't stop kissing me and doing that thing he's started doing with his fingers between my legs, I will die happy and unashamed.

When we crash through the door into his enormous bedroom, I assume he's going to take me to the bed, like he did last time. Instead, he crosses the room to what I thought were the windows, but actually turn out to be bifold doors leading out onto a roof terrace I hadn't even realised was there.

He puts my feet back on the floor and concertinas the doors, opening one side of the room out to the night with a dramatic flourish, then says, 'What do you think?'

It's a small space, only about half the size of his cavernous bedroom, but it's intimate. There's running water that I can hear but can't see amongst all the plotted plants, and it lends a crispness to the heat of a summer day that has not yet cooled. Tall potted plants and small trees circle the edges, curving to create an arbour that frames the centre of the sky. Even this close to the city centre, I can see the stars, and with the rest of the world blocked out, I can easily imagine that if

I lay down on one of the benches on the deck and looked up, I might feel as though I were miles away from anywhere.

What I really think is that it's a little slice of paradise.

What I actually say is, 'The one the Primus has is bigger,' because I'm a bastard like that.

'Maybe,' Drake replies, 'but I actually know how to use mine.'

He scoops me back up into his arms, nuzzles into my neck and says, 'Shall I demonstrate?'

'You want to fuck me on your roof terrace?' I ask. 'What are you, some kind of pervert? Want the neighbours to watch?'

'Says the woman who just flashed her backside to my head of security.'

'I did not,' I say. 'Drake, please tell me Kulika did not just see us foreplaying our way up the stairs.'

'She's seen worse,' he replies.

'With you in residence, I don't doubt it.'

Just like that, our impending deaths are forgotten, and we're playing again. Trading insults is what we do best.

To pass the time until I can think of my next one, I slip out of Drake's arms, then slip him out of his jeans and underwear, because I don't believe in inequality, particularly when it comes to nakedness. The bonus of this approach is that when I reach up to capture his mouth with mine, grabbing his exquisite backside as I do so, our bodies rub together in a way that makes him groan.

'Do you want to make me beg?' he asks.

'Yes, actually.' I lean back so I can run a finger slowly down his chest and over his stomach, stopping a fraction of inch away from where he wants to be touched. 'A little begging wouldn't hurt.'

With no preamble whatsoever, he drops to his knees and gets creative with his tongue. As far as begging goes, it's pretty good. All right, it's more than a little good. So good that my legs go wobbly and he has to catch me before I hit the floor.

'Duvet,' he says, coming up for air.

'I thought you wanted to be outside?'

'I do.'

He scoops me up in one arm and takes the duvet off the bed with the other, then he shoves the benches to the edges of the terrace, lays the duvet down on the deck and lays me on top of it.

'One night?' he asks between kisses.

'One night,' I confirm, smiling because I know where he's going with this.

'No consequences?'

'I should bloody well hope not.'

He laughs.

'And you're not going to be weird about it?' he asks, recalling the question I asked him the first time we did this, back when we thought we could just fuck it out of our systems and get on with our separate lives.

'Killian,' I whisper, 'if you know anything about me by now, it's that I am always weird. Now shut up and kiss me.'

The pain gets worse through the night. It starts with surges of burning, then sharp lances of heat, then a penetrating and constant searing pain that never lets up. Just when I feel like it can't get any worse it does, but I feel better in Drake's arms, so that's where I stay.

I'd rather spend our last hours doing more of what we did earlier, but I'm buckled over with pain, so I don't have much choice in the matter. I try to push Drake away, worried that my skin will burn him, but he curls himself around me and won't let go. He just holds me tight and murmurs to me softly, pressing cooling kisses to my skin through the night as I try to contain the pain. He says things so beautiful that I can't believe they're real, then I worry that I'm hallucinating and they *aren't* real, then he presses his lips against my burning throat and I know he's really here, holding me until the very end.

I can think of worse ways to die.

37

I WAKE UP with the dawn.

This is mildly surprising, but dying and healing in cycles like this is a novelty for the Silver, so it isn't an exact science. I'm sure it'll happen later today, or tomorrow even. The good news is that I'm feeling better for the small amount of rest I managed to snatch after falling fitfully asleep, so perhaps we'll even get another round in before the end.

'You feel cooler,' Drake murmurs, kissing my neck. He's still curled around me, his chest pressed against my back, his arm draped protectively over my stomach. 'Feeling better?'

'Better than I did a few hours ago.'

'Do you think you could eat?'

'Maybe.'

In fact, I can't remember the last time I had anything except blood.

'Breakfast, then,' Drake says, rolling me over for one last kiss, but he stops short of delivering it and instead asks, 'Why do you still smell of him?'

'What?'

'You still smell of the Primus.'

'I drank his blood, remember?'

'Days ago,' Drake says. 'I wouldn't expect it to be hanging around in your body like this.'

'I don't know. He's the Primus. Maybe he has weird blood.'

'Maybe.' He lets the subject drop, but he's clearly not satisfied, because I still don't get that kiss. 'Shall I carry you downstairs?'

'I'm not an invalid,' I say.

'You're dying,' Drake points out reasonably. 'If you're ever going to accept a little help, now is the time.'

'You're dying too,' I remind him.

'Only because you are. I can feel through the bond that you're not doing well, but I feel fine.'

'Well, good for you,' I say bitterly.

'Will you just let me help?'

I do, because I don't have much choice, but I refuse to be carried. Instead, I hold onto his arm as I walk unsteadily across the terrace, through his bedroom where we throw on some bathrobes, along the corridor, down several flights of stairs – tripping more than I care to admit – and into the kitchen. There's a private chef there already, waiting to take our breakfast orders, because of course there is. It's not even six am, but from the lumps of dough lined up along the counter, I guess she needs an early start to have time to work on the bread.

'Do you have freshly-baked bread every day?' I ask Drake.

He shrugs. 'I like eating bread, and Irina likes making it.'

'I do,' she says, smiling at me. 'It's very therapeutic, you know.'

'I just can't imagine having a chef in my own home,' I say.

'This *is* your home,' Drake reminds me, nudging me with

his elbow.

'Not for long,' I remind him in turn.

'Long enough to enjoy it once or twice, I hope.'

We're sitting around a coffee table in his plant-filled conservatory, tucking in to Irina's freshly-made croissants – I'll say that again in case you didn't quite catch it: *freshly-made croissants* for fuck's sake – when Drake's phone buzzes. He glances at the screen, then puts the phone back into the pocket of his robe.

'What?' I ask.

'Dr Ross wants to talk to us about your blood results.'

I sit forward in my chair, meaning to get up – after a croissant and another bottle of blood, I'm feeling more than well enough to spring into action – but Drake gently pushes me back down again.

'It can wait,' he says.

'No, it can't. If she's got my blood results, then maybe she'll be able to tell us how long we have left. If we don't go now, then we could die just sitting here.'

'And would that be the worst thing in the world?' he asks. 'We're going to die either way, so you might as well enjoy your croissants. The blood results can wait.'

I look around at where I'm sitting and who I'm sitting with.

'You know what?' I say. 'You're right.'

I reach out to take Drake's hand in mine, and he squeezes it gently.

We don't talk much. We don't eat much, either. We just sit side by side in the early morning light, listening to the distant clanking of Irina in the kitchen as we keep each other company, knowing that we might not have the opportunity to do so again. It's peaceful, and it's comfortable, and it's not like any time I have spent with Drake before, and I realise that's because I'm no longer fighting it. It's something of a revelation, and I can only wish it didn't come so late.

It would be perfect, if it weren't so bittersweet.

Back in the Dregs' underground lair, Tabitha now has her own lab, containing all the stuff that used to be in the lab in her back garden at Nash Lee. The only thing that surprises me about this is that they didn't ask her to move in sooner. She's bustling around behind the new wooden bench wearing a lab coat, chewing a pencil and squinting into a microscope with a disgruntled expression, as though the instrument has personally offended her.

'Give us the bad news, then,' I say. 'How long have we got?'

'I don't know,' she mutters. Then she finally looks up at us and says with a cheeky smile, 'You wearing lipstick all the time now, hen?'

Kulika handed me a tube this morning when Drake and I were on our way out of the mansion. It's a shade of pinky peach that does nothing for my skin tone and reminds me faintly of spam, but at least it covers up the silver.

'Better than wandering around like a reject from sixties sci-fi,' I say. 'Tell us about the blood results.'

'Well, that's the thing,' Tabitha says, shoving the pencil she's been chewing into her hair to join the pipette and spill that are already in residence. 'I've been looking at them all morning, and I can't make sense of it.'

'Make sense of what?' I ask.

'The thing is...' she says, and she looks as though she's struggling to find the right words. 'Can I take a keek at another sample? I'll pop it right on the slide, so I won't keep you long. I just want to be sure.'

I agree, but I don't like the sound of this. If the news is so bad that she needs to check my blood again before she can tell me what she thinks is going on... Well, that's *bad* bad.

Tabitha layers up with latex gloves and sticks yet another needle in my arm, but she only takes a couple of drops this time before transferring them to a slide and slotting them under her fancy electronic microscope. When she's fiddled with it for a while and made the necessary adjustments, she looks up and strips off her gloves.

'Last night, when I first looked at it, your blood was a disaster,' she says. 'And I mean, a complete disaster. It was full of the infected cells, and not much else. Then I looked at it again. And again. And again, and every time I did, it had changed. Suddenly, there were fewer of the infected cells, as though your blood was fighting back.'

'So I'm... what? Curing myself?'

'No, nothing that drastic, I'm afraid,' Tabitha says. 'But your blood seems to have stabilised overnight, both the sample I took last night and the blood circulating in your system right now. You're not out of the woods – you won't be until we can get you that cure – but you're in a kind of stasis. Something's happened to slow the speed of replication.'

'Well,' I say, 'you did drain out all my blood before I left. Wasn't the whole point of that to give me more time?'

'No, you don't understand, hen. The replication has stopped entirely. There's *something else* in your blood, and it's interfering with the replication process. I don't know what the new substance is, though. I've never seen it before. It's similar to normal blood cells, but it's... weird is the only word for it. It's almost... magical.'

'Magical?'

'Well, it isn't scientific, I can tell you that much for certain. It seems to be fighting against the poisoned cells and preventing them from using the new blood you're drinking. It's the weirdest thing I've ever seen. Look.' She swivels her computer screen to face us, so we can see what she's seeing through the microscope's camera. 'And, weirder still, it's silver in colour, like it's some kind of Silver superblood.'

Drake gives me a look and I know that he's thinking the same thing as me. Somehow, the Primus's blood in my veins is fighting with Khalyed's.

'And if there was more of that stuff in my blood,' I say speculatively, 'then would it be able to cure me?'

'No,' says Drake.

'Potentially,' Tabitha says at the same time. 'Why? Do you know what it is?'

'No,' Drake says again. 'You can't.'

'Not even if we'll both die otherwise?' I say.

'Is one of you going to tell me what's going on?' Tabitha asks.

'She drank the Primus's blood,' Drake says.

'Oh, Jack,' says Tabitha, like a disappointed parent.

'What?' I say. 'It's not like I did it on purpose.'

'Tripped and fell on his vein, did you?' she replies.

'No! I drank it from a cup. And anyway, it's not as if there was any scent-marking involved, so we don't have to worry about haematopsychosis, do we?'

Tabitha shifts uncomfortably at this unwelcome reminder of her fraudulent research into the subject.

'I didn't mean it like that,' I say.

'I know, hen. And I am sorry about that whole episode, Baron. I don't know what I was thinking.'

'The Primus gave her his blood without her knowledge,' Drake says to Tabitha, glossing over her apology. 'He's trying to claim her.'

Tabitha's eyes widen a little and she exchanges a worried look with Drake. That's how I know it's worse than I realised.

'What exactly does this whole claiming thing entail?' I ask. 'Are we talking adoption, or indentured servitude, or what?'

'Whatever he wants, hen,' Tabitha says. 'The issue isn't so much the symbolism of him claiming you as it is the person who's doing the claiming.'

'Meaning?' I ask.

'Meaning the Primus makes the rules,' says Drake. 'His claim on you means whatever he says it means.'

'But why claim Jack?' Tabitha asks. 'Why her in particular?'

'Because it's what he does,' Drake says, exasperated. 'You can't really say that he has a superiority complex, it's more that he is genuinely superior. Because of that, no one ever says no to him, so he just takes whatever he wants, and he tends not to want anything until someone else wants it first. In any other circumstances, he knows I'd fight him on this, but if his blood is the only thing that can cure Jack…'

'You think he knew what would happen when he fed it to her,' Tabitha says.

'Of course he did. He's put me in an impossible position.'

'So either you let him claim her and you both live, or you resist him and you both die.'

'Exactly.'

'Hello?' I say. 'Excuse me, but you both seem to have forgotten that I'm still in the room, that it's my person we're talking about being claimed, and that I'm certainly grumpy and stubborn enough to make up my own mind, thank you so very much.'

'And?' Drake asks.

'And I don't want you to die.'

'Do you *want* him to claim you?' Drake asks, looking a little pained.

'No! I just don't see that we have much of a choice but to go along with it.'

I can see his jaw working as his teeth grind together. 'No,' he says. 'We'll find another way.'

'There is no other way. Khalyed is gone. All the samples of his blood are gone. We can't get any more.'

'But we can still make the original serum, correct?' he asks Tabitha.

'Yes,' she says, 'but without Dr Khalyed's blood, I can't make a cure.'

He's quiet for a moment, then he says, 'What if I can get his DNA?'

'Drake,' I say, 'if you're about to tell me that you've been sitting on a stash of his blood this whole time—'

'Not his blood precisely,' he clarifies. 'But his blood*line*. He had children, before he was turned Silver. If we can get their blood, and introduce the serum to it, then would it interact the same way?'

Tabitha thinks on this for a while, then she says, 'Potentially.'

'Then it's worth a try.'

'You'll need to move quickly,' she warns us both. 'All I can tell you is that Khalyed's cells aren't replicating *at the moment*. I can't tell you how long that's going to continue, so I want to test your blood regularly, Jack. At least daily, to start with. And in the meantime, you'll need to take it easy, and keep drinking, little and often. There's so little viable blood in your veins that you'll have to replace it constantly. All right?'

'All right,' I agree, but grumpily. It's great that I'm not dying right this second, but taking it easy isn't really my style. I'm an all or nothing person, and I'd rather just be well or totally incapacitated. Being stuck in the middle sounds utterly tedious. I guess I'll have to get used to it. 'Can you do anything about the pain in the meantime?'

'Does the healing help?' Tabitha asks, looking between the two of us.

'Um, Yes. A bit.'

I am deeply uncomfortable talking about Drake's healing mojo with Tabitha. She, however, is apparently not.

'Then keep doing it,' she says. 'I'll see you back here this evening for your next draw. And you might want to speak to the chief,' she says to Drake. 'He could help with tracking down Dr Khalyed's descendants.'

We say our goodbyes and leave the lab, heading off in search of Boyd. Apparently he doesn't even have an office in this place, which is in itself an indication of how much he's changed since last year. Unfortunately, it means we need to walk all over the damn complex to find him. When we finally track him down, he tells us Carlotta and Mikey have slipped away. Apparently they ran as far as the river, then their scents disappeared into the water – an old trick of Winta's – and Quentin and Rolf haven't managed to pick them up again anywhere along the bank. Either they swam for miles, or they hopped on a boat. Either way, for the moment, they're gone. Now that Leclercq's dead, I'm not sure there's much point in wasting the Dregs' energy chasing the others down. Without Leclercq, I don't think they'll be coming after us again.

Boyd agrees to marshal the help of the Dregs to track down Khalyed's ancestors, and by then I'm at the end of my strength. After an hour or so wandering around underground, by the time we finally get back to the surface, my legs are feeling less than sturdy.

'You're tired,' Drake says. 'I can call a car.'

'I want to walk.'

'But you're going to burn yourself out. You heard what Dr Ross said.'

'Yes, thank you. I was there in the room. You don't need to mother me, Drake.'

'I promise you, Valentine,' he says. 'That is the very last

thing I have in mind.'

Then he pushes me up against the alley wall, caging me in his arms.

'It's broad daylight,' I point out.

'So?'

'So we might be in an alley, but we're in the middle of Oxford, you're the baron, and anyone could see.'

'And everyone who I'd care to keep this from already knows that I've silvered for you,' he points out, 'so what do we have to hide?'

'Everyone?' I ask, because a handful of the Dregs doesn't seem like everyone to me.

'There was only one person I wouldn't have told,' he says.

'You mean the Primus.'

Anger flares in his eyes and I know I'm right on the money. Drake was trying to keep his feelings secret, and I fucked that up by barging into Solis Invicti HQ and airing all our dirty laundry. Great work, Jack.

'He can't have you,' Drake says.

'He won't get me,' I insist, reaching up to cup his cheek in my hand. 'Not unless everything else fails. We've already decided that.'

'But he wants you.'

'What he wants is irrelevant. I don't want him.'

'You say that like it matters.'

'Hello? Consent is a thing.'

'Not with him. He's the Primus. Did you not hear me in there? He takes what he wants.'

'Not from me,' I say, but Drake doesn't seem reassured.

'You're sure that's what you want?' He looks away for a moment, as though he's genuinely worried I'm going to change my mind. 'After all, he *is* the Primus. He's rich, he's good looking, he's pretty much the most powerful man alive —'

'It sounds to me like you're the one who wants to fuck him.'

He smiles a little at that. 'But you don't?'

I think of those cold blue eyes and I shiver.

'Not even a little bit,' I say. 'Power doesn't do anything for me.'

'I'm pretty powerful,' he teases, curling a strand of my hair around his finger in a way that makes me wriggle. 'Ancient Silver. Baron of Oxford. Bachelor billionaire.'

'And look how long it took you to get me into bed,' I say. 'For me, power's a turn off, not a turn on. I like you better when you're just... Killian.'

Apparently I've said the magic word, because at that he leans down and puts some serious effort into smearing my lipstick. I'm too blissed out on his scent mark and the soothing wave of his healing mojo to care. He is possessive in the way that he kisses me, as though he's trying to prove to us both that we get to choose this, and that not even the most powerful Silver in the world can come between us.

The problem is, I'm still not cured.

Maybe Drake's right about the blood of Khalyed's descendants. Maybe Tabitha will be able to make a cure that will expel Khalyed's blood from my veins and leave me shiny and new. But maybe not.

If there's no alternative, I'll go to the Primus if I think it'll save Drake. I've done it before, and I'll do it again. I'll throw myself on his mercy. I'll do anything he asks. I will not let Drake die for his pride.

Drake must be thinking the same thing, because he pulls out of the kiss and says, 'Please don't do anything rash without talking to me first. However bad it gets, just talk to me first, Valentine.'

That gives me pause. I'm not inclined to ask anyone for permission, particularly not Drake. I prefer to do what I like and ask for forgiveness later.

But then he says, 'Please,' with a pitifully desperate look in his eyes, and somehow I find myself agreeing.

'Okay,' I say.

'So when he comes for you, you'll tell me?'

'Yes,' I promise, hoping I won't come to regret it. 'That's assuming he even contacts me at all.'

'Oh, he will,' Drake insists. 'You can be sure of that.'

Thank you so much for reading this book. I really hope you enjoyed it, and I appreciate you taking a chance on an indie author. If you'd like to read more from me, then I have suggestions!

***

Join my Readers' Club and receive a FREE short story!

www.josiejaffrey.com/subscribe

***

If you enjoyed *Valentine's Day*, why not read *Killian's Dead*? It's the short story prequel to the *Seekers* series, following Jack as she first meets Winta and discovers the Silver.

***

Please leave a review!

If you enjoyed *Valentine's Day*, I'd be so grateful if you would please review it. Book reviews can make a huge difference to the success of a novel, particularly those of self-published authors like me. If you have time to leave a review, even if it's just a sentence or two, then I'd really appreciate it.

***

Get in touch!

I love hearing from readers! If you'd like to contact me, you can do that through my website, Twitter or Instagram.

Acknowledgements

First and foremost: huge thanks to Adie Hart, my editor and general sounding board for everything Silverse-related, my co-editor at Indie Bites fantasy magazine, and a generally wonderful friend and fellow author, who makes this whole writing thing feel much less lonely.

Thanks to the incredible Jen Sugden, who not only writes outstanding stories, but champions mine to everyone she knows. I am so grateful for your support and your friendship.

Thanks to the amazing Silverse Squad for everything they do to help promote my books. It's tough getting your work seen as a small indie like me, and I couldn't do it without you all.

And thanks always to my husband and son for everything.

CONTENT WARNINGS

General warning for violence/murder.

General warning for blood/gore, including blood drinking, description of injuries, dead bodies, forensic investigation.

General warning for sexual content (consensual).

Some swearing (up to and including 'fuck').

Abuse of alcohol; alcoholism due to depression.

Abuse of drugs, non-consensual drugging, and death caused by drugs (off-page).

Torture of adults (on-page) and children (in past, discussed).

Intense scenes of drowning.

Terminal (fantasy) illness and discussion of impending death and suicidal ideation.

9 781913 786465